Opening Act

A Rock-and-Roll Romance

D0873480

Opening Act
A Rock-and-Roll Romance

Dish Tillman

Book One of the Encore Series

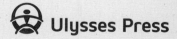 Ulysses Press

Published in the United States by
Ulysses Press
P.O. Box 3440
Berkeley, CA 94703
www.ulyssespress.com

ISBN 978-1-61243-301-1
Library of Congress Control Number 2013957409

Printed in Canada by Marquis Book Printing

10 9 8 7 6 5 4 3 2 1

Acquisitions Editor: Katherine Furman
Managing Editor: Claire Chun
Copyeditor: Andrea Santoro
Proofreader: Elyce Berrigan-Dunlop
Cover design: what!design @ whatweb.com
Cover photographs: man and woman © Coka/fotolia.com; title
    background © Dimec/shutterstock.com
Part title illustration: © JelenaA/shutterstock.com

Distributed by Publishers Group West

PART ONE

CHAPTER 1

Loni was having the loveliest dream. It was set sort of in the nineteenth century—except she drove her car to the café—and she was having tea with William Blake. (Well...*she* was having tea. He was drinking something green from a vial, which made him shudder after every sip. He offered some to Loni, but she said no thank you.) As they drank, the great poet instructed her on the trouble with her life. "There is no space left for the silences," he warned her. "And in the boom and clangor of your waking world, madness stirs, and rises, and ventures forth to claim you. Listen," he said, holding a finger aloft and looking outward. "It comes. It *hungers*." And Loni listened, and she could hear it: *thoom...thoom...thoom...*

Thoom-thoompa-thoom, tha-thoom, it continued, and Loni thought that was a little dancey for the tread of a dooms-day beast. She rolled over, and a sharp blade of sunlight pried under her eyelids. She tried to shake it away, but it held fast. She sat up and rubbed her eyes. She was awake, but the *thoom-thoompa-thoom, tha-thoom, tha-thoom* persisted.

It was Zee's freakin' speakers. Right up against the wall their bedrooms shared. Now that she was up, she could even feel the wall vibrate.

She got out of bed, pulled the oversize T-shirt she slept in down around her thighs from where it had ridden up during the night, stormed out into the corridor, and banged on Zee's door.

Zee opened it; she was fully dressed but only half made-up. One eye was lushly outlined, the other naked and pale. She held an eyeliner brush in her hand. "Morning," she said brightly. "Whassup?"

Loni could barely contain her anger. "Do you *have* to play your music so *loud,* and so *early*?" she said, gritting her teeth. "I mean, does it not occur to you that *someone* may be trying to *sleep*?"

Zee looked perplexed. She gestured at the knob on her stereo receiver. "It's only on four," she said. "Plus, it's, like, almost ten o'clock."

Loni felt the anger begin to wash out of her. "It is?"

Zee nodded, cocked her head toward the digital clock on her wall, then went back to her mirror and resumed applying her eyeliner. "You really should get a job or something. As for me, I've got an interview at eleven."

Loni was reluctant to let go of her fury. "Well, fine. But for the record, the volume may only be on four, but four is *too loud*."

Zee looked at her and sighed, then reached over and dialed down the knob. The music receded into a kind of raucous whisper. "That's one-and-a-half," she said. "Work for you?"

Loni folded her arms. "It's like a hive of bees, but I'll take it. I just don't see why you have to fill every hour of every day with this...*noise*," she said, snubbing her nose at the cradle holding Zee's iPod.

Zee laughed as she put away her eyeliner. "You knew I was a music lover before you moved in. I mean, you *knew* that. You used to give me crap about it, make fun of me. Told me I spent all my money on concerts and downloads. And now you move in with me, and you're *surprised* I play music all the time?"

"I wouldn't mind *music*," Loni said, still standing firm but watching jealously as Zee donned a crisp blue blouse and fastened its buttons. "It'd be nice to, I don't know, wake up to a Debussy étude or a Bach invention. But this hard-rock garbage…"

Zee laughed as she donned a trim suede jacket. "This isn't *hard rock*," she said, emphasizing the words as if she couldn't believe someone had actually said them. "It's indie folk rock, if it's anything. *Grief Bacon* by Overlords of Loneliness."

And in fact, Loni was starting to recognize it now. It wasn't difficult—it was the album Zee had been playing more or less nonstop for the past nine days.

"And," Zee added as she slung her bag over her shoulder, "you'll remember, please, you promised to go with me to their farewell gig tomorrow night."

"I remember," Loni said, annoyed with herself for having agreed to go. It had been a weak moment, one night after a few too many cocktails and too much soul-sharing. It was so easy to get too wrapped up in a roommate's life.

"And the after-party," Zee said as she headed for the door.

Loni moved aside to make way for her. "Surely you're not going to hold me to *that*."

Zee whirled on her. "The after-party is the whole *point*. This is my last chance to meet Shay Dayton before he goes off on their big nationwide tour. By the time they come back home, they won't be a local band anymore—they'll be *famous*. I won't be able to get anywhere *near* them." She fetched her keys from her bag. "I've been their fan since *day one*. I deserve a little private time with them before they go mega."

Loni furrowed her brow. "But you already know the drummer. You went for coffee with him. You *told* me."

Zee flapped her bag shut again. "Right. But I haven't met Shay Dayton."

"Shay Dayton. That's the singer, right?"

Zee rolled her eyes, incredulous that anyone wouldn't know this. "Yes, Loni. He's the front man. Welcome to our planet. I hope you enjoy your stay here."

"But wait." Loni followed Zee to the door of the apartment. "You went for coffee with the drummer. That's kind of a date."

"No, it's not. It was purely platonic."

"Does *he* know that?"

"How should I know?"

Zee reached for the doorknob, but Loni put her hand on the door. "Let me get this straight. You threw yourself at this drummer guy—"

"I did not *throw* myself at him. I—"

"You told me how you met. You *threw* yourself. Then he invited you out for coffee, now he's invited you to the after-party for this concert, and you're telling me the whole point of this, all along, was to use him so you could meet *another guy*?"

"Not 'another guy,'" said Zee, gently removing Loni's hand from the door. "Shay Dayton." She looked Loni straight in the eye. *"Shay. Effing. Dayton."*

"You're a menace," Loni said with an appalled laugh. "This poor drummer. What a dupe."

"He'll be fine," Zee said with a dismissive wave. "He's going on tour with the country's hottest new band. He'll have women falling all *over* him." She opened the door. "Wish me luck on my interview."

"Who's it with?"

"Optometrist. Clerical support."

"Sounds...exciting."

Zee laughed. "God, you're an awful liar!" She blew Loni a kiss and strode out of the apartment.

Loni went and sat on her bed for a few minutes, wondering how she could fill her day. There was nothing on the agenda. She had no compelling reason to even get dressed. She could, if she wanted to, sit on the couch and stare at the TV all day.

But she didn't want that. Trouble was, she didn't know what she *did* want.

It had been a full month since she'd gotten her bachelor's degree in Romantic Poetry, a degree that suited her for pretty much zero in the real world. Her only realistic option was to continue as an academic, get her master's, and teach. She even had a patron who was willing to help her out: Byron Pennington, her first poetry professor, who had shepherded her through her degree and had now invited her to be his teaching assistant while she worked through a graduate program. It was a very attractive offer; she was lucky to have it. Most people in her position would jump at it. And she might never find anyone else in her life who was as supportive and encouraging as Byron. She'd be a fool to turn him down.

Plus, she couldn't live with Zee forever. She'd intended to move in for only a few weeks, till she figured out what to do about her future. But she was no closer to a solution now than she had been when she first got there. And though Zee was being very patient and generous—Loni could only afford a pittance for rent—it was tough on them both. They'd been best friends in high school, but then Loni had gone on to college and Zee hadn't. She'd jumped right into 9-to-5 employment, mostly at the administrative support level. They hadn't seen each other much during Loni's college years, and now their world experiences were vastly different. It was getting harder and harder for them to find common ground.

So it seemed like an obvious move to say yes to Byron and become his TA. The problem was that he'd accepted a post as head of the Poetry Department at St. Nazarius University, so taking the gig meant moving with him to the West Coast. Something about the idea frightened Loni. She liked Byron, of course, and she trusted him. But to be uprooted from everything and everyone she knew for a new life where she was entirely dependent on him made her balk.

She could, of course, stay right where she was and become a graduate student at Mission State, but she'd be an orphan. Byron had so completely taken the role of her advocate on the faculty, that there was no one else she really even knew. It was like she'd burned those bridges without even realizing they were there.

And then there was the big problem.

The one that kept her awake at night.

There was something she really wanted—*deeply* wanted, in the most private recesses of her innermost whatever ("soul" being a word she stringently avoided, it having been debased by excessive and trivial usage)—and that was to write. She wanted to be a poet herself. Not to teach the skills to others. Not to forever live in academic awe of those who actually did it. She wanted it for herself. Just thinking about it made her flush. She could *feel* her face go red, and she fell back on the bed and buried her head in her pillow.

It was so embarrassing. It seemed like every girl went through a phase around fourteen or so when she wrote poetry. Usually in a special journal that she also decorated with drawings of daisies, broken hearts, or unicorns. The poems had titles like "My Tears Like Wine" and "Wind-tossed Is My Love." Most girls outgrew it. But not Loni. She'd just kept on writing. That's why she'd pursued an academic career. A young woman writing poetry is a cliché. A young woman *studying* poetry, however—no one laughs at that. No one actually *respects* it very much, either, but at least they don't laugh.

Even now, Loni had a briefcase under her bed that was filled with notebooks of her verses. (She never composed on her laptop. She thought it was an affront to the Muse.) Every once in a while, when she was certain no one else was around, she'd take it out, flip through the pages, and engage in some strenuous self-criticism. And, occasionally, some self-congratulation. Some of her poems were actually pretty good. She even considered trying to sell them to magazines.

But that seemed like a big risk—opening herself up to blatant rejection, and for what? A little shard of glory and a paycheck of, what, twenty-five bucks? If she was lucky enough to get paid at all? And the big publications, like *The New Yorker*, didn't really go in for the kind of poetry she liked—the old kind, filled with roiling lines and vivid imagery.

She gasped and pulled her head out of the pillow. It had been getting hard to breathe in there.

She rolled over on her back and stared at the ceiling. There was a crack running along its entire length, from one side to the other. Sometimes she would lie on her back, stare at that crack, and challenge herself to write a poem about it. She'd worked out a decent first two lines, but inevitably by the time she got to the third, she fell asleep.

Well, it was morning now, so why not have at it? There was no one around, and if what she really wanted was to write, why wasn't she writing? She had a flashback to her dream. It had already faded away to almost nothing, but she did remember William Blake telling her something about the value of silence. Okay then, it was plenty silent right now.

She pushed her torso over the side of the bed, reached down, and pulled the tattered briefcase from its hiding place. She opened it, withdrew the topmost notebook, and settled back on her pillow, holding the notebook against her knees. She opened it to the last scribbled-on page, grabbed a pen from her nightstand, and had a good look at the two lines she'd written so far:

A hairsbreadth divide that does not divine—meaning
gutters when division uncouples a nullity—

The dashes were a device she'd picked up from Emily Dickinson and had never been able to give up.

Looking at the lines now, she realized how unhappy she was with the word "uncouples" and remembered that this was why she hadn't gotten any further. There was certainly something better—something more appropriate to both the meaning and the meter...

Suddenly a tremendous battering noise shook the room. She jumped up in a flourish of alarm, then recognized the sound as a jackhammer. She went to the window, parted the curtains a few inches, and peered out. A pair of helmeted workers were just outside, methodically busting up the street in front of the building.

Her attention was pulled away by a knock on the door. So much for silence. It was no use trying to escape noise anywhere in this insane asylum of a world. She opened the door and found the landlady, Mrs. Milliken, on the stoop.

Loni was always a little taken aback by Mrs. Milliken's appearance. Apparently she'd spent nearly thirty years driving eighteen-wheelers across the country, and the left side of her face—the one exposed to the sun from the interior of the truck's cabin—was leathery, lined, and mottled by brown spots. The right side of her face, by contrast, was creamy pink and comparatively smooth. In the right light, Loni was sure she could frighten small children.

Mrs. Milliken looked over Loni's shoulder into the apartment. "I thought Zee would be home," she said.

"No," said Loni, raising her voice to carry over the sound of the jackhammer.

Mrs. Milliken frowned. "I was going to tell her about the work being done in the street. I just found out. They told me there's a burst water main or something."

"Is it going to interfere with our water pressure?" asked Loni, who hadn't showered yet.

"I was going to tell Zee," said Mrs. Milliken, not meeting her eyes, "that there may not be any water pressure for a couple of hours. I guess I'll have to call and leave a message on her voicemail."

"I can tell her," said Loni.

Mrs. Milliken turned away. "Or maybe by the time she gets back, it will all be fixed. It depends how long she'll be gone."

"She should be back around lunchtime."

"If she's gone for a few hours, she may never even know." And with that, Mrs. Milliken drifted away.

Loni sighed. She'd never met anyone quite so passive-aggressive as this creepy-faced landlady. Mrs. Milliken had never once spoken directly to her or even so much as said her name. Apparently she wasn't too keen on Zee having someone live with her—even as a visiting friend, not a subletting tenant—and had decided to respond by pretending Loni didn't exist at all.

Someday, Loni thought, *I am going to make that woman look at me and call me by name.*

But not today, obviously. The noise from outside was just too much to allow her any thought processes at all, much less crafty ones.

She went to the bathroom and tried the faucet. A trickle. There was no hope of hiding from the din in a nice, hot shower.

She went back and sat on her bed. She felt a little swirl of hopelessness. It was no good trying to insert her earbuds and drown out the noise with her iPod; nothing in her music library—filled as it was with piano concertos, string quartets, and art-song recitals—had the power to block out a jackhammer at close range.

Then she thought of Zee's iPod. Maybe she hadn't taken it with her.

This was unlikely, of course. Zee didn't go anywhere without music blaring. But Loni didn't remember Zee having her earbuds in when she left for the interview.

She went down the hall and entered Zee's cottony mess of a room. It was as though her laundry pile had exploded, strewing shirts, bras, and panties all over the floor and fixtures. Across the mountain range of clothes, Loni saw that the iPod was not in its cradle. Zee must have had it in her purse. But, in turning to go, her eyes fell on Zee's CD player, atop which were a few discs. Zee still bought CDs, when she liked an album enough to want to possess it physically—to value it as much as artifact as art. Loni picked up the topmost disc.

Grief Bacon, by Overlords of Loneliness.

There were five faces on the cover, in a kind of modernist design—tilted at odd angles, with unnatural lighting. The one at the forefront must be the lead singer Zee was always going on about. Loni cocked her head appreciatively. Not bad...if you liked the square-jawed, alpha-male type. She herself preferred the bespectacled, intensely intellectual sort.

But he had brooding eyes, this Shay Dayton. Nothing wrong with brooding eyes.

Of course, that was probably just Photoshop.

She turned the CD case over.

The back cover was the same as the front, only with all five members' faces now bloated out of proportion. *Definitely* Photoshop.

And in the place where the title had been on the front cover, was the word "Kummerspeck."

She took out her smartphone and Googled it.

Kummerspeck—A German word meaning "excess weight gained from emotional overeating." English translation: "Grief bacon."

She let out an involuntary bark of laughter. She had to admit, that *was* pretty witty. Maybe she was being hasty in dismissing Overlords of Loneliness so quickly. She put the disc into Zee's stereo and began playing it—turning up the music loud enough so that it cloaked the worst of the jack-hammer. She sat on Zee's bed, listening and holding the CD case in her hands. She stared into Shay Dayton's eyes, almost daring him to win her over.

And…he didn't.

She'd expected a whole cycle of songs about loss and longing and appetite, as promised by the title. But there was only one tune, "Feed Me," that even came close, and it seemed to be mainly about sex in a way Loni didn't really want to think too hard about.

The other tunes all seemed to be standard-issue rock songs, some a little more driven, others more like ballads, but the lyrics were completely unremarkable. There was a song titled "Never Till Next Time," but the title was the cleverest thing about it. The bridge was utterly pedestrian:

No use making promises I can't keep
No use going to bed when I can't sleep
No use pretending I'm not in too deep
I say never, but if ever
You crooked your finger I wouldn't linger
I'd be back in your thrall
Back at your beck and call.

It wasn't horrible, but there was nothing behind it. The song felt as though it was written merely because the singer had to sing something. She felt no actual longing behind the words, no real desperation, nothing approaching the fever of romantic obsession. It was typical pop-music posturing.

She felt a series of vibrations from the pocket of her terrycloth robe and realized her phone was buzzing. She jumped up and turned down the stereo, then pulled her phone out and answered it.

It was Byron. "Didn't wake you, did I?"

"No. It's after ten. Please."

"Sorry. I never know. I never see you anymore."

"Well, not because I'm *sleeping*." She walked to the kitchen. "Plus, there's this jackhammer thing going on here that would wake the dead."

"Is that what that is? I just thought we had a bad connection."

She fetched a cup from the cabinet, then a bag of green tea. "It's driving me crazy. I can't think straight."

"Well, good. 'Cause I'm giving you a reason to get away from it. Come to lunch with me."

"Today?" She dropped the tea bag in the cup.

"Today," he confirmed. "We've got something to discuss."

"Can't we do it over the phone?"

"I'd prefer not to. Especially with that racket going on. What's the matter, you're suddenly too busy for your sad old professor?"

"No, no," she said, going to the sink to fill the teapot before remembering there was no water. "It's just, I haven't taken a shower."

"So take a shower."

"Can't," she said, putting the pot back on the stove. "The jackhammer is for the plumbing. Everything's off for God knows how long."

"Well, how dirty can you be? Seriously."

She sniffed the sleeve of her T-shirt. She was a little sour, but not really offensive. "My hair," she said, running her hand through it.

"You're welcome to come over and use my shower," Byron said, then quickly added, "or wear a scarf. Or a hat. Aren't girls supposed to have these tricks?"

Loni decided to ignore his offer. "It's just…I *feel* gross. Whether I am or not."

"Look," he said, and she could tell he was getting a little irritable, having to cajole her while all this noise was getting in their way, "you're the one who, when we were reading Shakespeare and Spenser and Sidney, told me it was your dream to live in Elizabethan London."

"Well…it was. It is. Everything about it." She grimaced. "What's that got to do with anything?"

"No one ever bathed in the sixteenth century. They slept in their clothes and only changed once every two months or so."

"That's disgusting."

"That's Elizabethan. So use that vibrant imagination of yours. Just throw something on, and come to lunch. Pretend I'm Philip Sidney and you're the queen."

"I'm pretty sure Elizabeth I changed her clothes more than every two months."

"When Elizabeth I died there was half an inch of permanent makeup on her face. So don't even."

She gasped. "You're lying!"

"I'm not. She never washed it off. Just kept applying new layers."

She laughed, aghast. "Liar!"

"Google it. And meet me at noon at the Glass Onion on Ferris."

She Googled it. He wasn't lying. Also, after her death the queen's coronation ring had to be sawed off her finger because skin had grown over it. Loni was delightedly horrified. She wondered if Byron knew *that*. Probably. He was such a wonderful repository of bizarre facts and anecdotes.

She pulled on a cotton dress and sandals—not exactly Elizabethan—and spritzed herself with plenty of the sea-mist perfume her mother had given her for Christmas. Finally, something from her mom was actually coming in handy! (Usually Loni wore no scent at all, which she'd told her mother at least five hundred times.) Then she pulled back her hair into a ponytail and put on a purple beret she'd bought at a carnival on an impulse and which she'd looked at the next morning and thought, *I will never wear that*. Never say never, she reminded herself.

That made her think of Overlords of Loneliness—"Never Till Next Time"—and sent her back to Zee's room to take the CD from the player and put it back in its case. As she dropped it back on Zee's stack, Shay Dayton's brooding blue eyes caught her attention once more.

She wrinkled her nose at him. "Sorry, buddy," she said. "Not gonna work on this girl."

///////////

It was a beautiful day. There'd been a swift and sudden rain shower while she drove to the restaurant, but it had cleansed the air, swept away the humidity that had hung over the morning, and left behind a slight sharpness, as showers sometimes do. Loni and Byron sat at an outdoor table, and Byron was wearing his robin's-egg-blue shirt, which Loni had once complimented him on—after which he seemed to wear it more often than not.

She felt a little stir of something in her chest…a suspicion. It wasn't the first time she'd had it. And she felt herself suddenly glad she wasn't at her freshest and most attractive. They engaged in the usual small talk—faculty gossip and the like. One of the TAs, a guy Byron despised and Loni occasionally defended, had been caught in a sexting scandal and had been fired, but he was fighting the dismissal. "I guess he doesn't mind the department board reviewing the 'evidence,'" Byron had sneered.

Loni had said, "Maybe he's got nothing to be ashamed of," which had made Byron blush. But the waiter arrived, and after they ordered Byron's manner turned suddenly serious.

"Do you remember Tammi Monckton?" he asked.

"Sure. She was your TA when I first started studying with you." She knit her brow. "What about her?"

"She took a sabbatical to write. I just heard from her. She's finished her project and now she's looking for a publisher."

Loni felt a flash of envy. Someone who had been bold enough to live her dream. "Good for her," she said, and tried to drown her jealousy with a few gulps of iced tea.

"And she wants to come back," Byron said.

Loni licked her lips and put the glass back down. "Pardon?"

"She wants her job back. I told her I'm moving to St. Nazarius, and she doesn't care. She's been at a writers' colony in Maine. She doesn't have any roots. She'll go to the West Coast, drop of a hat."

"She wants to be your TA again?"

He nodded.

They sat quietly for a moment as Byron allowed Loni to process this. Then he reached across the table and placed his hand over hers. "I told her I'd offered the position to someone else. Someone who hadn't yet accepted or declined it."

Loni nodded.

"And I'm not retracting the offer. You're my first choice." He paused, then withdrew his hand. "But."

"But...?"

Their waiter appeared and set their salads before them. Byron waited till he'd gone, then smiled a bit crookedly and said, "You're very young. And I'm very fond of you. So I've allowed you to go all this time without giving me an answer. Even though it isn't really fair to me."

Loni gulped. "I'm sorry. I didn't think..."

"I know. As I said, you're young. But I leave in two-and-a-half weeks, Loni. Fine, fine, I know you, you're brilliant, you're gifted. I want you on your terms. I want you to be comfortable—happy, even. So I haven't pressed you." He sighed and shrugged his shoulders. "But now it's not just unfair to me; it's unfair to Tammi."

Loni looked at her salad. "I see."

"Now I've upset you. Please don't get all gloomy. This is the reason I didn't want to talk about it over the phone. Let's have a nice lunch and enjoy ourselves. My treat, by the way."

"Thank you," she said, barely audible.

"But I need your answer very soon. That's all."

"How soon?"

His face momentarily reddened, and Loni realized she'd insulted him. He was trying so hard to be accommodating, and she was treating him like he was some horrible surgery she kept putting off. "Four days," he said. "I told Tammi I'd give her my answer this weekend. Which means you have to give me yours before then."

She nodded. "I will. Promise."

"Growing up is hard. I understand that. When you're young, everything is wide open. You have a seemingly infinite number of possibilities before you. And then," he said, smiling sadly, "you start making choices, and with each choice, a door closes. But that's how it is, Loni. That's what it means to be an adult. You make choices, and you say good-bye to the possibilities those choices preclude."

"I know," she said, using her fork to toy with her salad. "You're right."

He sat back. "Anyway, that's all I'm going to say about it. Now, tell me what your crazy roommate's been up to."

Interviewing for a job, came immediately to mind. *Closing doors. Growing up.* But instead, she told him about Zee's misadventures at a recent strip-Twister party, and by the time the second course came he was almost choking with laughter.

CHAPTER 2

Zee was a fairly normal-looking girl. She was an average size and had naturally curly hair that she was always straightening in imitation of the girls with naturally straight hair (who were always curling theirs). She looked great in casual clothes and was always running around in shorts and a hoodie. She got a lot of attention from guys, who liked her sporty, easy-going style.

But her obsession with music seemed to derange her. Loni had seen it happen before. Zee would go into her room to get ready for a concert, and she'd come out wearing a black leather bustier, her hair all teased, and wearing enough mascara around her eyes to give the *Exxon Valdez* spill a run for its money. She had a tattoo on her lower back of a burning kitten—the residue of her infatuation with another band she didn't like anymore (called, perhaps obviously, Flaming Kitteh)—and she usually tried to cover it up, but on concert nights she didn't bother. The only good thing about that tattoo, as far as Zee was concerned, was that it had taught her not to make lifelong commitments to rock-and-roll bands. If she hadn't learned that lesson, probably the only un-inked skin she'd have left would be on her scalp, under her hair. Some of her friends, alas, had never learned that lesson. Looking at them, Loni wondered, *Where exactly are you going to get a job?* Not to mention the piercings. Zee, who had been in the workforce for a couple of years, knew to shy away from too many of those, something her wilder friends had not twigged to. Loni imagined what it would be like, twenty years from now, when the bagger at her supermarket was a middle-aged woman with a cobra tattoo around her neck and a Diet Coke can through one earlobe.

So in that respect, Zee was more conservative than her concert-going friends. But tonight when she came out of her room, slinging her bag over her shoulder, Loni had to gasp.

"How do I look?" Zee asked.

Loni groped for some euphemisms, but they failed her. "Like you were ridden hard and put away wet," she said.

Zee grinned and said, "You're so sweet," then gave Loni a peck on the cheek. "But we gotta get going here. Seriously, Loni. Get dressed."

Loni took up her own purse and said, "I *am* dressed."

Zee looked at her, appalled. Loni, seeing this, gave herself a quick reappraisal and couldn't figure out what was wrong. She was wearing designer jeans, a filmy tank top, and a burlap-colored hoodie. She thought she looked awesome. Badass, even.

"What's wrong?" she asked.

Zee gave her a wary, sidelong look. "Nothing. I mean." She grimaced. "If you're sure."

"I'm sure."

"It's just…this is a *rock concert*, Loni. Not a meeting of the Daughters of the American Revolution."

Loni swung her purse at her and hit her in the arm. "Just because I don't look like a sex worker!"

Zee laughed. "No worries there. Not a man alive who'd pay for *that*."

"Only because I'd charge more than the seven-dollar special *you're* obviously offering," Loni shot back as she followed her out the door.

They laughed together as Zee locked the door behind them.

//////////////////

In the cab to the concert, Zee was obviously feeling celebratory. It was turning out to be a great week for her. The interview had gone well, and she'd been asked back for a follow-up the next morning. Now she was on her way to see her favorite band, with an invitation to party with them afterward.

She fiddled with her right earring, a big black quartz alpha symbol (her left was an omega), which annoyed her by continually pulling itself out of its clasp. "Now, remember, you have to stay with me," she said. "We can't risk getting separated."

Loni furrowed her brow. "What do you mean? How can we get separated? Aren't we seated together?"

She snorted. "There's no seating, duh! It's all standing room. For dancing. Or moshing, or whatever. Seriously, you've never been to Club Uncumber?"

Of course she'd been to Club Uncumber. It was one of the city's only hipster hangouts. It was impossible to have a dating life in town without getting dragged there at least once. But the few times she'd been there she'd avoided the main floor. The noise from the bands had always been so loud she could feel it resonate in her pelvis. Instead she opted for hanging out by the bar, where she tried to have a conversation with whichever guy had brought her there. It had been like trying to make small talk in a jet engine. So her experiences at Club Uncumber hadn't exactly been memorable.

"Don't worry, I'll keep an eye on you," she said, imagining Zee up in front of the stage, jumping up and down and flailing her arms like she was trying to signal a ship from a deserted island. It would all be to attract the attention of Shay Dayton, and no doubt there'd be dozens of other frenzied, convulsive girls doing exactly the same thing, limbs flying in all directions. If Loni stayed by Zee's side, she'd risk getting her eye poked out or her kneecap busted.

"You won't be able to 'keep an eye' on me," Zee insisted, turning to her. As her head swiveled, the alpha earring came loose again. As she fumbled with it, she said, "This is Overlord's *last regular gig* there, for, like, *ever*. And everyone who's ever been a regular will be jammed in there to say good-bye."

"I'm sure they'll be back," Loni said with a slight roll of her eyes.

"Yes, but then they'll be *visitors*," Zee wailed. "They won't be *ours* anymore. It's like, we've nurtured this band all by ourselves, from their very first gigs back in the old days when Kelly Ramos was on rhythm guitar, before he, y'know, got married and moved out of state. Idiot." She sneered. "And we've stuck with them and supported them and loved them and watched them grow, and now we're releasing them into the world." A little tear brimmed on the lid of one eye. An actual, human tear. Loni couldn't believe it. It seemed to be having some trouble falling—it probably wasn't up to surmounting that mother lode of mascara.

But Loni didn't mock her; she had a feeling that Zee wasn't so much celebrating the success of the band she loved as she was mourning the death of the community that had built up around them. Possibly, she didn't even realize she was doing that. But it was clear: once these local boys went national, there wouldn't be any reason for their fans here in town to come together anymore. No need for them to stay in touch, even. They'd inevitably drift apart. Zee would almost certainly invest all of her enthusiasm and emotion in some new band, but she was getting a tad old for that kind of thing now. And the new band almost certainly wouldn't be as successful as Overlords of Loneliness. Zee had just lived through a golden age, a period of her life that she would always look back on as being filled with joy and excitement and the thrill of one good thing following another.

That's why Loni had agreed to come tonight. She didn't like Club Uncumber, and she wasn't a fan of their kind of music, but she knew how much this final hurrah meant to Zee. And, if she was honest with herself like she always tried to be, she was a little bit jealous. She'd never had a sense of community like Zee had with her fellow Overlords fans (who called themselves Underlings of Overlords, or just Underlings for short). She kind of wanted to be there to see them in their final burst of glory—and maybe get a little vicarious rush from it herself.

The low drone of the cab's radio switched from an announcer's voice to the opening chords of a song, and Zee lurched forward and said, "Turn that up, please! Driver, please turn it up!" Her alpha earring flew off again and landed on the floor. She didn't appear to notice, so Loni just picked it up and put it in her pocket. If Zee missed it later, she'd give it to her.

The driver, a jowly old woman who looked as though she'd rather just do whatever this crazy girl said than argue, dialed up the knob. Loni recognized the tune. "For God's sake," she said, as Zee settled back into the seat next to her, wiggling her butt ecstatically to the throbbing bass line. "This is the Overlords, isn't it? This is one of the same ten songs you've been playing incessantly for a week now. We just heard it five minutes ago before we left, and we'll hear it again when we get where we're going. What, you've got to hear it now, too?"

Zee looked at her, her eyes wide and compassionate, as if sensing that Loni would never understand, and pitying her for it.

//////////////

Club Uncumber wasn't any more inviting than Loni remembered it. In fact, it looked like it hadn't been cleaned since she'd been there more than a year ago, and it hadn't exactly been a model of sparkling fastidiousness even then. The walls had been painted over too many times—currently they were black and red—and had a kind of mottled look to them, like no one had bothered to scrape off whatever had fixed itself there before slapping the next layer of latex on. When she walked, her shoes experienced a very subtle pull from the floor, as though decades of substances both mundane and unnameable had created a permanent layer of stickiness. Loni crossed her arms to prevent herself from touching anything but had to reach out her hand at one point to get a stamp, in case she wanted to go back outside and then return. She couldn't imagine why she'd ever want to do that, and she didn't relish the idea of having her hand touched by something wet that had been pressed against the skin of two hundred other people. With a petri dish like that, the club could revive the bubonic plague. But she also didn't want to look like some kind of high-strung nerd either, so she just gave in and prayed she wouldn't wake up the next morning with a rash or a cough...or bald.

Zee was almost hopping up and down in excitement. In fact, forget "almost," she *was* hopping up and down, though Loni could now see that it was in time to the music. The closer they got to the ballroom, the more she could feel the bass thrumming in the floorboards. Despite Zee's earlier insistence that they stick together, she now seemed to forget about Loni entirely and went plunging on into the ballroom, which was brimming with people. Loni followed, clutching her purse in front of her like a breastplate so it wouldn't get snagged behind her by dozens of stray elbows and spiky accessories.

She found a suitable corner, next to an ancient video game that had been unplugged but not hauled away. Loni pressed herself against it and loudly emptied her lungs—she hadn't even realized she'd been holding her breath—then took in the scene before her.

Club Uncumber, she knew, had once been a dance palace called Diamond Jim's way back in the 1940s, and you could still see the bones of that earlier venue in this one. The bandstand was gone, but its platform remained in place, and the high ceiling with its frescoes of the stars in the heavens was still there, as were the massive colonnades covered with colorful mosaics. But instead of boasting nattily dressed gents swinging big-skirted girls across the floor to nimble, jaunty jazz tunes, Club Uncumber was now dark, dank, and almost tomblike. Looking out across what had once been the dance floor, where legions of shaggy-haired hipsters now crammed together, jerking and bouncing like the band had its instruments wired to their central nervous systems, Loni couldn't see anything except a sea of silhouettes caused by a battalion of tiny, piercing cell-phone screens.

The band on the platform at the moment wasn't Overlords of Loneliness, Loni realized at once. They were the opening act, a four-man guitar combo with a drummer and a frighteningly skinny female singer who crammed the microphone so far past her lips that Loni was sure it would get hooked behind her teeth. The drummer was fairly restrained and kept looking over at the iPad he had perched on a music stand next to him—what, was he on Twitter or something?—but the guitarists were slashing out chords like they got five bucks for each one they hit and only had ninety seconds left to do it.

Loni tried to locate Zee in the crowd. It wasn't really possible. Too many girls were the same size, the same shape, and had the same hairstyle. The way everyone milled about made it like trying to count baby chickens. Or more appropriately, baby roaches. Loni sighed, succumbing to the easiest way to seem busy when alone in a crowd, by checking her phone. She hated herself a little for giving in to the urge, but she gave in to it all the same.

She was surprised to see that there was a voice mail from Byron. She hadn't even felt the phone vibrate. Well, she wouldn't, would she? Not with being jostled by the crowd so much and with the competing vibrations in the floor being so overwhelming. She tried to listen to Byron's message, but of course she couldn't hear a thing.

She texted him: *Saw you called, can't hear voice mail, at a concert. What's up?*

She kept her phone in her hand so that she could feel when Byron replied, and looked back at the stage. The band—whose name, they'd just announced, was Nowhere Fast—now launched into a power ballad. Unfortunately, the singer's voice was a plaintive but rather detached wail, so that the effect was less like a woman lamenting the loss of a love than like one calling for someone to please, please help jump her car battery. Loni watched, telepathically willing her to put a little more feeling into her performance, till she felt her phone buzz in her hand.

She checked its screen and saw that Byron was calling again. She blinked in surprise. Hadn't he understood what she'd said?

She waited till the ringing stopped. Then she texted him back, *Can't take call, can't hear anything, too loud at club. What is up?*

By the time she sent it, Zee had found her. "You're just going to stand here against a wall, aren't you?" she said.

Loni shrugged. "Is something wrong with that?"

"Yes, if you're still doing it when Overlords start playing. Because that will mean you have no human feeling anywhere in your entire body. But it's okay, I'm not complaining. If you stay here, I'll know where you are and won't lose you."

"I'll stay right here, then."

Zee slipped her tiny purse from her shoulder, opened it, and pulled out a crumpled ten-dollar bill. "Here," she said, pressing it into Loni's hand. "In case you go to the bathroom, the table with all of Overlords' swag is right there. Get a copy of their CD."

"But you already have one," Loni said, holding the money away from her, unwilling to take it.

"It's not for me, it's for you." She grinned and closed Loni's hand around the bill. "A gift."

Loni shook her head. "I don't need one, I can just listen to yours."

"Only if you're planning to live with me forever. Which you *said* you're not."

She frowned and tried to give the cash back. "I can download it."

"Except you won't," said Zee firmly, backing away from her and lifting her arms to avoid contact with the cash. "I know you." She dropped her arms and crossed them. "Look, we're going to the after-party, where you can get them to sign it. *All* of them. They can't sign a download. And anyway," she said, letting her eyes glance across Loni's unfashionably large purse, "it's not like you haven't got room in that thing. You could smuggle a *dog* in there."

Loni hit her with the purse in question, and Zee reacted like she'd been hit by a freight train. They laughed, just as Nowhere Fast announced their last tune and thanked everyone for being a great crowd. Zee squeezed Loni's forearm. "Overlords next!" she cried, and she scriggled away through a knot of already-drunk hipsters who seemed more like frat boys in disguise.

Loni stuck the bill in her jeans pocket, then felt her phone vibrate again.

It was a text from Byron. *Call me need 2 talk 2 u*

She groaned in exasperation. Byron wasn't *that* much older than she was—he was only thirty-four—but in some ways he was so clearly of an earlier generation. Very few of Loni's friends actually used a phone *as a phone* anymore. She couldn't remember the last time she'd made an honest-to-God call to anyone she wasn't related to. Instead she texted. *Everyone* texted.

Can't talk, like I said too loud here, what's going on?

The lights went up, minimally, and many of the patrons started to file out to the three bars stationed in the lobby and on the mezzanine. Loni noticed that this was just what Zee had been planning for; as the ballroom emptied out, she scooted up to the front of the room, just before the stage, where a few other diehards were also staking their claims. They stood edgily together, legs wide apart, each defending her turf—or his, as there were a couple of guys in the mix as well. Loni wondered if it was wrong that she assumed they must be gay. Why else position yourself right where your face will be at the level of some dude's crotch?

For a moment, Loni thought the turf-holders might edge into a scuffle, or even an outright brawl, but they managed to keep their composure, only emitting a few warning snarls whenever one of them seemed—whether inadvertently or not—to encroach on another's territory. This wasn't very entertaining to watch, and Loni began to feel thirsty. She hated watery concert-venue beer, which always came with about two inches of foam in flimsy plastic cups that puckered when you increased the pressure of your grip even slightly, sending beer slopping over the edge and onto your clothes. But maybe they had something in a bottle? She'd pay premium if she had to. It was going to be a long night.

She guessed the line for the mezzanine bar would be shorter, so she climbed the crumbling marble stairs, passing a variety of pint-size human dramas on the way—weeping girls, bellowing boys, people bumping into one another while glued to their smartphones and then barking in fury at one another. She found the line still pretty long, but there wasn't much to be done about it. She took a place in it and waited.

As she inched her way forward several people came to stand behind her, which made her feel much better about the whole thing—she might have to wait, but they had to wait *longer*. Then her phone vibrated, and it was Byron calling yet *again*.

She blurted out an expletive, then looked up to see if anyone had reacted to it. Of course they hadn't, which made her feel even sillier. What on earth was wrong with Byron tonight? Why was he not getting that she *could—not—hear*?

On impulse, she pressed Talk, then put the phone to her ear.

"Byron?...Hello?...Byron, are you *there*?" It was no good. Even without the band's clangor, the place was noisy as hell. She couldn't make out a thing. She gave a little grunt of exasperation, then gave in. *"Hold on,"* she yelled, and left the line. Muttering darkly under her breath, she clattered back down the stairs, pushing through the crowd to the front door. The cool night air gave her a little slap in the face, knocking some of the anger out of her, but not enough.

"Hello?" she said. And now—even with the hiss of the outdoors and the hum of traffic, it was just barely possible to hear him.

"Hello," he said. "Listen, we need to talk."

"Clearly," she said. "Given the extraordinary lengths you've gone to get me on the phone."

"I just want to know whether you've come to a decision yet."

Her head felt as though it was going to rocket right off her shoulders. "Don't you think I would have called *you* if I had figured it out? We just talked yesterday! Just yesterday, you said I had till the weekend!"

"Which is now two days away." There was a short pause. "Plus, I can't believe you actually need that much time."

"What?"

"When I gave you three days, I thought you'd say you didn't need them. I didn't honestly think you'd grasp at them like some kind of life preserver. I never dreamed you'd insist on every last second of indecision you could get. I gotta tell you, it hurt my feelings. Like being my TA is such a fate to be dreaded or something."

"You didn't say any of that at the time!" She started pacing up and down the sidewalk in front of the club.

"Well…no. I was kind of in shock. Plus, I felt I had to be cool about it. I mean, I did offer you that time."

"Yes, you did!"

"Only now Tammi's putting some pressure on *me*. She needs to know whether I'm taking her or not. She's got another offer and they want to know her answer by Saturday."

"Then I'll tell you *my* answer by Saturday."

"Yes," he said, and she could tell by the way he twisted the word into two syllables that he was gearing up for a little spray of sarcasm. "You're obviously devoting a lot of very intense consideration to it."

"What's *that* supposed to mean?" She realized she was pretty much yelling. She'd suddenly become the kind of girl she hated: the one storming around in public, being all dramatic and bitchy to some poor schmuck on the other end of a phone call.

"You're at a *concert*," he said. "A *rock* concert, from what I'm able to tell. Your future weighing in the balance, mine as well, and you go rushing out for a night on the town." He laughed, and she could hear the derision in it. "I have to say, you have bouts of immaturity that sometimes make me wonder whether I've made the right choice in mentoring you."

"Then un-mentor me. Call Tammi and tell her the job's hers."

"You don't mean that." He seemed suddenly chastened.

"Don't tell me what I mean."

"Don't be so angry! For God's sake. Listen to yourself."

"Fine, I will. And you listen to this."

She mashed End on her phone's screen and longed for a bygone era when you could actually slam a phone down. She stood with the phone in her hand and just concentrated on not screaming. Her breath was coming hard and ragged, and she felt her face begin to swell. She didn't want to go back into the club like this, so she found a dark spot near an alley, melted into it, and had a furious, sixty-second cry, then pulled herself together and strode back into the club, displaying the stamp on her hand like it was a weapon she might fire off if anyone tried to stop her.

She went back up to the mezzanine, where she found the line for the bar even longer, which did nothing to improve her mood. She waited as the line moved forward agonizingly slowly. And this time no one even came to stand behind her. She was the last jerk and had to wait the longest.

By the time she was up front and able to order a drink, the lights were flashing, and a flurry of excitement stirred the air in the club.

"Do you have any bottled beer?" Loni asked the bartender, who looked like he was about eleven.

"No, just tap," he said.

"Anything else besides that?"

"Soda. Also tap."

"I mean, anything alcoholic."

"Electric dream shots," he said.

She blinked. "What?"

He nodded to a rack of what looked like plastic test tubes filled with neon blue experiments.

"How much?"

"Six dollars."

She laughed. "You have got to be kidding me."

The speakers came alive, and she heard someone from the ballroom saying, "Right—it's now, it's happening—the main event, the final hometown appearance of Haver City's hometown heroes…"

"Beer's fine," Loni said, feeling defeated.

"…before they leave us to pursue fame, fortune, cultural immortality, and their rightful place in the Rock and Roll Hall of Fame…"

"That'll be eight dollars."

"…people, give it up for…*Overlords of Loneliness!*"

She forked over the cash from her purse. The roar of the crowd was crazy-making; the speakers magnified it to the point that it felt as though her brain was being scrubbed with a potato brush.

The bartender handed her the plastic cup, and when she took it from him, it puckered at her touch, slopping the beer over the side and onto her sleeve.

"I hate concerts," she muttered, and she headed back down the stairs.

///////////////

She reached the ballroom just as the band was gearing up for its first tune. The two guitarists were plucking away and the keyboard player was running some trills. Lockwood Mott, the drummer, Zee's friend, gave a friendly staccato hello on his hi-hat.

Shay Dayton stood alone behind the mic. Loni hadn't realized that the band's front man was *only* a vocalist. She'd presumed he played an instrument as well, probably guitar, as that seemed to be the rock-god cliché. But he had nothing… nothing, she now realized, to hide behind. No instrument to connect with, to form a kind of closed system—a protection from insecurity and rejection. The lead guitarist—a rangy-looking, bearded black guy—was striding across the stage now, running through a few riffs, as if to prove Loni's point. For him, the audience might not even have been there. And the rhythm guitarist, a diminutive woman sporting a buzz cut and a wife beater, was also wrapped up in contemplating her fretboard. But Shay Dayton stood with his hand on the mic stand, looking serenely out at the whooping crowd. No barrier between him and them. He was open to anything they hurled at him. Tonight, what they hurled was love, but even so Loni was impressed by the courage it took.

She took a sip of her beer. Bitter, flat, and warm, it was like drinking used bathwater. She headed back to her little hiding place by the video game to watch in peace.

Shay Dayton raised a hand to still the crowd. Loni thought he was kidding himself, but it worked like a charm. Then he said, "Thanks for coming out tonight." An explosion of enthusiastic hoots followed. He gestured again for them to be silent—he seemed to have a kind of natural authority. "As you know, this is our last regular Haver City gig. In a couple of days we'll be off on our first national tour, opening for the legendary Strafer Nation." The applause that followed was so thunderous that Loni felt it resonate in her teeth. "And after we've conquered America, who knows? Europe, Asia, Australia—*the universe*." He blurted out a movie-mad-scientist laugh, and it was kind of lame, yet everyone *howled* at it. "But no matter how far we go, we'll always come back here—for *you*. You made us, and we won't ever forget that. Our hearts will always be here, in this city, in this community, in this room right now, in this time we're sharing at exactly this moment."

Loni almost couldn't hear these last few phrases because the roar in the room had swelled, seeming to push the very walls back. And while it was still at its height, Shay Dayton turned and signaled the band, and they launched into their first tune.

It was a song Loni recognized from having heard Zee play it constantly over the past two weeks; it was the opening tune on *Grief Bacon*. She didn't know its title, but the words had been drilled into her head. Which actually turned out to be a good thing, because between the crowd's continued noise and the club's crappy sound system, she wouldn't have been able to make them out otherwise. But they came to her, playing in her head as Shay sang them on the stage, leaning into the mic stand, pivoting it like a rocket launcher.

> *Born on a Friday, torn away, borne away*
> *Abandoned on a Saturday, battered, scattered, latter-*
> *day*
> *Undone on a Sunday, and still I knew that one day*
> *I'd waken on a weekday*
> *And find you.*

He sang with tremendous conviction, investing the words with a meaning Loni wasn't sure they entirely supported. But it was obviously working for the Underlings. As he stepped closer to the platform, several girls—possibly Zee among them, Loni couldn't tell—outstretched their arms, as if ready and willing to grab him by the waist if he got too close. It was obviously all theatre. Any one of them, if she wanted to, could easily have hopped up on the stage and been right there with him—but they held back out of a kind of tacit agreement, preferring the suggestion of erotic hysteria to actually giving in to it.

There was probably a book to be written there, Loni thought. A scholarly study of the ways in which rock concerts—once celebrations of anything-goes anarchy—had become ritualized over the years. But the thought of any academic pursuit immediately brought Byron back to mind. She'd hoped the noise of the band and the press of the crowd would help banish him from her thoughts, but the conversation they'd just had was still vivid in her mind—and heavy in her heart.

She was angry, of course. Very angry. She didn't like being jerked around the way Byron was obviously trying to do with her. At the same time, she had to admit, she was being a little provocative. He'd been her mentor, her champion, her confidante, and her advocate. What must it feel like for him now to be reduced to begging her to make up her mind about coming west with him? Her insistence on taking all the time to decide he allowed her was basically saying she needed to convince herself he was worth it. He would almost *have* to find it insulting.

And yet…why *didn't* she want to follow him? She'd as much as admitted she had no certain future here, and Byron was obviously on his way up in academia. It would benefit her enormously if he brought her with him. Yet she resisted.

Possibly this was simply a matter of sheer bloody-mindedness. She'd never liked being told what to do, never liked being pushed in any direction, even resented anyone having *expectations* of her. She knew this was childish and she had to outgrow it. And to a large extent, she thought she had.

But if not that, what could it be? What was it about Byron's generous offer that made her put on the brakes? She really did owe him a lot. And he was very sweet to her, to be so supportive and to give her so much room. Why couldn't she repay that with unconditional trust? Or just simple loyalty?

There was something, though…something just below the surface that she didn't want to think about, and as she stood in the semidarkness, her head blasted by sonics and her body jostled by revelers, she felt, oddly, that she was close to letting it come out…plunging through the blocks and distractions she'd placed in its way, to realize…to realize…

"Loni!"

She snapped out of her introspection to find Zee descending on her, just as the last chords of the tune were ringing out—a signal for the crowd to raise their arms in ecstasy.

"Can you believe we're *here*?" Zee cried, clutching her arm in glee. "This is *history* we're seeing! History *right on this stage*!"

Loni wasn't quite willing to go that far, though she was impressed by the way a room filled with dyed-in-the-wool hipsters had been persuaded to drop their attitude of world-weary ennui long enough to leap about like overstimulated five-year-olds. "Tell me about the band," Loni asked.

Zee was only too happy to oblige. "Shay Dayton you know, of course," she said, "though this is the first time you've seen him in the flesh, right? Man, I *envy* you. I remember my first time. Like seeing Jesus."

Loni resisted the urge to point out that no one either of them knew had ever seen Jesus, and said, "Go on."

Zee nodded her head toward the lead guitarist, who was beaming an incandescent smile at the crowd now, no longer seeming to need to hide behind his instrument. "That's Baby Cleveland," she said. "And that's not a nickname, either. It's his real, honest-to-God birth-certificate name. And that," she said, pointing out the rhythm guitarist, "is Trina Kutsch. She used to be in an all-female band called the Beneluxe Countries, but she quit because she said they played like 'girls.' She's pretty badass. Actually, she scares me a little." Loni shot her an amused look, and she added, "In a good way."

Then she cocked her head toward the keyboard player, who was taking an awkward bow. "Jimmy Dancer. Kind of a quiet, intense guy. But man, when he plays, he's like a wizard or something. And of course," she continued, and her voice suddenly got a weird little vibe in it, like she was having to try hard to keep up her energy, "you've heard me mention the drummer. Lockwood Mott."

Yes, of course Loni had. Lockwood Mott, with whom Zee had shamelessly flirted as part of her long-range plan to meet and seduce Shay Dayton. Loni gave him an extra degree of scrutiny. He was a big, genial-looking, dark-eyed guy whose hair was longer than it should be, which in Loni's experience was the telltale sign of the career single guy.

"He looks very nice," said Loni.

"Oh, he's sweet," said Zee, with maybe too self-conscious a note of casualness. She was obviously feeling some guilt about leading him on and was putting up a defense of breezy dismissal. But Loni had known Zee a long time and could tell it wasn't really working.

She was about to press the issue when the band began its second tune, and Zee squealed with delight and hurried back to the stage. She must have coerced a fellow Underling into holding her spot.

The new number was a very rhythmic, funk-type tune, but once again the lyrics seemed to be more the product of attitudes and posturing than of any real poetic impulse.

Hammer's hard but needs a nail
Woman's soft but she's not frail

What the hell was that supposed to mean? Each line on its own, while not exactly revelatory, at least made sense. But they didn't belong together. They were talking about two separate things. Loni imagined the songwriters just stringing together whatever sounded good and working with the meter. She'd known poets who did the same thing.

There was one line, however, that gave her a jolt.

The one who gets the bruises
Ain't the only one who loses.

That just catapulted her right back to Byron and the angry words they'd exchanged over the phone. She wondered if he was now obsessing over them, just as she was. It would be harder for him not to. He was probably at home, alone, with nothing to distract him, while Loni had this uproarious concert.

Not that the distraction was doing her much good.

She looked up at Shay Dayton, whose hips ground seductively to the beat of the music and whose hair hung in his face till he came to a pause in the phrasing and could toss it back, revealing his soulful blue eyes again. The women were driven to shrieks of ecstasy by his every gesture. Loni herself was completely immune. She wished she weren't; she wished she *could* see whatever these other women were seeing. It would be so…*therapeutic* to lose herself in the pantherlike stalking of some lean, shaggy-maned rock idol. But to her it all seemed a bit ridiculous, a kind of pseudo-pagan charade. Shay Dayton might have the looks, and the moves, and the sexual magnetism, but to what end? What was he *for*, exactly?

She supposed the same could be asked of the type of men she *did* find attractive—the thin, bespectacled brainiacs, whose laserlike focus and relentless pursuit of even the most theoretical argument could be exhausting, if not irritating, to most people Loni knew. But she was thrilled whenever one of them respected her enough to speak to her on his level. She felt *ennobled* by the way they challenged her. She was pretty sure that she, herself, didn't have a first-rate brain, but because of her exposure to so many contentious intellectuals, she was no slouch in the smarts department. And she knew it. And she liked it. And she wanted a guy who liked her for it, too.

But most of those guys either distrusted her—apparently unwilling to believe someone who looked as hot as she did could really be interested in them, and must therefore be subtly mocking them—or dismissed her—apparently unwilling to believe someone who looked as hot as she did could really understand a thing they said, and must therefore be pretending.

It was too bad, because it's not like those guys got a lot of female attention. Loni thought again of Byron, who'd been more or less single for as long as she'd known him. Since he never mentioned any exes, he had probably never had a significant relationship. She pictured him at home now, watching some documentary on the Sundance channel and eating microwave popcorn in the dark. In a way, it was too bad he was as old as he was. Just a couple of years younger, and he'd have been the perfect guy for her. She respected his mind, and he respected—and molded—hers.

This train of thought, which was just getting back on the tracks she'd laid earlier, was interrupted by the end of the second song and the beginning of a third. Loni's beer was gone, and the thin plastic cup felt like the shell of a dead insect in her hand. She wanted to be rid of it, even if just to replace it with a new drink, but the room had gotten more crowded. She wasn't certain she'd still find her place open when she got back to it.

And then something stopped her—arrested her. This new tune was a ballad, and Shay Dayton had taken the mic from the stand and now held it in both hands before his face, his fingers interlaced, like he was in prayer. And his singing...his singing was wonderful. He had such a beautiful, creamy tone in his mid-range. It was criminal that he sang so often at the top of his register, like some keening banshee.

But, again, the lyrics came up short.

Fireflies glow brightest when the darkest hour is here
Your memory is whitest in my blackest days, my dear
Sustain me in my trials while I climb up from despair
Give me hope that when I reach the end I'll find you
   waiting there

Loni had better work than that in her junior high school journals. In spite of the sheer splendor of his voice, she was embarrassed for Shay Dayton. But he clearly wasn't embarrassed for himself. In fact, the further he got into the tune, the more shamelessly he played to the crowd. This was a man who was very much aware of his power over his audience and had no reservations about milking it. The pleasure Loni had found in his voice receded as his swagger—his self-infatuation—became increasingly apparent.

And the more he acted out, the more wild the response he got from Zee and her pack of crazed Shay devotees. In fact, one of them did in fact get up on the stage now—then immediately compensated for such boldness by shying away from Shay, as though suddenly afraid of him. *Again with the phony ritual,* Loni thought in disgust. And when Shay sauntered over to the girl, grabbed her by the waist, and grinded into her, staring intensely into her eyes, during the band's instrumental passage, before passing her—near swooning—back down to the crowd, Loni couldn't take it anymore.

She left her dark little corner and went out to get another beer. Something warm, bitter, and cloying would be a relief after Shay Dayton's ambrosia overload.

////////////

As the show went on, Loni was so over the whole scene that she'd began to feel apologetic about the way she'd left things with Byron. She could not relate to this crowd on any level, and the singer's over-the-top, cringe-worthy theatrics just made her long for a nice, bracing talk with a man who actually spoke his mind (and had a mind to speak of). Whatever Byron might be guilty of, he'd always been straight with her. She always knew where she stood with him.

Finally, after three increasingly rapturous encores, the band retired from the stage and the lights went up. The gaggle of girls at the front of the stage stampeded out of the ballroom. One poor guy, walking with a cane, was actually knocked over.

Zee, however, was not among the exiting herd. Instead she made her way over to where Loni waited by the disabled arcade game.

"What's *with* them?" Loni asked, cocking her head in the direction of the herd of girls.

"They're on their way to the load-out door, at the back of the club," Zee explained, "so they can see the band when they come out."

"But not you?"

Zee waggled her eyebrows. "Bigger prospects for me. After-party, remember?"

Loni frowned. "Listen, I think I should go. I had kind of a fallout with Byron. I don't want to leave it there tonight. I should go and see him."

Zee grabbed her by the wrist. "Oh, no. You promised to come with me."

"I know. But this is...I don't know. I think my future's on the line."

"So's mine," Zee said. "One future at a time, here."

"But it's already pretty late, and I—"

Zee tightened her grip enough that Loni actually winced in pain.

"Listen," she said, almost seething, "you have all the time in the world to talk to Byron. He's not going up in a puff of smoke. But I have exactly one small window of time to get to that after-party and meet Shay Dayton. After that, the opportunity is gone, and it will *never come again*."

"I didn't say it would," Loni said, trying to withdraw her hand. "But you don't need me for that."

"I *do* need you for that," she insisted. "I'm not walking into that party alone. Think of how that would look."

"I have no idea what you're talking about. I've walked into plenty of parties on my own."

"I'll look like I'm *on the prowl*," Zee said, making a face.

"But you *are* on the prowl."

Zee squeezed her again. Loni yelped. "I don't want to *look* like it. I'm there because of Lockwood Mott. If I walk in alone, it'll seem like I've come there just for *him*. If we're together, it muddies the waters. Gives me room to maneuver."

"So you can maneuver yourself into the path of Mr. I'm-Too-Sexy-for-My-Pants Shay Dayton."

Zee looked momentarily stunned at Loni's quasi-blasphemy—as if the idea of any woman not losing her mind over Shay Dayton were beyond her ability to conceive. But then a sly grin crept over her face. She was obviously realizing that

Loni's disdain for the front man made her *exactly* the right friend to show up with.

"Byron can wait," she said. "He's waited this long. You're coming with me. Now."

As Zee dragged her out of the ballroom, along with the last few stragglers from the show, Loni said, "What do you mean, 'He's waited this long'?"

"Nothing," Zee said, emerging into the open air. "Look for a cab. We'll go have a drink first, to give the party time to get going before we make our entrance. There's one—*taxiiiii*!"

CHAPTER 3

"This is it?" Loni asked, after a swift, desperate look at the departing cab's taillights. "You're sure?"

Zee checked the address on her phone—or rather rechecked it, as she had every thirty-five seconds on the ride over. "I'm sure," she said, sounding not sure at all. "This is exactly what he gave me."

They looked up at the building in front of them. It wasn't tall—just a five-story walk-up—but it compensated for its compactness with its ominous exterior. It was grimy and gray, its windows either boarded over or blacked out by tattered curtains.

"We're actually supposed to walk in there?" Loni said, looking now at the dim, cluttered lobby beyond the front door. A drooping houseplant sat just inside, looking as though it were gasping for its last breath. "We're supposed to just walk in there and go up those stairs and knock on a door because some guy—"

"Not 'some guy'! Lockwood Mott! The drummer for Overlords of Loneliness!"

"—because Lockwood Mott, the drummer for Overlords of Loneliness, told you there was an after-party here," Loni went on, undeterred. "Did he mention what kind of after-party, exactly? I mean, is it just for the fans, or are serial killers welcome?"

Zee grabbed her by the arm. "Please, I *just* need you to stick with me till I meet Shay Dayton, then you can leave. I *promise*."

Loni looked around at the empty, yawning neighborhood. Battered chain-link fences, a darkened strip mall, and a sinister-looking Laundromat were all she could make out. "Yes, I'm sure I can just come back down here and hail a cab, no problem," she said. "That will totally happen."

"Call ahead for one. Don't be such a *baby*."

"Me?" Loni laughed. "*You're* the one who's afraid to go to a party alone."

"I *told* you," she said, leading Loni into the building. "I'm not *afraid*. I just don't want Lockwood to think I'm there for *him*."

"Then you shouldn't have flirted with him in the first place."

They crossed the lobby toward the inner door. "I didn't 'flirt' with him. Well…not per se. It was sort of pseudo-flirting. And anyway, if I didn't, I'd never have gotten this chance to meet Shay Dayton. This party is only for the *top tier* of Underlings."

The inner door resisted a bit, until Zee gave it a yank. "So, you used one guy to get to another," Loni said, shaking her head. "Feminism marches on."

They started up the stairs. "I'm sure he didn't really take it seriously," Zee said, barely audible over the squeaking of the steps. "I'm sure he knew it was just a little game."

"Of course. Guys always thoroughly understand what women mean when they come on to them."

"I don't know why you're being so horrible to me."

"Because you've dragged me to this war zone of a neighborhood to chase after some preening windbag of a rock star."

"Oh, you filthy bitch!" she said shrilly, then dropped her tone so as not to draw anyone out of the doors they passed on each floor. "Shay Dayton is the voice of his generation, and Overlords is *the* next big thing in music!"

"You could get a job writing their press releases."

"You just watch. This is *literally* my last chance to get to meet him before he's a celebrity. By the time they get back they'll be superstars and will have whole *teams* of people keeping fans away from them."

"I wish they had a team or two right now," Loni muttered, but it was too late in any case. They were on the fourth floor, and she could already hear the music, chatter, and clamor seeping out from Apartment 414.

They found the door hanging ajar, so Zee gave it a little push and it swung open.

They were immediately hit by a wave of smells: alcohol, cigarette smoke, perfume, fried food. A little pocket of warmth tumbled out to envelop them.

People were strewn everywhere, lounging on couches, poured into armchairs, seated cross-legged on the floor, or— Loni noted with distaste—secluded in corners, in pairs, making out. Everyone was engaged in either earnest chatter or languorous appreciation of the music, which, Loni was grateful to note, was an old Moody Blues album. She didn't think she could take any more Overlords tonight.

The lead guitarist greeted them at the door. The shyness Loni had noted earlier seemed to have fully evaporated in the afterglow of the show. "Hey, ladies," he said with a wide grin, "welcome to my pad. I'm Baby."

"Baby Cleveland, I know!" Zee blurted, as if it were the answer she had to give in order to get to heaven. "We were at the show! You guys *rocked*!"

He gave them a courtly little bow, then gestured for them to come in. "Enter my inner sanctum," he said, "and partake of anything you find therein. Just please note, I promise you joy, but I cannot promise you clean."

A moment later, Lockwood Mott noticed them. He left the pale-looking girl he'd been talking to and came over to greet them. "You made it!" he blared. "Come on in!" And before they could obey, he grabbed Zee and pulled her into a bear hug and gave her a large, wet kiss, the body language of which was oh so very *this-is-my-lady*.

From within his burly arms, Zee smiled at Loni, as though not at all concerned, but her panicked eyes told the exact opposite story.

When he finally released her, Zee took a moment to pop all her limbs back in their sockets, then turned and said, "This is my friend Loni."

"Welcome, friend Loni," said Lockwood, shaking her hand with uncalled-for vigor. "Come on, let's get you fräuleins some adult beverages!"

He grabbed Zee's hand and pulled her after him. Zee shot Loni a pleading look, so Loni felt compelled to follow.

She found herself stepping gingerly over sprawled-out partygoers, propped up on their elbows or draped over throw pillows—or over one another—drinking liquids of various strange hues: milky green, sky blue, crimson. She waved away acrid smoke, screwed up her nose, and managed to knock only one glass out of someone's hand. To be fair, the guy was waving it around as he told a very animated story, but she apologized quickly and moved on before he could react.

She could see the kitchen at the far end of the apartment and presumed that was where the drinks must be. Despite herself she felt she could use one—just one—to help quell the feelings of not-belonging and not-wanting-to-belong that were now gripping her like a too-tight sweater. She really ought to be used to those now. She'd felt this way ever since grade school. Whenever people gathered together to hang out, laugh, and relax in their own company, something inside her got a little more starched, a little more rigid, and she'd end up standing off to one side, all by her lonesome, longing to be back home with a book.

They'd come tantalizingly close to the kitchen, where bright fluorescent light shone like a miner's headlamp in the dark apartment, when Lockwood Mott suddenly pulled Zee over to a small circle of bearded, sullen musician-types and hugged her to him so hard that her eyes seemed to bulge out. "This is the girl I was telling you about," he said. "This is the fabulous *Zee*." And the musician-types looked at Zee as though not 100 percent convinced of her fabulousness—or maybe they were just jealous of Lockwood for scoring such a hot number when they were all stag—but either way, it was clear Lockwood had completely forgotten Loni's existence. And even though she would much rather be forgotten than drawn into that little scenario, something about it still stung. Rather than stand around awkwardly outside the circle, she continued to the kitchen on her own. She could feel Zee's eyes casting after her, like lassos trying to draw her back.

The kitchen was so bright that Loni couldn't avoid seeing what a complete dump it was. There were cans and bottles and fast-food boxes piled everywhere. A few hipsters lingered among the debris, chatting in cool, muted tones. Something about Loni's jagged energy must have made them uncomfortable, because they soon ambled back out to the party, leaving her alone.

She took a beer from the refrigerator, popped it open, and had a sip. Her face contorted as it went down; she really didn't like beer. Too sour. She was a fine wine girl, and champagne was her favorite. But it was silly to think of champagne in a place like this.

She leaned back against the kitchen counter as she drank, slowly and without pleasure. She wondered how much longer she had to stay. She'd promised not to leave until Zee had met the infamous Shay Dayton, but that could be a good, long while. It was clear Lockwood Mott wasn't going to let her out of his sight—hell, out of his *grip*—any time soon.

She sighed. And she wondered, once again, what it was about rock front men that made girls like Zee dissolve into puddles of romantic sap. She herself had been relatively unmoved at the Overlords concert, even as Zee wailed and writhed and moaned at the foot of the stage. The music hadn't been bad, really. The songs were very well constructed, and some of them had a complex harmonic structure. Shay Dayton's voice was fine, though he appeared not to know how best to use it. But the lyrics still bothered her. So simplistic— she might even say pandering. And the way he had strutted across the stage—thrusting himself at the audience like he was the yummiest dessert anyone would ever taste—had been mortifying.

Of course, Loni had been the only one in the auditorium who appeared to think so. Maybe the problem was with *her*. She was willing to consider it. But only because she was fairly certain she could convince herself otherwise.

She was turning the issue over in her head when someone entered the kitchen—lean and muscled, in a threadbare T-shirt and ruined jeans, with dark hair tumbling down around his shoulders—and Loni realized, almost matter-of-factly, that it was Shay Dayton.

She blushed guiltily, as though she'd been caught at something, but of course the singer couldn't have any idea she'd just been thinking about him.

She turned away from him and, pretending not to have recognized him, leaned against the refrigerator. With great concentration she took out her phone and checked her e-mail.

But this wall of private business meant nothing to Shay Dayton, who leaped right over it. "Hey," he said.

She looked up at him, as though seeing him for the first time. "Oh. Hey." She looked back at her phone.

He extended his hand. "I saw you come in," he said. "I'm Shay."

She felt a little twinge of pleasure at this. It was nice that he was letting her pretend she didn't know who he was. She shook his hand and said, "I'm Loni."

"Welcome, Loni." He leaned against the butcher-block table that had clearly made its way there from IKEA.

They stood staring at each other for a moment. Loni began to feel uncomfortable. What was going on here? Was he coming on to her? Was her pose of ignorance of who he was some kind of *challenge* for him?

She was just starting to get a little irritated—and a little panicky, too, if she was honest about it—when he gestured past her and said, "Sorry, I just need to get in there."

"Oh," she said, suddenly embarrassed. She moved away from the fridge. "Sorry."

"No worries," he said, opening its door now that Loni had stepped aside. He bent over and looked inside. "Jesus, what the hell is going *on* in here?"

She peered in after him and said, "Whoa." The shelves were packed—beer bottles, jars of pickles, mayonnaise, five different kinds of mustard, Worcestershire sauce, capers, aromatic bitters. "Doesn't he ever throw anything away?"

Shay crouched down and started rooting around inside. "This is kind of amazing. He's got eight thousand things in here, and not a single goddamn thing to eat."

Loni crouched down next to him. "What are you looking for?"

"Eggs," he said, moving aside an ancient-looking box of Arm & Hammer baking soda.

Loni blinked. "Eggs...?"

He chuckled and looked up at her. "Someone dared Trina—our rhythm guitarist—to see how many raw eggs she could eat before she ralphed 'em up. She's already downed half a dozen and isn't slowing down. They sent me for another carton. It's all going down in the bedroom, if you're interested."

"I am the opposite of interested," she said.

He laughed, and said, "Yeah, I get that."

At that moment Baby walked in, and Shay stood up. "Hey, dude," he said, "you got any more eggs? Trina's working a bet."

Baby thought a moment, then said, "I think I got some pickled eggs somewhere. Probably way past code. I think I bought them in, like, 2008."

Shay looked at Loni, who looked back. Then she laughed and said, "Don't you dare."

He shrugged. "She's just going to throw them up anyway."

"I want no part of this."

By this time Baby was on a stool, rummaging around in a cabinet above his stove. "Here they are," he said, taking down a glass jar from deep within. He stepped down and looked at it, then scowled. "I don't like their color."

Shay looked at Loni, and laughed. "All right, you win. I can't."

"I'll take them to her," Baby said. "She should at least do the sniff test first."

He left the kitchen, leaving Shay and Loni alone together. Shay reopened the refrigerator, took out a beer, and pried off its cap.

"Cheers," he said.

"Cheers right back," she replied, clunking her bottle against his. She considered adding, *And best of luck on your tour*, but decided against it. She didn't want to appear to be an Underling.

"Were you at the show tonight?" he asked, as if reading her mind.

"What show?" she asked, casually tossing back her hair.

He smiled at this, and she realized she was trying *too* hard to be nonchalant.

"The Bolshoi Ballet at the Civic Center," he said. "Heard they were *phenom*."

She pursed her lips to keep from smiling. "Very droll. Yes, I was at your show." Then she added, "A friend took me," to make it clear it hadn't been her idea.

"Oh, good," he said. "This party's kind of a thank-you for our local fans. Just want to make sure we don't have any freeloaders crashing."

She almost gasped. "Do I *look* like a freeloader?"

"The best freeloaders don't," he said, smiling.

She put down her beer and slung her purse higher up on her shoulder. "Well, if you have any doubt, I can always put your mind at rest by leaving."

He raised a hand to calm her. "No, no. I don't want that. I was just joking."

The tension had ratcheted up rather suddenly, and Loni was aware that she was *pretending* to be offended more than she felt any actual offense. She had to wonder why she was doing that—and how she could manage to scale it back without looking like some kind of idiot.

Fortunately, at that moment Trina, the rhythm guitarist, ran past the kitchen, clutching her mouth, followed by a quartet of whooping guys. Baby entered the kitchen a moment later, screwing the top back on the pickled eggs, and said, in a completely casual voice, "Yeah, turns out these are no good," before dropping the jar in the garbage.

When he turned around and left again, the tension was broken. Shay and Loni laughed together, long and hard.

When the moment subsided, each took a swig of beer. Then Shay said, "So you're not a fan, then."

She blushed again. "I didn't say that."

"You didn't say *anything*. That's how I can tell." He smiled again, and she felt it harder and harder to resist that smile. Its complete unself-consciousness was winning her over. "Most fans make fools of themselves when I walk in a room. They gush and babble on and on and keep *touching* me. It can be very embarrassing." He gave her a brief, appreciative nod. "This is kinda cool."

She tossed back her hair again, like it was a whip she was using to keep him at arm's length. She didn't like the way he was forging a little society of two with her. She suspected this was a trick he pulled on a lot of people—he was simply too smooth at it.

"Well, you won't get that from me," she said boldly, determined not to let him think he had any power over her. "I mean, you sing well enough, but that's all you do. Any good rock-and-roll front man plays an instrument, too."

"Mick Jagger," he said with a grin. "Robert Plant. Roger Daltrey. Jim Morrison."

Apparently he'd been hit with *that* criticism before. "The exceptions that prove the rule," she said, and she knew it was lame even as it came out of her mouth. "And your lyrics," she added, eager to change the subject.

"What about my lyrics?" he said, a touch defensively.

Loni had said, "your lyrics," meaning *the band's* lyrics; but by the way he responded, it was clear they were really *his* lyrics.

"Well," she said, not quite as eager to press her point now but too far in to withdraw, "they're a little…conventional. First love, lost love, unrequited love, blah blah blah." She made a face.

"What's wrong with love?" he asked, utterly sincere.

She blushed again and wished she could stop doing that. "Nothing's wrong with love. It's the way you position it. It's so…shopping mall."

He scowled. "I think you're being a little hard on me. I have to keep the market in mind, you know. I have to sell CDs, you know. I have to sell downloads."

"But that's not rock-and-roll! Rock isn't about *the market*. You should be ashamed, selling out your talent that way."

It was his turn to go red in the face—though seemingly from anger, not embarrassment. "That's an interesting thing to say," he said between clenched teeth, "while you're eating our food and drinking our booze. All paid for by my 'selling out.'"

"I haven't eaten any of your food," she said with a sneer. "And this is cheap beer, and I don't want it anyway." She put it down.

"What *do* you want?" he asked, and it was not entirely a friendly question.

She glared at him. "I want rock to be what it was meant to be. It's revolutionary. An *art* form. It has the capacity to change the world. In fact it *did* change the world. All those people you mentioned, Jagger, Plant, Morrison. They didn't sit around fretting about *the market*. They tapped into the subculture of the great poetic visionaries. They studied William Blake, they learned to—"

"'Hear the voice of the Bard, who present, past and future sees,'" he said, interrupting her, "'whose ears have heard the Holy Word that walk'd among the ancient trees... calling the lapsèd soul, and weeping in the evening dew, that might control the starry pole and fallen, fallen light renew!'"

She stared at him, unable for a moment to respond. She hadn't expected him to throw Blake back at her like that. It completely derailed her rant. And it did something more. It made her feel...*what*? What was that small vibration, at the very base of her spine...?

Before she could put her finger on it, Zee burst into the kitchen, followed closely by Lockwood Mott, who said, "Oh, hey, Shay, there you are—got a sweet thing here just dying to meet y—"

Before he could even finish the sentence, Zee hurled herself at the singer. "Oh, my God, *Shaaay*," she wailed, "I can't believed I'm *meeting* you, ohmi*gawd*, I am your total *biggest* fan I swear I listen to *Grief Bacon* constantly I know every song *by heart* I was at the concert tonight singing along with *everything* of course not like you because your voice is *incredible* and you are a *god*..."

By this time she'd backed Shay into a corner, and Lockwood had a look on his face that said he was finally figuring out why Zee had been so friendly.

Loni had promised to stay until Zee met Shay Dayton, and since that had just happened, she was free to go. She edged around Lockwood—who was partly blocking the door but was too paralyzed by his sudden epiphany to move—and slipped out. She took one final look over her shoulder and saw that Zee had grabbed Shay's arm and was stroking it like a pet cat.

And Shay himself?

He wasn't looking at Zee. He was looking at *her*. Watching her go.

She felt a momentary jolt at that, but, buffeted again by the warm, close, confusing dimness of the party, she was soon able to shrug it off.

She made her way through the apartment and out the front door. As she descended the stairs, she phoned for a cab.

///////////////

While she was waiting on the curb, she noticed—with a little jolt of alarm—someone else standing on the street. She turned, and saw that it was the band's keys player. What was his name?...Jimmy Dancer. Onstage, he'd struck Loni as aloof and wary—a natural outsider—and seeing him here, outside the party, having a cigarette in the dark, she felt a sudden kinship with him. She was an outsider, too.

"Those will kill you, you know," she said, nodding at the cigarette.

He shrugged. "With any luck."

She didn't know how to reply, so she turned back toward the street to watch for the cab.

"Kinda surprised to see you go so early," he said.

She half turned her head. "Me? Why?"

He raised his eyebrows. "Didn't Shay talk to you?"

Suddenly on alert, she replied, "A little. Why?"

He shrugged again. "Well, I guess everyone strikes out sometime. Even the Hall of Famers."

She turned all the way to face him. "What do you mean?"

"Just that he noticed you the moment you walked in," he said, after taking another puff on his cigarette. "And I've seen that look before. He spots his prey for the night, he stalks her, he moves in for the kill...he bags her." He took another drag, then nodded in apology. "Metaphorically speaking, of course."

Loni felt a little glow of heat in her forehead. "Well, he didn't bag this one."

Jimmy Dancer grinned. "Sweeeeet," he said. Apparently there was more than a little jealousy of Shay's sexual prowess among the other members of the band—or at least the one behind the keyboard.

Loni gave a little grunt of distaste and turned back to the street. She suddenly realized that Shay must have seen her enter the kitchen and then *volunteered* to fetch more eggs for the stunt going on in the next room, knowing it would give him the perfect excuse to sidle up to her.

She felt stupid. She felt manipulated. And she was grateful that she had bucked against the unwitting attraction he'd whipped up in her, grateful for the little bursts of pettiness and snarkiness she'd been unable to suppress. How could she have known they were a survival mechanism?

She was so upset, she actually considered making a pass at Jimmy Dancer. Going home with him instead? Now *that* would show Shay Dayton.

But of course, why should she let Shay Dayton be her motivation for *anything*? He was nothing to her. Less than nothing.

Besides, the probability of Jimmy Dancer having nicotine breath was a deal-breaker.

The cab arrived a few minutes later. During the ride, she considered calling Byron. It wasn't too late. But she felt strangely unmoved to dial his number—despite having protested so strongly to Zee, just a few hours earlier, that she needed to talk to him.

At home, she shucked her clothes and collapsed into her pillow. Exhausted, she fell immediately to sleep. And her last thought about Zee and the concert and Overlords and Shay Dayton was a firm, if drowsy, *Never again.*

CHAPTER 4

Eventually Zee felt the call of nature and excused herself to use the bathroom. Shay was only too glad to give her permission to go.

"I won't be long," she said, getting up from his lap and wagging a finger at him. "You just stay right here."

"Hey," he said, extending his arms—one of which held an empty beer bottle, "where would I go?"

As soon as she rounded the corner to the hallway, he leapt to his feet and scuttled across the party to the kitchen.

Trina was there, getting another Smirnoff Ice from the refrigerator. "Leave it open," Shay said. "I'm goin' in right after you."

She obligingly stepped away from the fridge and popped open her bottle. "Man, I can't get the taste of that goddamn rotten egg outta my mouth," she said. "Like eating a dog's cancer tumor." She swallowed a mouthful.

Shay removed his beer and closed the fridge. "Why do you keep letting people talk you into that kinda behavior?"

She wiped her mouth on the back of her hand and said, "Well, you know my nickname—'Kid Daredevil.'"

"Yeah. But nobody actually calls you that."

"They will before I'm finished with 'em." She took another swig, then made a face and said, "Blaagh. Still there."

"Listen," Shay said, prying the lid off his beer bottle, "if five Smirnoffs haven't done the job, a sixth isn't going to help."

She looked at him and emitted a little defeated grunt. "You're right." She set the bottle on the counter and said, "I should try a couple shots of Jägermeister." She left the kitchen, and a moment later Shay heard her cry, *"Hey, who moved the bar cart?"*

He took a swallow of beer and left the kitchen, peering down the hallway to make sure the bathroom door was still shut. Then he rushed out the front door, bolted over to the stairwell, and loped up the steps, two at a time, to the roof.

It was a warm night with a brilliant half-moon. A handful of people had spilled out of the party and come up for some privacy and quiet among the vents, chutes, and smokestacks. Seeking out a relatively obscure corner where Zee wouldn't easily find him, he came across Lockwood, seated with his feet dangling over the edge, serenely smoking a doobie.

Shay sat next to him. "I gotta wonder," he said, "if it's a really good idea to get high when you're perched five stories up."

"No wondering about it," said Lockwood. "It is an absolutely terrible idea."

Shay set his beer down beside him, then lowered himself and swung his own legs over the edge. "Share?" he asked, extending his hand.

Lockwood passed him the joint.

Shay took a hit, passed it back, and said, "So, this girl you invited…"

Lockwood laughed. "I was a conduit, man. A means to an end."

"I'm guessing I was the end?"

"All signs point to yes."

He sighed. "Sorry, man."

Lockwood shrugged. "I should've seen it coming. I *did* see it coming."

Shay cocked an eyebrow. "Then…why?"

He bounced his head from side to side. "Ahhh, you never know. I coulda been wrong."

Shay put his arm around Lockwood and gave him a squeeze. "You're twice the man I am. You know that."

"Everyone knows that." He took another toke.

"You're a genius. You're funny, and wise, and generous, and…and everything. You're a man's man."

Lockwood gave him a sidelong, suspicious look. "What do you want?"

"Why do I have to want something? I just love you, man. I'm just giving you some *love*." He squeezed him again.

"*What—do—you—want?*" Lockwood repeated, more deliberately.

Shay gave up the act and let go of him. "Rescue me from her."

He laughed. "Me and what army?"

"Any army you want. Just hire them. I'll pay for their ammo and transport. Fuck it, I'll buy an aircraft carrier."

"You can't afford an aircraft carrier."

"I'll pool my credit cards."

"You only have two. Both maxed out."

Shay sighed. "Man, I need a new band. We all know each other too well." He gestured for the joint, and Lockwood passed it to him.

"Besides," Lockwood said, "you seem to have rescued yourself."

Shay shook his head as he sucked in, then after exhaling said, "No, she'll find me. And she'll never let go. She's like a terrier on a pants leg."

"What about the other one? The one she came in with? I thought you were making some progress there."

"Gone." Shay sighed. "Walked out as soon as yours got me cornered."

"Huh." Lockwood shook his head. "Chicks, man."

"Chicks, man," Shay agreed.

After a longish pause, Lockwood said, "Probably just as well, though."

"Just as well, though, what?"

"That the other one left."

"Oh, yeah? And your reason for saying so?"

Lockwood gave him a come-on-now look. "You know perfectly goddamn well."

Shay grimaced. "Pernita doesn't own me."

"Fuck if she doesn't."

"She *doesn't*. Everything between us is totally NSA. We established that right up front."

"That was just a gambit, man. You *must've* realized that by now. That was just till she got your signature on the dotted line. Now she rules your skinny white ass."

Shay resisted the urge to argue back. What he really wanted was to drop the subject entirely. The fact was,

Lockwood was right, and Shay hated to admit it—even to himself. He hated to admit he could have been so naive, so stupid, that he could be *played* like a goddamn violin.

"We should go back to the party," he said.

"We should," Lockwood agreed.

"The fans, and everything."

"The fans," Lockwood echoed.

They sat exactly where they were for eleven minutes more, till Zee stumbled up behind them.

"*There* you are," she said, plunking herself down next to Shay. "I wondered where you'd gone to. You said you weren't going to move."

"I suddenly felt all flushed," he said. "I had to get some fresh air."

"Poor baby," she said, and she felt his forehead. "Better now?"

"Much," he said, and he turned to Lockwood and mouthed the words, *Rescue me!*

She sniffed the air and said, "You guys getting high?"

Shay shot Lockwood a look that said *absolutely not*.

Lockwood surreptitiously moved the joint out of sight and said, "I was. Downstairs. Came up for air."

Zee looked around. "You didn't happen to see my roommate up here, did you?"

"Your roommate?" Shay said, suddenly on alert.

"She's not downstairs anymore. I thought, since everyone seems to be coming up here, maybe she did, too."

"You and Loni live together?"

"Mm-hm." She looked at Shay. "You know her?"

Shay affected a nonchalant look. "I was talking to her in the kitchen, when you introduced yourself."

"You were?" She giggled. "I didn't even notice."

"Didn't notice a lot of things," Lockwood muttered so that only Shay could hear.

"Where did she go?" Zee asked.

"I'm pretty sure she left."

She slumped her shoulders. "Honestly, that's *so* like her. To just leave me here. I mean, I told her she could, but that doesn't mean she *had* to."

"She seemed kind of...uptight," said Shay.

"Oh, don't even get me started! Her idea of fun? You wouldn't believe it. Your average librarian is a she-wolf by comparison. I don't even know what she'd do if she didn't have *me*. I drag her everywhere. Not that she ever thanks me."

"You're a good friend," he said. "In fact, you're a real philanthropist, Zee...Zee...sorry, what's your last name again?"

"Gleason."

"You're a real philanthropist, Zee Gleason." He raised his beer bottle to toast her and took a swig.

"Oh, you *are* smooth," murmured Lockwood, who knew exactly what Shay was up to.

Suddenly Shay clutched his pocket. "Sorry," he said, "phone just vibrated. Won't be a minute." He got to his feet, pulling his phone from his pocket as he did so, then strode away from them, speaking into it. "Hello?...Yeah, I heard from him...Did you confirm for Friday...?"

When he was far enough away, he slipped behind a duct and took the phone from his ear, ending the pantomime of having gotten a call. He opened Facebook, and typed ZEE GLEASON in the search bar. When Zee's page popped up (God, was there *nothing* that woman wouldn't do in front of a camera? Shay had to roll his eyes.), he clicked on the link to her Friends page, then searched for LONI.

Nothing came up.

That was odd. He searched again, thinking maybe she spelled it in some other way—like a dude, LONNIE. Or maybe all Welsh or something; LLONI. A few other variants were equally unsuccessful. But he was on the hunt now, and he wasn't going to let a bad scent put him off the trail.

As he returned to Zee and Lockwood, he wondered why he was even bothering. Loni really *did* seem a little too uptight—not to mention a little too quick to take offense. Both being things he really hated in women. Yet he seemed ready to overlook them in Loni's case. Likewise her superior attitude and her transparent bullshit about not knowing who he was. She was full of herself in ways Shay usually found repellent.

Yet he was the opposite of repelled. In fact, he couldn't seem to get her out of his head.

Was it because this was the first time in a long time that a woman had walked away from him? Was it as simple as that? Was he merely reacting to a rejection, like some goddamn Neanderthal? *Grunt, I will* make *you love me.*

Or was it that he'd grown tired of being chased and flattered and fawned over? After all that sickening sugar, a little vinegar tasted surprisingly...*sweet.*

Zee and Lockwood were exactly as he'd left them. He'd hoped they'd have shimmied together, closed up the space between them, but they'd kept it open for him. In fact, they didn't appear even to be cognizant of each other. Zee was staring dreamily in one direction, Lockwood sternly in the other. With a sigh, Shay sat back down between them, picked up his beer bottle again, and downed a slug.

"*That* was awkward," Lockwood muttered.

"So, I was saying," Zee said, chirpily resuming where she'd left off, "Loni's gone and left me, and now I don't know *how* I'm going to get home…or to, y'know, *wherever* it is I'm going next." She smiled coquettishly. "I guess I'll just have to hope someone comes along to help me out."

"Really sucks that she left you hanging," Shay said. "What kind of person does that?"

"I know, right?" she said, inching closer to him.

"I mean, she must be a total bitch."

"Well, not total. She's just got major issues."

"Like what? Wait, don't tell me. She's one of those tech-phobes who, like, hates Facebook and shit."

"Well, she doesn't *hate* it, exactly, but she doesn't use her real name 'cause she doesn't want people from her past finding her and 'bothering' her."

"'People from her past'?" he said, shaking his head. "Man, that is lame. I mean, what is she, twenty-two? Who's she talking about? Her ex-nanny or something? Who's got a 'past' at twenty-two?"

Zee laughed, and grabbed his arm as if to keep from rollicking herself right off the roof. "You're so funny," she said.

She wasn't laughing anymore, but she wasn't letting go of his arm, either.

"So, what, does she use her porn name or something?"

She looked at him, in the moonlight, and it was clear she'd been trying to steer his attention in quite another direction. "Hm?" she asked. "Porn name?"

"You know. Like, you take your first pet's name, and the name of the street you grew up on, and that's your porn-star name. Tell me you never heard of this."

She giggled. "Really? This is a thing? Oh, my God. My porn-star name is…" She thought for a second. "Bubbles Fairbanks." She squealed in delight. "What's yours?"

"Tyler Montana," he said.

She screamed and slid her other arm around his. She was now attached to him like a barnacle. "Oh, my *Gawd*, that's a *total* porn name! I am so *dying*!" She pressed her face against his shoulder and groaned happily into it.

He was growing a little uncomfortable with her invasion of his private space—hell, she was all but crawling under his shirt—so he turned to Lockwood and said, "What's *your* porn name, man?"

Lockwood gave him a sidelong glance, then looked back ahead and said, "Wilbur Forty-Third Street."

Shay laughed, but Zee didn't. Then there was a spell of quiet that seemed like it might go anywhere.

"Soooo," Shay said, trying to get back to the point without drawing too much attention to it, "your roommate uses her porn name for Facebook?"

"No," she said dreamily, as though falling asleep. "The name of some English poet. *So* lame."

"Which English poet?"

"I don't remember," she said, sighing into his ear. Then she yawned theatrically.

"But English, right? What century?"

"Who knows?" she said. Then she blinked her eyes at him very drowsily and said, "I'm getting so *tired*. I need to find a bed soon."

Lockwood apparently couldn't help himself. He openly barked out a derisive laugh, as if he couldn't believe his ears.

"Where'm I gonna find a bed?" she asked, dropping her voice, as though to leave Lockwood out of it. "Hm? Any ideas, Tyler Montana?"

"I'll drive you home," he said.

She perked up immediately. So did Lockwood.

"You will?" she asked.

"You *will*?" Lockwood echoed.

"Sure. Why not? Gentlemanly thing to do."

All drowsiness seemed instantly gone from her. She looked like she was about to say something, then appeared to think better of it—as though, with things going her way, why risk it?

"You ready now?" he asked.

She nodded eagerly.

He got to his feet. But the sudden head rush as he stood up, and the effects of the pot he'd smoked, combined to make him momentarily thick-witted, dulling his strategic instincts. And in that moment, he revealed his hand. "She'll be there, you think?" he said, regretting the words as soon as they left his mouth.

"Hm?" Zee said, as she brushed the grit from the roof off her ass. "Who? My roommate?" Suddenly she stopped brushing and looked straight at him, her mouth hanging slightly open.

He tried to adopt a blank expression, but he was too baked to manage it. He must have looked as busted as he felt. Zee didn't say anything; she didn't have to. It was suddenly, blindingly clear where his real interest was—where it had been all along. She burst into tears and fled across the roof and back down into the building.

"Oh, man," he said.

"This is truly amazing to me," said Lockwood, who had swiveled around to watch the scene, so that his legs now stretched across the rooftop. "You throw away more talent in a night than I manage to attract in a year."

"I wasn't...this wasn't about..." His tongue felt too big for his mouth. He couldn't make it say what he wanted it to. He wasn't *sure* what he wanted it to.

"I liked this one, you know," Lockwood said. "She's a flake, okay, fine. But she's sweet and she's got a lot of energy and she loves our music. And she's got a shit job where she makes no money, but she doesn't complain because *we're* around to remind her life is worth celebrating."

"I'm so sorry, man. Really. I just...whoa." Shay ran his fingers through his hair. "I can't even figure out what just happened here."

Lockwood got to his feet and stood up with a grunt of effort. "What happened here," he said, his voice a little winded, "is that you are a lightweight."

"I can hold my drink," Shay protested. "And my weed."

Lockwood shook his head. "That isn't what I meant." He started across the roof.

"Where you goin', man?" Shay called out, feeling suddenly sad at the idea of being abandoned.

"To rescue *her*," he said, without stopping.

And a few seconds later, Shay was alone.

And the moon shone on, gorgeous and relentless.

CHAPTER 5

Shay woke up from a restless sleep with the sun slicing into his eyes. He rolled over and tried to block it out, but it diabolically insinuated itself through the crook of his arm and the folds of his blanket, to splash once more onto his face, like acid.

"Goddammit," he murmured, and his tongue felt like it was made of wet sand.

He pulled the covers over his head, blocking out the evil sun. He moaned in contentment and relaxed back into semislumber. But in a matter of minutes he jolted awake again, gasping for breath; he'd run out of oxygen under there.

He threw back the covers, angry at the cosmos for conspiring to deny him the only thing he wanted in the whole goddamn world, which was to sleep for the next several hours—to sleep indefinitely, really, until something worth *not* sleeping for came and shook him out of it.

He'd stayed up too late and partied too hard. When he'd finally stumbled home and collapsed into bed, his mind had raced in too many directions, his stomach had roiled, and his legs had twitched nervously. He looked down at his legs now: numb and white, like the legs of a corpse—even his elaborate tattoos looked ashy and shriveled. One foot still wore a sock. The opposite heel was wrapped in his boxer-briefs, like a bandage. Apparently, he'd been too wrecked when he'd undressed to be able to get them all the way off. He'd gotten them down to his ankles, but then the sharp right angle of that foot must have thrown him for a loop, so he'd just given up and left things as they were.

Of course, his morning wood was right there, staring him in the face. Didn't seem to matter how totaled he got the night before; there was always that one bit of himself that was up and at 'em come sunrise. He wished he knew its secret.

He made a smacking noise and probed his mouth with his tongue. His teeth felt furry. He groped around the side of the bed for a water bottle, but when he found one he knocked it over and spilled its contents all over the floor.

"Fucking fuckety fuck pants," he said, and then he quietly laughed, because he had no idea what that even meant.

He lay back on the pillow, his head clanging like a chapel bell.

Apparently it had been a good party. If and when he could manage to remember any of it, he was sure this assessment would be borne out.

His phone interrupted his attempts to pluck strands of memory from the fuzz of his brain. He searched the covers for his phone, and by the time he found it, his bed was in complete disarray. He sat in the middle of it, naked but for his T-shirt and sock, with the underwear wrapped around his foot. "H'lo?" he croaked into the phone.

"Wow," said a velvety voice. "Must've been some throwdown."

He ran his hand through his hair. His fingers almost snagged in its unkempt mass. "Must'a." He wiped the sand from his eyes. "Morning, P'nita."

The woman laughed. "You're still in bed, aren't you?"

"No," he lied.

"It's all right. As long as you're alone."

He didn't say anything.

"You *are* alone, aren't you?"

He lay back on the pillows, scratching his stomach with his free hand. "Let me check."

"Don't bother, I can check for you." A small pause. "I'm downstairs."

He went completely still. "What?"

"I'm in front of your building. I have coffee and cinnamon rolls. Let me in, please."

He was blasted into full wakefulness. He somehow managed to get onto his feet, straighten out his boxer-briefs, pull on a pair of jeans that was lying on the floor outside the bathroom, and drink a full half-quart of water within a ninety-second span. Then he padded over to his front door and buzzed Pernita in.

He gave his apartment a quick scan, as he wasn't 100 percent sure there *wasn't* some girl there, flouncing around in a towel, having just used his shower and now puttering around, waiting for her hair to dry or something. But no, he remembered now. He hadn't scored last night. He'd tried. But she got away. Got away *early*.

The memories were just filtering back when Pernita appeared at the top of the stairs, and he quietly cursed her under his breath. This was just such a typical move of hers. So...*proprietary*. She acted like she owned him. They'd been very clear, at the outset of this...this *thing* they had together, that there were no expectations, no obligations, no anything.

It was just for fun. Nothing more. Shay had thought he'd won the lottery: a hot babe who thought about sex just like a guy did.

Except…she didn't.

In fact, she thought about sex in the worst way possible, as a bait and switch. She'd said what she had to say to get Shay where she wanted him, and ever since, she'd been taking over his life by degrees. Relentlessly encroaching on every square inch of it.

He fought back with the only weapons at his command: rudeness, brusqueness, silence. He never said please or thank you, never complimented her, never called her by anything but her name (no "honey" or "babe" or "sugar"—*God*, no). If she was aware of this tactic (and she probably was), she chose to serenely ignore it and to sail on into his harbor as if she were the queen of it. Which she almost was, by this point.

Whenever Shay had had too much and was close to shutting the whole thing down, she seemed able to detect it with a kind of sixth sense or something. She would avert the danger simply by bringing into their conversation the one word that would instantly reset him to zero:

"Daddy."

This morning she looked like she always did—crisp, burnished, sparkling. She could've just walked out of a salon or a spa or both. Her leather jacket was so supple it might have been her own skin. Her jeans were so distressed Shay wondered how they stayed on—he'd thrown out jeans in better condition than those—so of course they probably cost her six hundred bucks.

She breezed past him into the apartment—she never waited for an invitation—pausing only to give him a quick smooch, then glided into his kitchen and set down the carton and the bag she'd been carrying. "I don't suppose you have any clean plates," she said, glancing at the pileup in his sink. "Never mind, I'll use paper towels."

Shay happened to know for a fact that he had no paper towels either, but he was content to let her root around in his kitchen for a while, looking for some. He sat down at his rickety kitchen table and yawned, while Pernita clattered and thunked through his drawers and cabinets. He was in mid-yawn—his jaw stretched as far as it would go—when it hit him.

Loni.

That was her name. The one who had gotten away.

The one who had pretended not to know who he was. How goddamn lame was that?...Adorably lame. He'd wanted to kiss her right then.

But no, she'd been in full emotional armor. She was having exactly *zero* of Shay Dayton and all his...Shay Dayton-ness. And she was ready to tell him so, too.

A spitfire.

And *hot*.

Pernita screamed and jumped back a few paces. Then she looked at Shay and said, in a very firm tone, "After breakfast, I'm taking you out to buy some roach motels."

"I won't use them," he said. "They're not humane."

"Well, no wonder you have a roach issue."

"I bought a thing," he said, gesturing with his thumb. "It's plugged in over there. It's supposed to drive them out with sonic waves that are inaudible to human ears."

She rolled her eyes in exasperation, then said, "Audio electronics are not the answer to *all* life's problems."

He pretended to look shocked and said, "You take that back!"

She laughed, then left the kitchen in disgust and said, "Never mind, we'll just eat out of the box."

He didn't want to face her across the breakfast table. That was too disturbingly domestic. Fortunately, his laptop was right there, so he flipped it open. By the time Pernita was seated, it was between them—a shield, a barrier, a partition.

She opened the box of cinnamon rolls and very carefully took one out. It was a difficult maneuver, given her spectacularly manicured nails, which were approximately the length of the cockroaches she'd just disrespected. "What are you looking at?" she asked.

"Facebook," he said. It was true. The news feed page had been the first thing to pop up.

That jogged his memory, too. The night before, at the party—the girl who wouldn't leave him alone. He'd checked her Facebook page. Why was that—?

Oh, right! He'd been trying to find Loni. Because she was the girl's roommate.

But—what had the girl said? Zee, that was her name. What had *Zee* said? Loni was on Facebook under the name of an English poet.

"Anything new to report?" Pernita asked, biting gingerly into the cinnamon roll.

"Nah," he said, not looking up at her. He opened up Wikipedia and typed ENGLISH POETS.

"You should try these," she said, licking some icing from her lips. "They're totally exquiz."

He winced. "Exquiz" was one of the expressions she used that threatened to trigger his sniper gene. "In a minute," he said. "Ready for some coffee, though."

She obediently fetched a steaming Styrofoam cup from the bag and slid it over to him. "My friend Maesha posted the sweetest video this morning," she said. "Kitten playing with an armadillo. You should see it. Maesha Vance. Go to her page."

"I'm not friends with her," he said, irritated that the search resulted in a list of English-*language* poets. Of which there were about twelve million.

"You don't need to be. She shares everything with everyone. Total social-media exhibitionist. Maesha Vance. M-A-E-S-H-A."

"I don't want to see a kitten playing with an aardvark," he said, trying BRITISH POETS.

"Armadillo," she said.

"Arma-anything."

She raised an eyebrow. "Well. *Sommmme*one's obviously found his inner snark this morning. Hungover much?" She slid the cup closer to him. "Coffee's getting cold."

There was no Wikipedia list of British poets. What the hell! He tried ENGLISH LITERATURE and got a page with a wall of text that went on for ten miles.

He closed the laptop and took a slurp of coffee. It surged through him like lightning, and he felt immediately better.

Pernita smiled at him. "There we go. Little color back in your cheeks."

He hated when she was right. He shoved aside the laptop and took another chug from the coffee. It was definitely revivifying. In fact, he could feel his brain cells start to wake up and percolate.

"I've told you about Maesha before, I'm sure," she said, going in for her second cinnamon bun. "She's the one who's been screwing Rob Kerringer."

"Who's Rob Kerringer?"

She put her hands on the table, as if his ignorance had sapped her of the strength to lift the cinnamon bun. *"Rob Kerringer,"* she said with more insistency, as if this would make a difference.

"Who is Rob Kerringer?" he repeated, imitating her.

"I can't believe you don't know who Rob Kerringer is," she said, raising the bun to her lips again.

"I can't help what you can't believe." *British poets, British poets,* he thought. What did he know about British poets? Just Shakespeare, really. Shakespeare and John Lennon. Did John Lennon count?

"Rob Kerringer is the tech billionaire," Pernita continued. "He's the one who invented Sited. You know, the app that lets you insert yourself into any photo you're taking, while you're taking it?" She bit off a mouthful of the gooey bun, then said, her voice thick with chewing, "I cannot *believe* you don't know this."

"I've never heard of Sited," he said. "That's a stupid app. It's embarrassing."

"Well, Daddy doesn't think so. He's one of Rob's investors." She smiled victoriously at him, as though playing a trump card. Which, of course, she was.

Shay shrugged and said nothing. He was thinking back to his chat with Loni in the kitchen, when she'd berated him for his terrible lyrics. She'd mentioned a poet then, hadn't she? Someone Shay had surprised her by knowing. How did that happen? He didn't know anybody.

"That's how I met Maesha," Pernita continued, licking the frosting from her fingers. Either she was oblivious to Shay's complete lack of interest in this subject, or she just didn't care. "Launch party for the app. You'll be doing lots of those, you know. Whether you like it or not."

He shrugged again. "If I have to."

William Blake! That was it. Loni had mentioned William Blake. Suddenly Shay was certain that this was her Facebook name. He would have bet money on it. He knew enough from his college psychology classes—and from his own, unsystematic studies of human nature—that the things people mention to you within the first ten minutes of meeting them are inevitably the things most important to them. Hell, how long after meeting someone new did Shay mention the band? Like, nanoseconds.

"You *do* have to," Pernita said, looking around for something to wipe her fingers on. "Don't worry, you don't need to say much. You can just stand there and smolder. Be the sexy, mysterious front man. It's good for your image. Far better than if you talked."

And then there was the shocked way Loni reacted when Shay had tossed off those Blake lines, like he had the poet's whole output right there on his personal hard drive. She didn't need to know that the only way he knew those lines was because Bono recited them in U2's "Beautiful Ghost."

"No, you just leave all the talking to me," Pernita said. She reached down to the floor, picked up a discarded T-shirt that had been lying there for God only knew how long, and wiped the frosting from her fingers onto it. "I'll do all the talking for you."

Shay snapped out of his private thoughts. "You?" He was shocked that Pernita was picturing herself as part of Overlords of Loneliness's parties and press junkets.

She nodded and took a sip of her own coffee. When she finished she licked her lips and said, "Problem with that?"

"Well...yeah. You're not part of the band, is all. If the band has a spokesman, it should be a band *member*."

She smiled at him, as if amused by his childishness. "Okay," she said. "You'll do it yourself, then?"

He frowned. He knew he had it in him. He *could* represent Overlords of Loneliness. But—he hated admitting it *again*—Pernita was right; he was better off as the sexy, silent front man. His awareness of his strengths was sufficient to convince him of that. He'd have far more impact as an image—an icon—than as a personality.

He shook his head.

"Lockwood, then?" Pernita said, cocking her head. "Lovely, genial, easygoing Lockwood? He's your choice?"

Of course he wasn't. Lockwood was too sweet-natured for the job. He lacked the killer instinct to *make* people pay attention to what he was saying.

"Baby, then? Or Jimmy?"

Baby was a featherweight, and Jimmy came off as a sociopath. Shay folded his arms in frustration.

"Trina, then! It's settled."

For a moment he felt like his chair was collapsing under him. Was there any greater recipe for disaster than letting Trina speak for the band? She had all the tact and finesse of a T. rex.

Pernita winked. "Me, then? It's settled? Honestly, honey, it's a bargain when you think about it. Most bands have to hire a PR firm and shell out thousands to get someone to message for them. You don't have to do that. I told you, when I convinced Daddy to take you on, you were getting the complete package. Not *just* the most successful band manager in the music business, but a *team*. Meaning, *moi*. I've just graduated with a master's in Communications with a special focus on entertainment. I'm fresh, I'm young, I'm hot, and I'm smart as a whip. I mean," she concluded, looking at him with deliberate boldness, "where would you be *without* me?"

He understood her meaning. She was pretending to ask where he'd be now, without everything she'd done for him, but in reality she was threatening him. Where would you be, she was saying, if I dumped you now? Where would you be if I walked away and took Daddy with me?

Shay wasn't stupid. He knew he was trapped. And he knew *she* knew it, too. That's why she'd agreed to his, in retrospect, ridiculous no-strings-attached rule before their first roll in the hay. She knew he wouldn't be able to cry foul when she quietly changed the rules to *hers*. Which is exactly what she'd done. She knew that nothing in his life meant more to him than Overlords of Loneliness, and she'd given him the means to take them right to the pinnacle of commercial success. "Daddy," after all, was the near-legendary Halbert Hasque, whose string of clients weren't just pop-idol gods, they were millionaires to a man. He could do the same for Shay.

And all Shay had to do was let Pernita invade and lay claim to every single corner of his life. To own him entirely. To run him exclusively. Well...let her try. She obviously thought she had him where she wanted him. But he had his own ideas. There were still some small corners of his life that were safe from her, and he meant to keep them that way.

She'd turned up her nose, for instance, at attending the concert's after-party. She was far too self-important to allow herself to mingle with mere *fans*. So that meant last night had belonged to Shay alone, and he had every intention of building on it. But not right away. Pernita—appeased by his obedience and rendered sweet by the sugar of the cinnamon buns—came over, sat in his lap, and put her arms around his neck.

He knew exactly what that was prelude to. So he went there, without a grumble, and hey, why shouldn't he? Pernita was a lot of fun when she finally let *him* take charge.

And he did take charge. In the bedroom, with her sprawled out beneath him, naked but for her designer scent, she looked like a fragile little china doll. He could almost believe her to be vulnerable, breakable.

But then he pressed into her, and her hip bones, which jutted out from her taut, smooth stomach, stabbed into his thighs; they were sharp as hatchets. And the nipples of her pert, creamy breasts scraped across his chest like sandpaper. Pernita only looked soft and frail—all you had to do was touch her to realize she was a woman of wire and glass.

So he felt no hesitation in going at her like a locomotive. He knew she could take it. And when she wrapped her legs around him and urged him on, faster, harder—well, he was only too happy to oblige.

To oblige *her*, that is. He skillfully, energetically brought her close—closer—to the convulsive brink of a tantric Niagara Falls, and then pushed her over, and watched her fall, flailing and howling in wild ecstasy.

But he didn't follow her. As soon as she fell limp, he reined himself in and declined to finish. This was one more thing he refused to give up to her, if possible. He'd choose when, and with whom, he'd ride the joy train. This took a degree of willpower he didn't usually have at his command; but at least today, his killer hangover made it easier.

Did she have any idea? If she did, she pretended otherwise. But then *everything* about their lovemaking was pretense. For example, the way, at the height of their thrashing across the sheets, she accused him of "punishing" her. But it was never really punishment. It was a charade of punishment, her little gift to him so he could exorcize his anger and give him the illusion of power. Yes, he took control of their sex life, but only because she let him. That was Pernita in a nutshell. For her, submission wasn't even submission. For her, it was just another tactic.

////////////

Afterwards, while she was in the shower, he crept back to the kitchen table and opened his laptop again. He went to Zee Gleason's Facebook page, pulled up her friends list, and searched it for William Blake.

And there he—or rather she—was.

There was no photo of Loni. Instead the profile picture was an image of one of Blake's paintings, of a muscular angel. On the ABOUT page, there was no information on birth date or current city or anything else remotely personal. There was only this passage:

> *He who binds to himself a joy*
> *Does the wingèd life destroy;*
> *But he who kisses the joy as it flies*
> *Lives in eternity's sunrise.*

He grinned. There was no doubt in his mind. There might be other people, other Blake devotees, who had Facebook pages like this, but there was no way that Zee Gleason, of all people, could know more than one.

He clicked ADD FRIEND and put in a simple message:

Tell me more.

CHAPTER 6

The alarm on Loni's phone bugled to life. She snapped out of a sound sleep, groped around her nightstand for it, and, when she found it, tapped Snooze, again wishing for a tangible object she could slam down on.

As she lay in the warmth of her bed, enjoying the act of putting off her day, she wondered why she had bothered to set her alarm at all. Force of habit, probably. It wasn't as if she had anything she had to get up for…any place to go, anyone to see, anything to do. And something about that utter emptiness caused a little wriggle of discontent in her breast that wouldn't let her go back to sleep. It was a paradox: the pointlessness of getting up was upsetting her so much that she might as well get up.

She sat on the side of her bed and looked at her phone. She had the urge to check her text messages and e-mails but was afraid there would be something from Byron, and she wasn't sure what she'd say to him. She wasn't even sure how she felt toward him. Was she still mad at him? Had she even *been* mad at him? Everything about last night was sort of hazy. That brain-scraping concert. That absurd party…

She felt a sudden need to use the bathroom. She got up, opened her bedroom door, and went out into the apartment wearing just the oversize T-shirt she always slept in. She was just passing the couch when something on it moved, and she nearly leapt through the roof. She backed away and gave a startled shout.

There was a man lying there. A *big* man. He was curled up with his face against the cushions, so she had no idea who it was. She was pretty sure she didn't know anyone this beefy. Was he an intruder? It seemed unlikely. Why would anyone break in just to crash out on the sofa? Also, he was fully dressed, but he'd removed his shoes and set them by one of the couch legs. So, obviously no marauding thug.

He'd stirred at the sound of her voice and now quarter-turned his head and looked at her.

"Oh, hi," he said.

And she *did* recognize him. That is, she realized she'd seen him before. And very recently. She just couldn't remember where.

"You scared the hell out of me," she said.

"Sorry," he said, rolling all the way over with a grunt of effort. He sat up and scratched his head.

"Who the hell are you?"

He looked at her and sighed, as if tired of being the guy no one ever remembers. "Lockwood Mott," he said. "You're Loni, right? We met last night."

"Oh," she said, as it all came back to her. "Right. Sorry! What are you doing here?"

"I just wanted to make sure your friend was okay. She was a little...shaky last night. I figured I'd stick around just in case."

"Zee? Is she all right?" Before he could answer, she said, "Wait, wait...I really have to pee. Just hold that thought." She hopped over to the bathroom and tried to turn the doorknob, but it had been locked. She rapped on the door. "Zee? You in there?"

"Uh-huh," came the reply. "Getting ready for my follow-up interview."

"You be out soon?"

"Couple minutes."

"Just, kind of a pee emergency here, is all."

"I said, a *couple minutes*," she snapped through the door—and Loni was taken aback. She'd never heard Zee sound so abrasive before.

She went back to the living room, where Lockwood Mott was slipping on his shoes. "I heard that," he said. "She's obviously fine. I'll just head out."

"No, wait," she said, gesturing for him to stay. "I'm sure she wants to thank you."

He smiled at her like she was naive or something. "You're sure of that, huh?"

Loni glanced back at the bathroom door, then looked back at him. "What happened last night?"

"Nothing," he said, finishing tying his laces.

She blinked. "Nothing? She got upset over nothing?"

"The worst kind of nothing," he said, sitting up again.

Loni sat down in the chair across the coffee table from him. "Oh," she said. "Didn't work out with...what's his name. Shay Dayton. That it?"

"Got it in one," he said, sitting back and yawning.

"Well." She gave a little sigh of admiration. "*You're* one hell of a stand-up guy, aren't you? Considering how you must've imagined the night would go."

"Hey." He shrugged. "I invited her. I was responsible for what happened to her while she was there. Just doing the gentlemanly thing."

"That's what I mean." She beamed a smile at him.

He shook his head. "No one should be *thanked* for being a gentleman. It should be, like, every guy's default setting."

"Well, there are a lot of should-be's in the world."

He nodded. "Got it in one again."

There was a small silence. Loni opened her laptop, which was on the coffee table between them, figuring she might as well check her mail while Zee was finishing. Then she remembered her manners, looked back up at Lockwood, and said, "Get you a coffee or something?"

He made as though to get up. "Nah. I should head out."

"No, really. Just wait to say good-bye." She looked over her shoulder and called out, *"Zee?"*

"ONE. MINUTE." was the snarled reply.

Loni looked at Lockwood in surprise. "What exactly happened to her?"

He raised his eyebrows. "Not really my place to say. But I gotta wish you good luck with her."

"Me? Why me?"

He rose to his feet. "Forget I said anything."

Zee came out of the bathroom, fully made up and dressed except for her stockinged feet. She saw Loni and Lockwood and came to a halt. "All yours," she said to Loni, while looking at Lockwood.

"Nice to see you again," Loni said, and she scurried to the bathroom.

///////////////

After Loni had entered the bathroom and shut the door, Zee turned to Lockwood. "Thanks. It was sweet of you to stay. You didn't have to."

"Don't mention it."

She gave him a look that made it clear that would be her preference, too. "Sorry I was such a mess."

He dismissed this with a wave of his hand.

"You didn't tell her anything, did you?" she asked, nodding toward the bathroom.

He looked shocked at the idea. "Not my story to tell."

She grinned in thanks. "You want some coffee?"

"No, no," he said. "Gotta run. But..." He half turned, and gave her a sly look. "Check on you later?"

She shook her head. "You don't have to."

"I know. But can I?"

"Really. It's not necessary."

"Right. But *can* I?"

She wanted to be angry, but somehow found herself laughing instead. "You can try," she said. "I can't guarantee I'll be here."

He winked. "Chance I'll have to take."

Then he gave her a courtly little bow and left the apartment.

Zee sat down in the chair Loni had just vacated and pulled her boots from under the coffee table. When she looked up, she noticed that Loni's laptop was open and that her Facebook page was up. As she pulled on her boots, she noticed that there was a new Friend Request. She suddenly went very still—her boot still only halfway on her foot. She had a gut feeling about that Friend Request…a very bad gut feeling. She looked up at the bathroom door. Still shut. And then something came over her…a kind of willful evil. She reached over and clicked on the Friend Request icon.

And yes. She was right.

There he was.

Shay Dayton.

And there was a message from him.

"Tell me more."

A sort of red haze blinded her for a moment. Her fingers seemed to dart across the keyboard of their own volition. Before her mind had caught up with them, they'd denied the Friend Request, erased the message, and blocked Loni's—or rather "William Blake's"—page from any further incursions by Shay Dayton.

She heard the toilet flush and then the faucet turn on. She sat back and finished pulling on her boot. A moment later Loni reappeared.

///////////////

Loni wasn't surprised to find Lockwood had left, but she was a little perplexed by the strange look on Zee's face: wide-eyed, like she'd been caught with her hand in the cookie jar. "Everything okay?" she asked, drying her hands on the back of the T-shirt, where it hung over her derriere.

Zee got to her feet and crossed the apartment to fetch her purse. "Mm-hm!" she said brightly. "Just running late for my interview!"

Loni looked at the rooster clock that hung in the kitchen. "You have half an hour. And you said it's only fifteen minutes from here."

A little spasm of what looked like guilt distorted Zee's face. "Have to stop at the pharmacy first. Pick up a prescription." She laughed—a brittle, nervous laugh. "You know how slow they are."

Loni had no idea what was going on, but she was willing to take Zee at face value. "Okay. I thought for a minute you were mad at me or something."

The weird laugh again. "No, no." Then she looked toward the door, the way a prisoner might look at an escape hatch.

"Lockwood's nice," Loni offered, trying to be casual.

"Mm-hm." Zee looked back at her, and her eyes looked almost desperate. "Late," she said again.

Loni shrugged. "Okay. See you later." She felt that something was definitely wrong and was anxious to set it right before Zee left. "Want me to whip up something for lunch?" she asked as Zee headed for the door. "Ramen noodles with my special sauce?"

Zee shook her head. "Lunch date in town," she said with a brief, apologetic smile. And with that, she was out the door like a shot.

Loni looked after her for a while, as though she might pick up some clues in the aura she left behind, but ultimately it was useless. Something had traumatized Zee last night, and she meant to keep it a secret from her. Well, as long as Zee wasn't mad at her...Loni must have just imagined that.

She sat down in front of her laptop. Her Facebook news feed stared her in the face, but it couldn't really rouse her interest. She knew it would only depress her to see updates from all her friends about the vital, purposeful lives they were leading, while she lingered on in a state of something like inertia.

The whole day was spread out before her. The only thing that might possibly fill even a little part of it was Byron. Should she see him or not? She decided to think about it while showering. Afterward, feeling refreshed, she stood before the mirror and buffed her hair dry, and decided, *not*.

It was shaping up to be a nice day; a little overcast, but the yellowish tinge to the otherwise gray clouds seemed to deepen the green of the lawns and trees outside her window. She'd spend the day just walking and thinking and taking in whatever life she could. It was like that Blake line: "To see a world in a grain of sand and a heaven in a wild flower, hold infinity in the palm of your hand and eternity in an hour." It had been a long time since she simply looked around and marveled at the simplicity of everything, and its wonderful connectedness.

When she picked up her phone, she saw there was a voice mail from Byron. She chose to not even listen to it. She had picked out her mood for the day the same way she'd picked out her clothes—a summery halter top and old, comfortable jeans. She wasn't changing either one, or allowing anyone to change them for her. She popped the phone in her backpack, then swung the backpack over one shoulder and left the apartment.

In the vestibule she found the landlady, who was picking up the advertising circulars that had collected on the floor by the mailboxes.

"Good morning, Mrs. Milliken," Loni said, very deliberately using the woman's name in the hopes that it might prompt Mrs. Milliken to return the favor. But no go. She just looked up at Loni with her bizarre two-toned face and said, "Oh. I thought it was somebody."

"No, nobody at all. Just me. One of the people who actually, y'know...lives here."

"If it was somebody, I'd have to speak to them about these flyers," Mrs. Milliken said. "Just because people don't want them is no excuse for throwing them on the floor this way."

"I agree."

"I do not run a barnyard. This is a respectable residence. People who rent here need to show some respect."

"You are so right."

"Also, the discarded rubber bands. This is not to be tolerated. The people who *do* take the advertising circulars are in the habit of removing the rubber bands and looping them around the inside doorknob." She reached into the pocket of her housecoat and produced a wiggling mass of colorful rubber strands. "Look at how many I found. You could barely turn the knob. In an emergency situation, that could mean life or death. *Life or death*," she repeated, for emphasis. "Plus, these things carry germs. Fortunately I'm well stocked on antibacterial soap. I'll need it after I discard these. Filthy." She put them back in her pocket.

"Well...there it is," Loni said, growing a little weary of the conversation now.

"I will have quite an earful to deliver, the next time I see any of my residents," she said, and the clear implication was that Loni was not a resident, was not even here, did not actually exist. She was basically just talking to thin air.

Loni reshouldered her backpack strap, which had slipped a little while Mrs. Milliken was droning on. She smiled and said, "Have a really great day," and scooted by the landlady out into the warm, humid summer air.

For a little while she was almost envious of Mrs. Milliken. Imagine a life in which the biggest problems you faced were discarded flyers and rubber bands. Or laundry room etiquette, which had been her ax to grind last week after someone complained about having her things moved from washer to dryer by someone else who wanted to use the former. Mrs. Milliken had gone right to work putting together a list of rules for residents who used the laundry room, which she had managed to tell Loni about while at the same time implying that the news didn't apply to Loni, because Loni was not a real human being on the face of the earth.

She laughed at the ridiculousness of it and wondered how Mrs. Milliken would react if she were facing a *real* problem—like, having to decide between two possible futures, one of which would uproot her and take her to the other side of the country, and the other of which was completely blank and uncertain.

Yeah, Loni would take rubber bands over that any day.

She had breakfast at the little French café on King Street—an omelet, a glass of fresh-squeezed orange juice, and a slice of baguette with two tabs of butter, which was one more than she usually allowed herself, but it felt like a morning to indulge. She wanted to avoid poetry because it reminded her too much of the decision facing her, so instead she flipped through magazines on her e-reader. When those began to bore her, she played Scrabble against the computer brain. She lost by a hair, which put her in a bit of a snit, so she left the café feeling worse than when she had arrived.

The sun was still lurking behind an iron wall of clouds, but that at least kept it from being too hot at midday. Loni strolled around Briscoll Park, trying to see the world in a grain of sand, but all she kept seeing were moms on cell phones ignoring screaming kids and dogs taking dumps under bushes. It would have been hard to find eternity in any of that. And she realized that at the back of her mind was Byron. She wasn't going to really be able to break through to a better mood until she at least knew what he was thinking right then. So she took out her own phone and listened to his voice mail.

"Hey, Loni—it's me. Sorry about last night. Million things to get done before moving, it's obviously deranging me a little. Give me a shout. Let's talk through whatever's still holding you back. Right. Later."

Well, that was pretty civilized. She smiled. The residual rancor and resentment of the night before seemed to dissipate like vapor. Byron. What a big goof. She should've known his panicky call trying to force her to decide had just been a nervous tic. She'd seen him go down that rabbit hole so many times. Obligations would pile up and he'd snap—become frantic and gibbering, running around like a chicken with its head chopped off. Then a few hours later he'd be over it and even laugh at himself.

He really was a sweetheart. But if that was the case, what *was* the thing holding her back? He'd been her friend and protector, her mentor and advisor, for so many years. He believed in her, he encouraged her, he celebrated all her successes with genuine happiness for her. Why *wouldn't* she want to continue that?

She didn't feel suffocated. That wasn't it. Just the opposite. She was a little bit *afraid* of being left on her own. Maybe that was why—because she *should* be left on her own then. Maybe she depended on Byron too much. But no, that wasn't it, either. She was only twenty-one. There was plenty of time to establish herself as her own woman. Byron could help her secure a firmer footing for that.

So…*why*?

And then, a bit of sun dribbled out from behind a bruise-colored cloud, and she knew. In fact, she realized that on some subconscious level she'd always known but hadn't allowed herself to admit it.

There had been a few incidents—two, really, plus a few near-misses—during her years as Byron's protégé, when things between them had gotten a little out of hand. A couple of parties where too many drinks were downed, and they ended up in a corner somewhere, locked together in crazy face-mashing. Byron had always called it off; he had always been the one to say, "All right, hold on—no, no, let's just leave it right there," because it was crossing a line. He was a teacher, and she was his student. Both times he'd been the responsible one who'd prevented it from going any further.

But now they weren't teacher and student anymore. If she went with Byron, she'd be his TA. They'd both be staff. And she knew—she'd always had a sense—that those inebriated snogging sessions had meant much more to him than they had to her. She'd just been acting out, letting go of her inhibitions. She'd done the same thing many times before, with other guys. Those times, it had happened to be Byron. Hadn't meant a thing.

She knew he couldn't say the same. Sometimes, the way he looked at her—the things he said to her, before he caught himself...

Well, all right then. *That* was what was stopping her. That was what was keeping her from making this decision. It wasn't about her career; it was about her personal life. She knew if she went to California with Byron, she'd be going not just as his TA but as his lover. Maybe not immediately, but it was inevitable. She wouldn't know anyone else out there, she'd depend utterly on him, and though he wouldn't ever press his advantage, she'd feel grateful to him. Indebted. Eventually she'd give him what he wanted. Of course she would.

This was all very clarifying. And she felt she was being very adult in facing it so squarely. It seemed to her that running away from this relationship would be the wrong thing to do. She liked Byron. She even loved him, in a way—though not in any way that might be considered romantic. He was sweet, and she was comfortable with him. Hadn't she even said, if he were only her age, he'd be the ideal guy for her? If her future depended on going to this next level, why not? It wouldn't be forever. And it would give her the time and the confidence to figure out where she could go from there.

She rounded the corner of her block with new determination. She'd figured it out. She'd decided what to do. She was going to St. Nazarius with Byron.

She was almost exhilarated as she turned up the walk to her apartment building. But then she stopped dead.

There was someone by the door—seated on the stoop.

Someone holding a slightly drooping rose.

Shay Dayton.

CHAPTER 7

After a seemingly interminable hour of shopping with Pernita that had felt like a year-long sentence he'd had to serve for unspecified crimes, Shay now had his place deliciously to himself. Pernita had been too eager to unwrap, spread out, and gloat over her new purchases to want to spend any more time in Shay's flea-trap of an apartment.

He tossed the bag containing the roach motels on his kitchen counter, then went to his couch and fell onto it backward, like a tree some logger had just cut down. It actually jumped back a whole inch and a half when he landed on it. He settled into the cushions, determined to grab himself a nice, restorative nap. It was, after all, not quite twelve hours since he'd taken his final bows on the stage at Club Uncumber. And then there'd been the party after, and he had no idea how late that had gone on. His memories of it were increasingly wispy, the further he delved into them.

His only certainty was that, had Pernita not burst in on him that morning and forcibly pulled him out into the rude, noisy, indecently brightly lit world, he'd still be asleep. He meant to make up for that injustice by slipping back into slumber right now. He'd worked hard the night before and played hard afterward. Now he needed to sleep hard to properly recover. But the morning had unsettled him. He'd been sullen and uncommunicative during the entire shopping expedition, barely managing to snort single-syllable responses to any question Pernita asked, but he'd been there all the same. He'd followed her to four stores in succession, sat and waited while she tried things on, and carried her shopping bags for her. It was pitiful. She snapped her fingers, and he jumped to attention. Just as he had this morning when she'd announced she was outside his front door. He'd nearly twisted an ankle vaulting out of bed to greet her.

So his snarling, frowning, and general surliness were pretty much irrelevant, as they fell on deaf ears. Pernita couldn't have been more oblivious to his sulking as she went on happily talking a blue streak, buffeting him with endless stories about her high-society friends and their utter unworthiness to be in her presence unless it was to kneel before her as her servants. When they'd parted, Pernita had seemed to swell in stature, to embody nothing less than vitality and life-energy—while Shay had felt diminished, like a balloon that had been left hanging overnight, withering to half its size.

She was, he realized, *allowing* him to treat her rudely, because she knew it was harmless. She knew it was no more than infantile posturing. He was hers, and she could do whatever she wanted with him. But why did *he* allow it? Of course he feared the implicit threat she always dangled before him: that if she were ever not 100 percent satisfied with how he treated her, she'd complain to Daddy, and then Halbert Hasque would come to his daughter's rescue by dropping the band she'd convinced him to sign in the first place.

But would he really? Hasque had spent a considerable amount of time and money putting together this national tour with Overlords as the opening act. He wouldn't just *replace* them at the drop of a hat…would he? Based on no more than a bit of whining from his spoiled daughter? He'd have to be a better businessman than that, to get where he was today.

And yet…Shay wouldn't risk it. He didn't dare. He still wasn't quite certain how Pernita had so completely wrapped him around her finger without him ever realizing she was doing it, but he knew she had to have had some pretty tremendous practice at that kind of thing, and he guessed Daddy was her first big conquest. He showered her with extravagant gifts, gave her complete freedom to go wherever she wanted, whenever she wanted, with whomever she wanted, and picked up the pieces afterward when (as was often the case) something interesting happened along the way.

Shay's only safe plan of action was to keep Pernita happy long enough for Overlords to get well into the tour and establish themselves as a powerhouse brand. Then he could afford to cut the cord, and if Pernita ran to Daddy and cried about the horrible rock star who'd done her wrong, Hasque would have to weigh that against the earnings Overlords was raking in for him.

That was, of course, presuming Overlords *did* hit it big.

Though if they didn't, that solved his problem, too. If Halbert Hasque couldn't make them into superstars, then Shay wouldn't need Halbert Hasque anymore and he could stop playing Pernita's games. But he wasn't going to let *that* kind of thinking poison his hopes. He believed in Overlords of Loneliness, and he was determined to make America believe in them, too. This was his chance—possible his only chance—and he absolutely had to make it work.

In the meantime, he'd do whatever he could to cultivate pockets in his life where he could be himself—places where Pernita's influence couldn't be felt. Fortunately, music was one of them. Pernita professed to be a fan of the band, but she seemed curiously uninterested in their actual material. Shay thanked God for that, imagining the hell his life would be if, for instance, Pernita wanted to collaborate with him on songwriting. And by "collaborate," of course, she'd mean do it all herself and then validate it by adding his name.

Thinking about songwriting and about private pockets of his life, his mind turned to Loni. She'd actually unnerved him with her critique of his abilities. He'd felt stripped naked when she'd done that, and not in the good way. It was like all his innermost insecurities about his talents—the ones he'd learned to bury deep and ignore—were all suddenly served up to him on a platter. He blushed now to think of the interviews he'd given in the local press, where he'd said he found songwriting "easy" and "as natural as breathing." Loni would snort in derision at that, no doubt. In her opinion, of course it was easy for him, because he wasn't trying to do anything but the bare minimum. Just produce tunes with a couple of hooks and a smattering of commercial appeal. And the music wasn't even his; it was Baby's and Jimmy's. He was just the lyricist. Which meant he wasn't an artist; he was merely a tradesman.

He rolled over on the couch, but a new position didn't ease his discomfort. He'd been stung by Loni's assessment of him and wondered why he didn't despise her for it. He usually didn't like people who exposed his insecurities and vulnerabilities. But there was something about Loni...he couldn't put his finger on it. She seemed insecure herself, vulnerable even. It was like she was speaking about something she knew firsthand. She intrigued him. "Tell me more," he'd written to her. And he *wanted* more.

Remembering the friend request, he found he couldn't wait to see whether she'd accepted it. He abandoned his nap, got up, and went to his laptop. He checked his Facebook page and there were a number of notifications, mainly from people congratulating him on the previous night's gig, but no new friends. He checked the status of his request and was astonished to see it had disappeared. Searching for an explanation, he figured maybe he must have missed a confirmation button or something, so he went back to William Blake's page to try again.

Except he couldn't get to William Blake's page. It wasn't showing up.

Which meant either Loni had shut it down, or...

... or she'd blocked him.

He sat back and stared at the screen.

His jaw hung open.

She'd...she'd *blocked* him.

Him.

Shay goddamn Dayton.

Nothing like this had ever happened to him. Not since... Jesus. Eighth grade?

His shoulders slumped.

"The *bitch*," he said aloud.

But it was a reflex. He should be angry. He *wanted* to be angry. He *wanted* Loni to be a bitch. To be the kind of woman so afflicted with a sense of entitlement that there was no man, no *anything*, on earth that could ever satisfy her. He wanted to be able to slot her into that category, close the lid, and dismiss her. Shove her to the back of his mental shelf and forget about her.

And he did try, for all the good it did him. He went online. He hopped around YouTube, watching videos of people falling off rooftops or car-crash compilations. Over his shoulder, he heard her say, "*This* is how you honor your talent?"

How had she gotten in his head? How had she *done* that? He hadn't spoken to her for more than five minutes.

He plopped back down on the sofa and sighed. He took his phone from his pocket, and before he knew what he was doing, he found himself dialing home.

God, he thought, *if anyone ever found out I got sad and called my mommy…*

"Hello, sweetheart," she said as she picked up the phone. "What's the matter?"

He threw his free hand in the air. "Come on, Ma. I can't just call to shoot the breeze?"

She laughed. "Just tell me what's going on. I have to leave in five minutes for my Zumba class."

"Nothing," he said. "Had our farewell concert last night."

"I know, honey, and I heard it went well. They showed some footage on the TV this morning."

"They did?" He was mildly impressed.

"Just a few seconds. But the man said it was a big hit." She paused. "Dad and I are so sorry we didn't come into the city for it."

"It's all right," he said, slouching down. "Not really your scene."

"Oh, now, you wouldn't know. You should've seen us during the eighties. We were total punks."

He definitely was *not* in the mood to have *this* conversation again. "I know, Ma. Sorry. And yeah, the show went well. But I'm kinda...well, wondering now whether we're ready for a tour. Whether we're up for it. We might just be local boys." He thought of Trina. "And girl." He thought of Trina again. "Boys."

"Oh, for heaven's sake. What's brought this on? You're not usually one for self-doubt."

He crossed his leg and scratched idly at his instep. "Just...got some feedback that made me think, is all. I know we're talented...but maybe. I don't know. Possibly I've been coasting. A bit."

"'Feedback,'" she repeated, with meaning. "Meaning, someone didn't totally entirely worship you the way you want. Probably a girl. Am I getting warm?"

"Ma, that doesn't make a difference, I just—"

"*Definitely* a girl." He could hear her laughing. "Honey, I'm going to remind you of something. Do you remember at your first junior high talent show when you got a standing ovation from the whole auditorium for that song you did from *Les Mis*?"

"Uh-huh," he said, scratching his other foot.

"And then two days later in the school paper there was one letter with a negative review, and you fell into a gloom for an entire week?"

He could feel his face reddened. "It wasn't a week."

"It was at *least* a week. And do you remember what I told you then?"

"Even if I could say yes, you'd tell me anyway."

"I told you then, and it's still true, that the problem with you is, you can be in a room filled with a hundred people who adore you and one who doesn't, and all you'll be thinking about is how to get that one person to see the light."

Well, hell. Mom had slam-dunked it there.

"So, how do I get over that?" he asked.

"At your age? Probably too late. You either just learn to live with it. Or…"

"Or what?"

"Or get that person to see the light. Listen, honey, Jess Niklaus just pulled up. She's my ride."

"Right. Lay down some righteous Zumba, Ma."

"Oh, honey, won't I ever. Love you."

"Me, too. Bye, Ma."

He slipped the phone back in his pocket, feeling marginally better even though his mom's advice wasn't really practicable. "Just learn to live with it." That was easy enough to *say*. It was like just learning to live with a hornet in your house.

And then there was the other alternative. Equally hopeless. There really wasn't much chance of getting Loni to see the light. She'd thrown up some serious barriers. Walking out on him. Blocking him. *Erasing* him from her history.

Unless…

Unless that had been a challenge. *Could* it have been a challenge? He'd grown so used to women hurling themselves at his feet that he'd forgotten some women liked to be fought for. Some women liked to be *won*.

Was it possible? Loni's behavior had such a resounding finality about it.

But if he didn't at least *try*...

He took his phone out again and texted Lockwood. *Hey bud how'd the rescue go?*

He waited for the reply.

And waited.

"Come *on*," he said, growing impatient. Then a slight vibration, and it appeared: *1477 londale blvd*

He blinked, then texted back, *Huh?*

A moment later the reply came: *Ur obviously texting to get her address so there it is*

Shay made a little exasperated noise. He was getting really, really tired of everybody knowing him better than he knew himself. He texted back *Thx* and then got to his feet.

What the hell. No time like the present.

On his way across town, he stopped and bought a rose from a kid selling them in the middle of an intersection. "Kinda dangerous to be standing out here," he said as he forked over three bucks.

The kid grinned a toothy smile. "Worth the risk, mister."

Shay took the rose and, as he strode away, thought, *Ain't it the truth.*

CHAPTER 8

"What are you doing here?" Loni asked. She tried to keep her tone neutral, but a hard edge crept into the last few syllables—her wariness getting the better of her.

He got up and smiled at her. "Hey. I was just thinking that...y'know, maybe if you didn't already have a stalker, I'd give it a go."

She readjusted her backpack on her shoulder. She didn't need to; it was just to distract her from smiling back. "I don't think stalkers are supposed to greet you at your door with roses. I think they're supposed to go through your garbage bins. Steal your mail, call your parents on the phone. All that."

He shrugged. "It's my first time. I'm not very good at it. Give me a chance. Promise I'll get better."

They stared at each other for an awkward moment. Then Loni nodded at the rose. "I take it that's for me."

He looked down at it, then extended it and said, "Oh. Yeah. Sorry." As she took it from him, he added, "It looked better when I bought it. I'd get a refund, but the kid's probably changed intersections by now."

"He saw *you* coming," she said, sniffing it. "Never mind. I think roses smell sweeter when they're dying. *Ow*," she said, and she passed the rose from one hand to the next, then shook her finger. "Damned thorn."

"Pleasure and pain," he said, not missing a beat. "I aim to provide the complete experience."

She gave him a dubious look. "I haven't signed on yet. You're still just a stalker wannabe."

He shifted his feet, then looked suddenly serious. "Look, I'm sorry if I offended you last night or anything. But what can I say? I don't give up easy."

What was he talking about? Give up what? They'd only chatted for five minutes. "Um. Okay," she said. "I guess."

"I didn't mean to come on too strong. Creep you out."

Again, what? Five minutes in a kitchen? "No, no."

"I mean, I get the message. You like your privacy. But. Y'know. I like *you*."

She felt a little flurry of doubt. She couldn't understand what he was talking about, and it alarmed her a little. "Well. Fine. That's…fine."

He seemed to sense he was losing her. "Look," he said. "The truth? I get women hanging all over me, all the time. I mean…not to brag or anything."

"No, of course not," she said in a slightly mocking tone. "I think of humble, I think of Shay Dayton."

He laughed. "No, really. I'm always getting told what a god I am. Sorry, but that's the word they use. Your roommate—she used it last night. I'm a 'god.' It gets a little…old." He ran his fingers through his hair. It was a very erotically charged gesture. Loni wondered if he knew that and did it on purpose. Probably. "You're the first woman—really, this is not bullshit—the first one who's ever told me I'm a slacker, I'm not doing it right, not taking it seriously, I should be ashamed of myself."

She felt her face redden. "That was an asshat thing to say," she apologized. "I was—it's just, I didn't know anyone at that party, I was feeling a little insecure, so I went all Xena to cover it up. Really. I have no business telling you to be ashamed."

"No," he said, waving down her apology, "you had a point. I haven't been able to get it out of my head. And since you blocked me, I thought the only way I could get any clarification from you was to come in person. I hope you don't mind."

She didn't know what he meant by "blocked" him. She presumed it must be some hipster term for rejection, though she couldn't remember rejecting him, either. Unless that's how he saw her leaving the party after he'd marked her as his property for the night. But she wasn't supposed to know he'd done that. "I don't mind, I guess," she said. "I'm not sure what you mean by 'clarification.'"

"Just...what you think I'm doing wrong, and how I should fix it." He stuck out his thumb and gestured toward the street. "You want to go and get a coffee or something? I mean...if you're free."

She felt herself balk. She'd been out all morning. She was tired.

"Or," he said, "if not, I mean...you can just write down your thoughts, then throw them away. I'll find them later, when I'm rooting through your trash."

She laughed. "All right, fine," she said, as if giving in to an irritatingly insistent child. "*One* coffee."

"I won't pick your brain too hard," he said, as they headed back down the walk together. "It's just, I've got this tour coming up..."

"I've heard," she said, sticking the rose in her backpack as she walked. Its head bobbed out of the folds, like a baby in a papoose. "Opening for Strafer Nation. Not too shabby."

"I'd really like it to go well." They turned onto the sidewalk and headed toward town. "It's my one shot at...well, *everything*. And I've got a great manager; he's put together everything from the *business* side of things...I mean, as far as that goes, we're set." He fell silent.

"But..." Loni said, prodding him to go on.

"The artistic side of things. *That's* got me worried."

"Because of me?" she asked. And though she was sort of appalled—she'd never meant to cause him such indecision—she realized she was also kind of flattered. He took her seriously. He'd listened to her, and what she'd said had stuck in his head.

Unless...unless this was also just pretense. Unless this was just another sly way of getting her guard down. There were guys like that, who'd say and do anything to get into a girl's pants. Tear down half of civilization, and go whistling happily away afterward.

He shrugged. "No one else has ever given me any negative feedback before. Usually I figure it's 'cause I'm just that good." She laughed, surprised by his arrogance, and he smiled at her brilliantly, as if confirming it. Then he frowned. "But sometimes, in the middle of the night, I have this sense that I'm getting away with murder. You're the first person who's made me think that in broad daylight." He grimaced and cocked his head. "Well...not quite daylight. But you know what I mean."

She was taken aback. She hadn't been prepared for this kind of responsibility. He was essentially asking her to give him the critical feedback he'd need to make Overlords of Loneliness ready for the national stage. What did she know about it? What did she know about *anything*?

She was about to demur, as politely as possible, when a sudden shower surprised them. Loni gasped as the downpour hit her, and Shay whooped in alarm and went loping away. She followed him, gasping but laughing, too, till he found a huge maple tree and took shelter under its branches where she hurried to join him.

Shielded by the dense foliage of the bows above them, they leaned their backs against the trunk and caught their breath, intermittently laughing.

"Is it just me," he said when he could speak again, "or did that just totally come from goddamn nowhere?"

"It's not just you," she said, and she opened her backpack and started rooting through it—taking care not to injure the rose, which looked a little limp after the sudden jog. "I think I've got an anorak in here. Folds up into a little pouch. I've been carrying it around for exactly this kind of emergency."

"Thanks," he said. "That's really sweet. But then what'll keep *you* dry?"

She couldn't help it. She laughed. So hard she actually dropped the backpack.

And then she realized, *Oh, my God.* She was learning something about herself. Something she'd never suspected. She *liked* guys who could make her laugh.

It wasn't a phenomenon she'd ever encountered before. All the wiry, nervous, furiously intense brainiacs she'd been attracted to all her life—they were invariably so deeply, relentlessly serious. Every moment she'd ever spent with them, it was like the fate of the world hung in the balance. Each word had to be weighed, each thought parsed and processed before it could be spoken—because goddamn it, it *mattered*. Ideas were everything, and they came so swiftly—it was like riding the intellectual rapids. She enjoyed it; the risk of capsizing was worth the thrill of sharing the raft with them. It was *exciting*. It was also exhausting.

But none of those guys had ever made her laugh. None of them had ever done anything so deeply subversive as to playfully skew what she said, turn it around so its meaning was upended—and just for the sake of making her smile. Shay Dayton had been doing that more or less constantly since he accosted her at her front door this morning. It was extremely disorienting...and wildly charming. She hated that it made her so helpless before him—he could obviously see how easily he could take the stuffing out of her—but she also kind of wished it would never end.

"You're right," she said, leaving her backpack at her feet and leaning back against the tree again. "It's not fair if only one of us is dry."

"I didn't say that," he protested, mock-serious. "I think it's entirely fair. As long as the one who's dry is me."

She bit her lip so she didn't laugh again, but it was an effort to keep it down. "You're *so* gallant," she said when she trusted herself to speak again. "I can see why women fall all over you."

"You mean it took you this long?" he said, acting like he was appalled. "It wasn't, like, immediately apparent the first time you set eyes on me?"

She gave him a hard look. "You like to talk about yourself, don't you? Even when you're joking."

He twisted his mouth to one side. "Okay," he admitted. "Busted."

"I mean, we talked about you last night in that filthy kitchen. And since you showed up at my house, we've been talking about you nonstop."

"Performer's weakness," he said, again turning serious. "We're very vulnerable onstage, you know. Because there's no hiding. We're there to be accepted or rejected, and what's being accepted or rejected is all that we've got—it's us. So we're always looking for reassurance—vindication. Some sense that we're good enough." He shrugged. "What can I say? It's pathological."

"Aaaand *still* we're talking about you," she said.

It was his turn to blush, and he did it ridiculously well. It was like watching a cartoon where a character's face reddens from the neck up, like a thermometer level rising. He turned away and dragged his shoe across the dirt. Which was also very charming.

But is it an act? she wondered.

"Sorry," he said, appearing to mean it.

"It's not a big deal," she said, and she moved away from him a little, but only because the rain had started to seep through the leaves onto where she'd been standing. "I mean, this isn't really a social call. You came to ask me for some feedback on your work, which is a bit different." She tossed her hair back, which was her defense mechanism when she was feeling awkward or insecure. It wasn't really working this time, probably because her hair was damp. "But in the future, if there's ever anyone you're interested in, you should probably remember that. Show some interest in *them*." She shook her head. "Sorry, *her*. One of my pet peeves. Plural pronouns to avoid gender specificity. I hate it, and I hate when I accidentally do it. *Her*. Show interest in *her*. Encourage her to talk. And *listen*. Don't just wait for her to finish."

He gave her a sly look. "So." He cleared his throat. "Where you from?"

She laughed. "Oh, God. You're pathetic at this. *Practice* first."

"I'd rather learn by doing," he said merrily. "Like you, with non-gender-specific pronouns."

The rain seemed to be lightening up. He stuck his hand out, palm up, and drew it back largely dry. "If we make a dash, we can probably get to the café on Magnolia," he said. "It's only two blocks."

She shrugged. "I'm game."

"Ready?"

She picked up her backpack. "I'll follow you."

"So you can check out my ass?" he said with a leer.

She snorted. "I've seen you flounce all over a stage. Your ass is old news to me."

"Well, I can't say the same, so maybe *you'd* better go first."

She hit him with the backpack. The rose lost another few petals. "After you, creep."

He lit out, leaping over puddles in an impressively athletic fashion, whereas Loni chose to do a little twinkletoes dance around them, which got him to the café a full minute or more before she did. He'd just chosen a table and was sitting down when she burst in and shook off the rain, though there wasn't that much of it. The storm really was tapering off. If they'd waited another five minutes, it would undoubtedly have stopped altogether. But she was glad they hadn't waited. The dashing through the rain—with him—was kind of exhilarating. She felt in a mood for…she didn't know what.

And that, she reminded herself, was dangerous. So before she sat down, she made up her mind to be all business. This whole thing was steaming out of her control, and she meant to put the brakes on.

A wan-looking waitress appeared and eyed them woefully. "What can I get you?" she asked in a monotone.

"Green tea," said Loni. "Please make sure the water's boiling first."

He raised an eyebrow. "Very holistic," he said, then looked at the waitress and said, "Triple espresso."

"We don't do triples," the waitress said.

"Then two doubles."

"Jesus," said Loni as the waitress slunk away, "you're going to be awake till next Thursday."

"Nah," he said, sitting back in his chair. "I sleep really well. Always have."

"All your clean living, no doubt."

"I'm not lying. Really." He gave her a meaningful look. "I can prove it, if you want."

Whoa. Time to rein it in.

"So," she said, putting her backpack on the floor. The rose seemed to gasp in relief. "Your lyrics."

He visibly tensed, the veins in his neck suddenly pronounced. "What about them?"

"That's what we're here to talk about, isn't it?"

He gave her a wide-eyed look, as if to say, *Is it?* Then he shrugged and said, "Hey, I'm just here to listen." Then he shot her another knee-weakening smile and said, "*Listening.* That's my new superpower."

"Well, I'm not here to lecture you," she said. "I mean, you know what to do. Lyrics are poetry. Poetry's not easy. Every word is crucial. Every *syllable*. You can't fake it." She took a paper napkin from the wire holder and started tearing it into strips. "Take William Blake. He didn't settle for clichés or placeholders. *You* should know that. You know your Blake."

He looked hastily down at his fingernails. "Not as well as you do."

"Oh, *very few* people know him as well as I do." She paused, hoping that didn't sound as douchey to him as it did to her. She cleared her throat and said, "Take that song of yours—I can't remember the title. It's on your album. The lyric says something like, 'You've devastated me'…"

"'Pulverized,'" he said, and he followed by singing, "'You're devastation, you're uncreation, you're bitter obliteration.'" He smiled. "Kinda proud of that one, actually."

"Fine. I mean, if all you want is to keep meter and rhyme going." She dropped the pieces of napkin and crossed her arms over the table. "But think about it. 'Devastation' and 'uncreation' mean two different things. 'Devastation' means destruction, the opposite of creation. But uncreation is different. Uncreation is sort of like…erasing."

He shook his head. "I don't get what you mean."

"Because you're not *thinking* hard enough," she said. "Look, when you destroy something you've got the pieces left, right? The debris. The ruins. But when you uncreate something, you've got nothing. You've wiped it from the world." She shook her head. "Two different things. Yet you use them as synonyms in that lyric. Just because they sound good together."

He opened his jaw and looked at her as though he was going to say something, then after an awkward silence he merely said, "Go on."

"I mean, okay, if you want to say this woman is doing *both*, fine. But then you have to *say* it. You have to make it clear that she's unmade you in every way possible."

He pursed his lips, but she could tell there was a smile behind it. "Mm-hm," he said, nodding.

"Also, 'bitter obliteration.' Yes, it sounds nice. But it doesn't quite work. 'Bitter' in what way? Who's bitter? The woman destroying you, or you? Or are you referring to the act itself? Because obliteration—well, it can be violent and nasty. But bitter? How so?"

He raised his eyebrows and took a deep sigh. "Wow. You're good at this."

"I'm sorry. I'm just telling you what any poet—or any decent songwriter—would say. *Will* say. If you want to enter the ranks of the greats, you've got to—"

She was interrupted by the arrival of their tea and espresso—which the waitress set before them as though it were the last act she would commit before her own bitter obliteration.

When she'd gone, they took a few self-conscious sips. Then Shay said, "You know a lot about songwriting."

She shrugged, licking her lips. The tea was too hot. "Just as an end-user. A listener. I know the good stuff when I hear it."

"What's the good stuff? For you?"

She thought for a moment. "Okay. You know Cole Porter, right?"

He cocked his head. "Kinda. Old musicals and shit?"

"Old musicals and shit that we still listen to *today* because he wrote the high holy fuck out of them." If he was going to try to intimidate her with profanity, she'd hit him right back, double-barrel.

He slowly turned one of his espresso cups with his fingers. "Example."

"All right. You know the song, 'Bewitched, Bothered and Bewildered'?" He looked uncertain, so she sang a few bars, and he said, "Oh, right…yeah. Everybody knows that. Right." He nodded in acknowledgment. "Great song."

"*Great* song. And it's a love song, right? How many love songs do you think Cole Porter churned out in his life? Dozens. Scads. So he gets to this one, and the bar is set pretty high. What's he got left to say? How does he convey the feeling of falling in love, *again*, without going back to all the ways he's already conveyed it? So—it's fairly genius—he takes these three unrelated words—bewitched, bothered, and bewildered—each of which had a completely negative connotation in the era where he's writing. I mean, before the 1940s, if you said someone 'bewitched' you, it was not a compliment. It was an accusation."

"Seriously?" he asked.

"Seriously. Anne Boleyn got her head cut off, because King Henry VIII accused her of bewitching him. It was all he had to say to get her sentenced to death." She screwed up her mouth. "Well...okay, not *all*. But it was one of the biggies."

"But, it means something else entirely today."

"Because of this song," she said. "Because Cole Porter put those three negative, unpleasant, *uncomfortable* words together, and he made them work together to express the disorienting, dreamlike, delirious feeling of being in love. He actually *changed the way* that we think of those words, changed their *meaning* after hundreds of years, just by the way he used them together. Shakespeare did this, too. Shakespeare did it in his *sleep*." She closed her eyes and recited, "'Weary with toil, I haste me to my bed / The dear repose for limbs with travel tired; / But then begins a journey in my head / To work my mind, when body's work's expired: / For then my thoughts—from far where I abide— / Intend a zealous pilgrimage to thee, / And keep my drooping eyelids open wide, / Looking on darkness which the blind do see."

She looked back at him and caught him staring at her. She blushed self-consciously. "Don't get me started on the sixteenth century," she said. "We'll be here all day."

She thought for sure he'd make some double entendre quip about that, but instead he sat silently, seemingly lost in thought. Then all at once he finished off his first double espresso in one big gulp and moved on to his second. Loni had barely sipped her tea. It was still too hot.

"It's not easy to do," she said, unnerved by his silence. "It's *work*. But we're here, in the twenty-first century *still* talking about Shakespeare, *still* talking about Cole Porter, because of it. Right? You want them to be talking about Shay Dayton in sixty, seventy years? Or four hundred?"

He gave her an oh-hell-yeah look.

"Then you're going to have to have something new to say. Wait...no. There really isn't anything new to say. What I mean is, a new *way* to say it. And good luck with that." She was about to mention the struggles she'd encountered in her own poetic endeavors but decided against it. She wasn't ready to reveal that to anyone. "This is a very noisy era we live in. Everyone's talking at once. Hard to find anything new for your own voice."

He sighed deeply and finally said, "You're supposed to be helping me."

Her shoulders slumped. "I'm just managing your expectations."

"I feel like canceling the whole goddamn tour."

"No, don't do that," she said, with a little edge of urgency in her voice that caught her by surprise. What did she care if Overlords of Loneliness went on tour or not? She wasn't even a fan. "Look," she said, "let's try an experiment. Tell meeee... tell me what it's like to fall in love."

He raised an eyebrow. "Um. It's..." He scratched his head and winced, as though he were uncomfortable with being put on the spot. "Like, it's dizzying. You feel all upside-down and everything. And yet it's like the world was *meant* to be upside-down."

She nodded, gently encouraging him. "Fine. But...not entirely original. What else?"

"Also…kind of like, I dunno." He took a deep breath, then let it out all at once. "An illness. A fatal illness."

She vigorously shook her head. "Been done. Been *over*-done. Try again." She leaned across the table and looked him square in the eye. "*Think*. Not about being clever. About *being in love*. What does it *feel* like?"

He gazed back at her for what seemed like far too long a time. She wondered if other people in the café were watching them but didn't dare break her eye-lock with him to check. Finally he said, "It's like being naked."

She sat back again with a disappointed sigh. He was back to sexual innuendo. Too bad. She'd had a little tingling of hope for him.

"No, not naked," he said, remaining very still—like he was in the grip of his thoughts. "*Invisible*. Like…like everyone can see right through you. See everything inside you *and* behind you. It's like…like you're just wide open. And you don't want to be. But you are."

She perked up. "Go on."

"I had…this is stupid." He folded his arms over his chest, suddenly self-conscious.

"Nothing is stupid. Not in the creative process. You never know where it's going to lead. Go on."

"I had this aquarium, when I was a kid. One of the fish in it…its skin was—what's the word? You could see through it."

She almost said *translucent*, but she stopped herself. She wanted him to find it.

He did a little mental searching, then said, "Translucent, I guess."

Bravo, she thought.

"Anyway, it would swim around, and there inside it, you could see its little heart was pumping and the blood was rushing through its veins. It was wicked cool." He paused, then gave her an embarrassed shrug. "Like that. Being in love, I mean. Only…it's not just your heart. Your head. Everything in your head feels like it's exposed. To everybody. All the time."

"And it's terrible," she said.

"And it's wonderful," he added. "It's terrible-wonderful."

They smiled at each other. Loni felt giddy, like she might float away. Then she got a grip on herself and cleared her throat. "Okay. Let's try another experiment, based on that." She took another napkin from the wire holder, then opened her backpack and pulled out a Sharpie. "I'm going to write a line. Then you write the next one." She sat with the Sharpie poised over the napkin and thought a moment, then wrote:

I live in a glass house, and it's not thrown stones I fear

She handed the napkin and Sharpie to Shay. He looked at it for almost ninety full seconds.

"Don't overthink it," she said encouragingly. "Go with your gut. You can always revise later."

He gave her a wary look, then wrote something and passed it back to her.

She turned it around so she could read it.

But the hurled glances of passersby

She raised her eyebrows. Interesting. Not what she'd expected. But it worked. She pondered for a moment, then wrote:

*My feet are its foundation, and its hearth becomes my
   heart*

She gave it back to him. He swiveled around and read it.
Then he looked up and said, "We're not rhyming?"

"Worry about that later. Right now, let's just go for
imagery. And truth."

He stared at it for a bit, then added something and slid
it back to her.

Casting light on my folly in every part

She pursed her lips and looked up at him.
"Rhymed anyway," he said. "Couldn't help it."
She took up the Sharpie and wrote the next line.

I live here alone, bathed by moon and burned by sun

She passed it back to him, he read it and added to it
almost immediately.

Exposed to the world, yet truly seen by none.

"It's good," he said excitedly, not waiting to read the
expression on her face. "It's good, isn't it?"

She cocked her head. "It's not bad. There's definitely
something here." She took up the Sharpie, ready to rise to
the challenge.

But at that moment the waitress appeared again and
placed their bill on the table, dolefully saying, "Sorry, I'm
closing out now; the next server is taking over. You can stay,
but you have to start a new tab."

"Oh, let me get this," Shay said, reaching for his back
pocket.

"No, don't be silly," said Loni, plucking up her backpack.

But before she could open it, he'd already produced his wallet and slapped a twenty-dollar bill on the table. The waitress took it and walked away, heavy-footed, as though heading toward her own execution.

The interruption had killed the delicate creative magic they'd had going. Loni seemed suddenly foolishly aware that they were two grown people, in public, who'd been madly scribbling on a napkin. "Well," she said, checking the time on her phone, "I'm not sure—I mean, about starting another tab..."

"No, no," he said. "I understand. I'm really grateful. Thanks for taking the time."

She tried to think of something else to say but couldn't. The uncomfortable silence between them was fortunately broken a few seconds later when the waitress returned with Shay's change. She placed it on the table and said, "Thank you, come again," in the kind of doomed tone that made it seem as though she held no hope of seeing anyone again, ever.

Shay slipped the change into his wallet. Loni, embarrassed by his generosity, busied herself by gathering up her backpack again, not wanting to watch him handle his money.

"Thank you," she said, as she got to her feet. "For the tea, I mean."

"You hardly touched it," he said, rising as well.

She took the cup and downed about half of it. "Mm," she said, making a little agony-face as she put it back down. "Still too hot."

He laughed, then said, "Come on. I'll walk you home."

"Oh, that's *so* not necessary," she said, not sure she wanted to spend any more time with him. They'd forged some kind of connection while they were collaborating on the napkin, and she wasn't sure what it meant—or if it meant anything at all, other than how flattering it was to be taken seriously by a guy who looked like Shay Dayton.

"I insist," he said, and he went to the front door and held it open for her.

When they were outside, Loni noticed the heavy cast to the sky. "It's going to rain again. You don't need to walk me home, honestly. You'll get caught in it."

"It's all right," he said, his voice sagging with resignation and dragging his feet. "Bound to happen."

She looked at him, completely perplexed. What the hell was he doing, shuffling after her, suddenly so glum? "No, seriously," she said. "You should go home." She held out a hand. "I can feel drops already."

"It always rains on me," he said miserably. "I got struck by lightning once. It was awful. I lived."

Suddenly he smirked, and she understood what he was doing; he was mimicking their woebegone waitress. He was "doing" her.

She laughed. "Idiot," she said. "There's no time to be stupid."

"Oh, I make time," he sighed, again channeling the waitress.

She slipped her backpack over both shoulders and gave him a little wave. "I'm going to try to beat the storm. You should, too. Thanks for the tea."

"Oh, no," he said, snapping back into his own persona as Loni skittered away. "A gentleman keeps his word. I said I'd see you home"—he started galloping after her—"and goddamn it, I'll see you home!"

They'd gotten about two-thirds of the way when the heavens opened and a really terrific downpour struck. The rain seemed to be beating the earth with watery fists. Within seconds, both Loni and Shay were drenched.

When they reached Loni's building, they spilled into the vestibule and nearly collapsed with relief. They half laughed, half gasped, and leaned back against the walls, catching their breath. Outside, the storm continued its angry pounding. A peal of thunder sounded from somewhere far off.

"That was *fierce*," said Shay. He looked so diminished, so bedraggled, like a puppy just out of its bath. She felt a twinge of almost maternal affection for him as she slipped her backpack off her shoulders. The rose, alas, had not survived the storm. It was no more than a battered stem.

"It was like being assaulted," she said.

"Nah," said Shay. "Not nearly that good."

She snorted a laugh as she twisted the moisture from the ends of her hair. "You're filth, you know that?"

He grinned proudly. "Sweet talker!" Suddenly he snapped to attention, looking worried. "Dammit," he said, and he reached into his jeans pocket and pulled out his phone. He fiddled with its screen.

"Is it all right?" asked Loni. She didn't need to worry about hers; it was safe in her backpack.

"Seems to be. But I can't risk it getting any wetter." He looked at her and arched his eyebrows. "Guess you're stuck with me."

She was about to tell him no. That he could borrow her anorak, which would keep him and his phone safe and dry—well, safe and no wetter—all the way home. It was, after all, the ideal solution. It was like God had inspired her to put the anorak in her backpack just for this moment, since she'd never had cause to use it herself.

But somehow, crazily, when she opened her mouth to tell him this, what came out was, "Come on inside, I can throw your clothes in the dryer. Maybe by the time they're done, the storm will have stopped."

///////////////

Loni gave him a fluffy pink terrycloth robe—another gift from her mom that she never, ever used—and he emerged from the bathroom with it tied loosely at his waist, so that his bare chest protruded. She was surprised to see that the tattoo that started at his wrist and ran all the way up his arm also splayed brilliantly across his pectorals. She didn't know what was more titillating…the chest itself, or all that gorgeous ink.

He sashayed up to her like a runway model and dumped his wet things into her arms. His hips were practically in her face. Really, it was like he couldn't help himself. In the mean-time, she'd changed into a dry pair of jeans and a rugby shirt, toweled her hair dry and pulled it back into a ponytail. She hoped she looked severe and unfeminine enough to put him off a bit.

"I'll be right back," she said, and she left the apartment, scooted down to the laundry room, and threw his clothes in the dryer. It hummed steadily as she made her way back upstairs, where she found Shay seated on the couch, his bare legs stretched out and his feet on the coffee table, holding a bottle of beer.

"Hope you don't mind," he said. "Helped myself."

She sat across the table from him. "Two double espressos, now a beer. And it's not even three. You must have an interesting metabolism."

"Oh, it's up for anything," he said. Then, with a wink, *"Any. Thing."*

She couldn't think of a way to respond to that, and she didn't feel like sitting there with him, face-to-face, with the rain coming down like drumbeats. It was all feeling a little too intense…too primal.

She said, "Be right back," and then went to the kitchen to fix herself another cup of tea. She really didn't need one, but it would keep her busy for a while.

She filled the kettle, set it to boil, and was just taking a ceramic cup down from a shelf when the whole apartment was shaken by a crack of thunder. It was so loud that Loni was startled into dropping the cup, which smashed at her feet into hundreds of jagged shards.

"God*damn* it," she cried.

"What is it?" he called from the living room.

"Nothing," she called back. "Just—*damn* it. What a freaking spaz!" The mess was between her and the kitchen door—and also between her and the broom closet. Since she hadn't bothered to put on shoes, she couldn't get out—and she couldn't clean up, either. "It's just, I'm sort of trapped."

"What?" he asked.

She tried to tiptoe through the wreckage, but she was still too shaky from the incident and backed up again. What a stupid, girly predicament to land herself in!

Suddenly he was at the kitchen door.

"Oh, wow," he said, looking at the debris all over the floor.

She pointed. "The broom's just in there."

He looked at the closet door, then back at her, and made a little face. "Sorry. I don't do housework."

She felt her forehead pinch in anger. "Then hand it to *me. I'll* sweep it up."

He grinned. "I have a better idea." And he stepped forward, maneuvering his bare feet through the shards. "I'll sweep *you* up."

"Are you mentally defective?" she cried in alarm. "You'll cut yourself to ribbons!"

"I have very tough soles," he reassured her, and suddenly—so quickly she barely registered it was happening—he had her in his surprisingly strong arms, and his face was incredibly, disorientingly close to hers.

A moment passed. The beating of the rain was drowned out by the thrum of her heartbeat in her ears. He lowered her a little, toward the stove. "You might want to turn that off first," he said, in a voice so soft, so gentle, that Loni thought she would've done anything he suggested. She reached out and flipped off the burner beneath the kettle.

Then he carefully stepped back through the shards—never once flinching or jerking—and carried her back to the couch. He laid her onto it, and when she was safely delivered there, he tried to get up—

—but Loni wouldn't let go of him.

She pulled him onto her and slipped her hands beneath the fluffy robe. It was all the encouragement he needed to reciprocate and he gently lowered himself down next to her. The sensation was immediate and arousing. His body was so *hard*—like he was sculpted from marble. All the men she'd been with, up till now, had been soft and doughy...pillow men. Thinkers. Shay was a doer. Action, activity, had armored him in muscle.

She realized, with a twinge of guilt, that Zee could walk through the door at any moment. Zee didn't have any real claim to Shay. She didn't even really *know* him. Still, Loni felt as though she was betraying her roommate at least a little. But then he kissed her, and she tasted the espresso, tasted the beer—it was dizzying. His self-confidence, his eagerness... she felt herself challenged to meet it with her own. He pulled the rugby shirt over her head in one big *whoosh*. She felt the sudden ping of the cool air against her skin and was gratified by the way his hands roved over her—and the grunts of approval he emitted in appreciation of her taut, firm flesh.

He began working on the fly of her jeans. Not wanting to fall behind, she gathered up the robe around his waist and cupped her hands around his buttocks—they, too, were like sculpted marble—and guided him into her; not that it took much guiding. He was a man who knew exactly what he was doing and where he was going. The suddenly hooded look that came over him couldn't hide the intense, fiery concentration beneath it—at least until he buried his face between her breasts.

What was happening? It had been only an hour ago that she'd made up her mind to give herself to someone else. Now here she was, falling into intimacy with someone entirely different—someone she'd only just met. She'd lived her entire life in thrall to the power of words, and the courtship dance she and Shay had engaged in that afternoon had been almost entirely verbal, so it was a shock to her now that the sheer energy of Shay's come-on—and her response—had completely pulverized her capacity for language. She couldn't form a coherent thought—not with Shay thrusting with so much rhythmic fury that the couch actually moved beneath them, jumping backward at half-inch intervals. She thought at one point he might run them right through the wall—despite the fact that she never felt out of control. She felt, rather, that she was riding a wild and untamed beast that was entirely under her command. Never mind the apparent violence of their lovemaking—or that the way they were crying out might be mistaken by passersby for victims of an attack—the thrashing passion that drove them was entirely mutual.

It wasn't till Shay had sent her skyrocketing through the roof of the building and out into the rain like a Roman candle that she realized, in a flash of clarity—possibly aided by a flash of lightning—what she was doing with him. She was testing her resolve. She was looking for something to stand up against Byron, to see whether his offer was worth it.

And now she had her answer. He was on the floor below her, where he'd fallen after finishing, all tangled up in pink and looking vacantly, but happily, at her face.

She sat up. It was all so clear now. So unambiguous, so *apparent*.

And look…the rain had stopped, too.

Everything was calm.

Everything was right.

////////////////

It was while Shay was showering that Byron called. Like he'd sensed something had changed.

"Just wondering where your head is," he said. "No pressure."

She sat down and sighed. "Thanks. Actually, let's meet. Today." Might as well get this over with. Before her courage ebbed or she talked herself out of it. She was clever enough to do that, clever enough to fool herself into betraying her own interests. She'd done it before.

"Oh," he said with a little peep of surprise. "Today, huh? Uh…my schedule's a bit tight. Unless you're available right now."

She looked at the door to the bathroom. She could hear Shay gargling an Overlords tune in the running water.

"Now's good," she said. The sooner the better. She was already feeling a worm of self-doubt.

"I've only got half an hour. Coffee?"

"Coffee's fine," she said. "The Mambo on Eleventh?" It was close to campus. Might as well make it convenient for him since it wouldn't be anything else.

"Great. See you in ten."

////////////////

When Shay came out of the bathroom, shrouded by steam and back in the fluffy robe, she was already strapping on her backpack. "Listen, I've got to go out," she said. "Sorry."

He looked a little surprised but nodded in understanding. "I'll get out of your hair," he said, and he looked around the apartment. "My clothes...?"

"Damn it! Still in the dryer," she said, grabbing her keys. "It's just down the stairs to the left. Can't miss it." She hesitated a little, then went over and pulled him into a kiss. "Sorry. Really."

"No worries," he assured her, grinning. "See you later?"

She smiled back but couldn't bear to say anything. It didn't seem right—not till she'd closed the book on Byron first.

She gave his neck a squeeze, then headed out the door.

CHAPTER 9

Shay took a moment to reflect on what a bad idea it was to ever turn your back on a woman. Odds were, next time you faced her, she'd be in an entirely different mood. Hell, sometimes it happened *without* you turning your back on her. He didn't know what had suddenly unnerved Loni and made her go all rigid and distant. Whatever it was, he had to figure it didn't have anything to do with him. Those barriers had been pretty much broken down. And a sweet job he'd done of it, too.

He felt a little silly, standing around a strange apartment in a disheveled pink bathrobe, so he padded out to the hallway to go and fetch his clothes from the laundry room. The minute the door clicked behind him, he realized, *I have no key to this place*. He turned around and tried the knob. The door wouldn't open.

Shit.

He sighed. He was still too blissed out from the way things had gone with Loni to be annoyed by his stupidity. He just resigned himself to it and continued to the staircase, then lightly skipped down the steps to the basement. He crossed the cold concrete floor to the dryer and pulled his clothes out. They radiated warmth, further easing any small irritation he might've felt. He was dopey and happy, and his warm clothes made him dopier and happier.

The trouble was, he had nowhere to put them on.

It would have to be there, then.

He looked around. The basement extended some twenty feet in both directions, but there didn't seem to be anyone around. He shrugged, doffing the pink robe, which he folded up and placed atop the dryer.

Then, standing naked by the machines, he sorted through his clothes, in search of his underwear. He had to pull each item apart separately before he discovered they'd gotten caught in one of the legs of his jeans. He'd just reached in and grabbed them when someone behind him said, "A-*hem*."

He turned, and there at the bottom of the stairs was an older woman who looked like she might've been the mother of Batman's enemy Two-Face. Beneath her iron-gray hair, one side of her visage was leathery and snarled, the other smooth and fair. Shay had no idea how that had happened, but the effect was definitely eye-opening.

"I thought I heard someone come down to the laundry room," she said, "so I decided to see whether my rules are being followed." She nodded briefly at the wall beyond the machines. Shay glanced that way and saw an eleven-by-seventeen sheet taped to the wall that read LAUNDRY ROOM REGULATIONS FOR RESIDENTS OF 1477 LONDALE. "I suppose," she continued, "I will have to add a new one. No displays of genitalia."

Shay quietly extracted his boxer-briefs from his jeans and covered his crotch with them. "Sorry," he said.

"This is not a rule I would've thought I had to specify," the woman went on, her nostrils flaring. "I suppose while I'm at it I might as well add a few others, purely as a preventative measure. Like no starting fires in the sink. Also, no cannibalism."

"I just got locked out," he said, flashing her a winning smile. "Of my friend's place."

"Didn't you knock?"

"My friend had left already."

The woman kept staring at him. Shay said, "If you turn your head, I can be dressed in a few seconds."

She took a breath, as though such a request was a great burden to her, but did as he asked. Though as he slipped on his briefs and then his pants, he could see from the corner of his eye that she was watching him from the corner of hers.

When he'd slipped on his T-shirt and socks, he took up the pink robe and extended it to the woman. "I wonder if you'd do me a favor," he said, and he shot her another smile. He was hitting her with all the wattage he had at his command, and he knew from experience that it was considerable. "Could you return this to my friend for me, with my thanks? I'm very sorry to put you out and to have taken you by surprise this way." He grinned shyly and let his hair fall into his face. "You certainly caught me at a...well, *vulnerable* moment."

The merest hint of a smile curled one end of her lips. "Oh," she said, as if reluctant to give way to him, "you look like you can take care of yourself."

"That's right," he said. "I'm a big boy."

She muttered, "No argument here," and Shay knew she was putty in his hands.

"My friend is Loni," he said as he put the robe in her arms.

She looked at him blankly.

"Loni in...uh..." He realized he didn't know her apartment number. Or her last name. "Second floor," he said. It was all he had.

She continued to regard him as though he weren't speaking at all, like she was still waiting for him to begin.

"Zee Gleason's roommate," he said, in a burst of inspiration.

"Oh," she said, smiling. "Zee. Of course I'll return it for you. As long as you promise not to go giving old ladies heart attacks anymore."

He took a quick look around the basement. "I don't see any old ladies here."

She giggled—this rusted old battle-ax actually *giggled*. Shay thought, *Damn, I'm good.*

After a bit more shameless flirting, he headed back upstairs. Fortunately, Loni had asked him to leave his shoes outside the door, as they'd gotten caked with mud, so he grabbed them from the floor. He gave the knob one more try, just in case he'd made a mistake the first time. When the door still wouldn't budge, he headed back down the stairs.

On the stoop outside he put his shoes back on, then went whistling away into what was turning out to be a beautifully sunny day. He was feeling a little hungry and realized it was way past lunchtime. There was a Vietnamese joint ahead that looked kind of promising.

And then something terrible occurred to him.

He clapped his hands over his pockets.

Empty.

"Fucking hell," he said.

////////////

Zee came home in an irritable mood. She'd had two interviews with the optometrist now, and she still had no indication of whether she could hope to get the job. She'd been glad to get called in a second time, but at the end of her nearly two hours there, the doctor and the office manager were still acting as though they were waiting for her to do something to convince them to make her an offer. She had no idea what they wanted. She doubted even they knew.

And then she'd had to suffer through an excruciating lunch with her friend Chynna, who'd brought her four-month-old baby along and spent the whole meal tending to it, bragging about how wonderful motherhood was and how much money her chiropodist husband was making. Yeah, but not enough to pick up the tab, Zee noticed. They'd ended up going dutch even though Chynna had picked the restaurant and it was not a cheap one.

She dropped her purse into a chair and looked through the mail, which she'd picked up on her way in. Bills, bills, fucking bills. They never stopped coming. She'd better get a new job soon. Some of these were second and even third notices. She didn't want the electricity cut off.

She tried not to be frustrated with Loni over her inability to pay much toward rent. As roommates go, she wasn't a bad one. She bought her own food, made no mess, and used barely any of the utilities Zee paid for. In fact, when Loni left in a few weeks for California—which Zee was sure she'd do, she had no realistic alternative—Zee's monthly expenditures would barely change. Loni left almost no footprint on the place she lived. It was actually kind of eerie when she thought about it.

But even if that weren't the case, even if Loni were costing her an arm and a leg…well, given the sabotage Zee had pulled on her this morning—cutting her off at the ankles with Shay Dayton—she felt she owed her a little slack. Not that she regretted doing it. It was so like Loni, who had everything—an education, a career waiting for her, even a guy who'd mapped out that career and guided her through it and who was plainly crazy for her—to drift through these last few weeks like it was all nothing much and she might not even want it after all. Like there weren't people who'd kill to have what she had. (Not that Zee was one of them. Probably. Not usually, anyway.) And then, to just blithely walk through a party for twenty minutes and leave Shay Dayton panting after her, *Shay Dayton*, who she *also* didn't want. Shay Dayton, whom Zee would've sold her soul for, and maybe even already had…

She shook her head. Never mind. Nasty incident, all over now. She'd had her petty revenge, and they could put it behind them and pretend it never happened. She tossed the bills onto her desk and looked up.

The apartment had a vacant resonance to it. She could always tell when Loni wasn't here. Even when she was just napping or reading, she gave off a very slight but detectable vibe. Zee wondered whether she'd miss Loni when she was gone. They had a lot of history together, and even though they'd gone down different paths, you couldn't ever replace that…

There was a rap on the door. Zee turned and opened it and found the landlady there, holding a big pink robe. What the hell?

"Oh, there you are, Zee," she said. "I thought I saw you come back. I was in the side yard, with the verbena."

"Hi, Mrs. Milliken. What's up?"

She handed her the robe with a sly smile. "Just returning this to you."

Zee balked at taking it from her and was about to explain it wasn't hers when she recognized it as Loni's. It was that one she made fun of her for owning—calling it Loni's "Pepto-Bismol robe." What on earth was Mrs. Milliken doing with it?

As if having heard her thoughts, the landlady said, "It's from the young man. He got locked out, you know, apparently wearing nothing but this." She broke into a smirk, the first Zee had ever seen from her. It was not a comforting sight. "Caught him stark naked in the basement," she said. "Polite boy, under the circumstances. I'll give him that. And very pretty, though I don't much care for tattoos."

Zee felt a little dizzy at the onrush of all this information. She managed to cobble together a possible scenario. Loni must have had a man over. A tattooed man. A man whom she'd gotten naked with. And whom she'd left wearing her pink robe, for whatever kinky reason. And then he'd—what—got locked out? Hidden naked in the basement? What the *hell*?

"Thanks," Zee said. "I'm...uhhh...thanks." She shrugged. "I'll see Loni gets it."

Mrs. Milliken just smiled and nodded, and left without another word.

Zee crossed the apartment to Loni's room and dropped the robe onto her bed. She walked back down the hall, a little unsettled at the idea that Loni had taken advantage of her absence to bring some guy in here and cavort with him for however long. She couldn't say *why* it bothered her. If you'd asked her a week ago, she'd have said it was exactly the kind of thing Loni needed to do more of.

Then she saw the phone and the wallet, lying right there on the kitchen table.

And somehow she knew.

Even before she examined them, she knew.

She knew why it bothered her that Loni had had a guy over.

Because she knew who the guy was.

She opened the wallet and found the driver's license tucked away there.

And sure enough.

SHAY M DAYTON

Everything around her went strangely, frighteningly still. Like the whole earth had just paused in its rotation.

Loni, who had everything handed to her, even things she didn't want—had just gotten what Zee wanted without even trying. She hadn't even been derailed by Zee going behind her back and working against her. It really was true, wasn't it? Everything just…*fell* into Loni's lap. A degree. A job. Two men. One of them *Shay Dayton*.

She felt a kind of uncontrollable fury whip up inside her, like a funnel cloud. She didn't know what to do with it. But if she didn't do *something*, it would blow the top of her head right off. Fortunately, this explosive charge was diffused by Shay Dayton's phone, which now started to vibrate.

She picked it up. The screen said, PERNITA, and there was a photo of a beautiful brunette with high cheekbones and too much makeup.

Zee did something without thinking, without wanting to think.

She tapped TALK.

"Hello?" she said, and her voice was barely a whisper.

"Baby?" said a voice at the other end. "I'm outside your building again. Can you let me up? I think I left one of my shopping bags there. The one from Ornello's? At least I'm hoping it's there. If not, I left it at the store."

Zee couldn't speak. It was a woman calling Shay Dayton "baby."

"Hello?" the woman said. "You there? Say something, sugar! I didn't exhaust you *that* much this morning, did I?" She laughed lasciviously.

Zee had to sit down. Apparently, Shay had romped with this girl in the morning and then with Loni just a few hours later. She knew he was an animal, but for God's *sake*. Suddenly it seemed that Shay Dayton was putting out for every woman in town—*except her*.

"I'm sorry," she said. "Are you calling for Shay Dayton?"

There was a long pause. Then, "Who is this?"

"I'm—it doesn't matter. Is...is he something to you? Shay?"

An even longer pause. "Who might be asking?"

Zee considered how to proceed. "He…he was here earlier. He left his phone. And his wallet. I'm feeling a little…I'm feeling like an idiot." None of this was strictly untrue, she was pleased to note. "If you give me your address, I'll bring them by, and you can return them to him."

"Why don't you return them yourself?" said Pernita, her voice like razor blades.

"Because," Zee replied, "based on this call, I never want to see him again." And that was true, too. In just the heat of a single moment, she had ceased to be an Underling.

"I'm in my car," Pernita said. "You give me *your* address, and I'll come by and get them."

"I'm at 1477 Londale," Zee said.

CHAPTER 10

The doorbell woke Shay from his nap. He sat up, and a sudden head rush made him feel momentarily swoony. The sun was still very bright. He wasn't entirely sure what day it was. The doorbell rang again. He lurched up from the couch and staggered down the hall to the intercom. "Yeah?" he said into the speaker.

"I've been calling you" was the tinny reply.

Pernita. He sighed in defeat.

"Lost my phone," he said, scratching his chest. Luckily he had left a set of spare keys with a neighbor, or he wouldn't have even been able to go home.

"Can you buzz me up?" she said. "I think I left a shopping bag there."

"You didn't," he said, scanning the place to make sure, but he buzzed her up anyway.

She appeared at the top of the stairs, looking as polished and fresh as she had several hours before—like she'd walked through a time vortex from 8 am straight to 4 pm.

She pecked him on the cheek and dropped her handbag on his orange-crate end table. "Silly," she said, "how'd you manage to lose your phone?"

He went and sat down. "Don't know," he said, yawning. "It happens."

"I think I'd lose my mind if I ever lost mine," she said, looking around the apartment. "I don't know who I'd even *be* without it." She looked up at him. "The bag doesn't seem to be here. You sure you haven't seen it? Blue, with orange lettering? 'Ornello's'?"

"I remember the bag," he said with just a hint of pique. "I carried it halfway across town for you." She shot him a challenging look and he moderated his tone. "Pretty sure you took it with you when you left."

She looked at him for a while, to the point at which he began to feel uncomfortable. Then she came over and sat in the worn leather armchair across from him.

"Have you tried retracing your steps?" she asked.

"Hm?" he asked, confused.

"Your phone. Walk yourself through your morning. Where did you go, after I left you?" She raised an eyebrow, which had the force of a gunshot. "You told me you were staying in to sleep off the concert high. So whatever got you up and out of the apartment must have been something pretty...singular."

She was, Shay thought. But he said, "I just felt restless. Went out."

"Where?"

"Just *out*," he said, and irritation crept back into his voice. "I don't know."

She smiled, but in a way that wasn't reassuring. "No need to bite my head off. I'm just trying to help you remember where you might've left your phone."

"No worries," he said, slouching down in the chair. "Sure it'll turn up."

The smile grew wider and colder. Then she said, "Oh, I know it will." Then she reached in her purse and pulled out his phone. She laid it on the table between them. "Your wallet, too," she added and she plucked that from the purse and tossed it on top of the phone.

Shay felt his face burn like a pepper under a broiler. He opened his mouth, but no words came out.

"She doesn't ever want to see you again," Pernita said, still smiling. "The girl on Londale Avenue. Apparently you neglected to tell her you were in a...nonexclusive relationship."

"Goddamn it," he muttered.

She sat back, and her smile relaxed somewhat. "Honestly, I don't understand why you insist on hiding these things from me. Your little 'adventures.' I mean, when have I ever said you couldn't have them? That's been the agreement between us from the start, and I've never...I mean, I can only *imagine* what it must be like, the morning after a big concert. All that energy and power and testosterone still surging through you, looking for release." She raised her eyebrows again. "Silly me, I thought I'd helped you work that off this morning. But I guess you had a little extra, huh?"

He looked down at his hands, resting on the arms of the chair. He used his thumb to push his cuticles back. He couldn't bring himself to look at her.

"Maybe hiding them from me is the *point*," she continued, unwilling to let it go and let him stew in his misery alone. "Maybe it's not exciting for you unless there's some degree of subterfuge involved. Maybe the secrecy is what makes it *hot*." She shrugged. "I don't know. Men are a mystery to me."

He imagined the floor opening up and swallowing him, chair and all, plunging him down to drown in a deep, salty sea. It was a comforting fantasy.

Finally, she got to her feet with a little grunt of exaspera-tion. "Maybe someday you'll learn to trust me," she said, and she came over and kissed the top of his head. He remained completely motionless. "I'm not your enemy. In fact, I'm the best ally you'll ever have. At some level, I'm sure you know that." She turned and fetched her purse from the end table. "Meet me for drinks tonight," she said as she slung the strap over her shoulder, "and I'll prove it. Working on a little scheme that, if it pans out…well, let's just say, you'll be happy. Mambo Room, six thirty. We can go to dinner after, if you're free." She winked at him.

I'm not free, he wanted to say. *I may never be free again. You've got me completely sewn up tight. I'm trapped, and I'm suffocating.*

And then…she was gone.

He waited till he heard the front door click shut behind her before he moved. And then all he did was to reach for his phone, and hold it in his hands. He was stymied. His impulse was to call Loni and explain. But he couldn't do that; he didn't have her phone number. He couldn't even look it up; he didn't know her last name. He knew, in fact, next to nothing about her. He didn't even know if she had a job. If he knew that, he might be able to reach her there.

Suddenly, her criticism of him—that he talked only about himself—came roaring back to bite him in the ass, and hard. She'd been right. He'd spent what he thought was a wonderful, exciting, life-changing afternoon with her, and when he thought back on it, all he could remember was talking about himself. His tour, his songwriting, his insecu-rities, his desires. Loni had liked him; he'd sensed that. She'd wanted him; she'd made that plain. But he didn't really know her at all.

He felt a sudden welling up in his chest, like he might cry. He was belatedly realizing what a totally self-centered prick he really was. And now it was too late. He couldn't reach Loni by phone or text, and he couldn't reach her by Facebook, because she'd blocked him. He had no other way of getting to her, short of camping out in front of her building. He was afraid to do that, because what if she saw him and called Pernita? He had no idea what had gone on between them. There might have been some horrible female-bonding thing, where Pernita had set herself up as Loni's protector should the predatory Shay come after her again. It was certainly within Pernita's powers to do that. She could manipulate the devil into handing over the keys to hell while he went off to live in a cardboard box beneath the freeway.

There was only one slender thread that might still work for him.

He called Lockwood.

"Favor," he said.

Lockwood sighed. "Man, I am so *not* your pimp."

Shay blushed. It was embarrassing that Lockwood just presumed this had to do with a woman. Even more embarrassing that he was right.

"Pernita got to Loni," he said.

Lockwood let loose a stream of profanities. "You're a piece of work, you know that? You can't even keep it in your pants long enough to get this tour started. The tour that makes or breaks us. You're just determined to break us *before*."

"This is different," he said. "This girl...Loni. Dude, I think this is it. This is...I don't want to be all melodramatic or anything..."

Lockwood laughed. "You? You're like a goddamn Hollywood diva. On your *best* days."

Shay gritted his teeth and soldiered on. "Listen, I just can't lose this one. Not yet. There's something there. Something *real*, man. We have a kind of...*connection*."

Lockwood snorted. "You're talking, but all I hear is *blah blah blah*."

"I know, I know. It's a string of clichés. That's the point. I need to get beyond that. I need to figure out what's there behind all the blah blah blah. Because there really is *something*."

"Well, what the hell am I supposed to do about it?"

"You're still friends with the roommate, right?"

"Zee?" he said, and barked a laugh. "You expect *her* to help you? Are you out of your fucking *mind*?"

"It's all I've got left. Just ask her, man. Ask her to please, please, please tell Loni that I can explain everything if she'll just agree to meet me one more time. Time and place totally up to her. Loni, I mean."

He sighed. "Fine. I'll ask. Just...don't get your hopes up. The girl's not your biggest fan, you know."

He was a little surprised to hear him say this. Surprised and hurt. "She used to be."

"Yeah, and then she got to know you. Put *that* in your pipe and smoke it."

"I will. I promise. Just do this for me, and I'm humble for the rest of my life."

"Fuck that bullshit. What am I, stupid?"

"No, you're my best friend. Best friend *anybody's* ever had. Thanks, bud. Seriously, I cannot express how much I owe you."

"I can," he said, before hanging up. "And I'll be invoicing you regularly, so be ready."

/////////////

Zee was feeling restless and uneasy. She was still upset by the inconclusive way her second interview had ended and was now saddled with additional guilt over the way she'd handled Pernita, allowing her to think that *she* was the girl Shay Dayton had hooked up with, not Loni. Pernita had intimidated Zee almost to the point of paralysis. The girl was so beautiful, so polished, so poised—everything about her screamed *finishing school*. But there was also something about her that seemed chiseled out of granite. That girl was *hard*. She had money and power and glamour—everything poor, plebeian Zee lacked. Zee felt like an idiot for having ever thrown herself at Shay. What could he possibly have seen in her, when he had a girl like *that* to turn to?

And yet, Shay had pursued Loni. Pursued her, caught her, and taken her down. Though wasn't Loni, too, someone who outclassed Zee by miles? Loni, with her upper-class cheekbones and her perfect vowel sounds and her computer brain? In a different way, she was as intimidating as Pernita. Zee had known Loni since they were both gangly, insecure adolescents, so she had never realized it before, but Loni had grown into a woman to be reckoned with. If, however, she had to bet money on a cage match, Zee would choose Pernita.

She was clearly used to getting everything she wanted and trampling over anyone who got in her way. Loni was still too sweet, too sympathetic. She was still someone who *listened* when you talked.

Whereas Pernita had made it clear to Zee—in phrases so sweetly worded and so pleasantly modulated that it was only later that Zee realized the lethal force behind them—that if she ever came anywhere near Shay Dayton again, Pernita would rivet her ass to a concrete block and then kick it off the nearest pier. So, in a way, Zee had done Loni a *favor* by letting Pernita win. She'd pretended to be angry and hurt by the revelation that Shay Dayton was in an open relationship with another woman—and after all, Loni probably *would* be hurt and angry—and had told Pernita she never wanted to see him again. Pernita would no doubt go back to Shay, return his phone and wallet, and relay the news that he'd fucked up his chances with *that* particular piece of tail, and Shay would never come sniffing around Loni again.

So Loni would be safe from Pernita. Zee had *helped* her.

Right? And she should be pissed at Loni anyway! Right? Loni knew how fanatical Zee was about Shay Dayton, but she just went ahead and did whatever she did with him anyway. Probably with not a single thought about Zee and how that would make her feel.

Except…except if all that were really true, why did she have to keep telling herself it was true? Why did she have to keep repeating to herself that *she* was the one who had been wronged and she had nothing to apologize for, if she in fact really *had* nothing to apologize for? If she was really helping Loni, and not just taking even more revenge on her for getting between her and Shay Dayton, why did it take so much *convincing*?

Maybe because the Shay Dayton she loved was a fantasy she had concocted from seeing him onstage and on album covers, but the Shay Dayton Loni knew might be a real person?

She felt itchy in her own skin and wished she could get out of it somehow. But when the opportunity came, she balked. She got a text from Lockwood Mott. *Hey just checking in u ok?*

She considered not responding, but after a few minutes of lying on her couch pretending everything was totally fine and failing, she decided what the hell, and texted back, *Fine thx.*

He replied: *How did interview go?*

She wrote back, *OK.*

U get the job?

Don't know yet.

There was a slight pause, and she wondered if that was it. She was surprised by feeling a little flurry of hope that it wasn't. But when he texted back, *Movie?*, she drew up her shoulders. She may have wanted some attention—distraction from her seething brain—but not *that* much. She certainly didn't want to have to *see* Lockwood Mott. He wasn't exactly a guilt-free association for her.

Cheer u up, he texted before she could think of a reply. *Totally NSA.*

She grimaced and texted back, *Thx sweet but v busy.*

He replied almost instantly. *Understand tk care.*

Zee considered several replies but rejected all of them and was still staring at her phone, wondering if he'd say anything else, when Loni let herself in. One look at her roommate's face was all it took to snap Zee out of her funk. "Oh, my God," she said, sitting upright. "What the hell happened?"

Loni strode angrily into the apartment, her face flushed and her eyes puffy from tears. "Nothing," she said, and her voice actually cracked. "Can't talk about it now." She threw her purse into a chair and headed for her bedroom.

"Anything I can do?" Zee asked as Loni swept past her. "Get you a hot tea or something?"

"Thanks, I'm good," Loni said, then went into her room and firmly closed the door behind her.

Zee blinked and felt her heart begin to skitter.

Something had obviously upset Loni—upset her *deeply*.

Zee couldn't imagine what that might be. Her first impulse, naturally, was to assume that Loni had discovered some of what Zee had been doing behind her back. Possibly Shay had mentioned being blocked from her Facebook page, and Loni had figured out Zee was responsible. Though if that were true, Loni was the type who'd confront her with it immediately. She wasn't shy about that kind of thing. But she'd come in and barely acknowledged Zee, as though anything to do with her was the furthest thing from her mind.

That at least made Zee feel safe in her little nest of deceit. Still, seeing Loni so distraught—having her right here in the apartment, probably collapsed in tears on the other side of that door—made her incredibly uncomfortable. What if she came out again? What if she wanted to confide in Zee, come to her for consolation, or unburden herself to her closest friend? What if she wanted to talk about Shay Dayton?

She felt a surge of panic. The idea of Loni in an extremity of distress counting on Zee, *trusting* Zee, when Zee knew perfectly well she'd betrayed that trust not once but twice today—blocking Shay from Loni's Facebook page and pretending to *be* Loni to Pernita—well, it would just be more than Zee could bear.

She texted Lockwood: *Changed my mind movie sounds gr8*.

A moment later, he texted back, *Fantastic*, and followed with the theater and show time. Zee quietly picked up her purse and crept out of the apartment. She was halfway down the stairs when she realized she hadn't even asked what the movie was. Not that it would've mattered. She'd have said yes even if it was some typical car-crash-and-explosion dude-stravaganza. The only thing that mattered was that it offered her an escape.

//////////////

Loni lay on her bed, feeling utterly destroyed. She'd known Byron would be upset when she turned down his offer after having kept him hanging on for so long, but she had no idea he'd be so completely, off-the-wall deranged about it.

"How can you do this to me?" he'd raged at her, his face the shade of purple Loni associated with heart-attack victims.

"I'm not doing anything to *you*," she'd said. "I'm making a choice about what I think is best for *me*."

He'd laughed bitterly. "What the hell do *you* know about anything? The only thing you know about life is what I've taught you. I *made* you, little girl. God*damn* it!" He'd gotten up at this point and stormed around the table, causing other patrons at the coffeehouse to look up in alarm.

"Well, then," she'd said, trying to keep her own voice as neutral as possible, "that's even more of a reason for me to go out on my own. I can't expect you to be responsible for me forever."

He'd sat back down then and put his face into his hands. And he'd *sobbed.*

Byron Pennington, her mentor, had bawled like a baby.

And when, after a few minutes, she'd reached across the table to comfort him, he'd reared back and snarled at her, like some kind of vicious raptor. "I don't need you," he'd said with a sneer. "I don't need your airs and your pretenses, that way you have of making people feel like you're doing them some kind of fucking *favor* when they put themselves on the line for you. Do you know how many times I've risked my own neck to get *you* ahead? And all the thanks I've ever gotten for it is that attitude you have that it's the goddamn least I can do."

She'd felt that one, felt it against her face like a blast of radioactive wind. It almost flayed the skin from her skull.

"That's not true," she'd said, leaning back in her chair as though recoiling from a frontal assault. "I'm grateful for everything you've done, I've always *said*—"

"Oh," he'd interrupted her with a dismissive wave of his hand, "you're *always* on form, I'll give you that. You dot your i's and cross your t's, and say please and thank you and speak when you're spoken to. No one can fault you on that. But," he'd continued, leaning across the table, like a panther preparing to pounce on its kill, "it doesn't begin to hide the egoism at your core. The massive sense of *entitlement* that makes you feel every good thing that happens to you is something you're *owed*. Well, *fine*, then." He'd abruptly sat back and pushed his chair away from the table. "Go your own way. You're so fucking confident. Let's see how you do without some idiot mentor running on ahead, clearing away all the obstacles for you so that you never even know they were there."

By this time, Loni had been unable to speak. She had been so completely taken aback by the ferocity of his attack—by the fact that he was attacking her *at all*—that she'd had to focus merely on breathing. She'd felt, honestly, as though she might pass out—just fall out of her chair in a mortified swoon and lay in a heap on the floor.

After he'd gotten up and stormed out—leaving her with the bill, she didn't fail to notice—she'd sat for a long time, just recovering from the shock and horror of it all and trying to pull herself together so that she could get up from the table and walk home without trembling like a leaf. But it was a hard job. Her mind kept boomeranging back to all the terrible things he'd said—the accusations, the condemnations. Was it possible that he really thought of her that way? Was it possible she really *was* that way? If what he'd said of her was even remotely true—if someone she'd considered her friend and protector could say such things about her—then what about the people in her life she was even *less* bound to? Zee, for instance; what did *she* think of her, in her private moments?

The thought of Zee reminded Loni of yet another mortification to come. She'd have to tell her about her morning with Shay. She couldn't begin to imagine how Zee would react to that. The girl had spent weeks plotting to meet and seduce him, and then at the crucial moment Shay had targeted Loni instead—completely shutting Zee out. That had to have been humiliating for her. If what Lockwood Mott had implied was true, she'd left the party an emotional wreck. The news that Shay and Loni ultimately *did* hook up wasn't going to help. The truth was, Loni had barely spared a thought for Zee the whole time she had been with Shay. What did *that* say about her? Well, whatever Zee might think about her, she was going to think worse of her now.

And that wasn't even factoring in the possibility that her morning's adventure with Shay wasn't just a one-off. She'd felt something solid spring up between them—a kind of foundation on which anything might be built. A friendship, a romance—who knew? She couldn't be certain, and didn't even like to risk hoping, but she wanted to keep herself open to all possibilities.

It was that—the thought of some kind of ongoing bond with Shay—that eventually gave her the strength to pay the bill, get up, and make her way home. He was, after all, the reason she'd turned Byron down to begin with. Whether she and Shay went any further than they had this morning, he'd shown her that there was more to life than following a plan in lockstep. There were opportunities she'd never suspected, a wonderful randomness that she wanted to embrace. It was exhilarating to think about, but the thought of Byron kept getting in the way, shooting her back into the scene at the coffeehouse and horrifying her anew. She had to get past that—cry it out of her system—before she could move on.

When she'd finally reached home, Zee was there, almost as if she'd been waiting. But Loni couldn't talk to her now, couldn't even risk looking at her. Zee might see the guilt on her face. Her confession would have to wait till after she'd had her catharsis.

Now, at last, all cried out and feeling ready to get up and face the new world she'd created for herself, Loni rose from her damp pillows and went out to tell Zee everything that had happened.

But Zee was no longer there.

CHAPTER 11

The film Lockwood had chosen was a revelation for Zee. It was a Japanese martial arts movie set in the sixteenth century. It was a perfect combination of romantic chick flick and violent action film. The hero was a disgraced aristocrat still in love with the woman he'd been promised to since childhood, who was now engaged to a corrupt imperial official. There were powerful scenes where the hero and the woman communicated their still fervent love for each other across a crowded room with the smallest of gestures: a raised eyebrow, a sudden turn of the wrist, a barely audible gasp. And then there were scenes where the hero hideously disemboweled the official's minions in massive, slow-motion sword fights. Both Lockwood and Zee left the theater feeling completely satisfied.

Zee was feeling so good that she agreed to Lockwood's suggestion of an after-movie drink. They found a congenial-looking bar, where Zee ordered a light beer and Lockwood a stout. They tried to discuss the movie for a while, but it rapidly became comical. It was as though they'd seen entirely different films. So they naturally segued into other topics, and Zee asked whether Lockwood was ready for the tour.

"Not so much," he said, after licking a foam mustache from off the surface of his real one. "Still not leaving for another, what, ten days?"

"But you'll be gone for *months*," Zee said, in awe of his casualness.

He shrugged. "We get a week off at the midpoint, when I imagine we'll all come back here and catch our breath. But otherwise, yeah, almost five months on the road."

"Haven't you got, like, lists of things you need to pack and buy and arrange and whatever?"

He chuckled. "Nah. I mean, I probably should. But I know what's gonna happen. Two days before, I'll just start shoving crap into a couple duffel bags, and when they're full, that'll be it. I'll just go from there, and whatever happens, happens."

Zee shook her head. "That's crazy. You have to start thinking about things like, I don't know, weather. I mean, you could conceivably run into snow before you're through. Do you have boots? And a parka? Also, what if you're invited to some kind of Hollywood agent party or something? You'll need a jacket, probably a designer one, and some really hot shoes..."

Lockwood raised the palm of his hand to her. "Enough. You're starting to give me heart palpitations."

"I'm only trying to help. If you want, I can come over and show you how to sort through your—"

He gave a little yelp, interrupting her, then laughed and said, "Congratulations, you've just hit on the one way you can invite yourself back to a guy's place and be sure of getting turned down."

She smiled at that but blushed a little, too. She didn't want to encourage any reference to an attraction between them. She was aware she'd led him down that path before, but she was off it now, and she wanted him off it, too. Fortunately, he saved her the trouble of changing the subject by growing suddenly serious himself. "Listen," he said. "I hate to bring this up…I don't want to upset you."

Suddenly she wasn't so sure a change of subject was a good thing. "What?"

"It's just…Shay told me he hooked up with your roommate this morning." He gave her a wary, sidelong look. "Maybe you already knew that. But the thing is, it apparently didn't end so well, and he feels bad and wants to explain things. Make it right. But he has no way of getting in touch with her. He doesn't even know her last name."

"It's Merr—" Zee began, almost reflexively, before stopping herself. If Shay didn't know Loni's last name, she wasn't going to be the one to pass it along to him.

Lockwood saw this, and his mouth stretched into a tight little smile. She could almost hear him thinking, *Okay, so that's the way it still is.*

For some reason, this triggered a flash of anger. She took up her glass, then downed a mouthful of beer, and when she'd swallowed it she looked at him with as much easygoing sweetness as she could manage.

"Oh, really," she said, "you should just tell him not to bother. The thing is, you guys aren't the only ones bolting from this hick town. Loni's leaving, too. In just a couple weeks she's moving to California with a man she's been on-and-off with for years." With her forefinger, she drew a little squiggle in the condensation on the side of her glass. "Her old professor. I'm sorry for Shay, but I'm pretty sure he was just one last fling for Loni before she settles down to being half of a boring old academic couple." She looked at Lockwood with dewy eyes. "You'll let him down easy, won't you?"

He cocked his head at her, as though slightly surprised by her answer. Probably he'd expected her to fall to pieces or something. Which, granted, she'd sort of done just last night when Shay had made it clear his interest in her was only as an avenue to her roommate. But she'd been a little bit drunk then and was taken off guard. Neither one of those things was the case now, and she smiled at Lockwood to reassure him.

"I'll let him down easy," he said, smiling back. "Don't you worry about Shay Dayton. Dude always lands on his feet."

"So I imagine," she said, making the squiggle on the glass more elaborate. "I mean, it's not like he'll be lonely or anything." She shot him a meaningful glance. "From what I understand, there's this woman…Pernita, I think is her name?"

Lockwood actually blanched a little. "Yeah. Pernita Hasque." He picked up his glass and took an extra long swallow of beer, as though the mention of Pernita's name required it. "I figured you might've heard about her," he continued, after wiping his mouth with the back of his hand. "She had a little run-in with your roomie, I understand."

You understand wrong, Zee thought, but of course she kept this to herself. "Loni's not bothered by it," she said, and that, of course was true—but only because Loni didn't know about it.

"Well, good," said Lockwood with a sigh. "She's the daughter of our manager, the guy who put the tour together. Kinda important we keep her happy. Shay ever blows it with her, who knows, we might find ourselves stranded in Idaho or something."

Zee laughed. "Oh, come on now," she said. But the wheels in her mind were turning. *Is this true? Is Pernita just someone he has to put up with because of the band? Because if that's true...*

But then she caught herself. No, no, she wouldn't go down that rabbit hole again. Shay had made his feelings about Zee perfectly clear. She'd never lay herself out for that kind of rejection ever again.

"Well," said Lockwood, sitting back and slapping his thighs. "I told him I'd give it a shot. My duty's done, my conscience is clean."

"Doesn't really sound like there's any destiny there," agreed Zee. "Loni's going west with her adoring professor. Shay's heading east with his...whatever she is."

Lockwood laughed. "Cross between a dominatrix and an organ grinder. With him as the monkey."

She pursed her lips in pretend disapproval. "That's terrible."

"Hey, I'm not complaining," he said, shrugging. "Works out for me, anyway."

Zee took another sip of her beer. "Yeah. Just as well nothing happens to complicate any of that." She noticed that Lockwood's glass was now empty. "Another one? My treat. As thanks for the movie."

////////////////

Loni was in her room, idly flitting about online, when she heard the front door open. Zee must finally be home. She looked out the window. It was dark.

She went out to greet her. "Hey."

"Hey," Zee said, letting her purse slide off her shoulder onto a chair. Then she went to the sofa, dropped onto it, and started unlacing her shoes. There was something in her manner—a little wobbliness—that led Loni to believe she'd had a drink or two. Well, good. That might help take the edge off what Loni had to tell her.

"How are you feeling?" she said, taking the chair opposite her, with the coffee table between them.

Zee freed her left foot from its shoe and set to work on the right. "Fine," she said, and she smiled kind of woozily. "Went to the movies with...with a friend." She grunted as she tugged at the shoe. "Couple beers afterwards. Time is it?"

Loni glanced at the chicken clock in the kitchen. "Ten to nine."

"Wow. Day disappeared, dinnit?" She laughed a little.

"Well," said Loni, beginning the careful approach to the subject of Shay Dayton, "I'm glad you're feeling better. You seemed pretty upset last night."

Zee leaned back, draped her hands over her stomach, and sighed. "Yeah. Had better evenings."

"Lockwood Mott...he didn't tell me anything, but he sort of hinted that something at the party upset you."

Zee made a flapping noise with her lips, as if it couldn't be less important. "Done now," she said.

"I'm guessing," said Loni, preparing to utter The Name, "it had to do with Shay Dayton."

Zee actually laughed and gave Loni a merry look. "Wow, you are a total genius detective. What were your clues? Was it that I spent all night talking about him and then actually threw myself at him, or was there something else that totally hit you over the head?"

"All right," said Loni with a smile. "Yeah, of course it was obvious. Look, I'm sorry I'm even bringing it up. It's just, there's something I have to tell you…"

"Really," she said, waving a hand at her. "Don't bother. Everything I've found out since, I'm not gonna waste any more time being all Shay, Shay, Shay."

Loni paused. "'Everything you've found out since'?"

"Yeah. Kinda embarrassing. Turns out I'm, like, the last one to know."

"Know what?" Loni casually crossed her legs, trying hard to act like this wasn't something she was intensely interested to hear.

"What, you can't guess?" Zee shrugged. "Only that he's pretty much catted around the entire town. Bagged himself a boatload of bimbos in every freakin' zip code. And the kicker is," she added, while beginning to play with a loose thread on her shirt, "he's already in a steady relationship."

Loni felt the color drain from her face—*felt* it disappear, like water running from a leaky pitcher. "He…he already has a…"

"Yeah," she said with a little scoff. "Should've figured. It's the daughter of the guy who manages the band. New York debutante type. Pernita Hasque. Man, name like that, you don't need to ask any more questions, right?"

Loni cocked her head. "They're…they're a couple?"

"Apparently so. She's going on tour with them and everything."

"But...all those other women..." Loni felt something like a plaintive cry threatening to take over her voice.

Zee flapped her lips again. "*Rock star*, Loni. It's what they do. Guess the gal who wants the ring has to put up with the running around." Suddenly she sat up. "Kinda hungry. We got anything in the fridge? Or maybe order a pizza?"

Loni could barely speak. By a great effort of will, she was able to get out the words, "Not for me, thanks," and then got to her feet and returned to her room. She had just enough fortitude to shut the door behind her before she once again collapsed into a heap on her pillows.

What an *idiot* she'd been! What a stupid, ignorant, *willful* little moron.

True, she hadn't really counted on her romance with Shay Dayton going any further than it had, but she'd really thought it *might*. And even if it didn't, that very possibility made so many other things seem possible, too.

And now...now she knew that there never *was* a possibility. She'd fooled herself. *Let* herself be fooled. Shay Dayton had showed her what a stupid naïf she really was. He'd just sent her the signals he'd figured she'd wanted, and she'd eaten them up with a spoon and asked for more, please. He'd gotten exactly what he'd wanted from her, and now he was heading off on the road to superstardom, leaving her behind, devastated, having closed the door on the only road open to *her*.

How many women, she wondered, had fallen into this same trap? How many had let a dazzling smile and lightning-blue eyes woo them into lowering their guards? How many had let a few lines implying respect and admiration trick them into believing they were respected and admired? God, Loni had even made the *first move*. She wasn't just a victim, she was a willing accomplice in her own victimization. And worst of all, she'd burned her bridges behind her. How could she possibly go back to Byron now and tell him she'd changed her mind? She didn't even *want* to. The things he'd said to her, she couldn't ever forget them—certainly never forgive.

Suddenly, the walls around her seemed to close in—to suffocate her. All the lives she'd lived in this single day; the futures she'd projected for herself one after another; the array of selves she'd tried on like gloves, admired, and set aside; all were gone now. She had nothing left. No allies, no mentors, no friends, no lovers—no choices and no confidence. She was utterly and completely alone.

//////////////

A few hours earlier, Shay had entered the Mambo Room.

Pernita had said to meet her there at six thirty. He was deliberately twenty minutes late. In fact, he'd spent most of the past half hour in a bar two blocks away, having a drink to pass the time. He wasn't going to show up until he was damn good and ready.

But of course, Pernita didn't care. She caught sight of him as he entered and happily waved him over to where she was seated, at a tall table near the bar. As he made his way through the club toward her, he knew she wouldn't even mention his being late. Possibly she didn't even realize it. More likely, though, she saw his lateness for what it was: a pathetic little stab at resistance to her power over him, a small piece of childish acting out. She'd ignore it, as it deserved to be ignored.

He felt his face redden with shame. He really was pathetic. He'd sold himself to this woman and her father. He knew it, they knew it, and whatever sulky little fits he occasionally threw against them were as ridiculous to them as they were to him.

"Hey, sugar," Pernita said when he reached her. Since he didn't lean down to her, she craned her neck up to him and smacked him on the lips. "Do you know Rachael Blessing-Innes?" she asked, gesturing to the imposing-looking young woman seated next to her, whose hair was pulled back into a tight chignon and whose black skirt and jacket looked like sheet metal.

"I don't believe I do," Shay said, and he shook the amazon's hand. Her grip, surprisingly, was very loose. Maybe she just didn't think he was worth impressing.

"Rachael and I were at school together," Pernita said. And this was the problem with her: he could never punish her by making her wait for him, because for her, waiting was never a chore. There was always someone there for her to talk to, someone she'd gone to school with, or flown to Brazil with, or went skiing in Gstaad with, or started a colony on Jupiter with, or who the hell even knew.

Shay couldn't think of anything to say to this, and Rachael had chosen the moment to take another sip of her murky green cocktail. Was she drinking absinthe? If anyone had friends who drank absinthe, it would be Pernita.

For a few moments there was an awkward silence. Then Rachael put down her drink and said, "Oh, there's my party.

Got to run. Such a scream to see you again, angel lady." She got up from her stool—and kept on going. Shay was astonished. She easily cleared six feet.

"We've really *got* to stay in touch this time," said Pernita, air-kissing her, and since she was about seven inches shorter, there was plenty of air to kiss.

"I've got all your contact info," Rachael said, grabbing her clutch. "I'll text you tomorrow."

"Looking forward to it. Ciao, darling."

Shay shimmied around Pernita, making his way to the stool Rachael had just vacated. He paused long enough to scope out the party Rachael had gone to meet. Yep, it was just as he'd figured: a group of three other people, one man, one woman, one who might have been either but in a way Shay could only call gladiatorial, and all of them were hung with couture, boasting cheekbones that could shelter small cars from the rain.

Shay slipped onto the stool and deliberately avoided making eye contact with Pernita. Instead he scanned the room for someone who could give him another drink. It was a bit early-ish to get hammered, but he was with Pernita, so he'd need it.

"Hel-*lo*," Pernita said. "Why yes, I'm fine, thank you, sugar-pie. And you?"

"Sorry," he said. "Just want to grab a server so I can order a bev." At just that moment he locked eyes with a pert young blonde carrying a tray and signaled her over.

"You won't need to do that," said Pernita, who noticed the blonde as well and made a small countermanding gesture to her. The blonde nodded and turned away.

Shay felt his face blister with anger. He put up with a lot of this presumed ownership crap, but this was too god-damn far. He was a grown man, for Christ's sake, and if he wanted to have a drink, he was going to have a goddamn drink. He extended his arm to its full length and tried to wave the server back.

"Excuse me," he said tersely as he flailed in vain, "but I'll be the judge of what I need and when I need it." It was as surly a tone as he'd ever allowed himself to take with her.

She actually laughed at him. Laughed, and her eyes twinkled as if his rebellion just amused and delighted her like it was the ferocious growling of an adorable puppy. She placed her hand on his arm and forced it down. "Just relax," she said, a smile in her voice. "It's all taken care of."

"It is not taken care of," he said, still angry but being careful not to get any angrier. "I came in thirsty, I remain thirsty, and," he added, gesturing at the empty place on the table before him, "there is nothing here to quench my thirst. So, no. Very much *not* taken care of."

He was just tearing off the last syllables of this blister-ing complaint when the blonde reappeared, carrying a cham-pagne bucket, a bottle of Veuve Clicquot, and two crystal flutes. "Ah," said Pernita happily. "Here it is. I've had her keep it on ice while I waited for you."

If there was a little hint of a spike in that "while I waited for you"—and Shay thought there was—there was no way he could address it. He was too busy feeling abashed by the sudden appearance of this extravagant bottle, whose cork the server had now freed from its wire cage and was laboriously pulling from the bottleneck.

"I don't understand," Shay said, as the cork came free with a pop.

Pernita clapped her hands and told the server, "Well done!" Then she turned back to Shay and said, "Just a moment."

He gritted his teeth and forced himself to wait for the server to dramatically fill the two flutes—first pouring a little, then letting the foam subside, then pouring a little more, and so on. Why was it always this way with Pernita? Did she actually *like* making a fool of him? He ought to be enjoying this moment, anticipating what she was about to tell him, because it was almost certainly good news. And yet there was something about the way she did it, the way she insisted on always keeping him partly in the dark, always just a little bit off-balance—like she got some kind of charge out of prompting him to react one way, then turning things upside down to make him regret it.

Well, he wasn't playing along anymore. He'd just sit tight and not say a word till Pernita finally revealed whatever it was she had up her sleeve.

Eventually the flutes were filled. The server plunged the bottle into the ice bucket and departed. Pernita handed him one flute, while taking the other herself.

"Here's to fashion," she said, and she held her flute aloft.

Shay raised his as well, but there was no way he was uttering a syllable until he knew what the hell this was about.

"And to fashion photography," she added teasingly.

Shay just stared at her.

"And," she continued, "to the upcoming photo spread in *Details* featuring the hottest men's winter fashions as worn by rock music's hottest front men. Including," and here she chinked her flute against his, "a certain Shay Dayton."

His jaw dropped. "What?" he asked, forgetting to drink to the toast, though Pernita was now happily enjoying her first sip. "What—what are you even—what did you—"

"Daddy's friends with someone on the editorial board," she said, clearly giddy at how gobsmacked she'd made him. "He called in a favor. Not that it took much calling. You *do* have quite a look, you know."

"But...," he said, setting the drink on the table. He didn't trust himself not to drop it, he was that shaken up. "But, that's a national rag! And I'm just a local boy. Nobody's even heard of me."

She slid his flute closer to him, gently pressuring him to pick it back up and drink with her. "You're a nobody *now*," she said. "But by the time the issue comes out in November, you'll have played a bunch of East Coast dates. You won't be a local boy anymore."

"Yeah," he said, "but...I mean, I still won't *be* anybody. We're just the opening act for Strafer Nation."

"Which," she reminded him, "is an amazing way to bring yourself to the world's attention. Strafer has legions of fans, and you now get a shot at them. *Details* will support that. Hell, it may even be a *better* way of fixing you in the national eye."

His shoulders slumped. "I'm...speechless. Jesus."

She lifted her glass. "Shall we toast Daddy?"

He shook his head in disbelief, then took his glass and raised it. "Yes. Of course. To Daddy. Sweet creeping Christ."

"And to me," she said, as she drew the flute to her lips. "It was my idea, you know."

He stared at her, as though never having seen her before.

She laughed at him. "What, don't you remember? I'm an integral part of your team supreme." She gave him a teasing look. "Don't tell me you didn't believe me."

He took a deep breath, held it a moment before releasing it, and then chugged half the glass of champagne. When he set it back on the table, he couldn't suppress a belch.

"There'll be none of *that* in Manhattan's finest establishments," she mock-scolded him.

"What?" he asked, suddenly wary again.

"Manhattan. You know, New York City." He stared at her blankly, so she continued. "That's where the photo shoot is." He opened his eyes wide, and she added the kicker, "We leave tomorrow night."

"Tomorrow night?" He almost fell off the stool. "Are you freakin' *kidding* me?"

She shrugged. "Why is that a big deal? You've played your farewell gig, you don't have anything on the docket till the tour starts. Unless there's something holding you here you haven't told me about."

She gave him a steely look, almost a challenge, and Shay realized at once that she was talking about Loni. Somehow, she'd recognized that there was a real danger in her and had moved to take Shay out of her path. He was almost certain that if Loni had never entered the picture, Pernita wouldn't have lifted a finger to get him this photo shoot.

And the crazy thing was, she was right. Shay *didn't* want to leave town until he'd squared things with Loni, at least enough so that there was an opening for them somehow, somewhere, to pick up where they'd left off.

But he couldn't do that from New York. He'd have to do it face-to-face. He'd have to do it *here*. He couldn't leave. But he also couldn't tell Pernita that. He hemmed and hawed for a bit, then he said, "My parents. You're asking me to just pack up and leave town for six months without even saying good-bye to them." Even he could hear the phoniness of the outrage in his voice.

Pernita just grinned at him over the rim of her champagne flute. After she'd taken a sip, she said, "You can say good-bye to them over the phone. And when you tell them why you're leaving early, what do you think they're going to say? You think their feelings will be hurt? Honey, they'll be over the *moon*. Their little boy is on his way to becoming a superstar."

He shook his head. "They don't care about that kind of thing. They just want me to be happy."

She laughed. "First of all, they *do* care about that kind of thing. *Everybody* cares about that kind of thing. And second, how will this *not* make you happy? Do you know who else is in this spread? Just three other singers."

Shay examined his fingernails, trying to feign a lack of interest but sensing he wasn't doing a very good job.

"Don't worry, you don't *have* to ask," she continued, "because I'm going to tell you. Piers Brandy of Mission Misters. Kyle Abromovitz of the Happiness Vector. And Mitch Prentiss of the Mitchell Prentiss Band."

Despite himself, Shay felt his mouth open a little. Those were some pretty significant names. At least one of them was always peering out from the glossy celeb mags Shay passed on the corner newsstand every week. He was seriously, dangerously impressed. And yet, he resisted. He toyed with the stem of his flute, unwilling to look her in the eye. "I can't just *go* to New York. I haven't got anything to wear there. I can't show up looking like I do here. Especially in company like that."

She leaned across the table and placed a hand over his. "Baby," she said, in a tone of voice that let him know she was condescending to him and enjoying it, "little secret I learned: they have shops in New York. Some pretty good ones, even." She sat back. "Plus, that's already arranged. I've got a meeting with a stylist all set up for the morning after we get there. He'll be taking you in hand, shaping your complete look."

"Oh," he said, rolling his eyes, "and how much is *that* going to cost?"

She winked at him. "Little present from me."

He shook his head emphatically. "I can't accept a gift like that."

"Then look at it as an investment. You're my client. Well, you're Daddy's, but I'm on his team. So anything I do for you now, I reap the benefits of later." She ran her fingers up his arm. "Jesus, will you *cheer up*? I've just gotten you a spread in a national magazine, and all you have to do is get on a plane, instead of lying on your couch all day watching the Cartoon Network."

"Syfy," he said, gritting his teeth. "It was Syfy I was watching all day, and you *know* that, and it was only *once*."

She blithely ignored this and looked over her shoulder. "You hungry at all? We could put in our names for a table here. Let me just find our waitress." When she looked back at him, his face must still have been set in a frown, because she said, "Or we can go someplace else. Your call."

What he wanted to do most was escape her. Never mind that everything she was doing was taking him further along the road he'd always dreamed of traveling. The way she was doing it was making him feel more and more like a passenger than the man at the wheel. And he hated it. He wanted to get away from her—flee into the night. Find Loni. Explain. Make peace. Make love. But he was paralyzed. He needed something. Some sign from the universe. Some *prompt*.

"Baby?" Pernita said. "Thoughts? About dinner?"

He couldn't answer. He could barely breathe. He sensed, somehow, that this moment was crucial. What he did now would drive his future in one direction or another—toward the career he'd always wanted or the girl he couldn't even be sure of.

His phone vibrated. He almost couldn't believe it. He'd asked for a sign, and here it was. It *had* to be. He raised his finger to signal Pernita to wait a moment, then took his phone from his pocket. It was a text from Lockwood. *Sorry man Loni already has a guy, moving to Cali with him in a couple wks bummer but still, tour calling.*

He read it over a few more times, then put the phone back in his pocket and turned to Pernita.

"Dinner here's fine," he said.

CHAPTER 12

Pernita was right, of course. It took barely half the morning for him to pack up whatever of his life in Haver City needed transporting to New York. The rest he left in a pair of battered old suitcases to go on the van to Pittsburgh, where he'd meet the rest of the band to start the tour.

He'd been a little apprehensive about telling the others he was being whisked off to Manhattan for a magazine fashion shoot. He was sensitive about how, as the front man, he tended to overshadow the others in the band, and he often thought he picked up little currents of resentment from them…especially Jimmy. But in fact, they were almost unanimously excited for him—and for themselves.

"You know what this means for us, don't you?" Lockwood had said. "Your pitiful mug is somehow going to hypnotize gullible women and gay guys across our great nation to go straight to their smartphones and download *Grief Bacon*. We'll be millionaires by the end of the month."

"The spread doesn't run till November," he'd said, embarrassed.

"End of the year, then," Lockwood corrected himself.

Trina hooted and cawed like a whole stadium full of football fans and told him, "Just show that ass, Dayton. Whatever they tell you, *show that ass*. It's a superfine ass, and if you've got *me* fucking telling you that, you better fucking believe it's down."

Baby had, in his own laconic way, showed tremendous excitement, almost agitation. He'd muttered "Wow" seven or eight times, then said, "Opens some doors for us, you know?" Shay got a little nervous, hearing him go on this way, and told him to calm down, nothing was for sure.

It was, as Shay predicted, only Jimmy who'd felt obliged to spike his congratulations with a little acid. "Way to go, mic-man," he said. "Just don't forget while you're swanning around with the goddamn glitterati that we're the ones who make you look good."

His parents, too, proved Pernita right about them, which was maddening even though he'd known she was dead-on when she'd said it.

"But, sweetheart," his mom had said, "this is the most wonderful news *ever*. Of course don't worry about Dad and me. Just get on that plane and *go*. You know what they say: don't knock opportunity once."

He grimaced. "I don't think that's quite the way it's worded, Mom."

"Or however it goes. You know what I mean. Do you think you'll make it home for Christmas?"

He hadn't even thought to ask about that. "I'm not sure."

"Well, if not, maybe we can do the Skype. Dad got it working last month to see Cheryl's twins out in Nevada. Cute as all get-out. One of them knocked over Cheryl's computer and broke the Skype, though. So Dad keeps saying we can't use it anymore. I keep telling him, it's just on Cheryl's end, ours is fine. But you know how he never listens sometimes. Do you do the Skype?"

"I can manage it. And it's just Skype, Mom."

"That's what I said."

"No, you said *the* Skype."

"I know. That's what you said, too."

"No, I just said *Skype*."

She gave a little exasperated sigh. *"Same as me."*

"No, Mom, you said *the* Skype."

He realized he was rapidly spiraling into a conversational whirlpool of no return—an easy place to end up with his mom, so he always had to be wary—and strategically withdrew to an earlier point. "I'll find out about Christmas."

"We'd love to have you. Also let us know if you're going to be on the TV anytime."

"I will."

"Or the Interweb. We do the YouTube, you know."

"It's not *the* YouTube, Mom, it's…fine, yes, I'll let you know."

There was a pause. "You don't sound very excited, honey. What's wrong? You want to go, don't you? I'd certainly *think* you'd want to go."

"Yes, of course, it's…it's just. Well. You remember last time we talked, and I mentioned that girl I met?"

"Mm-hm," she said, in a way he could tell meant she didn't, not quite. But it wasn't necessary.

"Well, I'm kind of leaving with that whole thing in a bad place. My fault, really. And I don't have time to make it up to her, and…and in the meantime, she's moving out west, and it's just a big freaking mess. That's all."

"Oh, sweetheart. I'm sure there will be other girls. Lots of them, from what I remember about the club scene."

He absolutely did not want to hear any more stories about his mom's adventures in the club scene; they had already scarred his adolescence. "Yeah," he said, "but there's something about this girl. A thing I can't really describe. Like, she intrigues me. She shouldn't, but I can't help it. I...I think she may be, like, someone I'm meant to be with. Possibly. Sort of. Ish."

She laughed. "You men and your qualifiers! You know your dad never tells me he loves me? Not in those words. Whenever I ask him, he just grins and says, 'You'll do.'"

"I know that, Mom." He'd heard it often enough.

"Well, fine, Shay, let me play devil's advocate. You say this girl *may* be the one you're meant to be with. You're not sure, then."

"No. But I'd like to be. I have a feeling."

"Fine. Test it, then. Go to New York. Wade through all the girls that get thrown in your way. If you can make it through them and still be thinking of this one, then track her down and tell her so."

"Yeah, but..." He shifted in his chair and scratched his knee, a nervous gesture. He was hearing what he needed to hear, but it embarrassed him that he had to hear it from his mother. He felt like he was fifteen or something. "Here's the thing. She's moving west with another guy. To be with him."

She scoffed. "Oh, honey, you know that means exactly nothing. If this is a destiny thing, then who she's with now means less than zero."

He smiled. "It's crazy how you always make it sound so easy."

"Well, I'm a professional. Of course I make it sound easy. But it's not. Like they say on TV, 'Don't try this at home.'"

"Try what at home?"

"Giving yourself advice. That's what moms are for. What time is your plane, honey?"

"Six thirty–ish. Pernita's picking me up."

"This is the one who's the daughter of your manager?"

"Yep, that's her."

"Well. That's very nice of her." Shay's mom had a way of saying things about Pernita that sounded like the exact opposite of what the words meant. Like now, what she was really saying was, *How deviously grasping of that little witch.* It was amazing to Shay that she'd developed such a strong dislike for Pernita, despite Shay having said almost nothing about her, ever. Hell, maybe that *was* why. Mothers could read between the lines. It was kind of their superpower.

//////////////

Seated at the airport in the departure lounge, Shay felt restless and bored. Pernita was immersed in her iPad and exuded a kind of serene patience. It made him want to knock the thing right out of her hand. He readjusted himself in his seat, checked the flight number on his boarding pass for the eleventh time, and compared it to the one on the board over the check-in desk in case something had suddenly changed in the forty-six seconds since he'd last done this.

Everything still seemed in order, so he shifted again, then turned to Pernita and said, "By the way, I forgot to ask, what hotel are we staying at?"

She looked up at him with her usual didn't-Shay-just-say-the-cutest-thing look.

"In the city, I mean," he said, thinking she didn't understand him. "In New York."

"Idiot," she said, grinning. "You're not staying in a *hotel*."

Another layer of doom seemed to drop over him like a sheet. "I'm not?"

"Of course not! There are going to be plenty of hotels when we're on the road. This is our last chance to relax in the comfort of an actual home."

He blinked. "*Whose* home?"

She tweaked his arm. "Whose do you think? *Daddy's*."

"He's got a place there?" he asked, but he was thinking, *Of course he does.*

"I've told you before, Daddy's bicoastal. He's got a beautiful apartment on the Upper East Side, overlooking Central Park. You'll *love* it."

"Oh. Okay." He sat back. He was feeling strangely sorry he'd asked. It was like she'd told him, *We have the most beautiful cage for you to stay in. Everything you could ask for; you won't even notice the bars.* Testing this out, he said, "It sounds pretty convenient. I'm guessing I can just jump on the subway and head downtown. Kinda hoping to take in some of the clubs while I'm there."

"Oh, don't worry about that. We can use one of Daddy's cars for wherever we want to go. Also, he and I have put together a pretty tight schedule for you, parties and openings and things like that. We don't want to waste a minute of your time there. It's all about exposure, exposure, exposure."

She glanced at her watch. "Almost boarding time. I wonder what's delaying my upgrade request…"

She got up and went to harangue the gate agent. Shay stayed behind, alone in the crowd, and thought, *This may be my last chance. If I get up now and leave, I can be out of here before she even notices I'm gone. I can grab a bus and go somewhere new and start over and no one will ever find me…*

But of course he didn't move a muscle, except to restlessly shift in his seat, until the time came to board the plane.

/////////////////

Loni shouldn't have cared whether he was in town or not. She'd always known he was leaving anyway, so what did it matter *when* he left? But when she heard that he'd flown to New York the day after she'd made love with him—flown off with the woman he was apparently some kind of item with to shoot a magazine spread for some trendy magazine—she felt as if she'd been punched in the stomach. Maybe it was worse that a photographer had snapped a photo of them as they entered the airport and she got to see what this Pernita looked like. It was just as she'd feared. Pernita Hasque might've been sculpted out of soap and sprayed with sex. Women like that just weren't *natural*. Not that men ever cared.

She lay on her bed and just concentrated on breathing. In…out. In…out. It wasn't difficult, but if she didn't pay attention, she might…just…stop.

She examined her mental state with characteristic ruthlessness and realized that deep down she'd been kind of hoping that Shay would make some dramatic reentry into her life—come back and explain himself and make everything all right. Ask for a second chance, and…well, get one.

Schoolgirl, soap-opera stuff. The kind of stupidity she actually *mocked* in other people.

And here she was, lying limp on her bed because… because her life was not a fairy tale. Because she was an adult who made mistakes and didn't want to accept the consequences. Didn't want to do the hard work of getting back on her feet and making her life what she wished it to be.

But…that was the kicker. She'd thought with Shay she *had* been making those hard decisions. She *had* been in control. She hadn't thrown herself at him; he'd pursued *her*. And even then, he'd had to earn her respect. She knew now that it was all an act—him pretending to listen to her as she went on about poetry, about art, about creativity. He was just a practiced, polished seducer who instantly sussed out the way into any woman's heart. Or, rather, her pants. Better women than she had fallen prey to guys like that.

And yet…and yet…even now she couldn't let go of the idea that he *hadn't* been pretending. Admittedly she was young, but she wasn't entirely inexperienced. And she'd been completely convinced by everything he'd said to her, by the look in his eyes, the look *behind* his eyes. They'd engaged each other, met each other on a higher level. They'd *connected*.

Well, so what if they had? Tonight he'd gotten on a plane with a woman who had more invested in her hair than Loni spent on her entire education. That was the hard lesson of the world. Hearts don't matter, minds don't matter, *money* matters. Money and power.

She rolled over on her back, and found herself once again staring at the crack in the ceiling. Reflexively, the lines she'd written about it came back to her:

A hairsbreadth divide that does not divine—meaning
gutters when division uncouples a nullity—

Division had uncoupled a nullity with her and Shay, all right.

This was ridiculous. She got to her feet and swept her hair away from her face. Then, with a big gulp of air to summon up all her courage, she went out to the kitchen and made dinner. Chicken cutlets from a bag and frozen carrots. It was that kind of world.

////////////////

The next morning Zee got her long-awaited job offer, and after the first rush of euphoria, she plummeted into a weird kind of nervous moodiness.

"You should call Byron," she told Loni. "I mean it."

Loni laughed. "You're very sweet. But that bridge done be burned."

"No, I mean it," she said, sitting on the side of Loni's bed. She'd burst in to tell her the news and found Loni half awake, scrolling through e-mails on her phone. "It's not too late. It's never too late, not for anything."

"It's too late for this," Loni said, pushing herself up to sit propped against her pillows. "I told you the things he said to me. I can't just *ignore* them."

"But, you've said before, he goes a little crazy every now and then, loses his mind, and then an hour later he's all right again. What if that's what happened this time? What if an hour after he walked out on you, he was all regretful and everything? And wishing he could apologize? I mean, he's a poet, right? He's allowed to rage out sometimes. It's part of the whole artist thing."

"Then he could damn well *have* apologized. And he's not a poet. He's a poetry *professor*," Loni replied, then muttered, "which is more than I can hope to be."

"Except..." Zee balled her fists and play-pounded Loni's skull. "Come on, idiot. You can't *not* know how incredibly into you he is. He's probably killing himself over what he said and worried that if he tries to apologize and you shut it down, he'll have to go and...I don't know. Kill himself or something."

"Byron Pennington will never kill himself," she scoffed. "He'd never deprive the world of so much literary genius. He'd consider it cruel."

Zee sighed. "You're not taking me seriously."

"You're not *being* serious. You're just...look, a week ago, I had this big job lined up, my future was made. And you had nothing. Now, our situations are exactly reversed. You've got your hot new gig, and I've got a great big crater of zip, zilch, nil, nada. And you're a very sweet and very empathic girl who remembers what that felt like, and you want me to join you back on the other side of the fence." She stroked Zee's forearm. "I love you for that, really. You're a stand-up friend. But...it just ain't happening."

A funny thing occurred while Loni was saying this. Zee's face underwent a series of contortions, like she was in some kind of agony. Loni had no idea what was behind it. Could the girl not stand being complimented or something? Whatever the reason, she decided not to torment her any further with more comments on what a great friend she was.

Instead, she said, "And anyway, Byron's sure to have offered the job to the other woman he had lined up. He'd promised to let her know as soon as I made my decision, and I sure as hell made my decision. So that's it. The job's not even there for me to take anymore." Loni still hadn't found it necessary to tell Zee about Shay, and she felt a little bad hiding from her very compassionate friend that the true cause of her depression might actually be more from a one-afternoon-stand than the whole thing with Byron.

Zee's lower lip trembled. It looked to Loni like Zee felt personally responsible for her predicament, which was totally insane. Loni had made all her own decisions—every last lousy one of them.

"Well, then, at least call him to smooth things over," Zee said. "You say you've burned that bridge, but it can be rebuilt. I mean, you're going to need him, aren't you? He's, like, your only reference. Wherever you go, for whatever kind of job you end up doing, there's no one else you can have people call but him."

Loni was about to quip something back but stopped herself. In fact, Zee had a point. If she allowed Byron to remain banished from her life, she'd essentially be back to where she had been when she graduated high school. Everything that had happened since would be effectively erased, because the only human being on the planet who could testify to its value was someone she'd cut the cord to.

She heaved a big, resigned sigh. "Okay. You're right. I'll call him. I will."

Zee leaned in and gave her a hug, then hopped up and said, "I'm making pancakes. Interested?"

"Love some. Do we have any blueberries?"

"Bought some on my way home," Zee said, leaving the room and shutting the door behind her. "Because I knew you'd ask."

Left alone, Loni fondled her phone for a minute before opening her address book. She hovered her fingertip over Byron's number.

But she didn't press it.

Later, she thought.

After breakfast.

////////////////

But breakfast came and went, and still she procrastinated. Eventually she realized she was waiting to think up the perfect opening line. But of course there was no perfect opening line, because this whole situation was so completely *im*perfect. So in late afternoon, seated outside the apartment building on a rusty porch swing that made a sound like a tortured cat whenever it moved on its hinges, she called him. She'd just let the moment tell her what to say.

He answered in a hushed voice: "Hi."

"Hi," she said, sounding equally quailed.

There was an awkward pause. Then she said, "I just called to say, you were right. Not about everything, but about the job. I should've taken it. I should've gone with you. I'm sorry I let it go." She let a beat pass. "If it means anything to you."

He chuckled. "Well, there it is. You did it again."

"Did what again?" she asked, growing suddenly wary.

"Beat me to the punch. Did the right thing before I did. With even less cause. I mean, it just goes to show, you're a better man than I am."

"Oh, that," she said, relaxing again.

"Listen, you *know* me," he went on with a sudden tinge of urgency in his voice. "You know the way I fly off the handle. I mean, that's no excuse. But my point is, you know how little it really means. How afterward, when I get the demon out of me, it's all over. Just a lot of hot air and screaming. Sound and fury, signifying nothing. Like a really long fit of Tourette's, or something."

She laughed. "Yeah. I do know that."

"Right, then. I'd like for us to be friends. I'd like for us to stay in each other's lives."

"Me, too," she said, and she felt a little constriction in her throat. She commanded herself not to cry. Grown women did not cry. Not in front of men, anyway.

"Maybe we could meet for lunch or something. Before I head out west."

She was taken aback by the offer. She pushed the swing back a little, a nervous tic.

"Ye gods," he cried, "never mind! I'm sorry I asked!"

"What?" she said. "I haven't answered you yet!"

"Didn't you just scream bloody murder at the idea?"

She laughed. "No, that's the swing I'm sitting on. On the porch at my place. It's really, really rusted."

"For Christ's sake! I think my hair actually turned white."

"It *is* pretty unnerving," she said, moving the swing back to its resting position.

"*Stop* it, *Jesus*," he said. "It's like hearing baby seals get clubbed!"

She made an effort to keep the swing still. "That better?"

"Much. Bloody hell. You should hear my heart pounding." Another beat. "Well?"

"Well, what?"

"Well, lunch or something?"

"Oh!" She laughed. "Yes. Sure. Love it."

"Wonderful," he said, sunlight flooding back into his voice. "Now, do me a favor. Tell me, 'Byron, you're a contemptible asshole and I never want to see you again.'"

She knit her brow. "You *want* me to say that?"

"Yes. Because it's what I deserve. I *need* to hear it. It's my punishment. But I couldn't bear to hear it if I knew you actually meant it."

She laughed. "Byron, you're a contemptible asshole and I never want to see you again."

"Thank you," he said. "You're an angel."

///////////////

Byron called again that night, as she and Zee were flopped on the couch, watching the last bit of TV they could manage before dropping off to sleep.

"Hello?" Loni said, as she got up and shambled off to the quiet of her room, ignoring Zee, who was hugely mouthing the words, *Is that him? Is that him?*

"Hey, it's me," he said, rather adorably—as if she wouldn't know it was him from his picture smiling out from her phone. "I'm not waking you, am I?"

"No, still up," she said numbly. Though in fact she felt about two-thirds comatose.

"I just want to tell you, the job's still yours, if you want it."

Her eyes sprang suddenly open. "What?"

"I fixed it with Tammi. It wasn't easy, but I managed it."

"You didn't!" she cried, now fully awake and horrified. She sat on her bed. "Oh, Byron, you shouldn't have! That poor woman! What must she think of me?"

"Don't worry about that. It's all smoothed over. She's fine. We're both fine."

"But…Jesus, Byron! How the hell can you do that to someone? What did you even say to her?"

"I just told her the truth. Which is that, in this matter—in *everything*, really—everything to do with me, in every area of my life—it's you. It's always been you."

Loni was so stunned, she didn't know what else to do.

So she said yes.

PART TWO

CHAPTER 13

"Just one more," said Shay, as Paul poured him another tumbler of bourbon. It was what he'd said when Paul had poured him the last two...or was it three? It was, in fact, what he said most often to Paul, since they'd started their tradition of drinking after dinner.

It was surprising, this friendship. No one in Overlords of Loneliness had thought they would actually *hang out* with Strafer Nation. After all, Strafer Nation had been together and touring since the early nineties, and Overlords was only their opening act—one of dozens they'd seen come and go during their careers. Yet Strafer was a really friendly bunch. Shay had expected them to look down their noses at their tagalongs, but apparently they'd been on the road long enough, and racked up enough gold records and TV appearances and fan pages and whatever, to have the luxury of slumming with the kids nipping at their heels. Strafer Nation had nothing left to prove. Quite the opposite; they had plenty to share.

Case in point, Shay Dayton and Paul Di Santangelo. Paul was the Strafer front man and had been since dinosaurs roamed the earth. He'd also, in his time, been the kind of sexually turbocharged icon who'd inspired women to hurl their bras and panties onto the stage. He was in his forties now and still pretty hot, but noticeably less lithe than in his prime. When he got offstage after a full night of working, he groaned and winced and complained about his knees.

You'd think such a guy would be threatened by Shay Dayton, who warmed up the crowd for him with the kind of Lizard King moves Paul himself could no longer pull off without pulling a muscle. (And boy did it take some warming. Most audiences didn't know Overlords from Adam and greeted the opening set with impatience at best and outright hostility at worst.) Yet Paul and Shay had bonded.

Shay had arrived in Pittsburgh for the first gig of the tour looking vacant-eyed and shell-shocked from his ten days in New York. In the Big Apple, he had been alternately shoved into rooms filled with media people swilling cocktails and told to charm them, and brusquely escorted into back alleys where idling cars waited to speed him off to dinner at some unspecified locale while paparazzi—having caught the scent of the Next Big Thing—circled the block of Halbert Hasque's penthouse like hound dogs in heat. Shay quite literally never knew whether he was coming or going, whether his goal was to seduce or stand off, whether his next dinner companion would be a movie star at an awards ceremony or his chauffeur parked outside a fast-food joint.

Paul Di Santangelo had been through it all before, and often. So the older man had taken Shay under his wing and shared with him his wisdom...and the other benefits afforded to rock legends. Benefits like the way to get any mind-altering substance known to man ("You don't even have to ask," Paul had said. "Just think about it hard enough. People will *know*.") and a stream of eager young women who only wanted one brush with fame to hold onto (well, technically, a bit more than a brush) before disappearing into lives of drab anonymity.

And it wasn't long—Kansas City, to be exact—before Shay had extracted from Paul something more valuable than all of that.

"All right," Paul said as he set down the bottle of Woodford Reserve, which he had sent by the case to every hotel room booked for him in every city on the tour. "Let's have another go. Play a G major 7 chord."

Shay tossed back a mouthful of bourbon, then plonked the tumbler atop the Yamaha digital piano Paul traveled with for practicing and composing. Lately he had, almost casually, begun giving Shay lessons. Teaching him scales, basic chord structure, the circle of fifths, and certain chord progressions, like the 2-5-1 turnaround vital to so many standards and pop songs. Shay found it to be uphill work, but he was committed to mastering the instrument. He was also committed to hiding the ferocity of his ambition from Paul—he didn't want to look desperate.

Shay obediently played a G major 7 chord: G-B-D-F#.

"Now play a D7."

Shay slid his hand down the keyboard: D-F#-A-C.

Paul cocked his head and grimaced. "Remember what we were talking about earlier," he said. "You don't want your hand to be jumping around like that. You want to keep it as still as possible."

"Right, right," Shay said, going back and playing the G major 7 again.

"Now, play a D7, *without moving your wrist*," Paul told him, then had another swig from his own glass.

Shay thought for a moment, then moved his thumb up a whole step and his index finger a half step: A-C-D-F#.

"Exactly," said Paul. "You just take the A and C from the top of the chord and move them to the bottom. The tones are exactly the same, and your hand doesn't move."

"Right, right, I remember now," Shay said, feeling stupid he'd ever forgotten.

"Toast yourself, then," Paul said, lifting his glass.

Shay raised his tumbler. "Here's to me," he said, and he had another swig.

"Okay," said Paul, wiping his lips on the back of his hand. "Play that G major 7 again."

Shay did so.

"Now play a C minor 7 with a flatted 5."

Shay stared at the keyboard.

"It's the same principle," Paul said, encouraging him.

"I know, I know. This is just…trickier." In fact, he was completely blanking. He looked at the keyboard and tried to visualize the chord in question before reshuffling the notes to accommodate the G major 7 hand position, but he couldn't even see it. He wasn't sure whether it was too much bourbon or the pressure of being put on the spot by Paul Di Fucking Santangelo.

Finally he had to turn and say, "Sorry…stumped."

Paul chuckled and said, "No worries, that one's kind of a killer. Here." He came over, sat on the bench beside him, and played the G major 7 chord: G-B-D-F#. Then, just by moving his thumb, index, and third fingers slightly, he played the new chord: B♭, C, E♭, G♭.

"You make it look easy," Shay said.

"It is…after a lot of repetition. You've just gotta put in the hours. And then you get to the point where you can just drop your hand and play G major 7, D7, and C minor 7 flatted 5 one right after the other, boom, boom, boom." And he did so, with a perfectly still wrist.

Shay grinned. "Very cool."

Paul knocked his shoulder into his. "You've earned a break, Ludwig."

"No, wait, let me give it one more try," Shay said, eyeing the keyboard.

"No use. This late, and this drunk, it won't sink in. Go on, give it a rest till tomorrow. Or…whenever."

Shay became aware that he might be pushing at the outer edges of Paul's patience, so he relented. He took up his drink again and said, "You're right. Thanks, though. Here's to you, keyboard wizard." He tossed back a mouthful.

Paul did the same, then settled back into the radiantly purple hotel chair and said, "I gotta say, you're a pretty determined pupil. You really never studied before, huh?"

"No, never," Shay admitted. "Flute lessons when I was in grade school. But that never took."

Paul raised his eyebrows. "How very Jethro Tull."

"Yeah. I never knew about them back then, or who knows, I might've stuck with it."

"Well," he said, holding up his drink to the light and casually studying its refractions through the amber liquid, "you're well on the road to being able to compose a tune.

You've already got a knack for rhythm and phrasing, just from performing, so it should all fall into place. Hell, maybe by the end of the tour."

"You really think so? That soon?"

"Mm," Paul said, having another sip. "If you want. I'll give you a nudge here and there if I see you going wrong. If you don't mind the input."

Shay wanted to jump up and down and say, *Are you fucking kidding me?* But he forced himself to play it cool and merely said, "Thanks, that'd be great."

"Gotta say," said Paul, slumping deeper into the chair, "I'd have thought someone like you would be more drawn to the guitar. Most guys are."

"Well," said Shay, running his fingers up the keyboard (which, now that he'd turned it off, made no sound), "I might have, if I were touring with a guitar god. But I'm touring with you, so...piano it is."

Paul scowled. "Really? That's the deciding factor?"

Shay blushed, not wanting to be thought so callow an opportunist. "That, and the fact that my band's already heavy on guitarists."

Paul raised an eyebrow. "Oh. I thought...sorry, didn't you say you were interested in learning to play just so you could take a more active role in songwriting?"

"Yyyyeah," Shay said.

"But...you're obviously thinking of performing, too."

He felt busted. "I don't...I'm not...maybe." He shrugged. "I mean, we've got Jimmy on keys already, so...I mean, there's no real need. But..."

"You thinking of getting rid of Jimmy?" Paul asked.

"No, no. Nothing like that."

" 'Cause I gotta say, he doesn't strike me as a guy who's real happy to be here."

"He's always like that. It's just his way. He's good. Really. Totally committed."

Paul nodded. "All right, then. I just…excuse me for getting all sloppy on you, sport. But you've got the goods for this job, and by that I mean the pipes *and* the moves. You know how to work the stage like a champ. Last thing you need is to anchor yourself behind a keyboard."

"No, I wouldn't. Not as a regular thing, anyway. I think."

"You sound uncertain."

He shrugged. "Well…it's just, you think of a rock-and-roll front man, you think of an instrumentalist. Is all."

"You think of a *guitarist*," said Paul. "Be specific. And I don't need to be told that." He threw back the last of his bourbon, then reached for the bottle. "I've had to put up with that my whole career." He grinned as he poured out a new serving. "But then I never had your moves, so I was always grateful to be able to hunker down behind the keys."

"Yeah, you never had my moves," said Shay, reaching out his own glass for a topper. "You just had your three-octave range and your banshee wail. Poor fucking you."

Paul finished pouring and screwed the cap back on the bottle. "So," he said, leaning back into the chair. "Who is she?"

Shay choked in mid-swallow. "Who's who?"

"The girl," he said, smiling wryly. "The one who made you think you weren't a proper front man 'cause you don't play an instrument."

Shay could feel his face burning. "I never mentioned any girl."

"Oh," Paul said in a highly sarcastic tone, "my mistake. Apologies."

Shay sighed. "It's that obvious?"

"Maybe not to the average dude. But for me...man, it's like looking down the narrow corridor of time."

"You, too?"

"Mm," he said, taking a sip. "Ended up marrying her."

"Really?"

He nodded. "And I can honestly say, our nine years together were the happiest two years of my life."

Shay laughed.

"But don't let that discourage you," he added, raising his glass to Shay.

Shay shook his head. "No discouragement needed. She's already hooked up with some other guy. Moved out west with him. They're faculty at some university where they teach together."

Paul made a sour face. "Sweet fucking Christmas."

"I know," he said. "Thing is...I mean, I barely know her. But I just...I got the impression she's not *like* that."

Paul looked at his watch and stretched his arms behind his back—a clear signal he was calling it quits for the night. It wasn't even one o'clock, but Shay had to remember Paul had about twenty years on him, and they were twenty years of hard road.

"Your call, cowboy," Paul said through a theatrical yawn. "But my advice? If you're actually trying to learn to play piano because of her, then this thing ain't finished."

"You think?"

Paul got up and waved him to the door. "Go on, get the hell outta here. Let an old man have some peace."

//////////////

On his way to his room, Shay heard a tremendous crash spill out from behind another door followed by raucous laughter.

He went over to it and knocked. *"Hotel security,"* he called out.

Someone from inside shot back, *"Fuck you, flatfoot—investigate my ass."*

Shay laughed and shook his head. "Christ, Trina. You really are fucking crazy."

The door opened, and marijuana smoke billowed out, obscuring Shay's vision before he saw that it was Baby who was admitting him. Lockwood and two members of Strafer Nation were hanging out, smoking. The floor was covered with shattered glass. In its midst, Trina, completely unperturbed, brushed off her sleeves, then flopped onto the bed.

"What the *hell*?" said Shay.

"What?" Trina sneered, "Did we disturb the big fucking Yalta summit of douchebag front men?"

"I think you disturbed the entire breadbasket of America. What happened?"

Marty, the Strafer Nation drummer who had to be fifty if he was a day, said, "We bet Trina she couldn't make it all the way to the bathroom with the room-service tray on her head."

"Loaded with every glass in the place, from the look of it," said Shay, nodding.

"Every glass, *plus*," said Lockwood laconically. "We sent down for more."

Shay looked at Trina, who shrugged and said, "Hey, they don't call me Kid Daredevil for nothing."

"No one calls you Kid Daredevil," said all the others, including the Strafer Nation players, who had learned this refrain by now and had taken it up with tremendous enthusiasm.

Shay shook his head in disbelief and said, "Just to remind you, we have a long bus ride tomorrow with an actual paying gig at the end of it. For actual human people who have shelled out actual money to see us."

"Yes, *Fah*-thuh," said Trina in a truly execrable attempt at a British accent. "Shall we go to sleep now, and pray for Grandmama to be happy with the *aaaahn*-gels?"

"Pray that Halbert Hasque is happy with us, or you'll be able to find out how Grandmama's doing firsthand," he said.

"Whoa, is that a threat?"

"Nah. I know a threat would only turn you on."

Everyone in the room said, *"Oooohhh,"* and Trina threw a box of Cheez-Its at him. Unfortunately it was open, and tiny orange crackers spilled out all along its aerial arc, rendering it too lightweight to reach Shay's head. It fell to the ground several inches from his feet.

"Just try to wrap it up before the bus leaves," Shay said as he headed back toward the hallway.

When he turned to shut the door behind him, he saw Trina hanging off the bed, picking Cheez-Its off the carpeted floor and eating them. Jimmy said, "Trina, are you out of your goddamn mind? That floor is full of busted glass."

"Oooh, how *frightful*," Trina said, again in her British accent. As the door shut behind him and he continued down the hall, he heard her go on, "I must be *evah* so careful or I might—*ow!* Fucking *fuck! Owww!*"

///////////////////

Moments later, Shay was back in the relative privacy of his own room. Relative only because he was technically sharing it with Lockwood, who could come barging in at any time. But given the settled look he'd just had in Trina's room, that was unlikely. He dropped onto his bed, lay back, and worked his shoes off one at a time. Then he put his hands behind his head and looked up at the ceiling.

It had been nice, this leg of the tour. A little rocky, at first. He'd left New York more or less a broken man, with Pernita even more smotheringly proprietary of him than ever. The first few gigs had been rough as Overlords got used to being on the road and the wild variances between sound systems at different venues. (They'd learned pretty quickly the first rule of touring was never mind what the sound engineer tells you, insist he does it your way.)

And then, how the hell it had happened Shay couldn't imagine—possibly he'd been praying in his sleep or something—but Pernita had gotten bored and left. As much as she wanted to control his every waking movement, barring the ones he conducted behind the bathroom door (and given enough time, she might insist on monitoring even those), she found that the endless hours on the drab freeways frayed her nerves. She had a constant need of novelty, and whenever they arrived at their destinations—small cities in Pennsylvania, Ohio, Indiana, Illinois—the clubs awaiting them there were not remotely up to the caliber Pernita was accustomed to. So she left the group, though with plenty of assurances that this was just a temporary departure to attend to some pressing business and she'd be back very soon. She'd even left most of her luggage on the bus, as if it might check up on Shay in her absence. But the truth was, she'd essentially cut bait.

Just today, however, she'd e-mailed to say she'd be rejoining the band in Chicago, their last stop on this leg of the tour. That gave Shay less than a week to enjoy his liberty and the high times he'd been having with Paul.

Paul, God bless his crusty heart, had never once mentioned Pernita's name after she was gone. He seemed to have sensed how desperately Shay wanted to be free from even thinking about her. Maybe he even knew what Shay was going through. Certainly when they'd first met him, Pernita had thrown herself at Paul as though claiming him as a reward she'd earned in a past life. He'd managed to shrug her off gently, with complete aplomb, as though that kind of assault was something he'd grown very, very used to. There was even a look on his face, behind the twinkling eyes and pasted-on smile, that said, *Oh, yeah. One of your type. Hell if I can't handle you.*

But now that the first half of the tour was winding down, Shay felt a sense of anticlimax, almost of guilt. All this time he'd been free of Pernita, and he hadn't made even a token attempt to reach out to Loni. Possibly he wouldn't have been able to; he still had no contact info for her, nothing. But in fact, he hadn't even *tried*.

He supposed he'd expected that the tour and hanging out with Strafer Nation would all be so new and so novel and so fulfilling that it would drive Loni right out of his thoughts. He had certainly given it plenty of opportunity. But it never really kicked in. Probably because touring involved—much more so than he had ever dreamed—just freaking endless hours of transit. Sitting on that bus for hours on end, with nothing going on except fidgety Pernita beside him complaining and always having to pee, or alone with the two bands who seemed only interested in sleeping or smoking or playing cards or occasionally daring Trina to do something stupid (like moon a squad car from one of the windows), Shay had had acres of time in which his mind was unoccupied and restless—a free agent.

He'd tried to use that time constructively. He'd picked up a copy of *The Complete Poems of William Blake* while he was in New York and had tried to make his way through it on the long rides. Occasionally he did hook on to some passages that made the rest of the world disappear for a while, but most of the time he was too distracted by hunger or movement or weariness or passivity. He came almost to resent having committed himself to the book. It was just so goddamn *massive*. Like, more than a thousand pages. Before they reached Chicago it might just pull his arm out of its socket.

Despite his not-quite-ringing success with William Blake, Shay felt a modicum of hope. After Chicago, the band was returning to Haver City for sixteen days, just for a stopover, no gigs. He could rest up, check in with some OGs, and maybe get some news on what Loni was up to now. He knew Lockwood was still in contact with Zee, and even though Zee hated him, he might be able to use Lockwood to pry some intel from her.

And then there was the second leg of the tour, when Overlords would be accompanying Strafer Nation west, playing every burg from Boulder to Vegas and ending up—where else?—in Los Angeles.

Shay wasn't sure where Loni lived. He only knew it was in California. But if it was anywhere within driving distance of LA…and hell, even if it wasn't…

Well.

He'd see what he'd see. That's all he could project, from this far out. Play it by ear. Take it as it came.

The bourbon began to claim his consciousness. He shimmied out of his clothes and fell asleep as soon as his T-shirt cleared his head, even though the overhead light still shone brightly into his face.

CHAPTER 14

There was one in every classroom. Loni knew that. Of course she knew it. It's just that now, she couldn't sit back and wait for the drama to resolve. Now, it was *her* problem.

She stood before the class—composed almost entirely of women, with a few stray men who looked like they hadn't quite settled on planet Earth as a permanent residence yet—and tried to look authoritative and calm. She was neither.

"All I'm saying," said the student—one Ferry Shagall, an extremely tall, angular, and imposing-looking girl with ebony skin and copper-colored hair, "is that if somebody on campus found a poem like this on my website or something, they'd haul me in for a psych evaluation and probably hook me up with some kind of therapist. *And* charge my parents."

Loni sighed. "I still don't entirely see your point."

The work under discussion was a poem by Charlotte Dacre that read:

> *So full my thoughts are of thee, that I swear*
> *All else is hateful to my troubl'd soul;*
> *How thou hast o'er me gain'd such vast control,*
> *How charm'd my stubborn spirit is most rare.*
> *Sure thou hast mingl'd philtres in my bowl!*
> *Or what thine high enchanted arts declare*
> *Fearless of blame—for truth I will not care,*
> *So charms the witchery, whether fair or foul.*

Yet well my love-sick mind thine arts can tell;
No magic potions gav'st though, save what I
Drank from those lustrous eyes when they did dwell
With dying fondess on me—or thy sigh,
Which sent its perfum'd poison to my brain.
Thus known thy spells, thou bland seducer, see—
Come practice them again, and oh! again;
Spell-bound I am—and spell-bound wish to be.

"My point," said Ferry, as the other students in the class took advantage of the interruption to check their cell phones and send God-I'm-bored texts, "is that this woman is calling her lover a seducer and liking the idea that he may have drugged her. Am I right?"

Loni felt as though the girl was laying a trap for her. "Let's say you are."

Ferry shook her head. "I don't want your condescension. Just tell me: *am I right?*"

Loni felt a thin film of sweat form over her brow. "That... that would be my interpretation as well. Yes."

"Fine." Ferry sat back and extended her arms wide. "Why are we studying this poem, Ms. Merrick? What's our takeaway supposed to be? Everywhere I go on this campus I'm being exhorted to be rational, to take control, to be empowered, and yadda yadda yadda. Then I get to classes like this one, and I'm served up works like this—reveling in subjugation, powerlessness, abandonment of personal authority. Talking about *'perfum'd poison,'* for God's sake."

"This is poetry," Loni said, "not rules for living. That's not the way we *use* poetry."

"Then how *do* we use it?"

Loni felt her face flush. "There's...there's no single use for poetry. It's a whole palette of responses, of ways that it... that it impacts our lives..." *Oh, my God,* Loni thought. *I just used "impact" as a verb. This girl is really rattling me.*

"And it's not *just* poetry," Ferry said. "In my Women's Studies class, we've been reading Simone de Beauvoir. You're familiar with her, I take it?"

"Yes, of course," said Loni, though her familiarity was only slight.

"Well, all right, then. The way that woman *tore* through life. Rebellion, abortion, female lovers, constantly hurling herself against the authorities of the day. If I lived life the way she did, I'd be booted from this campus in a New York minute, and my parents would disown me into the bargain. But here we are in our safe little classrooms, having her parceled out to us in antiseptic one-hour segments and being quizzed on it later." She shook her head. "Maybe I'm not cut out for university life. Maybe university life *isn't* life." She looked up at Loni. "Do you see what I'm getting at here?"

"No," said Loni, having to hold on to the desk to keep from falling over.

"There's no *risk* here," she said. "This is, like, the place risk comes to *die*. People like de Beauvoir *roared* across the world stage. They took chances, they defied convention, they *lived*. And we here—here on this campus, in this classroom—we run along after them, collecting the rubble they left behind and fetishizing it. *Why?* What is the purpose of that, if it's not to inspire us to do the same goddamn thing, throw out the rule books and light out for parts unknown?"

She gestured widely, taking in the whole of her surroundings. "Where is *poetry* on this campus, Ms. Merrick? *Where?*"

Loni's throat had gone dry. She tried clearing it, but only succeeded in closing it tight.

The trouble was, she agreed with Ferry. She'd just never allowed herself to confront the issue before. She'd been smart enough to steer clear of it, for her own sake. She'd always worshiped the great visionaries and nonconformists—Blake, for Christ's sake!—but she herself had always kept to the safest, most brightly lit, most well-trodden path. She'd never taken a risk in her life.

Well…only once. When she'd thrown everything away because of Shay Dayton. And then, at the first sign that that might have been more dangerous than she'd thought, she'd come scampering back to the herd, to the security of the pack. And to the protection of her mentor. She felt a sudden welling up of shame.

But she had a job to do. So she summoned up all her resources and said, "Literature isn't supposed to be *useful*, Ferry. It can be, but ultimately its only real purpose is to illuminate shades of the human experience, to show us ways of being we otherwise might not have known or even suspected."

"As a substitute for actually experiencing them, or *being* them?" she asked. "Because, let me tell you, there's not a whole lot of love for varieties of human experience around this place. It's pretty much lockstep or locked-out, as far as I can tell. Which makes this worship of historic and literary rebels flat-out hypocrisy."

"We don't *worship* them," Loni said, trying not to let anger edge into her voice. "We *listen* to them. It's all a conversation. They speak directly to us, right off the page. They always will."

Ferry slouched in her chair and crossed her arms over her chest. "Well, if they speak directly to us, then why do we need *you*?"

Loni felt almost faint. She'd gotten some flak from this girl before, but never on this level. Possibly there was some atmospheric thing going on that was making her more contentious today than usual. "We're here as your guides," Loni said, in the most evenly measured tones as she could manage. "We're here to help you navigate…well, for instance, Charlotte Dacre's vocabulary and imagery. To clarify what it is she's done, what's *behind* what she's done."

Ferry narrowed her eyes. "You're *priests*, is the point. Right? Because, if you really meant what you said—that literature is a conversation, and poets speak directly to us—then there's no need for any intermediaries. You're here because… well, basically, you *do* worship these people. You *do* fetishize them. Because of some lack in your own confidence or abilities or whatever, you put yourselves between us and them— you *insert* yourselves into the conversation as intermediaries, and from that you draw some kind of sad, reflected glory."

Loni rubbed the bridge of her nose between her thumb and forefinger. "Oh, for God's sake. You're asking me now to justify the whole existence of academia."

"*Can* you? At least, with respect to the arts? Because if poets speak directly do us, why *do* we need you? Listen, do you think Charlotte Dacre, when she wrote this poem, was like, 'Okay, it's finished, now I'll turn it over to my vestal virgins so that they can spoon-feed it line by line to the rest of humanity and tell them exactly how it ought to go down'? Because frankly, I have to doubt it."

Loni shook her head. "You can't know what Charlotte Dacre meant."

"And you can?" She sat up and put her hands on the desk and laughed. "How can you possibly? How can you tell me *you* can understand a woman who lived her life like a lit match and I can't? What gives *you* insight into that kind of mind and not me?"

"You're confusing passion with poetry. That's only part of it. Poetry is also a discipline; it's work. It's *hard* work. It's not just fire, it's…" She searched for an appropriate analogy. "It's nailing fire to a page. So that it burns forever." Oh, hell. That wasn't right. It was a mixed metaphor, for one thing. Loni cringed at her own ineptitude.

But it seemed to quell Ferry's contrariness for the moment. She heaved a large sigh and said, "All right. Well. I'll consider that." She sat back in her chair. "Though I have to tell you, I hear poetry everywhere around me. You ever been to a hip-hop concert, Ms. Merrick? *There's* a conversation. No need for an intermediary, either. People hear it, they get it, they *respond*. And it's *useful* to them. It *does* give them ideas on how to live their lives. I'm sure someday there'll be a hip-hop unit in this department with someone like you standing up in front of a classroom deconstructing every phrase. And that's when we'll all know hip-hop is dead."

Loni felt something inside her snap, some essential support on which the entirety of her persona had been resting. She had just enough presence of mind to say, "Would you excuse me for a moment?" then get out the door and down the hallway to the women's room, where she stumbled into a stall and burst into bitter, angry tears.

////////////////

"I swear," she said at lunch later, over a crab salad and a Diet Coke, "that heinous girl actually made me *cry*. And I mean, I'm not some goddamn shrinking violet. I don't just fall to pieces like that. I still can't get over it."

Her lunch companion, a sandy-haired, rather gamine-looking TA named Kevin Morski, eyed her sympathetically as he chewed a mouthful of his grilled cheese sandwich. He swallowed and said, "It's not you. It's just the pressure of this place. I mean, you've not only got these classes to teach, you've got your other work for Byron *and* your own course load."

It was true. Loni's position as a TA was only part of her duties as a graduate student. She'd always just presumed that somehow, somewhere, she'd pursue a graduate degree, and Byron's offer of a job had made that possibility a reality. It was only now that she was actually living that dream that it began to seem like something she hadn't thought through very thoroughly. She wasn't certain she'd made a mistake, but she wasn't certain she hadn't, either.

The other TAs all seemed completely fine with the road they were on. Kevin, for instance, seemed never to question it at all. He was in fact much further along than Loni—only about a year from earning his degree, and was well into his thesis.

Loni liked him well enough. He was easygoing and generous with his time and advice, and he had a very dry wit. And yet he seemed to her to be...well, there was no way to disguise it, not quite a full human being. How could he be? He'd spent his entire adult life on college campuses, first as a student, now as a graduate student and TA, and soon he'd be on the faculty somewhere as a teacher and presumably hang on to that until he achieved tenure and lived out the rest of his days there. He had no experience of urban life—or of rural life for that matter—or of *any* life in which a man had to forge a place for himself in a community where not everyone was exactly like him. He'd curled up in his nice academic cocoon, and he would stay here till he died.

That had been Loni's plan once, too. It had seemed faintly romantic—and yes, a bit monastic—retiring from a vulgar, fractious, avaricious world to tend the fires of knowledge and the altar of culture so it could burn bright the day the lesser world finally consumed itself and would once again need the wisdom of the ages to rebuild. It had happened before; it seemed certain to happen again.

But she now knew the residents of this academic world well enough to have trouble aligning them with so heroic a mission. They were, if anything, *more* vicious and ambitious and double-dealing than the people she'd known in the outer world. There, the simple matter of having to coexist with other people very different from you demanded a code of behavior, of *civility*, that—while not universally embraced—was universally acknowledged. Not here. Here, it was flat-out cutthroat.

"Hey, hey," Kevin said, snapping his fingers in her face. "You still in there?"

"Sorry," she said, picking up her fork again. "Just thinking."

"Really lost you there for a sec. Where'd you go?"

Someplace you wouldn't understand, she thought, but she said, "No place in particular."

"Listen, you can't let this student of yours upset you," he said, before slurping up some iced tea through a straw. "I mean, when you think about it, her arguments aren't even internally consistent. She says academia is a 'priesthood' that has inserted itself unnecessarily between the poet and his readers. But later she says she'll know hip-hop is dead once it becomes fodder for academic study. So which is it? Are poets still vital, and we just block readers' way to them? Or do they only come under our watch when they've already lost their vitality, when they're museum pieces?"

"Either way," said Loni glumly, "it's not very flattering to us."

"She was trying to *offend* us. Or you, anyway." He patted her hand. "Oh, hon. Trust me. There are always going to be students who feel compelled to challenge you just because you're in a position of authority over them. They'll throw everything they've got at you, and it doesn't even matter if it's contradictory. On the other hand," he said with a sly grin, "there are students who'll want to *give* themselves to you— be ravished by you—for the same reason. Power can be an aphrodisiac." He winked. "That's where you can make up for the other kind."

Loni felt slightly ill. She thought of the gay men she knew in Haver City, men who had to navigate the difficult waters of competing *with* one another *for* one another, and the ferociously Darwinian arenas in which they did this—the pulsing dance clubs, darkened bars, and catalog-like hookup websites. Kevin had never had to subject himself to anything like that. He'd been brought to St. Nazarius by Leopold Kanak, the distinguished scholar who'd almost single-handedly built the university's Queer Studies department. Kevin had always been under Professor Kanak's protection—his *intimate* protection—but had also had a steady diet of other carnal experiences virtually delivered to his door in the form of young students eager to attract his notice.

That must be how she herself appeared—and not just to Kevin, to everyone. It was an open secret that she and Byron were now lovers. No one spoke of it, but not because it was scandalous; quite the contrary: because it was too commonplace to warrant comment. But it wasn't how she liked to think of herself, and she liked it less when someone like Kevin held up a kind of mirror to show her a reflection that was preening and self-satisfied.

"I wanted to run an idea by you," he said, having finished his lunch and shoved the plastic tray aside. "An expansion of my thesis. It's a sort of refutation of Foucault's idea that transvestism can function as either a sexual expression or merely as a gender identity. I think transvestism is *always* sexual. I mean, think about it. The 'trouser roles' in baroque opera were meant to show off the figures of the mezzo-sopranos who filled them—it was *risqué*. They were *designed* to arouse. Cherubino would've made all those old Viennese burghers in the dress circle pop a woody. And then there were the TV comedians in the sixties and seventies—Milton Berle, Flip Wilson—who dressed up like women, ostensibly for laughs. I say *ostensibly*, because I think it was actually an attempt—conscious or otherwise, but I think the former—to diminish the cultural power of transvestism by making it ridiculous. It was a political act meant to take that weapon out the quill of the gay arsenal. Ooh," he said, furrowing his brow. "I like that phrasing. Have to remember it. Anyway, I see the rise of explicitly sexual glam rockers—David Bowie, Marc Bolan—as a direct response to those comedians. A rebuke, and a poke in the eye." He gave her a sly look. "What they're poking *with* shall remain open to conjecture. Hah!" He gave her arm a nudge. "So…what do you think?"

Loni was somehow able to string together enough words to suggest that she thought it was a good angle, but she actually didn't know much about David Bowie, only a smattering about Foucault, and nothing at all about old TV comedians. She wasn't entirely interested in learning, either. She was too caught up in a sudden vision of herself in a few years, in Kevin's position, coming up with some ridiculous premise on which to heap thousands and thousands of words and thus earn herself an extended stay in this idyllic little claustrophobic paradise.

She found herself missing Zee and the nights that had always kind of bored her before, when they'd sit on the couch sharing a bottle of wine. Zee would relate in brutal detail all the indignities she'd suffered that day and whether, and how, she'd managed to give back as good as she'd gotten. Afterward they would go out to a bar or a club and erase it all from their minds with more cocktails, a game of darts, flirting, music. Loni had always considered those nights to be the equivalent of slumming for her, an almost anthropological exercise in seeing how normal people lived before she headed off to her ivory tower and spent the rest of her days in exalted research and inquiry. What an asshat she'd been!

She felt such a pang of longing that she thought of texting Zee on the spot, but she could think of nothing to say.

//////////////

Byron had promised to bring dinner home, but then he called and said he'd be late. There was a thing with the provost that would be politically advantageous for him to be seen at, blah, blah, blah. Loni found herself not even listening. It was fine that he wasn't coming straight home. She sensed she was in the kind of mood that would only annoy him, and she didn't feel sufficient desire to modify anything about her current state of mind just to avert his anger.

It had been nice in the beginning. He'd been so sweet, a kind of dutiful puppy dog who couldn't wait to see her at the end of every day. But as the term went on, he became distracted by his classes, his workload, and his own razor-sharp ambition—something about him that had surprised Loni—and he'd begun to take her rather for granted. It was as though he had a checklist of things he wanted to accomplish at St. Nazarius. A regular sex partner was one of them, and having ticked that off, he'd now turned his attention to the other line items.

After the first delirious couplings, sex had proven to be a kind of methodical thing, like their meals. No matter what she tried to whip up in the kitchen, and she'd taken on some serious challenges, he devoured it all as though it were a task to be gotten through, then thanked her and spent the rest of the night in front of his laptop. He seemed to be a man almost without a voluptuous impulse of any kind, an anti-sensualist. Food and sex were just there to propel him forward, but he never enjoyed them for their own sakes.

This at least made it easier for Loni, because she never really had to pretend any emotional investment once the lights went out. She told herself she was glad of it. She told herself that quite often, actually. Like she was trying to convince herself it was true.

Always, just off at the perimeter of her mind when she entered this particular realm of thought, were Shay Dayton's steely limbs, his damp hair hanging in her face, his urgent breath, his marble butt cheeks, his narrow hips working like pistons...

...but she'd retreat, force herself to back quietly away if she ever got too close to confronting those memories head-on.

She was itchy and edgy and distracted now. She sat down before her own laptop and checked to see what was new on Facebook. Just the usual stream of cat photos, vacation pics, political slogans. Nothing that could hold her interest. Feeling utterly daring, she checked the Overlords of Loneliness fan page. It wasn't the first time she'd done this since coming to St. Nazarius, but it was the first time she'd done it when she hadn't had a few drinks first.

There were some links to reviews of the tour so far, some concert shots, photos of events backstage and of the band members touring famous sites in the cities they visited. There were also a few videos. Loni found herself playing one.

It was for a tune called "Come Down Hard or Die Easy," which must have been new because she didn't recall it from

Zee's constant playing of *Grief Bacon*. The video was a little grainy and the screen very small, but it seemed to her Shay had grown in gravitas since she'd last seen him. He seemed to have tremendous focus. He wasn't strutting or preening or throwing his body around provocatively. He used it like a whip, jerking or snapping his head to accent the musical phrases. She listened closely to make out the lyrics:

> Only one way to play it
> 'Cause it isn't really play
> Only one way to work it
> If it's what you've got to say
> You won't make friends
> You'll only make foes
> But if you wanna be remembered, baby
> Everybody knows
> Come down hard or die easy
> Jump the barricade or quit the race
> Come down hard or die easy
> Live forever or leave no trace

The video ended with an exultant Shay reaching out his arms to take in the rest of the band—God, that *smile* of his—while the audience applauded appreciatively (though in Loni's opinion, not appreciatively enough).

She blinked a few times, then considered replaying the video. But once was sufficient.

More than sufficient, in fact.

It was uncanny. It was as though Shay had somehow been attuned to her, been riding her wavelength. This song was exactly in accord with everything she'd been thinking about all day, and that had maybe, perhaps likely, been simmering beneath her skin for months now. It was about risk, about taking a chance, making a roll of the dice. Like Charlotte Dacre did. And William Blake. And Simone de Beauvoir. And Michel Foucault. And David Bowie. And Shay Dayton. Shay Dayton was jumping the barricade every goddamn day on this tour.

While she hid. While she kept herself confined in this little rabbit warren where pale people like her pored diligently over the receding echoes of Charlotte Dacre and William Blake and Simone de Beauvoir and Michel Foucault. And, probably somewhere, David Bowie. As if that made for some kind of affinity. As if it made for some kind of equivalency.

She felt a sudden surge of boldness—a willingness to throw the dice, to take a chance, to *risk*. And so she did something she hadn't yet had the nerve to do. She went to the top of the Overlords Facebook page and pressed the Like button.

She sat back in her chair, feeling the thrill of the moment stir her.

And then...

And then she laughed.

If that was her idea of risk, she realized, it was the most pathetic thing she'd ever done. She closed her laptop, went into the next room, and flopped down before the TV where she half watched some documentary about the rise of Sinn Féin. There were lots of talking heads channeling intensity at the camera and occasional footage of explosions—enough to keep her from entirely disappearing into her own mind.

Something about the scenes of violence triggered more resolve in her. *Just look at the world*, it seemed to be saying.

The world where people believe that things—abstractions, even—are worth dying for. Where the phrase "life and death" actually *means* life and death.

Was she so reduced, so benumbed by safety and security and the road ahead being paved and well-lit, that she was willing to go through her entire life without ever stepping out of line and grabbing for something she wanted—*jumping the barricade*?

She bit her fingernail, bit it down to the quick, until it started to bleed.

She got up to get a bandage, and as she was applying it to her fingertip, it hit her. The answer. The solution. It hit her just like that, the way the most audacious plans sometimes form during the most mundane moments of our lives.

She looked up into the mirror over the sink, and she saw her new self looking back.

CHAPTER 15

Shay found Pernita already talking when he reached their hotel room on Michigan Avenue, and she didn't slow down a beat when he entered. He thought she must be on her Bluetooth, so he ignored her and busied himself with hefting his suitcase onto the bed and starting to unpack. It was a full three minutes before he realized she was talking to *him*. What the hell? She must have started when he get off the elevator. Had she *smelled* him coming down the hall?

He snapped to attention and tried to pick up the thread of what she was saying. By close listening and some speculative leaps, he managed to put together that she was *extremely* put out by an incident that had occurred in New York, where she'd thrown a small dinner party for a highly prized video artist, Monsieur Désastre, only to have him beg off at the last minute, claiming an illness.

"...but I've just heard from Portia Brookington that she saw him out that night—*out on the town*, Shay. At Gisellina's, in fact, *dancing* with Mitzi Planck-Overton, who of course wasn't invited to my dinner party because of that stunt she pulled at Gstaad last year with the K-Y Jelly on my DPS Spoons. I almost broke my leg on the slopes! Can you *imagine* the gall it took to *lure* Monsieur away from my party *in his honor*? To induce him to *lie* to me out of petty jealousy and a desire for revenge? Because *of course* she'd have known the news would get back to me. You don't go dancing at Gisellina's if you don't want to be seen and talked about. No, my finding out about it is the whole *point*. She's throwing down a *gauntlet*, and all I can say is, fine, if she wants Monsieur Désastre that much, she can have him, and good riddance. I only put up with him for the cachet. I still haven't forgotten the way he left Chloe Vassar's powder room at her fundraiser for ruptured silicon implants. I think the cleaning staff needed hazmat suits. Still, the *insult*, Shay. And the sense of *betrayal*. God only *knows* what Mitzi promised him to convince him to renege on me, though I can guess. And I'm reasonably confident her punishment will be a full course of industrial-strength antibiotics. But listen to me go on! This is no way to greet you after so long a separation, I know. I'm sorry, it's just on my mind because I only got off the phone with Portia minutes ago. But how are you, sugar-pie? You look so wonderfully *emaciated*. I wish we could do that fashion spread all over again."

"I'm fine," Shay said, willing himself not to go rigid as she closed in on him to give him a kiss. After she'd done so, she held him for a few moments, till he felt the need to break the silence—preferably not with a term of endearment. Finally, he settled on, "I *have* been eating."

She responded by squeezing his sides, which made him jump. "You're skin and bone," she said merrily. "But never mind, it's a look that works. Very heroin chic, and you managed to achieve it without heroin." She leaned back and gave him a searching look. "Right?"

He rolled his eyes. "For Christ's sake, Pernita. No. No heroin. Just a lot of traveling and performing and late nights." He realized that last bit was possibly incriminating, so he added, "Burning the midnight oil, rewriting parts, changing lyrics."

She shook her head, as if in awe at his dedication. "Well, all that ends now. It's the wrap-up to the first leg of your ascension to immortality, and I've got lots and lots planned for you, beginning with a major media cocktail party after the gig tonight."

"*After* the gig?" he said. "But we don't even go on till, what—nine o'clock? It may be well after midnight when Strafer finishes."

She smiled indulgently at his innocence. "Poor baby. You've been on the rural back roads so long, you've forgotten that not *everywhere* in America shutters the windows and rolls up the streets at ten thirty. This is *Chicago*. There's a whole stratum of nightlife here that doesn't even get going until one o'clock."

"Hooray," he said despondently.

"But you should get some rest," she said, breaking her grip on him with a final pat on his rump. "Long night for you, as you say. I'll be happy to unpack for you."

"No, it's okay, it'll only take a moment." The idea of her handling his things bothered him. She already had her fingers in too much of his business. Also, it was terribly transparent that she only wanted to snoop. This was a woman who never unpacked her *own* bags. Or packed them in the first place, for that matter.

"It's no trouble," she said.

"My point exactly," he countered, and turned to begin the task.

She stood behind him, hands on her hips—defeated, yet unwilling to give up entirely. Finally she said, "Well, as long as you're going to be up a few minutes more, I'll tell Daddy. He wants to have a word with you."

He whirled. "Your father's here?"

"Of course. Wouldn't miss it. Excuse me." She was already dialing her phone. "Daddy?" she said, as she walked into the next room. "Yes, he just got here...he's unpacking..."

Shay felt a sudden jolt of wariness. He'd met the elusive Halbert Hasque only three times before. Once during their initial negotiation, then at a small cocktail party Pernita threw when the contract was signed, and the last time at a reception in New York before the tour began. Never on any of those occasions had he impressed Shay as particularly genial. He seemed always to be multitasking. In fact, at the reception in New York, which was ostensibly in honor of Overlords and Strafer Nation (who were also Hasque clients), he'd been preoccupied with trying to woo a legendary theatre actor to his stable. (The actor's new play was tanking, and he reportedly blamed his management. Halbert, ever on the alert, had smelled blood in the water.)

The idea that Halbert Hasque actually wanted to *see* him—had expressed an interest in actually addressing him face-to-face on some matter—was disconcerting, to say the least. He steeled himself for the encounter and forced himself to continue unpacking.

At the bottom of his bag he found *The Complete Poems of William Blake*. Or, as he had taken to calling it in his head, *The Complete Poems of Will-my-arm Break*, because of its tremendous weight. He'd several times considered just jettisoning the book, but it seemed to be his only tether to Loni. And he felt the need for *some* connection with her, however slight or foolish. He flipped it open and sought out a shorter poem, one he could read before Pernita came back into the room. He settled on "The Lily."

> *The modest Rose puts forth a thorn,*
> *The humble sheep a threat'ning horn:*
> *While the Lily white shall in love delight,*
> *Nor a thorn nor a threat stain her beauty bright.*

Whoa. *That* was a little uncanny. It was pretty close to how he regarded both Pernita—beautiful, alluring, inviting, but with jagged edges you had to watch out for if you got too close—and Loni—all openness, brightness, receptivity. Pernita was shields-up, all the time. Loni was a lowered drawbridge.

He dropped the book and wondered if he was being a little too easy on Loni. After all, when he'd first met her in Baby's kitchen she'd certainly been shields-up. She'd exhibited a "threat'ning horn." But somehow he'd been able to see that for what it was: a rather endearing insecurity. Pernita's shields were all about keeping you away until you proved your worth. Loni's were about buying herself time to judge the risk to herself. Certainly once she'd gotten to know him, she'd relaxed, become all sweetness, all candor.

And yet she'd been playing him, hadn't she? She'd had another guy in the background the whole time. A guy she must've known she'd be moving to California with. She'd just been using Shay as one last no-strings-attached romp before she settled down to domestic life.

Except…that had been what Loni was supposed to be for *him*, too, one final fling before the tour. But she *hadn't* been that. Well, she had, but she'd also been so much more. He still had no idea how she'd managed to get so deeply into his head. But she had. She'd planted herself there like a seed, and her roots had been growing deeper inside him ever since.

Was it so impossible that she might be feeling the same about him? Yeah, sure, she ended up going to California, but *he'd* ended up going on tour. If he'd done so only out of confusion about what else he could do, hell, maybe it was the same with her. In any case, he was just a couple of days from being able to find out. Back in Haver City he'd have more than a week to coach Lockwood on how to draw the info he needed out of Zee: whether Loni was happy out west, whether she was in love, whether this was a permanent thing, or whether she was already restless and trying to get out.

And if that was true…if *that* was true…

His thoughts were interrupted by Pernita's return, still on the phone. "I don't care who gets in the way," she was saying. "I've told you what I want, so stop being such a whining little cretin and make it happen."

Shay felt the color drain from his face, and Pernita must have noticed it, too, because she lowered the phone and said, "Are you all right?"

"Man," he said with a nervous laugh, "I never knew you ordered your dad around like that."

"This isn't Daddy, it's Nancy Leboudreau." Then she put the phone back to her ear and said, "Why are you still here, Nancy? *Chop bloody chop.*" There was a knock on the door and Pernita headed for it, saying, "Text me when it's settled. Thanks, you're an angel. *Mmmwaah.*"

And with that, she slipped her phone back into her pocket with one hand while opening the door with the other. "Daddy!" she squealed, and she flung herself into Halbert Hasque's arms. Shay grunted in distaste. You'd think she hadn't seen him in months, yet Shay knew from an e-mail he had received from her that they'd had lunch together that very afternoon.

Halbert, a solid, square-built man with a shock of peppery hair, patted the small of her back and kissed the top of her head. "Hello, little girl," he said, pleased by her attention. *That* was how she controlled him, Shay knew well enough. It was only Halbert who hadn't twigged to the fact that his daughter played him like a violin. "Where's that young man of yours?"

Shay stepped into the vestibule and said, "Hello, Mr. Hasque," and extended his arm.

"Pleasure to see you again, Shay," he said, shaking his hand. Then he turned to survey the room and said, "Let's have a seat over there," gesturing to a table and two chairs.

"I'll just go finish unpacking your things," Pernita said with a look of triumph, and she instantly disappeared into the adjoining room.

Shay, feeling as stiff as if he'd been dipped in lacquer, waited for Halbert to choose one of the chairs, then sat in the other. Halbert looked him in the face and said, "I want to talk about the final night of the tour."

Shay nodded. "At the Palladium."

"The Hollywood Palladium, yes," Halbert said. "I have to tell you I'm changing the opening act on the bill."

Shay felt his vision momentarily blur, as if he were on the brink of losing consciousness. The Palladium was the biggest and most prestigious club on the whole tour, and LA by far and away the biggest city, and he'd been looking forward to that gig like he hadn't looked forward to anything in a long, long time.

"I'm bringing in a duo act," Halbert said. "A kind of neoclassical dark-wave Sonny and Cher. Maybe you've heard of them: Jonah and the Wail? Out of Atlanta?"

"I...I think I might've," Shay said, though he was having trouble making his voice actually work. "May I—" He stopped and cleared his throat, and when he spoke again it was with a hair more resonance. "May I ask why?"

"Because," Halbert said, "I'm changing the headliner as well."

Shay blinked. He looked into Halbert's big, broad, unreadable face and found himself completely unable to understand what he was talking about. "I beg your pardon?"

"I said," he repeated, "I'm changing the opening act, because I'm changing the headliner as well."

Shay blinked again. Twice. Unable to think of anything else to say, he asked, "Who?"

"A five-man ensemble. One I'm pretty sure you've heard of." The corner of his lip curled into a barely perceptible smile. "Overlords of Loneliness."

Shay now felt the floor drop away. Afraid he might faint, really honest-to-God *faint*, he clutched the arms of the chair tighter and held himself upright. "You're saying," he said, "you're saying...we..."

"You're headlining at the Hollywood Palladium. Congratulations, son."

"But...but Strafer Nation..."

He waved a hand in dismissal. "They never wanted that gig. They've already played that house any number of times, and Paul Di Santangelo is already bitching about how tired he is of touring, period. He wants to skip LA and go home to his girlfriend and kids, and he knows if he sets foot in LA he won't be able to leave until he's seen the eight hundred people who'd be mortally offended if he came to town without having breakfast-lunch-dinner-sex with him."

"And—and the Palladium just lets you change their bill around like that?"

He chuckled. "They owe me several favors. Several *large* favors."

"So...so you're booting Strafer, just like that? *Firing* them?"

Halbert shook his head and laughed. "This is not the reaction I'd expected. A word of advice, Shay: if you're going to get ahead in this business, you can't be worrying about your competition. *Screw* your competition. When the chance comes for you to get ahead, *steamroll* your competition. Whatever the hell it takes to get them out of your way."

Shay shifted in his seat. "Thanks. But we've, I don't know. *Bonded.* On the road."

Halbert nodded. "Yeah, yeah, whatever. Look, if it makes you feel any better, I never intended for Strafer to be on the bill in LA. But I had a clause in their contract stipulating they'd play it if I asked them to. Really, it was just a safety measure in case you Overlord boys flaked out on the road, or cracked up, or in some other way showed you weren't ready."

"And you think we *are* ready?" Shay said, sitting up a little straighter.

"Oh, I think you're ready. And frankly, so do the Strafer guys. Paul in particular is very complimentary. Of course, as I just said, he really, *really* doesn't want to go to LA. He calls it 'falling into the black hole.'" He laughed. "But he's not stupid. He wouldn't tell me you were ready if you weren't. He knows the consequences."

"Which are…what?"

Halbert made a low, rumbling noise in the back of his throat, and Shay decided maybe it was better not to inquire further.

And suddenly Shay realized with a sense of awkward stupidity that Paul Di Santangelo befriending him on the tour hadn't been entirely a matter of two like-minded dudes hanging out. Though Shay hoped it had been at least a *little* bit of that. But Paul's primary motive, he now understood, had been to keep Shay focused—keep his eye on the prize—and to hone his musicality and his performance skills in the process, so that he'd be tanned, fit, and ready for the Palladium. And of course Shay had drunk the Kool-Aid with gusto. Hell, he still would. He'd drink it and ask for seconds, please.

"But," he continued, thinking of a new worry, "we're still a pretty young band. Do you really think we can draw a respectable crowd to the freakin' *Palladium*?"

"That *is* a gamble," Halbert admitted, sitting back in the chair. "But I'm going with my gut. I think it's doable. And we haven't had much trouble selling you so far. All those radio interviews and reddit question-and-answer sessions and YouTube concert videos, they've done their job. And of course all the press you've gotten. You can thank my daughter for that. She's definitely your secret weapon, and she's far from being done with you."

As if prompted, Pernita stuck her head around the corner. "You tell him yet?"

Halbert nodded. "I told him."

She flew over to Shay, her arms flailing and a sort of sirenlike keening issuing from her lips. She threw herself into his lap and smothered his face with kisses. "Isn't it exciting? Isn't it the most exciting thing *ever*?" she said between smacks. "My God! We're going straight to the *top*! Oh yes, yes, yes, we are!" And more strangulation, and more kissing.

She didn't disentangle herself from him until another knock summoned her away. She bounded over to the door, opened it, and admitted a bellman who carried an ice bucket, a champagne bottle, and three flutes.

"Right there," Pernita said, pointing to the table where Halbert and Shay sat.

Pernita hopped back into Shay's lap as the bellman worked at popping the cork. As he did so, Halbert leaned in a little and examined the label, then made a sour face. And when, after filling Pernita's and Shay's flutes, the bellman turned to Halbert's, he put his hand over its rim and shook his head.

Pernita clicked her tongue and said to Shay, "Daddy only drinks certain vintages." Then she turned to her father and said, "I'm sorry, Daddy, the hotel doesn't have any Armand de Brignac. I did ask."

"Very well, I suppose I can choke down one swallow," he said, frowning. "For the sake of ceremony."

He allowed the bellman to pour about two tablespoons into the flute before loudly stopping him. And when the bellman had gone—heavily tipped—Halbert raised his glass and said, "To Overlords of Loneliness, and the continued success of their first national tour."

All three tapped their flutes together, which made a dull, clanking sound. Halbert winced, and Pernita preemptively said, "They don't send crystal up for room service. It's a policy," and they all drank.

Halbert took his pocket square from his jacket pocket and daubed his lips, as though to remove excess residue of the offending vintage. Shay openly stared. He'd never seen anyone actually *use* a pocket square before. Was he going to refold it now, and place it back? No, he was stuffing it into his interior jacket pocket. Probably he had an assistant waiting by the elevator with a supply of replacements in designer patterns.

Then Halbert rose to his feet and said, "Well, kids, I've got to be going. I'll see you at the Park West tonight."

"You'll be at the venue, too?" Shay said in astonishment.

"For a while. The first few numbers, at least. I've got a flight back to Manhattan." He kissed the top of Pernita's head again and showed himself out.

Halbert's chair was now empty, but Pernita showed no inclination to get out of Shay's lap and take it. She remained curled around his torso like a cat, which made it difficult for him to hold his flute, not to mention caused his hips to feel stressed to the breaking point.

Finally, when she reached over to refill his drink, he gently put a hand on her arm and drew it aside. "I think that's enough for me," he said. "Better have that nap you suggested earlier. Long night ahead."

She kissed his forehead and jumped out of his lap. He almost groaned with relief and tried not to hobble as he walked away from the chair. If she saw him do that, she'd think he was making a joke about her being fat or something. She was like that, always quick to take offense. Being around her involved a lot of walking on eggshells. Shay felt his happy days of on-the-road freedom slipping through his fingers, like sand. Maybe sand was all they ever really were.

"I'm going to hit the shops," she said, donning her Balenciaga hoodie. "I'll be quiet when I get back." She grabbed her tiny little postage stamp of a purse and said, "What time do you want me to wake you?"

"You don't have to; I'll use the alarm clock on my phone."

She sidled up next to him. "No, you misunderstand," she said, running her hand down the back of his neck. "What time do you want me to *wake* you?"

In spite of himself, he felt the front of his pants spring to life. "Oh," he said. "Um…whenever, really. Up to you." He was still playing his pathetic game of making no show of any commitment to her at all. Despite her obviously owning him lock, stock, and gonads.

She bit his earlobe and whispered, "I'll surprise you. Meantime, sleep tight." Then she headed for the front door.

He stretched his arms, yawned, and said, "Man, this has been one hell of a ride. I can't believe by this time tomorrow, it'll be half over, and I'll be on my way back to Haver City for some R-and-R."

She had pulled open the door, but now she released it and turned back. "Oh! I forgot to tell you."

He immediately went on alert again. "Tell me what?"

"We're not going back to Haver City."

He blanched. "We're not?"

"Oh, I should say not!" She put a hand on her hip. "You're headlining the Hollywood Palladium in just a few short months, sport. We've got less than a month before the tour recommences, and we're going to use them to head west and do a seriously intensive PR push. Interviews, photo shoots, parties..."

His jaw dropped. "But...but we've been working so hard already. The guys were really looking forward to the break."

She scoffed. "Oh, and they'll get one. They're going home. But not the front man. This is his job, honey! For Christ's sake. You want to be a superstar? You don't get there by loafing around for weeks at a time." She waved a hand in the air. "Hell, Strafer Nation isn't! They're spending these two weeks shooting a video, recording a tune for a movie soundtrack, *and* performing at an anti-Monsanto benefit in Omaha."

Shay felt the walls of fate close in on him...slowly, inexorably.

He was well on his way to achieving everything he'd ever dreamed of. If only it didn't suffocate him first.

CHAPTER 16

Zee arrived at Baby's apartment building. It looked less ominous with the sun out. In fact the whole neighborhood seemed quite a bit friendlier, if still a tad seedy. Since this was the scene of one of her most painfully embarrassing fails, she took the new light as a sign that maybe the way she saw things that night wasn't the way things would necessarily remain.

Jimmy Dancer was outside the front door, leaning against the wall, smoking.

"Hi, Jimmy," she said—a little tentatively, as he didn't look like he'd welcome any intrusion. "We met here before, at the Club Uncumber after-party. I'm Zee."

He turned his head toward her in a positively reptilian way and said, "I remember you," then issued a sheet of smoke from his compressed lips.

"Welcome back home," she said. "I hear the tour's going great!"

He inhaled another lungful, held it, then released it through his nose. "Depends," he said.

She furrowed her brow. "On what?"

"On if your name is Shay Dayton. If the answer is yes, then absolutely, the tour is going great. For the rest of us…?" He flicked the cigarette to the pavement, then ground it beneath his toe.

She frowned. "You don't like Shay very much, do you?"

He whirled on her, an expression of astonishment on his face. "What do you mean? Dude's like a brother to me!"

She felt a momentary flurry of fear, as if he might hit her. "Sorry. You just…never seem to have anything good to say about him."

"What I say about him," he shot back, while taking a crumpled pack from his jeans pocket, "is only 'cause I love the guy." He shook his head as he tapped out another cigarette. "Nothing good ever comes of getting everything you want, as soon as you want it."

She felt a sudden sympathy for him. "I can't fight you there."

"I *write* those goddamn tunes, you know. Baby and me."

"Of course I know that."

He lit up and took a puff. "Yeah, you do, don't you?"

"Shay writes the lyrics."

"*Some* of them." He turned and jerked his thumb toward the door. "You can go up, if you want. It's unlocked."

"Thanks." She stepped up onto the stoop.

"But nobody's up there."

She faltered. "They're not?"

He shook his head.

"But Lockwood invited me! Just a couple of hours ago."

He squinted his eyes as he considered this. "Oh. Yeah. I think maybe he's still there." He took a quick puff, then added, "No one else, though."

Zee climbed the stairs to Baby's place. The door was ajar, so she gave it a shove and went in. She found Lockwood slumped in a beanbag chair, reading an issue of *X-Men*.

"Hey," she said, setting down her purse.

He jumped up at the sight of her and tossed the comic aside. "Hey!" he said. "Look at you! You look *phenom*."

"Oh, please. I just came from work. I look like a Young Republican."

He approached her, and they executed a kind of awkward arms-here-and-there maneuver till they managed a quick, uncomfortable hug. Then Zee gently pulled herself away and said, "Thanks for inviting me. I'm just on my lunch break, though. So..."

"So you must be hungry," he said, pointing toward the kitchen. "Baby's sister made some fajitas. Not sure if they're ready."

"Thanks, that'd be great." She followed him as he crossed the apartment. "Where is everybody?"

He snorted. "They dared Trina to plank in the middle of Braithewaite and Maple."

She blinked. "But...that's the busiest intersection in town!"

"I know. That's why. Of course, she was out the door like a shot."

"What...what's she going to plank *on*?"

"Baby had an orange crate and an old amp. They took them along." They reached the kitchen. "Hey, look, they're all cooked and on a platter and everything. Think I'll join you." He took a couple of cracked ceramic plates from a cabinet and filled one with a trio of fajitas. Suddenly he turned and said, "Oh, sorry...mind if I use my fingers?"

She waved away his concern, and as he loaded a second plate she said, "Why didn't you go along?"

"Well, I knew *you* were coming." He turned to carry the plates out of the kitchen. "Grab a couple beers from the fridge, 'kay?"

"Thanks, but I still have to go back to work."

"I meant a couple for me," he said. "Get a soda for yourself, or whatever you want."

She shrugged, plucked a few cans from the refrigerator, and followed him.

They sat down together at Baby's highly stressed coffee table, one leg of which was bound together with guitar string.

"Mm," said Zee, taking a bite of the fajita. "Good." A little string of cheese fell onto her chin, and she scooped it up with her forefinger and sucked it down. In the meantime, Lockwood shoved almost an entire fajita into his mouth and swallowed it in a few doglike gulps.

They sat in silence for a while, eating. Then Zee said, "You could put some music on, if you want."

He grimaced. "No music. I don't want to hear a single goddamn note these entire ten days. I'm freakin' *worn out* by music."

She shifted uncomfortably in her chair, then said, "Thanks for inviting me."

"You already said that," he replied teasingly.

She blushed. "Well…it was nice of you. That's all. Your triumphant coming-home party and all…"

He shook his head vigorously. "This is just a hang, Zee. We're only back for the blink of an eye, so we're just chillin', reconnecting with some of our peeps. All very low-key."

She smiled. "I'm glad I made the cut."

"Hey. You were top of the list."

She finished her first fajita, then sat back to let it settle before tackling the next one. "So tell me about the tour," she said, popping open her cola.

He sighed theatrically. "Do you mind if I don't? I freakin' lived that business for nearly three months. Now I just want a little space that's clear of it." He shrugged. "Besides, I gave you all the high points in my e-mails."

"Thanks for those, by the way. They made me feel special."

"Well, if *that's* all it takes for *you* to feel special, then there's something extra fucked-up about the world."

She blushed again.

"I tell you what," he said. "Why don't you tell me what's goin' on in *your* life?"

She took a deep breath. "Honestly, pretty much work, is all. This new job, though it's not so new, anymore. Anyway, it really keeps me jumping. I'm on from nine to five, pretty much nonstop. Fortunately, there's not a lot of overtime required—I'm just clerical staff—but by the time I get home, I'm basically too burned out for anything. I haven't been to a club in weeks."

He clicked his tongue. "Shame."

"I'm not complaining, though. Glad to have it. Sure as hell glad of the paycheck."

Lockwood shoved another entire fajita into his mouth and worked it down. "And how's things at home?" he said, once he'd managed to swallow it. "You get a new roommate?"

"No," she said, making a tentative start on her second fajita. The way he was going, she had some catching up to do.

"I don't really need one anymore, with the job. Though the company might be nice. And for a while…" She paused, with the fajita before her lips, and looked up at him.

He took a swig of beer, then set down the can with a barely audible burp. "For a while, what?"

"For a while," she said in a low voice, "I thought Loni might move back. So I kept the room open for her."

"Wow," he said. "You're a real sweetheart." He took another swig of beer.

She nibbled a corner off her fajita, then said, "But now, I think…she's happier. Loni, I mean."

He nodded. "Good. Good for her."

She waited for him to go on, and when he started making tactical moves toward his third fajita, she said, "That… that's all?"

He looked up. "What's all?"

"You're not going to pump me for info about Loni?"

"Why would I do that?"

She felt suddenly embarrassed, as if she'd farted or something. "I just thought, maybe that's why you invited me here."

He gave her an astonished look. "I invited you here because I like you."

"And…and Shay Dayton didn't ask you to get the low-down on Loni from me?"

"Oh, hell yeah, he did."

She felt dizzy. "He did?"

"Yeah. And I told him to go fuck himself. He used me for that once, and nothing came of it. So I said, this is your goddamn deal, you play it out."

She raised her eyebrows. "Did you really?"

He shrugged. "Well. I was nicer about it, obviously."

"So...he's not expecting to hear anything from you? About Loni?"

"Knowing him, probably, yeah." He grinned. "But he'll be disappointed."

"He will?"

"Well, yeah." He raised his palms in the air. "I mean, I don't *know* anything."

"And if you did know anything?"

He smirked. "I still wouldn't tell him."

She smiled so hard, her face hurt. "Lockwood, you are so *totally* a gentleman."

He slammed down his can and said, *"You take that back!"*

She laughed so hard she actually belched. Which made *him* laugh.

When they'd both settled down, Zee had another few bites of her fajita, then said, "As it happens, Loni really *is* happy. Though not because of the teaching gig so much. It's 'cause she's decided to publish her own poems. Which is just incredibly major good news, because she's been scribbling them in private for, like, fifteen years, squirreled away in her room like a crazy person. Seriously, since *grade school* this has been going on. But anytime someone would ask to see them, she'd react like they were asking her to take off her underpants or something."

"Well, good for her," he said, eyeing his now empty plate. Then he looked up and said, " 'Scuse me while I head in for seconds." He got up. "You want anything?"

"No, no, I'm good."

When he came back and sat down again—his plate now wobbling under the weight of four more fajitas—she said, "So, is Shay not still with that Pernita woman, then?"

He groaned, then said, *"Slooowly I turned, step by step, inch by inch..."*

She laughed and said, "Excuse me, *what*?"

"Didn't you ever hear that? It's an old, old vaudeville routine. This guy's just out of prison for killing his wife and her lover at Niagara Falls. He's telling this other guy how he hid in their cabin and when they came in, he crept out of the shadows and strangled them. 'Slooowly I turned, step by step, inch by inch—and then I *grabbed* them, and I *throttled* them...' and so on. Only now that he's out of prison, he snaps back to that moment whenever he hears the name 'Niagara Falls.' And the joke is, of course the other poor schmuck in the sketch keeps saying 'Niagara Falls,' which triggers the ex-con to say, *'Niagara Falls!* Slooowly I turned, step by step, inch by inch...and then I *grabbed* them, and I *strangled* them,' and so on. Of course while he's saying it he's strangling the other guy, who's screaming, Stop it, stop it, you freak. He regains control of himself, and he's like, I'm sorry, friend, I didn't mean to hurt you, and the other guy says, Dude, listen, you can't go around getting all medieval on people just 'cause they say Niagara Falls, and then it's *'Niagara Falls!* Slooowly I turned, step by step, inch by inch...'"

Zee was laughing so hard she could barely breathe.

"So anyway," Lockwood said, nodding his head. "Yeah. That woman's name has the same effect on me."

"Pernita's?" said Zee, wiping a tear from her eye.

"Pernita Hasque!" he cried, and he jumped up from the table so quickly he toppled his fajitas onto the floor. "Slooowly I turned," he said, creeping toward Zee, who was too helpless with laughter to move, "step by step, inch by inch—and then...*I caught her! And I shook her! And I shook her some more!"* And here he actually grabbed Zee by the shoulders and gave her a good shaking. *"And...and I shook her some more after that! And...and then..."*

By this time, Zee had stopped laughing and was looking into Lockwood's face in confusion—not a *bad* confusion, by any means—a kind of dizzy, *happy* confusion. She wondered what Lockwood would do next and was surprised to find herself open to several interesting possibilities...

... When all of a sudden Trina Kutsch burst back into the apartment, her arms raised in triumph, followed by the other members of Overlords and a few hangers-on.

"Braithwaite and Maple have been *planked!"* she crowed. "This is why they call me Kid Daredevil!"

"Jesus, Trina," said Jimmy, plopping down before the TV and turning it on. "No one calls you Kid Daredevil."

Lockwood released Zee, who took a moment to compose herself. "Where's your amp?" Lockwood asked.

Baby ran his hand through his hair and frowned. "Wrecked, man," he said. "Plowed over by an eighteen-wheeler."

"Kid Daredevil having escaped in the *nick* of time," called Trina from the kitchen, where she had her head in the fridge.

"No one calls you Kid Daredevil," said Baby and Jimmy in perfect synch.

"Well," Lockwood said, "at least it was an old one."

"Yeah," Baby said, falling into the beanbag chair, "but I still *used* it…"

Zee gathered up her purse. "I should get going. Lunch hour's nearly up."

Lockwood walked her to the door. "You can come back later, after you get off work. We'll still be here, just hanging."

She smiled, slipping her purse strap over her shoulder. "Thanks, but like I said, I'm usually pretty wiped out at the end of the day. I only have enough energy to go home and collapse."

He scowled. "Seriously? What do you do about dinner?"

"Skip it, usually. Too tired to cook."

He looked momentarily uncertain, then said, "How about…how about if when you collapse tonight, it's into a chair at some swanky Italian restaurant? My treat."

When Trina exited the kitchen, bearing an armload of cold beers, she found Lockwood standing by the front door, a dopey grin on his face.

"Man, you should'a' been there," she said, handing him one of the beers. "It was fucking *crazy*. That truck just *exploded* into the orange crate and the amp, man. And I was, like, already on the meridian pumping my fists. You really, really messed up by sittin' it out, dude."

Lockwood popped open the beer, raised it to salute her, and said, "Actually, I really, really did just the opposite."

CHAPTER 17

Shay was learning that there were different ways to be a prisoner.

Take New York. When he'd been held captive there in Halbert Hasque's east side apartment with its magnificent view of Central Park, he'd been utterly miserable. The only time he could be on his own recognizance, going where he wanted and doing whatever he liked, was when Pernita was busy elsewhere. Whenever she'd leave the apartment for a hair appointment, or a shopping spree, or a lunch date, or whatever, Shay would watch out the window till she exited the building, got into a cab, and zipped away; then he'd let out a whoop of exhilaration and head out himself. And for a few glorious hours he'd be alone—*alone*—on the streets of Manhattan and be his own goddamn master.

Then Pernita would return, and once again he'd find himself utterly under her thumb, told where to go and how to dress and whom to talk to and when to sit down and when to take a piss.

But damn. Looking back? He hadn't realized how good he'd had it.

Here, in Halbert Hasque's mansion in Holmby Hills, he was much more a prisoner than he ever was in New York. And this was despite Pernita almost never being around during the day. She got up every morning, complaining of all the

258

plans she had, and of the seven thousand best, most intimate friends she *had* to see while they were in town or *God* only knew the consequences, and then she was basically gone. So in theory, Shay was freer than ever. Except...to do what?

In New York, all he had to do was step out onto the pavement, and the world of Halbert and Pernita Hasque would already be behind him. He could take four steps, buy a hot pretzel from a street vendor, chat up a girl or two. In a few more steps, he'd be at the subway, and any place on the island was just minutes away.

When he stepped out the door of the Hasque mansion here in LA, there was nothing but blue sky, green lawn, and black asphalt driveway for as far as his eyes could see. Once, feeling adventurous, he'd trekked all the way down to the boulevard beyond the driveway's gate (he'd had to shimmy over the wall because he didn't have the code to punch into the gate's keypad), but there had been no cab there waiting to whisk him to some new adventure. Certainly no subway.

In fact, there'd been nothing in any direction. Just houses the size of battleships and acres and acres of the crispest landscaping imaginable. He tried going it on foot to see where it took him, but where it took him was someplace so utterly like everything he'd seen everywhere else he'd been that he'd had to admit he was hopelessly lost and called Pernita to come and fetch him.

It didn't take long for her to reach him, either, because she was already out in her car. She'd come home, found him gone, and the housekeeper and gardener had both told her he'd done a runner. Shay then realized, too, that unlike New York, here the prison had extra guards. They posed as household staff, but as far as he was concerned, their real function was to watch him and report on his movements.

"I don't understand why you feel so *compelled* to leave," Pernita had complained as she drove him home. She reminded him of her father's swimming pool, his billiards room, his bowling alley, and his two separate home theaters with high-res monitors and DVD libraries of every film and TV show produced since the dawn of man.

"If it's such a goddamn paradise," Shay had said, "how come *you* never spend more than ninety minutes at a time there? Short of sleeping, I mean."

She always had a million excuses. Then he'd ask why he couldn't just have a car of his own; he'd even pay to rent one. And she'd say, Don't be silly, you can have *this* one when I'm not using it. And he'd say, When the hell *aren't* you using it? And sometimes when she seemed to sense his desperation reaching a certain pitch she'd say, Oh, you can have it tomorrow, and he'd say, Really, and she'd say, Of course. He'd make plans for everything he was going to do the next day, but then that day would dawn and just as he was getting ready to leave, Pernita would remember some *hugely* important errand she had to run and would he mind *terribly* if she came with him? And that would be that. He'd escape the house, but only for the smaller prison of the car.

Occasionally he broke down and accused her of trying to control him. Which led her to call him ungrateful and selfish and to cry, which was the big gun in her arsenal, the one she pulled out every time she felt backed into a corner. In fact, Shay was completely unmoved by her tears, but he let her believe the opposite. Better to save his implacability for a time when revealing it would score him an actual point.

But he didn't know if he had the strength of will to wait that long. As the busyness of the first few days of his stay receded—days filled with image consultants and hair stylists and wardrobe fittings—the flurry of activity was replaced by…nothing at all. Oh, the nights were always filled with some event or other, where Pernita trotted him out like a trained seal to smile and bark and clap his fins for the amusement of the crowd. But the days? The days passed in a manner he could only call glacial.

He'd already exhausted every entertainment the house had to offer. Always an excellent bowler, he'd managed a perfect game on his third day in Halbert's private alley, and after that there didn't seem much point. He'd watched the entire run of *M*A*S*H* on DVD and was still too emotionally involved in that experience to want to move on to something else. He'd had to abandon the pool when his skin burned and then started to peel. (Pernita had been furious at that and called in an emergency dermatologist to buff away all the dead skin and to refresh and tone what was underneath, as there was a big party that night *with cameras*, she'd said, he couldn't go there looking like his head was emerging from a cocoon.) Finally, he'd had to give up honing his billiard skills after he accidentally ripped a hole in the green felt of Hasque's pool table. In fact, he'd hung up his cue, turned out the light, and skulked guiltily away, hoping it would be several weeks before anyone noticed, by which time it would be harder to connect the crime with him.

The only thing left for him, then, was to eat. And Halbert Hasque's kitchen was better stocked than any he'd ever known—which was crazy, considering that Halbert himself was almost never there. What happened to all that fresh produce brought in three times a week when there was no one here to eat it? The mind boggled.

But then one night, when he was changing into an incredibly expensive Dolce & Gabbana suit for an appearance at some music awards pre-show party ("where there will be *cameras*," Pernita had again told him urgently, as if she ever brought him any place where there weren't any), he found he couldn't zip the fly. He dropped a few f-bombs trying to manage it, and Pernita flew over to see what the trouble was because for *God's* sake they were *already* running late. She exploded into affronted horror when she realized Shay had put on just enough weight to turn the Dolce & Gabbana suit into a hugely expensive hanger decoration.

After that, she ordered all the food out of the house except what she prescribed for him, which was all locally grown and organic, and on any given day filled about a third of one shelf of the house's commercial-grade refrigerator. Seriously, Shay was convinced he could hear his echo when he spoke into that vast, chilly emptiness. Pernita also rustled up a personal trainer to come in every morning and aggressively banish the unwelcome fat with extended sessions in the Hasque mansion weight room. Under ordinary circumstances that would have been the purest torment for Shay, but now, what the hell, it was something to do for two hours out of twenty-four. And at the end of his sixteen-day junket in la-la land, he had to admit he *was* looking pretty ripped.

He'd tried to fight the boredom by working on musical ideas. He'd asked Pernita if she could rent a piano for him during his stay, which was a huge concession for him. Up until then it had been a point of pride that he never asked her for anything, ever, and it was telling that on this one occasion when he did, the answer was no. "You don't need to be a musical genius," she said with a dismissive smirk. "You're a front man. You need to sing like an angel and look like a devil. And make everyone in the whole goddamn world know it."

He tried using a keyboard app on his laptop, but it wasn't the same as running his fingers over actual keys, so he eventually gave up the effort.

And then there was nothing left but Facebook. (Facebook and web porn, but he suspected Pernita of keeping tabs on his Internet history, so he was almost monastically sparing with the latter.) He would spend marathon sessions checking all his friends' personal pages to see what they were doing with their actual human lives in the actual real world where he used to live before it spat him out onto Mount Olympus. One day at the end of his stay, he sat down to begin one of these sessions, and a sudden urge struck him. He did something he almost never bothered doing: he checked the Overlords of Loneliness fan page.

And damn if he wasn't impressed. The last time he'd looked, just after the tour began, they'd had 275 fans, which he'd thought was phenomenal. Now they were at 8,011. He had to hand it to Pernita: she was really honest-to-God doing her job. She might kill him in the process, but she was getting the results she'd promised. He clicked on the list of people who had liked the page, wondering whether they were predominately male or female, black or white, young or old—any demographic trend at all. It wasn't that he wildly cared; he was just mildly curious and epically bored.

He skimmed down the list of Rita Dovermans and Nicholas Jelniks and Lakota Stains, and the pint-size profile pictures all sort of began to blend together, so that they meant exactly nothing.

And then he saw it.

Right there in the middle of that long roll call of Overlords Facebook fans.

William Blake.

William Blake, with the same profile picture of an especially buff-looking painted angel.

No. Fucking. Way. was his first reaction. It was simply too bonkers to think that after everything had gone so wrong between them, Loni would actually Like his band's page.

Ah, but then she'd blocked him, right? So she'd be assuming he'd never find out.

So why *was* he finding out? If she'd blocked him, William Blake should be completely and utterly invisible to him, wherever he—or rather, she—went on Facebook.

And that's when he realized the crazy, wonderful thing that had happened. Pernita had made him open a second account, under an assumed name, so that he could go around Facebook incognito, talking up Overlords and urging everyone to buy *Grief Bacon*. Pernita had several such accounts herself and was tired of doing all the hard work on her own.

Shay had chosen the name Bruce Banner, and that had been a good little rebellion against Pernita, because of course she didn't recognize it. The Incredible Hulk was far beneath her notice, at least until he decided to switch his tatty purple pants for Ermenegildo Zegna flat-fronts. But of course, he then realized everyone else in the world *would* recognize the Bruce Banner name, so he'd been too embarrassed to actually use it, until Pernita had forced him to the night before, commanding him to go online right that minute and do some word of mouth on his own behalf. She'd practically stood over his shoulder while he'd done so. Afterward he'd been so steamed, he'd just shut the laptop and gone to bed.

So when he opened it this morning, it was to Bruce Banner's account, not Shay Dayton's.

And Bruce Banner was not blocked by William Blake.

Just thinking that sentence in his head was so wonderfully goofy that it put him in a good mood. He only wished Lockwood or somebody was here to share it with. But instead, his excess of giddy good feeling caused him to do the next best thing. Bruce Banner sent William Blake a friend request.

///////////////

That night's event was a media cocktail party at a club in Venice called Hazzard. A certain Wendii Frontiac, who was apparently very influential with a particular stratum of LA ersatz-hipster society, had committed to showing up and taping a segment for her weekly webcast on what was trending in the city's nightlife. Pernita was beside herself. Apparently she'd been trying to get to Wendii Frontiac for *years*. The entertainment for the event was Jonah and the Wail. Halbert Hasque—again, running things in absentia—had flown them in from Atlanta to give an extra push to the Palladium gig coming up in a few months.

Arriving at the club fashionably late, Shay left Pernita to air-kiss all her very, very closest friends on the planet and then take her new outfit for a grand tour of the room. He made his way to the bar, where he ordered a good stiff tumbler of Scotch. Then he turned his attention to Jonah and the Wail, who were already playing.

It was pretty impressive stuff. Jonah, the male member of the duo, handled all the surprisingly lush and textured instrumentals himself, using only a synthesizer. Meanwhile the Wail, a wan, goth-looking female, sang spectrally into her mic, almost at a whisper, except for the occasional phrase where she went soaring up into the stratosphere, hitting a pitch so high Shay could swear he heard dogs barking blocks away. Obviously this vocal trait was the source of her stage name.

The compositions were very rich, very dark, very complex, and in unusual time signatures like 7/8 and 11/16. Shay was really enjoying listening to them, listening *hard*, and digging his way into their mysteries...

...but then Wendii Frontiac dutifully appeared, beaming laserlike ambition. She stuck a microphone in his face and chirpily asked questions like, "What's more important to you, music or image?" and "If you had to pick only one Overlords song to win over a new listener, what would it be?" and "Who's your greatest musical influence?" and of course, most important for this town, "Who are you wearing?" As Shay was by then slim enough to once again accommodate the Dolce & Gabbana, he was able to provide this satisfying reply.

Pernita, taken aback by Wendii's sudden appearance, had to practically vault across the club to reach Shay while he was still being interviewed. She needn't have worried, though; he acquitted himself exactly the way she'd rehearsed him (and re-rehearsed him, and re-re-rehearsed him). He was nearly finished by the time Pernita showed up. In fact, he was just mentioning (for the third time) the Palladium gig and the date. Completely off-the-cuff, he mentioned how excited he was about Jonah and the Wail joining them, and didn't they sound great?

But Wendii Frontiac's eyes had already lost interest. She turned aside and told her cameraman that was a wrap. So it was up to the lesser media in the room to give Jonah's singular soundscapes some love. Shay would do what he could to help. He was a fan.

He expected Pernita to wait for Wendii to depart before taking him aside and telling him the ninety-six ways he'd screwed up the interview but never mind, you did your best, baby, next time maybe you'll really listen to me. But instead, to his astonishment, she scampered after Wendii, trying desperately to engage her in a few moments of substantive trend-whore conversation. It was rare that Shay got to see Pernita pay homage to anyone else's authority, so it was worth a few nourishing laughs at her expense.

A few minutes later Jonah and the Wail finished their set. Jonah, who was a short, energetic guy with crazy hair and a glittering amber jacket, came down into the club. The Wail evaporated off the stage, probably to go back to her dressing room and, who knew, bathe in the blood of young virgins or something. Shay intercepted Jonah at the bar, where he was ordering a drink. "Nice set," he said, extending his arm. "Shay Dayton. Good meeting you."

"Hey, Shay," he said with a slight southern lilt, and shook his hand. "Likewise. Saw you from across the room."

He raised an eyebrow. "You recognized me?"

"Hard not to. Your face is goddamn everywhere these days." Jonah's drink, a glass of Johnnie Walker Red, was delivered. He raised it and said, "Cheers. Here's to the Palladium."

"To the Palladium," Shay said, and they each tossed back a mouthful.

Shay went on to say how much he liked Jonah's songwriting, and asked where he studied and for how long, and what he'd been doing since—and Jonah answered amicably enough, though downing his drink a bit faster than Shay himself would have dared. When he'd drained the glass, he smacked his lips, plonked it back on the bar, looked out at the crowd, and said, "What a fucking circus this is. All these tragic cases just dying to be seen. Because if somebody doesn't notice them they might fucking disappear into thin air or something. Pathetic."

Shay sighed. "That's kinda this whole burg, though, isn't it?"

"It's this industry." He looked at his watch. "Man, I cannot fucking *wait* to get out of here."

Shay took another, more measured sip of his own drink and said, "Well, you've only got one more set, right?"

"No, you don't understand," said Jonah, stepping away from the bar. "I mean I really *cannot wait*."

Shay blinked. "You're—you're going *now*?" He glanced back at the platform. "But…what about the Wail?"

"Marcia? What about her?"

"You're—you've got—you're supposed to be—"

"Look," he said, leaning in conspiratorially, "she'll be fine. Maybe she'll be a little embarrassed when she comes out to sing and finds there's no one there with her, and maybe she'll ream my ass tomorrow. But I'm not a fucking slave to this shit, and she knows it."

"But...your reputation, man. People will *talk* about this."

"Exactly," he said, fishing around in his pocket and producing a car key. "A helluva lot more than they would've talked about me otherwise. People *like* bad boys. What they don't like are guys who kiss ass. The guys who *want* approval don't get it." He grinned. "I don't fucking care what they think of me, and I show it. So of course they fall all over me."

Despite the lubricating the Scotch had given it, Shay's throat went suddenly dry.

Jonah cocked his head. "You wanna come?"

"Me?" Shay said. "Bolt on a party that's thrown in my honor?"

"Best kinda party to bolt from. *Really* drives the message home. What do you say?"

Shay laughed, not entirely sure he was serious. "No. No. I'm...thanks, but." He cocked his head. "Seriously. You're just...going to *go*?"

"Watch me," he said, palming the key and turning toward the door. "You stay here and wag your tail like a good little lapdog. See where the hell it gets you."

He walked a few steps, then paused, went back to the bar, borrowed a pen from the bartender, and scrawled something on a paper napkin, which he handed to Shay.

Shay looked at it. It was a phone number.

"Let me know when you're ready to break the chain," he said with a wink.

And then he was gone.

Shay wandered about the room in an incredulous daze for a while, until Pernita found him and told him not to walk around with his mouth open, he looked like a half-wit, and *snap to it* there were some people he still needed to meet.

Fifteen minutes later the Wail returned to the mic and stood forlornly alone until everyone realized she wasn't doing anything. Then there was a flurry of activity as the people in charge of the event (including Pernita) tried in vain to locate Jonah. Eventually, an upright bass player emerged from behind a closed door and hauled his instrument up on the platform to accompany the Wail in an abbreviated set of stripped-down melodies that was, Shay had to admit, no less compelling.

Later, on the way back to the Hasque mansion, Shay asked Pernita whether they'd hired the bass player in advance, and she admitted they had.

"Daddy's idea," she said from behind the wheel (she always drove). "Jonah's got kind of a reputation for flaking out mid-gig. It seemed smart to have a back-up plan."

"I'm amazed your dad would put up with that kind of shit from someone he reps."

She shrugged. "What can you do? Jonah's basically a genius. You work around the quirks."

////////////////

Pernita usually insisted on sex following a press event, as though it were her right—a kind of Roman triumph conducted beneath the sheets. But apparently tonight hadn't been enough of a success to meet her benchmark, what with Wendii snubbing her and Jonah taking a powder. When she joined Shay in bed, she gave him a perfunctory kiss, then turned her back on him and coiled up in bitterness, like a snake.

Shay had trouble sleeping, as he usually did after these kinds of events. Too many faces too close to his left a kind of psychic imprint on his consciousness, and he had to wait for all the intensely curious eyes, babbling mouths, and spectacularly coiffed hair to fade into mist before he could sleep. But tonight he had the added element of Jonah's advice to him. Was he *really* a lapdog, letting other people tell him when to sit, stay, roll over, beg? Was his true self getting lost in this by-the-numbers pursuit of rock stardom? Was rock stardom *worth* it? Or, as Jonah implied, was he going about it entirely the wrong way?

Eventually, after tossing and turning, he went down to the kitchen for something to eat. He'd managed to sneak a few hors d'oeuvres at Hazzard, snarfing them down while Pernita's back was turned, but he was still hungry.

There were only fruits and vegetables in the refrigerator. Pernita was still monitoring his diet like he was a racehorse. He took an apple from the shelf—what he wouldn't have given for a slice of cold pizza!—and sat down at his laptop to keep him company while he ate. When he opened the cover, he found Facebook still on the screen, opened to Bruce Banner's account.

There was a notification. He clicked on it.

William Blake had accepted his friendship request.

He smiled as he chewed on the apple. This was very, very intriguing. He had to wonder why Loni had said yes. She couldn't know it was him. She couldn't know it was *anyone*.

He went immediately to her profile page. And the first thing that struck him was her most recent status update:

> *Only three days till my reading in Santa Barbara!*
> *Please come if you're in the area. I'd love to meet you*
> *and would greatly appreciate your support.*

Beneath was a link to a bookstore, announcing that Loni Merrick (Merrick! Finally, he knew her last name) would be reading from her new self-published volume of poetry, *Venus in Retrograde*, at five in the afternoon.

The date was the day after tomorrow.

So that was why she'd accepted Bruce Banner's friendship request with no questions asked. Loni Merrick had entered the ranks of the audience whores. Just like Shay, just like every performer everywhere, she had seats to fill, and who knew, Bruce Banner might fill one of them. And with that, Shay decided that Bruce Banner would. In fact, it wasn't a decision; it was more like a sudden awareness of what had already been determined, somewhere else, by unseen forces.

He thought for a moment about the difficulties involved, but there was never for a moment anything resembling doubt. And sure enough, he came to understand that the unseen forces had been busier than he'd even dreamed. The unseen forces had laid it all out for him.

He went back upstairs, found his phone, found the contents of his pocket from where he'd emptied them when he'd undressed, and located the napkin with Jonah's number.

He sent him a text: *Hey it's Shay. I'm ready to break the chain.*

CHAPTER 18

"I gotta tell ya," said Jonah with a bit of a sneer. "When you said you were ready to break the chain, I didn't think you meant *this*." He flicked his cigarette out the window in disgust. "Driving to goddamn *Santa Barbara*. In the middle of the afternoon. To go to a *bookstore*." He turned to Shay. "Sure you wouldn't rather hit a crystal meth den in Compton at three a.m.?"

Shay shifted uncomfortably in his seat. "I told you," he said. "It's to see a friend. An *author*," he added, lamely. As if any literary credentials would impress Jonah Piercon.

He was growing increasingly uncomfortable with his decision to slip away to attend Loni's reading. Jonah was proving to be much more of a borderline sociopath than he'd realized from their brief conversation at Hazzard. But what could he do? Jonah had the wheels. Too late Shay realized he could've just rented his own car, on the sly. It would've been far less trouble than managing Jonah on the road. But until now, he'd thought it would be a kick to have a friend along, a partner in crime.

Unfortunately, Jonah's idea of crime was significantly more elevated than Shay's. He said, "Well, if we're gonna be swanning around Santa Barbara with the snobs, we might as well get ourselves tight for it. Could you pass me the party mix?"

The "party mix" was a small vial of white powder with a little silver cap that had a tiny spoon affixed by a slender chain. Shay had originally guessed it to be cocaine, but Jonah's nickname for it implied that there were additional ingredients as well.

Shay had buckled to peer pressure and taken a bump when they'd first gotten into the car. Now he was fiercely regretting it. He felt as though he was having a heart attack. That might just be the effect of Jonah's driving—he seemed to think it was against the law to go under seventy-five and was blithely oblivious to anyone who might be in his blind spot when he changed lanes—but the chemicals couldn't have helped. Shay cursed himself for being such a wuss. He'd always *hated* cocaine. "Fake fun," he called it; it made your heart beat faster so you thought you were enjoying yourself, but really, you weren't. It was all illusion.

He hated cocaine, and yet he'd taken cocaine—and not just cocaine: cocaine spiked with God knows what else. He'd refused any seconds or thirds, but of course by then it was too late. He was royally fucked up. He could only imagine how wrecked Jonah must be, though that guy's resistance was undoubtedly considerably higher. The way he went at it, it was clear he snorted this stuff for breakfast.

Shay passed the "party mix" to him but, worried about the increasing deterioration of his attention span, added, "Listen, it's not fair for you to have to drive the whole way. Why don't I take over?"

Amazingly, Jonah agreed. Probably because he was having far too much trouble unscrewing the vial's itty-bitty cap while simultaneously keeping the wheel steady. "Sure, thanks, bro," he said, and he immediately swerved toward the shoulder—almost clipping a Dodge Dart that was sailing alongside them.

He shifted the car into park and got out. Shay sat for a while longer in the passenger seat, because he wasn't entirely sure the car had stopped moving. It *looked* like the road ahead was laying steady and flat before them, but the feeling against his face was like g-force.

Jonah knocked on the passenger window. "Change your mind, bro?"

Shay snapped to attention, opened the door, and got out. "No, no, I'm still cool." And in fact the sudden snap of cool air against his skin made him feel a little more grounded. He shook his head vigorously, sending his hair flying, then stamped his feet against the gravel a few times—trying to shock his wits back into functioning. *Come back, come back,* he thought to himself. *Where are you, Shay, man? I need you!*

When he felt reasonably fit to drive, he got back into the car, shifted into gear, and pulled back into traffic. It was helpful to have a job, something to concentrate on. And in fact, his focus seemed very, very sharp. He had to pinch himself every now and then just to keep from getting *too* focused and forgetting other, peripheral activities like, say, breathing.

Jonah sat next to him, happily spooning up powder into his nostrils and emitting raspy little grunts of pleasure. Yeah, this was definitely not an ideal situation. And yet, any doubts Shay had had about undertaking it had been obliterated the day before, when the only media coverage from his party at Hazzard had been about Jonah and the Wail and its bad-boy mastermind who'd bolted after their first set. Wendii

Frontiac's segment on the party—which ran for an epic thirty-seven seconds, a small eternity in television—had been *all* about Jonah, the unpredictable boy-genius. In fact, Wendii even showed some footage of the Wail singing forlornly alone, backed by only the upright bass, which had happened *after Wendii had already left*. How she got those clips, Shay couldn't imagine, but given the intensity of her ambition, body bags might have been involved. He wouldn't put it past her.

As for Shay, who was the whole reason Wendii had been there at all, he only appeared on-screen once, and that was to say how great Jonah and the Wail sounded—a quote Wendii had only because he'd slipped it in right before she told her cameraman to cut. He'd barely made it into the segment that was supposed to have been all about him.

So in the end, Jonah had been right: the way to rock stardom wasn't by letting yourself become a performing seal for someone like Halbert or Pernita. The way to rock stardom was to do your own goddamn thing whenever you goddamn felt like it. Even Loni had known that. When he'd first met her in Baby's kitchen, she'd told him real rock musicians don't care about the market or publicity. They cared about their passion, about their art.

Well, all right, then. Loni was Shay's passion. That much had become clear. His mom had been right when she'd told him to see if all those women on the tour could make him forget her. They hadn't. He knew now that she was the real deal, she was the one. She was his passion, and he was absolutely goddamn following it.

He just wished he could be surer of it all turning out okay. Jonah, in the next seat, was well into an endless rant about the treatment of dairy hens, which so roused him to anger that at one point he punched the dashboard several times and came away with bleeding knuckles.

As for Shay, he kept thinking about the event scheduled for that night, dinner with Pernita and Halbert and a couple of record-label suits who it was vitally important for Shay to impress...or so Pernita insisted. Drinks were at seven. Loni's reading was at five. Presuming it lasted a half hour, Shay could conceivably make the ninety-minute drive back to LA in time for cocktails.

But wasn't the whole idea that he shouldn't *care* about the freakin' dinner and the asshole record-label execs? Wasn't that the whole point of everything he'd learned from Jonah?

Well, yes, it was. Except Shay had a sinking feeling that maybe to pull that off you had to be that way from the get-go. He had to doubt whether—having been so visibly Pernita Hasque's dress-up doll for show-and-tell all this time—he could suddenly go rogue with any conviction. But what did he care? He was on the open road, in his new friend's rented Mustang GT, and with Loni at the end of the line.

He settled back to enjoy the ride.

And then...there she was.

He thought at first she might be a mirage, an image reflected onto the window by the vibrant, shining picture of her in his mind. So he cupped his hands around his eyes and peered past the glass, into the bookstore.

And yes, it was her. Beautifully, unmistakably, irresistibly her.

And she was already reading.

He muttered a few profanities under his breath. He'd wanted to hear every syllable she uttered. But once they'd reached Santa Barbara it had taken them forever to find a parking space. They eventually settled on an illegal spot ("Let the rental company pay the ticket," Jonah had said. "Better yet, let Halbert Hasque!"), and then they'd wandered another agonizing chunk of time trying to find the bookstore. Shay had committed the address to memory, but then he'd gone and addled his memory with Jonah's heinous "party mix." It was really a miracle they'd found it at all, especially with Jonah insisting on stopping every twenty yards to point all around him and say, "No, seriously, *look*—isn't it *exactly* like being in a Ron Howard movie?"

But at long last, here they were.

And here *she* was.

Shay took a deep breath and tried to compose himself. His heart was still hammering like a woodpecker on a tree trunk, but he was pretty sure it was mostly from seeing Loni. Even so, he knew he must be a hell of a lot twitchier and more wild-eyed than usual. He didn't want her to see him this way. The thing to do was to slip into the bookstore and take a place at the back, where she wouldn't spot him. It was a pretty good-size crowd. About forty people filled all the chairs and spilled over into standing room near the door. It would be easy to sneak in unnoticed, especially given how intently she seemed to be reading, eyes burning into the slender volume in her hands.

Jonah was dithering a few paces behind him. Shay waved him over and then entered the shop. The door gave a little jingle, but Loni was too much in-the-zone to hear it and look up. He took a place sandwiched between a few other patrons, and Jonah followed, excusing himself more audibly than he needed to. A woman turned and shushed him. "We're not interested in hearing what *you* have to say," she sternly whispered.

"Then stop breathing," he whispered back.

Sweet creeping Christ on a moped, Shay thought. *Just get me through this.*

When they'd finally settled in, Shay turned his attention to Loni—Loni! That was actually *Loni* in the *same room* as him! Seated on a stool next to a table with a pitcher of water for her to drink with her own actual human mouth!—and tried to focus on the verses she was reading aloud.

> *The dampening of sinews, the heady stew of leaves,*
> *The aroma of corruption in the repining of pine,*
> *Fallen so long and time, measured out in moss,*
> *Slows and stills, and gives rise to wonder whether*
> *A forest no longer upright—a forest uprooted—*
> *Is a forest yet; and am I—undone—*
> *Yet myself, no longer standing tall*
> *But toppled by the blow of your abandonment.*

Holy shit, Shay thought. *This girl is really throwing down the heavy.* And while the audience applauded, he thought, *Wait—was that about me? I hope that wasn't about me.* Then a moment later he thought, *Jesus, how wicked cool would it be if that* was *about me?*

Loni, looking stupefyingly cerebral in all black—black turtleneck with the sleeves rolled up, black jeans, black-framed glasses—turned a page and continued.

"This is the oldest poem in the book," she said, "but at the same time, also one of the newest. I started it years ago, struggled...grappled with it, the way one does...and only recently did I get it into a choke hold." There was a ripple of mild laughter. "I call it, 'Fracture.'" Then she turned her eyes to the page and read.

> *A hairsbreadth divide that does not divine—meaning*
> *gutters when division uncouples a nullity—*
> *Constant ever, yet aspect alters:*
> *Your face in starlight—enchantment—*
> *Your face in daylight—error*

There was a little stir in the crowd. No one seemed to know exactly how to react to it. Someone started applauding, almost, it seemed, as a courtesy, and everyone else joined in, but it was tentative. Loni, seeming a little flustered, said, "Thanks—I know that's a strange one. And brief, for all the years it took to get it out. But trust me, it's exactly what it needs to be." The clapping grew a little more resonant after that, but it still came as a relief when someone accidentally knocked over a cardboard display of *Harry Potter*.

Once the laughter over that had subsided, Loni began the next poem. Shay tried to listen, but his mind kept wandering to his game plan. *I'll just wait till she's signing copies,* he thought. *I'll just stand in line and wait my turn, and when I reach her I'll say, "Make it out to Shay," and then she'll look up and meet my eyes, and then I'll smile, and I'll turn and go. I'll just go, and leave that seed planted for a while. Yeah, that's it.*

He was liking this plan, liking it so much that he didn't notice when someone sidled up and wedged between him and

Jonah. And when Loni finished the poem and the audience was responding, this interloper—a young skateboard-dude type—turned to Jonah and said, "Hey, you're the guy!"

"I certainly am," said Jonah, his eyes crazy bright.

"You're the guy on TV! The guy with the skinny chick—Noah and the Wail!"

"Jonah and the Wail," he corrected him. "It's all right this once. Don't let it happen again."

"The next poem," Loni said, "is a lighter one."

"I seen you on TV!" Skateboard Dude continued. "You were on, like, three channels!"

"Brother, I'm on every goddamn channel you can name, right at this moment."

"*Ssh,*" said a woman in front of them, over her shoulder.

"Didn't you, like, walk out on a gig or something?"

"*Your bravery in battle is your willingness to go,*" said Loni.

"I didn't walk," said Jonah. "I *ran* out."

Skateboard Dude laughed. "Yeah! I totally saw that! *Radical*, man!"

"*Ssssh!*" said someone else.

"*Mine is mine to let you,*" Loni continued. "*To arm you by retracting arms…*"

"Man, I'm only here 'cause my girlfriend dragged me," Skateboard Dude said. "Hell're *you* doing here?"

"Dying a slow death," Jonah said.

Skateboard Dude laughed.

A few more people shushed them—Shay included—and then someone appeared right in front of them, an older guy with glasses and a receding hairline and a face blazing righteous anger, blocking their view of Loni, who continued reciting, as if blissfully unaware.

"Do you mind shutting the hell up?" the guy in the glasses said.

"Are you talking to me?" said Jonah.

"Yes, you. Will you please shut your goddamn mouth?"

"You could always shut it for me," said Jonah mock-seductively, "with a kiss."

Some kind of animal rage roared up behind the older guy's eyes. He drew back his arm in what Shay knew was the windup to a punch, and Shay, not wanting Loni's reading to be interrupted by violence, stepped in between them—

—and ended up taking the punch himself, hard, on the side of his jaw.

"Oh, fuck—*ohhhh*," he groaned—as quietly as possible, despite the searing pain. He was still thinking of Loni, whose reverberating voice was even now sounding over the crowd, though more than a few heads had turned away from her to see what was the disturbance was.

"Get me out of here," Shay commanded Jonah with as much urgency as he could muster from his wobbly jaw. He was desperate that Loni shouldn't see *him* at the center of this ridiculous scene.

Jonah was only too glad to go, so much so that Shay might have suspected him of causing the whole scene just for that purpose. The older guy in glasses even held the door open for them, then gave them a few angry snorts as they passed through it, like a cartoon bull chasing intruders out of his field.

Shay felt like his entire brainpan had been jostled. He could barely see straight. Jonah had to lead him back to the car like he was drunk. When they passed a pair of Santa Barbara matrons who looked down their noses at him, presumably thinking he *was* drunk, Jonah accosted them with, "Get a good look, Stepford Wives, then hurry on home and hump your Mexican gardeners! Yeah, because *your* shit don't stink," which, perhaps predictably, set them running.

Shay was too disoriented to drive. He couldn't seem to focus his eyes—was he concussed?—so Jonah took the wheel, but not before another snort of party mix.

///////////////

As they sped back on the Ventura Freeway, Shay worked his jaw back and forth, then held it cupped in his hand as though afraid it might fall off if he let go.

Jonah laughed at him. "You should'a just let me take what was comin' at me. What the hell? That goddamn bookworm didn't look like he could punch his way out of a taco wrapper. Plus," he said, grinning, "my jaw's built up plenty of scar tissue, having been clocked so many times by Marcia. Most recently, yesterday. See any bruising?" He turned his face toward Shay.

"None. You mean, she actually hit you? Watch it, you're drifting to the right."

He corrected his steering and said, "Oh, she fucking *whaled* on me. I pretty much knew I had it coming, the way I left her stranded at...whaddayacall. Razmatazz."

"Hazzard. You mean, you *knew* she'd hit you?" He couldn't imagine the corpselike Wail exhibiting that much animation.

"Oh, we've been goin' at it hammer and tongs for years. You'd think we'd learn. Walk away from each other. But. Y'know. *That* never goes well."

"Jesus! I'd think you'd *want* to walk away from each other, *run* from each other, if it's as bad as that. You're drifting right again."

He swung back to the left. "Who says it's bad? I mean… yeah, it ain't pleasant. But…y'know. It's *feeling*, man. It's knowing you're *alive*. And while we're takin' swings at each other, we're thrashing it all out, getting everything off our chests we've been holding in all week, month, however long it's been. That kind of honesty, it *hurts*, you know? But it's necessary. So it kinda makes sense to throw it in when you're hurting each other physically, too." He gave Shay a sidelong look. "I'm sure you know what I mean. Gotta be the same for you and your…whatever her name is. Hasque's little whelp. Juanita."

"Pernita. And…actually. Huh." He fell silent, suddenly and astonishingly ashamed to admit that his relationship with her wasn't as spectacularly dysfunctional as Jonah's with the Wail. He tried to imagine Pernita hitting him. If she ever did that, he'd turn on his heel and walk away from her forever, star-making father or not. And if he ever hit her? Hell, he knew beyond a doubt he'd be locked up in a jail before the hour was up.

"You know," he said, realizing something else, "I don't think, in the entire time I've known her, that I've ever said *anything* honest to Pernita. Never anything that even hinted at what I was really thinking or feeling. And I'd bet cash money it's the same for her."

"Man," said Jonah, laughing in disbelief. "You guys, you're really fucked up."

So it had come to this: Jonah Piercon, one half of a living Punch and Judy sketch, had told him *his* relationship was the warped one.

But he was right, wasn't he? Shay knew it; he'd always known it.

What he *hadn't* always known was the thought that struck him now. From the moment he'd met Loni, they had been scaldingly honest with each other. Yeah, sure, maybe she hadn't mentioned her steady guy and he'd never mentioned Pernita, but the way they'd talked about everything else? There hadn't been anything in the way. No barriers, no evasions, nothing.

No wonder he'd immediately thought she was so remarkable. And this was the woman he'd just had to run out on, because he'd gotten into a freaking brawl at her literary event. What the hell kind of black cloud was he born under, anyway?

"You're drifting right again," he said.

////////////////

The excitement of the day took its toll on him, and in the monotony of traffic he fell asleep. He didn't wake up till LA was once again sprawled out before them. Traffic had thickened, so that Jonah was no longer able to barrel along at quite the speed of sound, but he was still maintaining a pretty hell-bent clip. He was also jumping around in his seat as if to the beat of some wild thrash-rock tune.

But...the radio wasn't on.

Shay began to suspect there'd been a little more party mix while he was asleep.

He looked out the window and saw, coming up fast, the ramp for Mulholland Drive.

"Uh, Jonah—isn't this our exit?"

"What? Oh, *shit*—" He swung hard to the right.

"Jesus, *wait*," Shay cried. "There's someone *there*—"

Jonah swung left to avoid a collision. The Mustang's wheels locked and they went skidding, at a harrowing speed, right into the highway's meridian.

///////////////

When Shay awoke in the hospital, he was on a gurney but still in his own clothes. So things couldn't be that bad. He swung his legs over the side and felt a little twinge in his chest. He'd obviously pulled or sprained something, maybe broken a rib. If it was the latter, that was a problem. The tour started up again in just a few days. He needed to be leaping around onstage. Maybe with enough painkillers...

He was just wondering how he'd manage this when Pernita entered the room, looking so shiny and burnished she might've been sculpted in copper. All at once it occurred to him, she must have come straight from the dinner with the record executives he'd missed because of his sad, stupid attempt to rebel.

He steeled himself for the first onslaught of her anger and outrage.

But, amazingly, she dropped her purse onto a chair and came up and hugged him. "Oh, sugar-pie," she said. "What a nightmare! I'm so glad you're all right." Then she stood back and smiled at him. "And a hero, too!"

He blinked. "A hero?" It hurt his jaw to talk. He gave it a quick massage.

Pernita nodded. "You were so quick on your feet. Calling for help so soon, the way you did."

Oh, yeah—it was coming back to him now. The crash. Jonah, slumped over the wheel. "Is he all right? Jonah?"

She nodded. "A little banged up. Some broken bones. He's got some physical therapy to look forward to. But he'll be okay in time for the Palladium." She ran her hand down Shay's arm. "I just shudder to think what would've happened if you hadn't been there. That man's got a self-destructive streak a mile wide."

This was emphatically not what Shay had been expecting. There were no questions about where he and Jonah had gone, or why. No demand that he account for his actions, defend his decisions. No furious accusations of ingratitude, of having missed the dinner she and her father had put together *just for him*. Could it be that Pernita actually *cared* for him? That the news he'd been in a crash made her realize the depth of her feeling for him?

He sure as hell hoped not. He couldn't imagine anything worse than Pernita being even *more* proprietary of him.

"Am I okay to go?" he said, having examined himself and found no bandages or any sign of treatment.

She nodded. "You're fine. They just gave you a sedative, 'cause you were apparently raving a bit when they brought you in."

"I was?"

"Yes. It's silly. You kept going on about whether a forest is still a forest if it's lying down. Or something. I think you must've bonked your head."

He took a deep breath. "Yeah. Probably."

As they made their way down the corridor toward the exit, he said, "Calling 911 is hardly the mark of a hero. It's what any idiot in that situation would do."

She gently brushed the hair out of his face. "Don't sell yourself short," she said. Then she slipped her arm through his and added, in a breathy little whisper, *"Hero."*

///////////////////

It wasn't till the next day that he figured out why she'd reacted the way she had. The news of Shay and Jonah's accident was a big local story covered by all the newscasts. There was footage of the wrecked car, some concert clips of both Overlords and Jonah and the Wail, and there was an interview with Halbert Hasque, who said that Shay reacted "like an absolute hero" and probably saved Jonah's life.

It was ridiculous, of course. Jonah's life hadn't been in any danger; he'd just been banged up. The only reason he was even unconscious was probably from all the "party mix" he'd ingested. (And in truth, the only favor Shay had done him was to take that vial of poison and hurl it far, far away before the ambulance arrived.) But of course, that wouldn't be a news story. The flat, unglamorous, messy truth of the matter—that Shay and Jonah had gotten exactly what they deserved for acting out the way they had—served no one. So why settle for the truth, when the razor-sharp mind of Halbert Hasque saw a way to make a fictionalized version profitable for everyone involved?

That's why Pernita hadn't been angry, or accusatory, or even curious. The accident on the highway was a much, much bigger boost to Shay's career than any dinner with record executives ever could have been.

CHAPTER 19

So, it turned out all those sappy songs about following your dream were just a load of bullshit.

Loni lay on the couch, staring up at the ceiling, and actually found herself missing her crack—the hairline fissure in her room at Zee's place, which had been the focus of so much of her scrutiny and analysis. If she'd had something like that still in her life, some proof of the inherent crappiness and shoddiness of everything, everywhere, then she'd never have fooled herself into thinking she could ever achieve anything, ever create anything lasting or beautiful.

By rights, she should hate Shay Dayton, too, with his yammering on about "jumping the barricade." But she couldn't. He, at least, had admitted it was a risk. You jump the barricade, you might get shot. And Loni was certainly feeling bullet-riddled at the moment.

She'd drawn a pretty fair crowd for her reading, standing room only, even. Props to social media. Mindlessly inviting everyone she knew—students, fellow faculty, friends from years gone by, not to mention a pretty good swath of people she didn't know at all (any unfamiliar name that floated her way on Facebook or Twitter)—had really done the job.

Too bad she couldn't say the same about her poems.

The reaction to them had been polite at best, bewildered at worst. Just the memory of all those blank faces staring at her whenever she looked up from her book—faces that seemed to ask, *Is that it? Do we clap now? Or is there more?*—made her want to pull the blanket up over her face and just hide there till the crack of doom or the zombie apocalypse or whatever.

She'd managed to sell nineteen copies, which hadn't sounded so bad till she factored in that she'd brought a box of fifty. Byron had told her she was nuts. "Fifty copies at a reading? Jesus, Loni, Seamus Heaney doesn't sell that."

"Well, no, he wouldn't," Loni had replied as she packed up her unsold stock. "Being dead."

It was the kind of cheap shot she usually refrained from scoring off him, but she was angry at his never having supported her from the moment she'd told him what she was doing. "For God's sake," he'd said, "what does the world need with *another* twenty-something chick poet? Do you *really* think you've got anything to say that hasn't been said countless times before by women *significantly* more gifted than you?" And when she'd accused him of cruelty, he'd gotten all shrill about it and said, "You stupid bitch, it's *kindness*. I'm trying to save you from the critical lambasting you're going to get when you go public with your little book of valentines."

And then, when she'd compiled the first manuscript, he—now contrite and so very, very sorry he'd *ever* said a thing to discourage her—asked to see it, and against her better judgment she'd let him. He'd immediately taken it to the kitchen table, sat down with it, and started reading while she did the dinner dishes. After five minutes, he'd taken out a red pencil and started marking it up.

She'd thrown down the dish towel, whirled on him, and said, "What the *hell* do you think you're doing?"

He'd looked up at her, completely astonished. "What? Do you want my help or not?"

"*Not*. Jesus, Byron, you asked to *read* it. I agreed to let you. That's *all*."

He'd looked down at the manuscript, then up at her again. "You're awfully goddamn confident for someone who actually wrote, 'the burthen of the insubstantial.'"

So she'd taken it away from him, and he hadn't read it again until it was printed in book form, at which time she could hardly stop him. His complete silence with regard to his opinion was deafeningly eloquent. And then, of course, he'd capped it all off by actually getting into some kind of *fight* at the actual reading. He had, in fact, actually physically *punched* someone. In a *bookstore*.

Not just that, but he'd been all *proud* about it, strutted around afterward like he was waiting for her thanks or something. Was he out of his mind? After dumping all over her work in private, he thought she'd thank him for going off like an ape at someone who'd just been *talking* while she read? She hadn't even been aware of any muttered conversation in the audience until Byron had drawn her attention by getting all *High Noon* over it.

She'd managed to keep her composure and continued reading through the entire incident. She wanted to pretend it had never even happened, but afterwards it seemed like it was all anyone could talk about. Not Loni's work—not the verses she'd slaved over, sometimes for years—but her Neanderthal boyfriend avenging her honor.

There'd been a moment, too, when someone had mentioned the guy he'd confronted being a musician, someone who was currently in the news. Loni knew that Shay Dayton was in LA doing publicity and had immediately thought, *Could it be?* But then some young blond guy had said another name, Judah or Jonah or something, and Loni felt ridiculous that she'd ever thought it a possibility that Shay could tear himself away from his celebrity dream life to come and see her, even if he'd known she was doing a public reading, which of course he didn't.

And yet just that flickering thought of Shay Dayton, that momentarily conjured image of lean, leonine Shay, with his careless grin and his what-the-hell attitude, served to make preening, self-important Byron look all the more asinine. What was she doing with him? Why had she put herself under his protection—his *control*? Had she really been *that* afraid of living life on her own terms?

She'd refused to speak to him on the drive back to campus, and when they got home she'd refused to sleep with him. So there she was on the couch, unable to get comfortable on its lumpy cushions and kept awake by contemplating the wreckage of her life. What she wanted, more than anything, was to get up and walk out. Leave all this behind and start over somewhere else.

But she couldn't.

There was no place for her to go.

//////////////

She'd just managed to drift off into a restless, fitful sleep when she became aware of someone in the room and sat up with a start.

It was Byron, in his wrinkled cotton bathrobe.

"This is stupid," he said. "Come to bed."

And so she gathered up the blanket, got up, and followed him to bed.

That was the way it had to be, apparently. The way it had been since she'd arrived here. The way she'd *chosen* for it to be.

Byron would call the shots for her.

Byron would tell her what to do.

PART THREE

CHAPTER 20

Zee stamped the snow off her boots, then entered the apartment, fell into the first available chair, and pulled them off. She massaged her toes to warm them up, then padded into the kitchen and put the teapot on to boil. When her phone vibrated, she took it from her pocket, checked the screen to see who was calling, and smiled. She tapped Talk and said, "Hey, rock star."

"Hey, clerical-support star. What's the weather there?"

"Cold. What's yours?"

"Not bad. We're in Portland. Forties here."

She grimaced as she got a cup down from the cabinet. "It should be colder there. That far north."

"Sorry. I'll put in a complaint for you."

"Tour's still kicking ass, though?"

"Tour's kicking major ass. We've built up what our esteemed manager likes to call 'momentum.'"

She took a teabag from a foil packet and dropped it into the cup. "Oooh, fancy talk. How's everybody? Baby, Jimmy, Shay?"

"All good. Trina, however…"

She smiled, anticipating a good story. "Trina, however?"

"Trina had the idea, at our last gig, to dive off the stage and do some crowd surfing."

"Ah?"

"Alas, the crowd did not have the same idea."

She gasped, then laughed. "Oh, no! What happened?"

"Fractured pelvis. Not serious enough for surgery, but she has to play tonight's gig sitting on a stool."

"Oh, my God! Poor Kid Daredevil."

He groaned. "You are the only human being on the planet who calls her that."

"Well, someone has to."

"No, Zee. Please believe me. *No one has to.*"

She leaned back against the counter to wait for the water to boil. "So next week is the Palladium, right?"

"Next week is the Palladium. You are correct."

"You stoked for it? Mr. Headliner?"

"I believe it is no exaggeration to say that I am stoked."

She sighed dreamily. "Wish I could be there."

"'Wish'?" he said in a flutey voice. "Did somebody say 'wish'?"

She furrowed her brow. "Um. Yes? Me, just now?"

"Well, then it's your lucky day, young lady!"

A beat. "What do you mean?"

"I mean, I am inviting you on an all-expenses-paid trip to beautiful *Los Angeles, California*, where you will be wined and dined by actual *rock-and-roll musicians* and probably later ravished by one of them. Certain conditions may apply."

She blinked. "Are...are you serious?"

"Do I ever kid?" He paused. "Actually, yeah, I almost *always* kid. But not this time. Really, I'm serious. I'd love to have you there."

"But...can you afford it?"

"Can I ever! *Rock star* here, remember." He dropped his voice a little. "Seriously, we may have to eat mainly fast food when you get here. But beyond that, I'm totally good."

She felt as though she might cry. "This...this is really the sweetest thing anyone's ever..." Her throat closed up and she couldn't go on.

"Aww, shut up," he said. "Shut up or I'll disinvite you."

She laughed a little but still found it hard to form words. When she was able, she managed to say, "Thank you. I accept."

"Sssssssweet!" he said. "Though I kinda knew you would. Me being a total fox in every conceivable way, and all."

"But...listen. Lockwood."

"I'm listening," he said, sounding suddenly wary.

"Yes, it's true, I'd love to be there, I'd love to see you."

A terse pause. "So far no problem."

"But I have a condition of my own."

He sighed. "My momma warned me about women like you. What is it?"

"If I'm flying to California, I want to go and spend a day with Loni first."

Another pause. "That's it? That's all?"

"Yes."

He laughed. "Jesus. Of course. What the hell. Not a problem."

"It's just..." The teapot began to whistle, so she took it from the burner and poured the boiling water into the cup. The teabag danced around the rim like it was being tickled. "She's in kind of a bad place right now. She could use some cheering up."

"Seriously? But wasn't she, like, publishing her poems and shit, and making this whole new career for herself?"

"Well, yeah." She stirred a couple of teaspoons of honey into the tea. "Only it didn't go so well. Her book kind of tanked, and she had a reading where everyone just sort of sat there. They didn't know what to make of her."

"In my experience, it's only the really original talents who have that effect. She should keep at it till they catch up to where she's at."

"Easier said than done. She told me it was awful. The only time she got any reaction out of them was during her patter between poems. Occasionally they'd laugh."

"Listen, she's just being excessively sensitive. You ever hear what happened at the first Overlords gig? They threw *bottles* at us, man. Some of them not even *empty*. Jimmy got clipped by one."

She took a sip of the tea, then made a face and smacked her lips. Too hot. She set it down to cool a bit. "Yeah, but… she said they were 'polite.' Like they were just humoring her. For Loni, that's worse than having a bottle thrown at you.

He snorted. "Forgive me, sweet thang. But as someone who's actually *had* a bottle thrown at him, I'm gonna say, that is oh so very bullshit."

She laughed. "Well. Maybe. Anyway, she's been in a funk for months. She doesn't really like teaching, she's bored…and I'm picking up that she's over her thing with Byron, too."

"Oh, yeah?"

"Yeah. She never actually says so. But…I've talked to her a couple of times. And when she mentions him, there's just this…deadness in her voice."

"Huh. That's very...huh."

"And I just feel...I feel a little...responsible." Her throat started to constrict again.

"You?" he asked, obviously surprised. "How can you possibly be responsible for *that*?"

And suddenly—without warning—something came right up from the depths of Zee's core and started spilling from her lips. "Oh, Lockwood," she said, "I'm such a lousy human being! The worst. I fucked it up for Loni and Shay. *I* did. I went behind her back and did completely vicious things. I was just...it was a craziness. A bad kind of...I...I thought I was doing the right thing. I mean—I guess I still would've done it anyway, but I really thought she was *meant* to be with Byron, and now I know she's not, and I'm the one who pushed her into that—"

"Now, wait," he said. "You may have acted out, yeah, but she's a grown woman, and her choices are her responsibility alone, and—"

"She's my *best friend*," she said, and tears rolled down her cheeks and plummeted onto her stockinged feet. "I'm supposed to be the one who *looks out* for her, and instead I'm the one who shut down her thing with Shay, and she's still *totally* into him. I mean, she almost never even mentions him, I've heard her say his name maybe twice, but both times it was like—like the sound of an open wound—I don't even know how to describe—"

"Whoa, whoa, whoa," he said. "Calm down!"

"I went on her Facebook account, and I blocked him," she said. "At the very beginning. Right after they met. Then

I pretended I *was* her to that Pernita woman and told her to keep Shay away from me. *I* did that. *Me*."

She paused to catch her breath, collect herself, and wait for his reaction. She knew what must be coming. He'd have to call it quits with her, take back the invitation to LA, hang up, and never speak to her again. Why had she lost control this way? Why had she *told* him everything, just out of the blue?

Because, she realized, she loved him.

And it was too late. Too late for that to matter.

"Okay," he said, in a very low voice. "Okay. So. You did that to her. Okay." And he emitted a long, low whistle.

"I know," she said. "I can't believe I ever…Oh, God, I wish I could just rewind and—and—"

"Well, you can't. You can only go forward. So." He took a deep breath. "What are you going to do?"

She sniffled, then wiped her nose on her sleeve. "What… what am I going to do?"

"Yeah. Y'know. To make it right."

She shook her head. "I…I don't know. How can I possibly? I…I don't have even a single idea."

"It's okay," he said, and she was amazed to hear a smile in his voice. "I do."

CHAPTER 21

"So, that's the tour," said Loni, leading Zee back down the commons toward the parking lot.

Zee took a deep breath and then said, "Ooookay. This is really a bit more...everything than I imagined."

Loni blinked. "What did you imagine?"

"That it would be...I don't know. Like the college campuses in the movies. All ivy-covered and green, with middle-aged men in bow ties and long coats running around." She looked around her. "This...this is like a whole town. I mean, it *is* a whole town. Traffic running through it and everything."

Loni sighed. "Spend a couple weeks here. You'll learn how small it really is."

"And these students," she said, as a pair of willowy, chattering blondes sauntered by. "They all look so...young. I mean, for God's sake. I'm not even that much older than them. What is that?"

"Pampering," said Loni without missing a beat. "This is a little cocoon. A little *cradle*." She gave Zee an admiring look. "And you're a grown-up."

Zee frowned. "Kinda makes me feel like I missed out on something."

Funny, I get the same feeling looking at you, Loni thought, but she kept it to herself. Instead, she said, "What do you feel like—for lunch, I mean? Lot of great little spots I can take you to. Italian, barbecue, Vietnamese…"

Zee gave her a sly, smiling look. "Could we just grab a sandwich and sit out here?" Loni was momentarily taken aback by the request, and Zee must have seen this. "It's just so beautiful and *warm* outside. Back home, there's six inches of snow. I'd love to just…*bask* for a while."

Loni shrugged. "Anything you say. You're the guest here."

So they grabbed a couple of chicken-salad-on-ryes at the student commissary and sat cross-legged on the lawn, Zee luxuriating in the sunlight like a cat. "This feels *sooo* good," she said after she'd wolfed down her sandwich. She lay back on her elbows, then turned to Loni and said, "You don't have it half bad here, you know."

Loni barked a laugh. "Oh, I don't know about that."

"You're not shut up in an office all day. You get to come out here and be in the sunlight. And you've got all these students to look up to you…"

"You mean to constantly challenge my authority. When they condescend to notice me at all."

"And you've got a guy who's into you."

"No, *you've* got a guy who's into you," Loni said, eager to change the subject. "And I can't tell you how happy that makes me. I mean, I knew he was a keeper, after that first time I met him when he showed up on our sofa. The guy walked you home 'cause you were upset, then stayed all night to keep watch over you."

Zee toyed with a few blades of grass. "God. And I was such a *bitch* to him."

"Never mind. He obviously knew you were worth waiting for."

Zee looked suddenly troubled. "That's the thing. I really don't think I am. I mean...*he* does. But...Loni. I don't deserve him."

"Shut up. You do so."

"No, I really *do not*." She appeared momentarily conflicted, as though struggling with something she wanted to say but couldn't bring herself to. Finally she relaxed and said, "Oh, what the hell. Maybe being with him will *make* me better." She turned her face back toward the sun. "In fact, it pretty much already has."

"Well, there you go," said Loni, swallowing the last of her sandwich and crumpling the paper wrapper. She was curious to know exactly what Zee meant by that last remark but felt it would be intrusive to ask. "Anyway," she said, popping open her Diet Coke, "I think a guy who actually buys you a plane ticket so you can go to his rock concert at the Hollywood Palladium is pretty much a dictionary definition of Excellent Boyfriend."

Zee gave her a big, excited grin. "That's not all he did."

Loni raised her eyebrows. "No?"

She shook her head. "He also threw in an extra ticket, so I could see the show with my best friend."

Loni almost asked, *Who's that?* before it occurred to her. "Oh," she said. *"Oh."*

"So, what do you say?"

Loni was very touched, and the idea of escaping the hothouse air of this campus was terrifically inviting. But her natural reticence kicked in, and hard. "I don't know, Zee. It's really sweet of you. But you know I'm not such a big fan of those things. The crowds and the noise and everything."

"You need something to shake you out of your funk," Zee said, sitting up. "Crowds and noise will do that."

She sighed. "And I've never been a big Overlords fan."

"No," said Zee with a funny look in her eye. "But a big Shay Dayton fan, maybe."

Loni felt the color wash from her face.

"Oh, for Christ's sake," Zee said. "I'm not stupid, Loni. And you're not nearly as mysterious as you pretend to be."

"How long have you known?"

"I've *always* known." She took her own can of soda now and popped the lid. "I won't say I've always *liked* it…"

"Well, that's why I never told you."

"I know. I get that."

"Also, really, except for that once, there was nothing to tell."

Zee shifted to her knees and scuttled over to Loni, then knelt next to her and put a hand on her shoulder. "Listen, Loni. 'Once' can be a very small word, or it can be a very big one. I think in this case, it's Door Number Two."

Loni had to grip the ground to keep from toppling over. Zee had just said something so wise—so *poetic*—that she felt it really might knock her flat.

"Come to the Palladium." She reached for her purse, opened it, fished around for a bit, then pulled out a small envelope. "Here's the ticket. And a parking pass. Lockwood also got you one of those. So you don't even have to worry about where to leave your car."

"I just don't know. I'm not sure I'm free."

"It's not till tomorrow night," she insisted, stuffing the envelope into Loni's shirt pocket. "Plenty of time for you to *get* free."

Loni drew her knees up to her chest. "Byron's out of town. At a conference. He gets back tomorrow. He'll expect me home."

Zee snorted. "Just two hours ago you told me he never even notices you anymore. You said last week there was a night you got home three hours late because of car trouble, and he hadn't even realized you weren't there. He thought you were in bed."

Loni felt a slight kick of panic. "That's another thing. My car. LA is a long drive."

"It's only an hour. And you said they fixed your car good as new."

She grabbed her ankles and buried her face in her knees.

"Jesus," said Zee, rolling her eyes. "You're hard work, you know?"

"It's the Shay Dayton business," Loni admitted. "I don't really relish the idea of reliving it."

"You're not reliving it. This is Los Angeles, not Haver City, and it's the Palladium, not Club Uncumber. And you're almost a year older, and so is he. And you won't even have to talk to him, for God's sake."

"I'll be in the audience. He'll see me."

"You ever been on a stage? At a rock concert? What he'll see is a big red blur."

Loni lay back on the lawn, her hair splashed around her head onto the grass. "This was your whole reason for coming here, wasn't it? You didn't just miss me and want to see my new life. You always had it up your sleeve to come and stir up things that had finally become…well, whatever the opposite of stirred is."

"Inert," said Zee. "Stagnant."

Loni shot her a look. "You're pretty zippy with the vocab lately. When the hell did that happen?"

"I lived with you for five months. Look," she said, getting up and brushing off her pants, "I have to get going. Lockwood's taking me to dinner and I need a nap and some pool time. Just text me when you figure out whether you're going to vegetate here in your academic compost heap or actually go out into the world you say you miss so much and risk getting your precious feelings ruffled a bit."

Loni glared at her. "I wish we'd sat closer to the Japanese garden. Then I could throw a rock at your head."

Zee dismissed this with a wave. "You throw like a girl."

Loni walked her to her rental car, but Zee refused to let her hug her good-bye, "because I'll see you tomorrow. Seriously. Loni. *Grow a pair.*"

Loni laughed, then, growing suddenly serious, she said, "All right. Fine. You win. Tomorrow night."

Zee grinned from ear to ear as she got into her car. "Text me as soon as you've parked. I'll tell you where I am and how to get there."

"Right, I will," she said, standing back to give her room to maneuver. "Whatever you say."

"Wear something hot," Zee tossed out the window as she pulled out of the parking space.

"*Almost* everything you say," Loni shot back as Zee sailed on out of the lot.

As she turned back to the campus, Loni felt that something fundamental had changed. The feeling she'd had that her life was running along a single track like a locomotive toward an unknowable end was now much more expansive. She suddenly saw her life as a palette of possibilities, an array of colorful travel brochures. She had only to pick a destiny and book the trip.

///////////////

Zee drove about four blocks before her giddiness and excitement became too much to contain. She pulled over to the side of the road, took out her phone, and texted Lockwood:

Mission accomplished. She's coming.

CHAPTER 22

The initial thrill was over. The head-spinning rush of having arrived at the Hollywood Palladium to discover OVERLORDS OF LONELINESS WITH GUESTS JONAH & THE WAIL blaring from the marquee had abated. Shay felt like he owned Sunset Boulevard. Hell, that he owned Los Angeles. Or the whole freaking planet, cosmos, space-time continuum, you name it.

Then had come the hard, unglamorous work of loading in, setting up, and running the line check—during which Shay had tried to not look overwhelmed at talking to a sound engineer he couldn't see, from a stage overlooking a dance floor that could hold three thousand people. He did his best, in fact, to act as though this sort of thing was old hat to him, that he went through it all the time. But in the silences, when the engineer was adjusting his levels, Shay could almost hear his knees knock.

Then there was nothing to do but wait. Most of the band wandered off to grab something to eat. Shay stayed on site, just in case anything else came up that needed attention or an opinion or a decision. He hunkered down in the greenroom, along with Lockwood and Marcia, aka the Wail, who sat in a far corner on a plush chair, her knees pulled up to her chin, reading a large leather-bound book—essentially throwing up a wall between herself and the two Overlords.

Lockwood, self-contained as ever, ate steadily from a bag of Doritos and washed it down with a Red Bull. Shay couldn't manage that degree of serenity—or any degree at all. He occupied himself by furiously skimming the Internet on his smartphone. He found a Buzzfeed page containing videos of teenagers' failed jumps from rooftops into swimming pools, which was usually the kind of thing that could keep him happily occupied for twenty minutes. Now, he was restless after five.

He almost wished Pernita hadn't gone out for a late lunch with her father. Having her around, pestering him, annoying him, being her usual controlling, abrasive self, would at least have given him a focus for all the anxious energy he was feeling. As it was, he had nowhere to direct it but back into himself. He was a rattling, twitching bag of nerves. Every so often he went out and looked at the house, trying to imagine it filled to the rafters with screaming fans. That was a bit much to hope for, but who knew? The interest generated by the car crash a few months before had faded, as such things always did, but maybe it had left enough of a residual impression to get people to mark today's date in their calendars.

He wryly laughed at the idea that he was now counting on that incident to bring in some bodies. Up till now, he'd treated the whole thing as an enormous embarrassment. When Halbert had floated the idea that after his opening set, Jonah would tell the audience to "Stay put for Overlords of Loneliness, featuring Shay Dayton, the man who saved my life," both Jonah and Shay had responded with *absolutely fucking not*. It was easy to take the high road when you were at some swanky bar with a couple of whiskeys in you. Now, on the Palladium stage looking out at the echoing vacuum he was expected to fill, Shay thought he might agree to screw the family dog onstage if it brought in one or two undecideds.

He returned to the greenroom and told Lockwood, "Now I know why Ozzy Osbourne bit off a bat's head onstage."

But Lockwood wasn't listening; he was staring at his phone, grinning. "Hm?" he said. "Sorry?"

"Nothing," Shay said, resuming his seat on the couch and putting his feet up on the coffee table. "What's got you so feline-faced? Text from the missus?"

"Yeah," he said, putting the phone back in his vest pocket. "She's on her way." He reached in the bag for another handful of Doritos. "Says she's bringing a friend."

"God bless her skinny white ass. Tell her to bring a couple more."

"I think one is sufficient," Lockwood said with a kind of weird lilt in his voice. "Provided it's the *right* one." He popped the Doritos into his mouth.

Shay blinked. It wasn't like Lockwood to get all coy. He assumed it must be the pressure getting to him. Of course, being Lockwood, he wouldn't get all edgy and frantic, the way Shay did. It figured he'd go the opposite direction and turn twee. Shay slumped back against the cushions. He felt the urge to say something valedictory, something to mark how far Overlords had come, how incredible it was that they'd made this journey together. But he was also wary of coming off sounding like some self-important asshat.

So all he said was, "Check out where we *are*, man."

Lockwood grinned and said, "Check it out."

They stared dopily at each other, until Marcia noisily turned a page in her book. Then Shay snapped out of it, checked the time, and got up to change into his stage clothes.

//////////////

Halbert and Pernita returned shortly after the doors opened, by which time Shay had sweat through his stage shirt, which enraged Pernita. She made him sit with his arms outstretched so that the shirt would dry, then lurked about with the attitude that she was the longest-suffering human being who ever walked the earth. Halbert kept going down to check the house, and every time he returned, Shay asked what the crowd was like, and he'd say, "Respectable," which was no fucking answer at all. Baby and Jimmy filtered back in, as casually as though this were just an everyday gig at some dive in Haver City, and got changed.

A wooden box arrived with three bottles of Woodford Reserve, and a note reading, *Break every fucking leg you've got*, signed by Paul Di Santangelo. Halbert immediately confiscated the booze, telling them sternly, "Afterward."

Shay sweat through his shirt again, but Pernita didn't notice.

It was twenty minutes to showtime when Marcia closed her book, got up wordlessly, and went to change. It was then that everyone seemed to notice that Jonah and Trina weren't back yet.

"They went off together," said Baby drowsily, as he played a hand of cards with Jimmy.

Shay felt his head lift off his shoulders in alarm. "Did *no one* think what a bad combination that was?"

Jimmy shrugged. "What were we supposed to do? Citizen's arrest?"

Halbert, working his phone, looked like he might kill somebody as he strode off.

Pernita smoked cigarette after cigarette after cigarette.

At seven minutes to showtime, Jonah led Trina in. She was purple in the face and choking.

"What the hell happened?" asked Shay, rushing to her.

Jonah cocked his head. "Dunno. She was okay, mostly, till I bet her she couldn't fit an entire twelve-pack of peanut butter cups in her mouth."

"Why the *hell* would you do that?" Shay said, pounding Trina on the back.

Jonah looked at him as though it was the stupidest of stupid questions. "To see if she could," he answered.

"Ssshwwha nncaahwme Knnh Dhrrdunnuh," garbled Trina.

"No one calls you Kid Daredevil," Shay screamed.

Marcia, now in her black shroud of a dress, stepped forward, suddenly transformed into the Wail. "Let me," she said, shoving Shay aside. "I'm trained in the Heimlich."

Jonah ambled off to get changed, as though nothing at all were out of the ordinary.

By this time Halbert had come back in and observed what was happening. He looked at Pernita and said, "We've got a bass sub standing by, don't we?"

"Yes, Daddy. In case Jonah bailed."

"Well, he can do as well for this one," he said, nodding toward Trina, and he put his phone to his ear to notify one of his assistants.

The Wail grappled her wiry arms around Trina's midsection and squeezed. Trina groaned.

"The sub plays an upright bass," said Pernita, "not a bass guitar."

"I'm sure he knows how," Halbert said. "Just give him Tina's when he gets here."

"*Trina's,*" Shay corrected him. "And shouldn't we be calling a medic or something, instead of worrying about a sub?"

"Hello, Jerry?" Halbert said into the phone, ignoring Shay. "Where's our bass sub?"

The Wail gave Trina another superhuman squeeze, and a fist-size mass of chocolatey peanut matter shot from Trina's mouth.

And landed on the front of Shay's shirt.

"Oh, for God's sake," said Pernita. "What the fuck is wrong with you?"

"*Me?*" said Shay in disbelief, shaking the glop off of him and onto the floor.

The Wail released Trina, smoothed out her gown, and stepped toward the door, just as Jonah emerged in his lounge-lizard jacket and spats.

"You ready?" he asked.

"Mm-hm," she said.

He gave her a little kiss, and then they headed out to the stage.

Halbert was barking into his phone. "Have the sub stand by, Jerry—but it looks like it may not be urgent after all." Then he tucked his phone back in his suit coat and turned to follow Jonah and the Wail.

"Hey," called Trina after him, as she pulled herself back together after her ordeal. "Hey, *you*. Thurston Howell the Third."

Halbert turned around and looked at her in disbelief. "Are you talking to *me*?"

"Yeah," she said, after quickly wiping her lips on the back of her hand. "For the record? You ever send anyone to touch my ax, I'll break all ten of his fingers. Then his face. Then *you*."

He looked at her in amazement. "Are you threatening me, little girl?"

"You want that?" she said, working herself up into a fury. "You want me to threaten you? Is that it? Go ahead, then—*dare* me."

"*Don't*," Shay interjected, raising a hand to quiet Halbert before he could speak. "Don't...do *not*...dare her."

The corners of Halbert's lips curled into a kind of sneer as he stared "Tina" down. "If you can put half of this crazy-lady passion into your playing," he said as he turned away from her, "we'll all be the better for it."

"Yeah," she said, shouting after him as he retreated, "I love you, too. In fact, talking to you now? I came *twice*."

Pernita was tugging Shay's shirt off him. "You can't wear this," she said.

"It's all right, I already managed to sweat through it worse than the first time."

"Never mind. I have a replacement. Where's my garment bag?"

"Around here somewhere," he said, and he grabbed her wrist before she could go in search of it. "Hey," he said, "what the *hell*? How does Trina, of all people, get away with mouthing off to your old man like that?"

She laughed, as if it were a silly question. "Oh, baby, he's not an *ogre*, you know. He makes allowances for personality types. And she's definitely her own category, there."

He released her, and she went looking around the green-room for her bag.

And he felt something come over him, a kind of dread. It was becoming clear that everyone else in his position—Jonah, Trina, all the others—were taken at face value and adjustments were made for their quirks and habits. Only he was being hammered into a new shape, molded into something he didn't even recognize as him. And only because he'd been idiot enough to allow it.

He tamped down the feeling for the moment. It wouldn't be at all helpful to let it cripple him now, not when he was just an hour away from taking the stage at the Hollywood Palladium.

That hour passed incredibly swiftly. Before he knew it, Halbert returned to announce that Jonah and the Wail had completed their set, and it was Overlords' turn to go on.

Pernita had found her garment bag stuffed next to the couch with Shay's replacement shirt crumpled within it. ("When I find out who did that, blood will flow," she'd seethed.) She'd hung the shirt in the bathroom and turned the shower on to steam out the wrinkles, but it was still a mess—it looked like a chamois. And it was damp, besides.

"I'll just have to wear the shirt I wore in," he said, going to his duffel bag.

"No, wait," she said, putting a hand on his shoulder. "That awful old thing…no."

He shot her an impatient look. "Well, we're sort of out of options here, Pernita."

"No. No, we're not." She had a wild, excited look in her eyes. "Lockwood," she said.

He looked up from his chair. "Hm?"

"Give me your vest."

Lockwood plucked at the arm holes of the burgundy vest he was wearing over his black T-shirt. "This vest? That I'm wearing?"

"Yes, exactly." She waggled her fingers at him. "Come on, come on."

"All right," he said, seemingly unwilling to argue with her in this state. "Just let me get my phone out of the pocket." He did so, then slipped off the vest and handed it to her.

She in turn handed it to Shay. "Put this on."

He gave her a you've-got-to-be-kidding look. "Over my bare chest?"

"Over your magnificently bare and beautifully tattooed chest, yes."

He stepped back from her. "No *fucking* way. I'll look like an idiot."

"You'll look like sex on two legs. Just *do* it."

He complied, hoping that as soon as she saw him, she'd realize what a dork he looked like and change her mind. But the look on her face immediately told him different.

"God, I've been wasting my time with you," she said exultantly. "All those fittings and couturiers. It's not about how you're dressed, it's about how you're *un*dressed."

Jonah and the Wail returned to the greenroom. The Wail took one look at him and smiled lasciviously.

"See?" Pernita said. "Oh, God, this is genius. I love being me."

"Fine," he said, realizing they were running out of time. "But believe me, Pernita, this is a *one-time* thing."

"Whatever you say," she said, in a tone that implied exactly the opposite.

As they headed down to the stage, Shay said, "I cannot *believe* I'm going out there like this," and hugged his chest as if embarrassed by his near-nakedness.

"Never mind," said Lockwood. "Just pretend you're Jagger. Or Morrison."

"I feel more like Borat." Shay noticed that Lockwood was staring at the phone he'd just removed from the vest in question. "What is it? Another message from the missus? She not make it?"

"No, she's here," he said. "But her friend isn't. And she has no idea why. Not responding to any texts or calls."

"Never mind," he said, slapping Lockwood's shoulder. "Zee's the important one, right? You got your lady in the crowd, and you're going out to wow her. Be happy, dude."

Lockwood gave him an unconvincing grin. Shay might have wondered what was behind it, but there was no time for that.

The moment had arrived for Overlords of Loneliness to take the stage.

CHAPTER 23

Loni really should have been out the door ten minutes ago. As it was, she'd have to count on traffic being light in order to get to the Palladium on time. Fortunately, she had a reserved parking spot waiting for her, thanks to Lockwood. That would save her a good chunk of time.

If only she could tear herself away from her mirror. It was just so maddeningly hard to know how to make herself look tonight. Obviously, she wanted to be completely irresistible, but she didn't want to look like she was *trying* to be irresistible. She wanted to knock Shay Dayton on his rock-star ass, while at the same time looking like she didn't give a damn what he thought. It was a real tightrope.

She applied a little bit more color to her lips, then decided it was too much and wiped it off. It was ridiculous, really. She wasn't even sure she'd *see* Shay. Given the choice—say, if Zee tried to bring her backstage after the gig—she'd refuse to go. She wouldn't pursue him, absolutely not. Let him come to *her*, if he felt like it. She had her pride, and as far as she knew, Shay was still involved with his manager's daughter. Loni wasn't about to go chasing another woman's man.

It occurred to her, as it did every time she thought of Pernita, that Shay wasn't the only one currently committed. She was still with Byron, though the thought of it kind of sank her heart in ways she wasn't prepared to examine too closely.

As soon as she thought of him, she heard the key turn in the front-door lock. It was as though he'd been waiting off-stage for a telepathic prompt. Loni sighed and figured it was for the best. Now she could at least greet him after his trip, instead of having him arrive home to an empty apartment. It would remove some of the sting of his having to spend his first night home alone.

She applied a little more lipstick after all, figuring what the hell, then grabbed her purse and her jacket and went down to greet him.

"Hi," she said brightly, and by the way he looked glumly at her—he set down his suitcase but stayed stooped over, as though bent double by fate—she knew this was going to be a difficult conversation. "How'd the conference go?"

"You wouldn't believe it," he said, trying to stretch himself out of his cramped posture. "Some pompous hack from the University of Chicago read a paper on menstrual imagery in Poe."

Loni waited, but nothing else seemed to be forthcoming. "Ah," she said. "And this is bad because...?"

He shot her a look of extreme annoyance. "For God's sake. I've *told* you that's one of *my* ideas. I just haven't been able to get around to it because of all this goddamn teaching work." He glared at her again, as though his class load were her fault, she being presumably too lazy to take it over for him.

She bit her lip to keep from sniping back. It would hardly help matters to begin an argument now, to point out that Loni had her *own* classes to teach, not to mention her own classes to *attend*, and by the way, the number of ideas Byron had for potential papers would keep a team of academics busy for a lifetime. Choosing the diplomatic approach, she just cocked her head sympathetically and said, "Sorry. That really sucks."

"I just want to have dinner and watch some mindless TV and forget the whole thing," he said, and he glanced toward the kitchen.

"There's some pasta salad in the fridge," she said. "And I bought a bottle of Chianti yesterday. I only had a glass, so it's almost full." She hitched her purse up over her shoulder.

He looked at her as though just seeing her for the first time. "You're going out?"

She nodded. "Zee's in town. Well, in LA. She invited me to a concert." That sounded insufficiently urgent for her to abandon him in his distress, so she added, "The Palladium. Her favorite band. She's dating the drummer."

He sighed, and it was the kind of sigh a biblical patriarch might issue over his errant children continuing to worship false idols. "For God's sake, Loni."

"For God's sake, what?" She looked toward the door, her avenue of escape. She should leave right now. She was already running late. Save this argument for later.

But she stood fast, rooted by something…a sudden flickering of angry rebellion.

He gestured toward her clothes. "Look at you. This is…I mean, I just don't understand what the attraction is to this cheap, noisy cesspit of a world you continually find yourself drawn back to."

She shook her head in disbelief. "What cesspit is that, exactly?"

"You know exactly what I'm talking about," he said, shifting his weight from foot to foot, like a boxer getting ready to jab. "The one your little vulgarian friend Zee inhabits. All that binge-drinking and crashing music and mindless, casual sex."

"Except for the crashing music, you've exactly described faculty life here."

He extended his jaw and breathed audibly. "And this," he said, snubbing his nose at her. "This air of superiority you put on whenever you get anywhere near the common herd. Like associating with them ennobles you or something."

"The...the 'common herd,'" she repeated, unable to believe he'd actually just said that.

"Not to mention the rank ingratitude it implies. I mean, for Christ's sake," and here he started pacing, growing more agitated with every step, "I *rescued* you from all of that! I *saved* you from a life in that stockyard world of human cattle and subhuman swine! I brought you here, to this place where your intellect and your sensibilities are appreciated, hell, *honored*, and where you can live the life you were meant to live—the life of the mind, pursuing inquiry and delving into the eternal mysteries. And here you are, in this...this world of *privilege*, and you seem to grasp at every opportunity to hurl yourself back into the gutter. Even embarrassing yourself by insisting on publishing your own tepid work and then *reading* it in public. Putting yourself on *display* for the derision of those cretins. What the hell were you thinking? Are you so *eager* to debase yourself?"

She bristled at this reference to *Venus in Retrograde*, the first he'd dared to make since the bookstore. "The online reader reviews have been good," she protested.

He barked a laugh. "Who do you think has been *writing* those reviews?"

Her jaw dropped. "No."

"Yes. *Somebody* had to salvage some scrap of dignity from that fiasco, even if it's only the *appearance* of dignity. Of course I did it. Like I said, I've *saved* you, and I *keep on* saving you. Every goddamn day. Hell, I even save you from *yourself.*"

She stared at him, mouth open, for a very long time. The entire world seemed to have gone very, very still. She could hear her heartbeat in her ears—her angry, stuttering heartbeat—but everything else was calm, like in an orchestra waiting for a cymbal to crash.

"If I'd known that's how you felt," she said, "I never would have come here with you. I never would have allowed you to have such influence and control over me." She shook her head. "You know my love for the Romantic poets, the ones who wandered the world finding the source of their art in all the things you look down your nose at: the lives of common people, their rituals and their communities, their songs and their sweat. Yet you think *removing* me from that world is doing me a *favor*. Taking me to this little insular enclave of fetishism and navel-gazing. I—I'm just completely astonished by your arrogance."

"Well, I'm completely astonished by your ignorance."

She headed for the door. "We can talk about this later. I have some subhuman swine to commune with."

"Oh, no, you don't," he said, grabbing her arm. "You don't walk out on *me* like that! Not with everything you owe me."

"I owe you respect, and gratitude, and that's *it*," she said, jerking her arm away. "And don't ever lay a hand on me that way again."

"You can't play *that* card," he said with a shockingly callous laugh. "Not after all the times you've spread-eagled for me in bed, like a goddamn bitch in heat—"

He made a move to grab her again. She batted away his hand, and he immediately lunged in with his other one. She backed away to dodge it and in the process lost her balance. She fell and hit her forehead on the metal edge of the coat rack.

"Oh, my God," he cried, "oh, God, *Loni!* Oh, my God, I'm so sorry! Loni! Loni!"

She sat up and gingerly felt her forehead, her fingers coming away bathed in blood.

"Oh, my God!" With fumbling hands, he unzipped his suitcase and pulled out a white T-shirt, then bundled it up and applied it to Loni's wound. "Oh, Jesus! Oh, sweet fucking Christ! I'm so sorry!"

"How bad is it?" she said, feeling quite amazingly calm.

"It's soaking right through," he said. "Head wounds, they bleed like crazy. Oh, Loni, sweetheart, I'm so fucking insanely sorry..."

"Help me up," she commanded him.

And he did. She gave him her left hand, while continuing to hold the T-shirt to her forehead with her right.

"Please, please," he said, "say you'll forgive me. Oh, my God. I can't believe this is happening. Sweetheart, baby, I'm so incredibly, overwhelmingly sorry..."

"Byron," she said.

"...You know how I get when I'm angry. I know that's no excuse, but, honey, you mean *everything* to me..."

"Byron!" she said, more pointedly.

"...You won't tell anyone about this, will you? We can keep this to ourselves. This would just be a goddamn feeding frenzy, and not just in our department. Honey, I'm sorry, I'm such a *shit*, I admit it. Please forgive me, everything will change, I *promise*..."

"*Byron!*"

He gulped down the rest of his rampaging apology. "What? What, sweetheart? Anything you say. I mean it. *Anything.*"

She looked into his eyes in a way that made him visibly shudder.

Then she said, "Take me to a hospital."

CHAPTER 24

Three encores, baby. *Three.*

They'd been prepared for two, though they thought that was wildly optimistic. For the third, they'd had to improvise. Shay called the Decemberists' "The Rake's Song," which they'd only ever played before in rehearsal as a warm-up, and which had a ton of lyrics that Shay ended up only imperfectly remembering. But it hadn't seemed to matter. The crowd had been really, *really* into them.

Possibly because everyone had seemed to ramp up their energy level tonight, starting with Trina. Maybe she took Halbert Hasque's parting shot to her as a challenge, but in fact, she focused less on her usual onstage grandstanding and instead poured all of her showmanship into her playing. Her performance was flat-out *blistering.*

So much so that Baby had been taken by surprise and upped his game. Then Jimmy, not wanting to be the only one holding back, had really thrown down some epic keyboard solos. As for Lockwood...well, his lady was in the audience, so *of course* he was going to go all-out.

Meaning that Shay had suddenly found himself surrounded by bandmates who were all in very real contention for the spotlight he himself usually held. He'd had to ratchet up his own performance accordingly, just to hold his own. In fact, he found himself actually grateful Pernita had sent him out wearing only Lockwood's vest, which had elicited some whoops of approval when the lights had come up. He even doffed it for the final two encores and sang entirely naked from the waist up, feeling like a shameless attention whore, but he was clinging on to his front man status by his fingernails here. Whatever it took, he'd do it, and worry about personal dignity later.

He retrieved the vest after the last encore and mopped his brow with it as the crowd—a very respectable size, as Halbert had said—stomped and wailed for more. This had been a freaking *great* night for Overlords.

Backstage, Shay handed the vest back to Lockwood. "Thanks for the loan, man," he said.

Lockwood looked at it with distaste. "Yeah, well, maybe you could have it dry-cleaned first. Or better yet, just throw it on the burn pile."

They both laughed—they'd laugh at anything right then. They were on top of the world.

"You see Zee out there?" Shay asked as they climbed the stairs back to the greenroom.

Lockwood shook his head. "I'm a professional, Dayton. I was *in the zone*, not checkin' out the room for any goddamn tail."

Shay laughed again. "You're full of shit, man."

Lockwood shrugged. "Yeah, all right. Sure I saw her. Watched her watching me, the whole goddamn time."

In the greenroom, Halbert had champagne flowing (still not his own preferred label, Shay noted), but Shay himself preferred to crack open a bottle of the bourbon Paul Di Santangelo had sent. He took his first few sips as he donned the shirt he'd worn from the hotel and simultaneously felt both the warmth of the liquor and the comfort of once again being dressed like a post–Stone Age human being.

Fans and press started filing in, and both Halbert and Pernita, visibly uncomfortable at milling about with common people, left the room. Overlords of Loneliness spent a dizzying half hour or so holding court, though during the process their members, one by one, slipped away to go back to the stage and break down their equipment. No one entirely trusted the house crew, especially Lockwood with his precious drums. He was the first to go.

Which was a shame, because Zee showed up a few minutes later. If she'd been a little quicker, she might have met him on the stairs. As it was, Shay caught her scanning the room for him and being perplexed at not finding him. He couldn't tell her where he'd gone just yet; he was still busy talking to his public.

His public. This—this here—was what he'd been aiming for, ever since he first took up a mic in his parents' garage, back in his senior year, along with a few like-minded friends—Lockwood one of them. And now he'd arrived. A headliner with his own band in the biggest city in America, at the end of a national tour, and sitting with a towel around his neck, drinking premium bourbon, and pontificating for the eager ears of rapt listeners.

"Yeah, sure, I have a vision for Overlords," he said in answer to some mundane question. "What I'd like is to bring back some of the wild, expressionistic elements to rock-and-roll, the way the great early bands borrowed from the Romantic poets...like, y'know, Blake and...well, Blake and whoever." Dang, that thought had petered out a bit. He'd realized it was going to when he was halfway into it. The only reason he'd even gone down that road was that the visitors to the greenroom had thinned out enough now that he thought Zee might possibly overhear him and report back to Loni that he'd been talking about William Blake. And then, after the last few fans had gone—one final girl actually lifting her shirt and having him unstrap her bra so that he could sign his name over the whole of her back—Shay was alone…with Zee.

It was momentarily awkward. He of course hadn't forgotten that Zee had no reason to think him anything but a selfish, manipulative shit. But the whole night had been such a joyride, and she was apparently so happy with Lockwood these days, that he set his apprehension aside and gave her a great big grin. "Hey there, Zee Gleason."

"Hi, Shay Dayton! Great concert. I mean, best I've ever seen you give. By a long shot."

"Yeah, well, we've really tightened up in all our time on the road."

"Jesus! You sure have." She looked momentarily awkward, then said, "I…I was hoping to have a friend with me tonight. I have no idea what happened to her."

"Never mind. It's enough that you're here. Lockwood's over the moon about it." He jerked his thumb toward the stairs. "You just missed him. He went down to help load out. No one's allowed to break down his kit but him."

"I know. The way he treats that setup, I get jealous sometimes."

Shay shook his head. "No need for that. If you could only hear the way he talks about you!"

She perked up but tried not to show it. "Oh, shut up."

"No, he really does." He took another sip of bourbon, then lifted the glass to her and said, "Pour you one?"

"Nnnno," she said, wrinkling her nose. "Bit strong for me. I'll just go down and see if I can find Lockwood."

"We've got champagne, too," he said, pulling the bottle from the bucket. "Looks like there's a mouthful left. Wet your whistle?"

She took a moment to consider this, then said, "What the hell. It's a night worth celebrating, right?"

"You slam-dunked that one," he said, and he emptied the bottle into a plastic cup and passed it to her. "Cheers," he said, raising his own drink, and they tossed back a mouthful together.

"Mm," Zee said, scrunching up her face and rubbing her finger along the bottom of her nose. "Tickles."

"Yeah. This doesn't, though," he said, holding up the bourbon again. "More like scorches."

She made a gagging face, then said, "Well, I'll leave it to you, then," and finished off the champagne. She set down the cup, got to her feet, and said, "Thanks for the drink."

He stood up and said, "No worries. Listen, I'm glad you were here tonight."

"Aw. You're sweet to say so."

"Not just for Lockwood...for all of us. You've been there since the beginning. And...and we really appreciate it. More than we can say, actually."

She appeared pleased by this. She seemed to summon up her courage, then said, "In that case, can I have a hug before I go?"

"Sure," he said, extending his arms, "though I warn you, I'm all sweaty."

She made a clicking noise, dismissing this, and wrapped her arms around him and squeezed.

"Thanks, Shay Dayton," she said in a low voice, "for *everything*."

Then she took up her purse and turned to go.

And there was Pernita in the doorway.

Zee said, "Oh, hi. Nice to see you again," and slipped by her down the stairs.

Shay smiled up at Pernita. "I think that's everybody," he said. "Soon as I change my pants, we can go."

But she was looking at him with such a thunderous expression that it stopped him in his tracks. What the hell was the matter now?

"You lying sack of shit," she said.

He blinked. "What?" he said, dumbfounded. "No, really. I *do* have to change my pants. These are all damp."

She glared at him with what looked like intense hatred. "Running around behind my back with that...that Haver City *slut*," she said. "How long has *that* been going on? How long has she been following you on this tour? Hm? The entire time I've been gone?"

This was the last thing Shay had expected of this day, and it instantly obliterated his mood. Yes, he'd arrived. Yes, he'd achieved everything he'd ever wanted, and had done it in just a few short years. But *this*, he now realized, was the price: attachment to this woman and her unfathomable whims, jealousies, and rages.

"Are you talking about Zee?" he said, gesturing toward the stairs. "She's with Lockwood, for Christ's sake. Ask anyone. I mean it."

Tears streamed down her face. "I can't believe anything you say. I can't trust anything you do. You've so—so completely *withheld* yourself from me—all this time—and now—now I know *why*..."

She was actually at the point of bawling. Shay was absolutely gobsmacked. He had no idea where this was coming from. "*She's with Lockwood,*" he repeated more insistently. "What the *hell* has gotten into you, anyway?"

She lashed out at him and struck him hard across the face.

"You've been playing me for a fool," she spat at him. "You and her *both*." She choked back a gasp. "And after everything I've done for you."

Shay stood there, reeling a bit from the slap, his face stinging. He recalled how a few months before, when Jonah had told him about his epic battles with the Wail, he'd wondered how he might react if Pernita ever dared to hit *him*. And he'd determined that he would simply turn on his heel and walk away forever.

And...he'd been right. That was exactly what he was going to do.

But there was something else he hadn't anticipated... something new.

When she'd slapped him, it was almost like...like she'd awakened him from some kind of dreamy half-consciousness. As if she'd broken a *spell*.

"Everything you've done for me?" he said now, in a very low, very feral voice. "I think you mean everything you've done *to* me."

She laughed, and it was a terrible, acid laugh. "Oh, easy to say so *now*. You know goddamn well you wouldn't be here without me. You'd be *nowhere* without me."

"I *am* nowhere," he said, realizing—with astonishment—that it was true.

"You ungrateful shit! *Headlining* the Hollywood Palladium. That's something you can look down your nose at now? You're suddenly so big? Well…I can bring you down."

"You can't bring me down any further than I already am," he said, his head suddenly filled with light—such clarifying, illuminating light. "You've manufactured me. You've chopped me up and stitched me back together like some kind of fucking Frankenstein monster. That's what I've become, you know. I'm your little pet project. Your *creature*."

At that moment, Halbert Hasque came back into the room.

"Daddy," she said, flinging herself into his arms. "He's hurt me…he's hurt your little girl." And she burst into racking sobs.

Halbert turned his saurian eyes on Shay, and Shay knew that whatever was coming, it wasn't going to be pleasant.

///////////////

Shay was forced to go down and deliver the news himself. Halbert refused to lower himself.

He stood at the load-out door, where everyone was hanging with the crew and having a few drinks, smoking a few joints. "Hasque has dropped us," he said.

Everyone laughed. Then, noticing the rigidity of his face, they stopped.

"Are you fucking kidding me?" Trina said. "After tonight?"

"He says tonight's success wasn't big enough to measure against our behavioral issues."

"That lousy fat fuck," Trina said, rolling up her sleeves. "You dare me to make him repeat that?"

"No one's daring you to do anything, Trina," said Baby morosely.

"The real blame is with me," Shay said. "For some reason, Pernita just went apeshit on me. She's convinced I've been fucking around behind her back the whole tour."

"Well, you pretty much have been," said Jimmy with a sneer. "And we've warned you about it."

He shook his head. "But, it's weird." He looked to where Zee stood with Lockwood. "Seeing *you* was the thing that really triggered it."

Zee's face drained of color. "Oh, no," she said. "Oh, shit. I think I know why."

"It doesn't matter," he said, trying to reassure her. "We're better off without her."

"Oh, *are* we?" Jimmy said, tossing a spent joint to the ground and stepping on it in a manner that suggested he wished it was Shay's head. "And how do you figure that?"

"She was too controlling. Hasque, too. We need to do things our way from now on."

Lockwood sighed. "We can talk about this tomorrow. We're all wiped out. We can use a good night's sleep before we decide what comes next."

Shay cleared his throat. "Yeah. About that." They turned to look at him. "Uh, he's kicked me out of his house, too. I need a place to stay tonight."

"You can bunk with me," Trina said. "Gotta warn you. I snore."

"And also," Shay said, really wishing he could some-how evade having to mention this, "he's cutting bait as of tomorrow."

"What the hell does that mean?" Jimmy asked.

"Meaning, after we check out of the hotel, we're on our own. He's not footing any of our bills anymore."

"Then how the fuck do we get home?"

Shay stared at them, then took a deep breath and said, "Like Lockwood says…let's get some sleep before we try to figure that out."

///////////////////

Shay went back up to the greenroom to grab his duffel bag. On his way down, he found Halbert Hasque at the bottom of the stairs.

"So long, sir," he said, and he headed backstage, toward the load-out door.

"That's it?" Halbert said, opening his palms. "That's all you've got?" When Shay turned to face him, he continued: "You're not going to say how happy you are that you're now free to tell me exactly what you think of me? What a lousy, evil, hypocritical shit I am, and you hope I die soon, pain-fully like I deserve? None of that?"

Shay was alarmed to realize that Halbert had played this scene before…and apparently actually *enjoyed* it.

"No, sir," he said, adjusting his bag on his shoulder. "You've given us plenty of opportunities and invested a lot of time and money in us. As I see it, we owe you thanks. And respect. And apologies for having let you down."

Halbert stared at him in disbelief.

Shay nodded his head, turned, and continued walking.

That's got to rattle him, he thought. *Halbert Hasque now knows I'm a bigger man than he is.*

EPILOGUE

Loni rang the buzzer a few times, but no one answered. So she took out her phone to send a text—*I'm here, I'm right outside*—but before she could do that, the door opened.

It was Mrs. Milliken, looking just as blankly uninterested from her leathery side and she did from her smooth one. It was like she'd last seen Loni yesterday, not nine months before.

Though, in point of fact, she'd never really *seen* Loni at all.

"Oh," said the landlady. "I thought it was somebody."

"Hello, Mrs. Milliken. It's me, Loni. Zee's friend? I'm back to stay with her for a few months. How nice to see you again."

Mrs. Milliken stepped away from the door. "If it was somebody, I'd have had to speak to them about not losing their keys," she said, and she drifted blithely back into the building.

Nice to know some things never change, Loni thought, and she caught the door just before it closed again. She was maneuvering her suitcase through it when Zee suddenly appeared behind her, slightly out of breath and carrying a brown paper bag whose contents clinked when she moved. "Loni! Hi! Sorry I wasn't here. I just ran down to Ray's Liquors to get some wine to celebrate you moving back."

"Oh, that's sweet," Loni said, "but you should've let me do that."

"Don't be silly. Here." She skittered around the suitcase and held the door open so that Loni could push the behemoth into the vestibule. "Jesus, what have you got in there, a grand piano?"

"I bought some new clothes in California," she said, pausing to catch her breath. "Shopping therapy."

"How the hell did you ever get it here from the airport?" Zee asked as she let the door swing shut again.

"I tipped the cabdriver to carry it for me."

"Jesus, Loni," Zee said as she opened up the interior door. "Women who look like you don't need to *tip* guys to get them to carry their bags."

Loni scoffed at the compliment and hauled the suitcase up the steps. "I could use one of those pulley systems the Egyptians had for building the pyramids," she cracked, pausing halfway up to catch her breath and wipe the sweat from her brow.

"Pretty sure I'm out of those," said Zee.

///////////////

When she'd settled back in, showered, and changed, Loni came out to the living room and joined Zee on the sofa. Zee had a bottle of chardonnay and two glasses waiting. "In honor of your triumphant return," she said.

"Not so sure I'd call it a triumph," Loni said as she flopped down onto the cushions. "More like a strategic retreat."

Zee poured her a glass. "So, you're really not going back?"

She shook her head. "No. Finally realized teaching's not for me. And since I quit as Byron's TA, I can't afford graduate school anymore."

"Couldn't you be somebody else's TA?"

"I don't know anybody else. And I don't *want* to, Zee."

"Well…what *do* you want?"

She shrugged. "Hell if I know."

Zee laughed. "Here's to that!" They clinked their glasses and sipped the wine.

"Mm," said Loni, settling back into the sofa. "Feels like I never left."

"So, was it awkward with Byron?" Zee asked.

"A little. He cried, which was embarrassing. Kept saying how sorry, sorry, sorry he was. Like he's been saying for three months." She drank another mouthful of wine. "And of course he begged me to come back."

Zee almost spat out her wine. "You're kidding!"

"I don't mean to *live* with him," she said. "Just to be his TA again next year. Funny enough, once I'd moved out, we got along much better than we ever had. He knows he's going to have trouble replacing me. No one wants to work for him, after…you know." She touched the scar on her forehead. It was really a very small one, far smaller than Zee would have thought given that it had taken eleven stitches.

"But…didn't he already have some woman lined up who wanted the job?" Zee asked. "The one he offered it to, before you took it?"

"You mean Tammi Monckton?" She shook her head. "He lied about that."

"What?"

"I called her," Loni explained. "A couple of weeks ago. I thought Byron might offer her the job again, and I figured she might have heard about the whole domestic violence thing and would maybe turn him down. So I thought I'd do the decent thing and talk to her, set the record straight, let her know the whole thing was largely accidental. She wouldn't have to worry about him going off on *her.*"

Zee nodded. "And?"

"And she didn't want the job. She never had. Byron had completely made that up to try to pressure me into accepting the position back when I hadn't made up my mind yet."

Zee's jaw dropped onto her chest. "You're *joking.*"

"Oh, there's more," she said. "He also lied about writing the online reader comments for my book. I went and e-mailed a thank-you to everyone who posted a review, just to see what happened. And I got back some nice replies. All from real, actual people."

When she could manage to speak again, Zee said, "He really is a steaming turd of a human being, isn't he?"

Loni laughed. "Oh, I wouldn't go that far."

"Well, *I* would. On your behalf."

She shook her head. "Don't bother. There's no punishment you could inflict on Byron that's worse than the one he's already suffering. He has to get up every morning and *be him.*" She raised the glass to her lips. "Trust me, the guy's his own worst enemy." She took a sip. "But enough about him. Let's talk about a *real* man. How's Lockwood?"

Zee curled her legs up under her and gave a coquettish little purr. "Fine. Still a total sweetheart."

"He's treating you right?"

"Oh, hell *yes*."

They laughed. "And didn't you mention he's got a new band in one of your e-mails?"

"Not so much a band," she said. "It's a small ensemble—more urban folk–type stuff. But really beautiful. It's just him, a pianist, and a bass player. They're called Agency of Record."

Loni smiled. "I like it." She raised her glass. "To Agency of Record."

"I'll drink to that," Zee said, touching her glass to Loni's.

"So, no vocals, then?" Loni asked after she'd taken a swallow.

"Oh, the piano player sings," Zee said, as she reached for the bottle to refill the now nearly empty glasses. "Really well, in fact."

"I'd love to hear them sometime."

"You can," she said, reaching over to top Loni off. "Tonight, in fact. They're doing a set at Jehoshaphat's."

"The coffee bar?" Loni said, holding the glass steady. "That's going to be interesting. Slugging down some java after a bottle of wine."

"They serve alcohol after six," she said, replacing the bottle in the ice bucket. "And Agency doesn't go on till nine. We can have dinner first."

Loni ran her finger around the rim of the glass. "So…no hope of an Overlords reunion then, huh?"

Zee sighed. "No. Unfortunately, that's pretty much dead. As I think I told you, when their manager stranded them in LA, Baby, Jimmy, and Trina just decided, okay, this is where we live now. So they started up a new band, hired a few new members, and now they're kind of a *thing* out there."

"Oh, yeah," Loni said, crossing her legs on the cushions. "What did you tell me their name was?"

"Kid Daredevil," said Zee. "Trina's the front man. Front woman." She waved her hand. "Front person. Take your pick."

Loni laughed. "She sings?"

"Kind of talk-sings, apparently. But well enough for it to work. She's more of an all-around stage animal than a singer."

"Well, good for them. And...they didn't ask Lockwood?"

"They did ask Lockwood," she said with a coy grin. "But he had better things to do."

Loni tried to modulate her voice to be as casual as possible. "And Shay?"

Zee shrugged. "Ask Lockwood. He'll know better than me."

She furrowed her brow. "Saying he'll know 'better' means you must know *something*."

Zee raised her glass to her lips, repeated "Ask Lockwood," and downed a mouthful of wine.

Loni was, of course, wildly curious to find out what Shay was up to. She'd Googled him intermittently over the past few months, but after the Palladium gig and a few solo sightings in LA, he seemed to have disappeared off the face of the planet.

But as eager as she was for news of him, she didn't want to *seem* that way to Zee. So she quietly finished her wine and counted the minutes till she could, in fact, ask Lockwood.

///////////

By the time they sat down at a table in Jehoshaphat's, Loni was mindful of having already drunk a half-bottle of chardonnay, so she ordered a sparkling water for the show. But the slight wooziness she was feeling seemed to swell into sudden hallucinatory intoxication when the musicians came onto the stage—and Shay Dayton was one of them. Shay Dayton, in a white collarless shirt and skinny black jeans, with his hair pulled back and knotted at his nape. Shay Dayton, who then sat down at the piano.

Shay Dayton sat down at the piano.

Loni turned to shoot an inquiring look at Zee, but instead caught her exchanging a thumbs-up with Lockwood, who sat grinning behind his drum set.

"Hi," said Shay into a mic that angled over the center of the keyboard. "We're Agency of Record, and this is our second Thursday night at Jehoshaphat's. Thanks for coming out. Tell your friends." A light dusting of applause.

Shay adjusted the mic a little, then said, "This first tune is kind of special to me." And he cleared his throat and played a few mournful yet achingly lovely opening bars. The bass player—an angular, dark-haired woman Loni didn't recognize—joined in, and then, very subtly, so did Lockwood on snares.

And then Shay sang.

I live in a glass house, and it's not thrown stones I fear
But the hurled glances of passersby
My feet are its foundation, and its hearth becomes my
  heart
Casting light on my folly in every part
I live here alone, bathed by moon and burned by sun
Exposed to the world, yet truly seen by none,
Exposed to the world, yet truly seen by none.

The words, which cascaded into the room, propelled by his rich, creamy tenor, burned Loni from the inside out. How…how was this even possible? The bass player took an extended, gorgeously resonant solo, and then Shay came back in to repeat the lyrics. He held the last note as the bass line spiraled away from him, and Lockwood's percussion retreated like the flap of a swallow's wings heading for the horizon line.

Loni realized she hadn't breathed for the entirety of the song. She exhaled now and felt light-headed, like she might float away.

After the applause died down, Shay said, "Those lyrics were a collaboration between myself and someone who is—who has been for some time—my muse, my inspiration, my…well, my anything else she wants to be. No terms, no conditions. All she has to do is ask."

And with that, he turned and looked right at Loni.

She felt her heart galumph around her chest, like a pony loping the perimeter of a corral. Her face felt scorched. Moments passed, and other people began to turn and look her way. Finally, Zee nudged her and whispered, "*Say* something."

Loni, panicking—but in the happiest way imaginable—said, just loud enough to be heard, "I'll consider the offer."

He smiled—sweet Lord baby Jesus on a Vespa, that smile!—and said, "Good enough for now." He turned back to the piano.

And the songs that followed! Brilliantly constructed, ingenious without being showy—the word that kept coming to Loni's mind was *athletic*. Shay's playing was spare but bold, and ravishingly masculine. His singing was shatteringly beautiful.

But it was the words! The lava flow of lyrics, all so wonderfully textured, so evocative, so *arresting*. Loni was thrilled down to the core. Each song was like listening to the pages of a diary, condensed into a few brief lines—reduced like a sauce till what was left was the most concentrated, most potent flavor possible.

She lost track of time. She lost track of herself. The room around her—the context of time and place, her orientation in the universe—all melted away like mist. There was only Shay, and his voice, and his melodies, and his words.

And then, "Thanks, you've been great. We really appreciate your enthusiasm." They were ending! "We're Agency of Record—Senga Florin on bass, Lockwood Mott on drums, and I'm Shay Dayton. We're here every Thursday. Stick around for Joanna Kehr."

And in the next moment, he was coming down from the stage and heading her way.

Zee got up and said, "Excuse me. I'm going to go give a smooch to Lockwood. I won't be long." As she stepped away she added, "Just thirty, forty minutes tops."

And then Shay was right there at the table. "Mind?" he said, gesturing at the chair Zee had vacated.

"Oh, I'm going to *insist* on it," Loni replied. When he sat down, she turned to him and said, "That first tune...what the *hell*?"

He grinned. "You remembered?"

"Clearly not as well as *you* did."

He shook his head and reached for his back pocket. "I didn't *have* to remember." He pulled out his wallet, opened it, and extracted a tattered paper napkin, which he gently opened on the table between them.

It was the very napkin on which they'd scribbled those lyrics, over tea and espresso that afternoon, nearly ten months before.

"You *kept* it?"

"Hell yeah," he said, folding it back up and replacing it. "Didn't think I'd let a document like that just get thrown out, did you? Future generations would never forgive me."

She rolled her eyes. "You haven't changed," she said—but affectionately, radiantly. "What makes you think future generations will care?"

He cocked an eyebrow. "One way to make sure they do."

She smiled. She didn't know what was coming, but she could tell by his impish expression that it would make her laugh. "What's that?"

"By producing them ourselves."

She was only half right; it made her laugh *and* cry.

///////////////

Hours later—after so much talk, and so much hand-holding and soul-baring, and a few moments in the parking lot where she thought she might go mad from happiness and just crawl inside his skin and live there forever—she was back at Zee's place, in her old room, in her old bed. This was at her insistence. She told Shay, *slowly* this time. Nice and easy. This voyage is a long one, and she wasn't missing any of the stops along the way.

She lay on her back and stared at the crack in the ceiling. Still there, still taunting her.

But no...not taunting her. *Teaching* her. Trying to wake her *up*.

Yes, it was a crack. It was still a crack. It would always be a crack.

But it was also still a ceiling. *One* ceiling. A crack couldn't change that. A crack couldn't even come close. All the crack did was lend it character. Depth. Interest.

She felt a jolt of inspiration, like her brain had been stung by a joy buzzer. She reached over to her nightstand, where she'd placed a copy of *Venus in Retrograde*, and grabbed the book, turning to the page on which "Fracture" was printed. She read it anew:

A hairsbreadth divide that does not divine—meaning
gutters when division uncouples a nullity—
Constant ever, yet aspect alters:
Your face in starlight—enchantment—
Your face in daylight—error

No, no. This was all wrong. She could see it now. She searched the nightstand drawer and found a pen, then began marking up the page, making changes. When she was finished, she sat back and read the result.

A hairsbreadth divide that does not define—meaning
lingers when division uncouples a duality
Constant ever, yet aspect alters:
Your face in starlight—hope
Your face in daylight—home

She smiled in satisfaction. *Time for a second edition*, she thought.

ABOUT THE AUTHOR

Dish Tillman is a writer and musician living in Chicago who, under another name, has published several novels and fronts a progressive alt-rock band.